EVIDENCE
OF MERCY

Books by Terri Blackstock

Predator
Double Minds
Soul Restoration
Emerald Windows

Intervention Series
1 | *Intervention*
2 | *Vicious Cycle*

A Restoration Novel Series
1 | *Last Light*
2 | *Night Light*
3 | *True Light*
4 | *Dawn's Light*

Cape Refuge Series
1 | *Cape Refuge*
2 | *Southern Storm*
3 | *River's Edge*
4 | *Breaker's Reef*

Newpointe 911
1 | *Private Justice*
2 | *Shadow of Doubt*
3 | *Word of Honor*
4 | *Trial by Fire*
5 | *Line of Duty*

Sun Coast Chronicles
1 | *Evidence of Mercy*
2 | *Justifiable Means*
3 | *Ulterior Motives*
4 | *Presumption of Guilt*

Second Chances
1 | *Never Again Good-bye*
2 | *When Dreams Cross*
3 | *Blind Trust*
4 | *Broken Wings*

With Beverly LaHaye
1 | *Seasons Under Heaven*
2 | *Showers in Season*
3 | *Times and Seasons*
4 | *Season of Blessing*

Novellas
Seaside

Other Books
Miracles
(The Listener/The Gifted)

The Heart Reader
of Franklin High

The Gifted Sophomores

Covenant Child

Sweet Delights

EVIDENCE OF MERCY

Terri Blackstock

SUN COAST

1

CHRONICLES

ZONDERVAN®

ZONDERVAN.com/
AUTHORTRACKER
follow your favorite authors

We want to hear from you. Please send your comments about this book to us in care of zreview@zondervan.com. Thank you.

ZONDERVAN

Evidence of Mercy
Copyright © 1995 by Terri Blackstock

This title is also available as a Zondervan ebook.
Visit www.zondervan.com/ebooks.

This title is also available in a Zondervan audio edition.
Visit www.zondervan.fm.

Requests for information should be addressed to:

Zondervan, *Grand Rapids, Michigan 49530*

Library of Congress Cataloging-in-Publication Data

Blackstock, Terri, 1957–
        Evidence of mercy / Terri Blackstock.
            p. cm.—(Sun coast chronicles)
        ISBN 978-0-310-20015-4 (softcover)
        I.Title. II. Series: Blackstock, Terri, 1957– Sun coast chronicles.
    PS3552.L34285E95 1995
    813'.54—dc20   95-33052

Published in association with the literary agency of Alive Communications, Inc., 7680 Goddard Street, Suite 200, Colorado Springs, CO 80920. www.alivecommunications.com

Cover design: Curt Diepenhorst
Cover photography: Superstock®
Interior design: Susan Vandenberg Koppenol, Lisa Connery

Printed in the United States of America

11 12 13 14 15 /DCI/ 51 50 49 48 47 46 45 44 43 42 41 40 39 38 37 36 35 34 33

*This book and all those to follow it
are lovingly dedicated to
The Nazarene*

ACKNOWLEDGMENTS

Special thanks to Chip Anderson, of Anderson's Optique in Jackson, Mississippi, for showing me his magic; to Carla Nowell, physical therapist at Methodist Hospital in Jackson, Mississippi, for helping me find authenticity; to Ellis Warren, pilot, for talking me through my landing; to Larry Morgan, aircraft mechanic, and Lane Smith, general genius, for helping me create my disasters; to the Cockrells and many others at First Baptist Church in Jackson, Mississippi, for their powerful prayers; to Greg Johnson, for sharing the vision; to the Phillips-Corry class, for leading me to the brink of awakening.

And to Ken, my spiritual leader, for helping me decide where to go from there.

PROLOGUE

He had waited for a new moon, for he needed the cover of darkness. Tonight was perfect. Dressed in black, he knew it would be virtually impossible for anyone to see him. The airport guard who patrolled the small building in the wee hours would never notice that anything improper was going on right beneath his nose. Not as long as he was swift and quiet.

Checking once again to make sure no one was near, he crept across the tarmac, past the private planes lined up like a military fleet, squinting to read the number and name on each fuselage.

Solitude was the fourth from the right, just as he'd expected.

With one more quick look around, he bent down and duck-walked under the plane, found the wheel well, and shone his small flashlight to find the spot he needed. Calmly he pulled the tool he'd brought out of his pocket, made the necessary adjustment, then flicked off the light.

It had taken less than thirty seconds to create the catastrophe that would finally make things right. Grinning, he hurried quietly back across the tarmac then broke into a jog for a mile beyond the airport until he reached his car. He'd parked it far enough away so he wouldn't be heard back at the airport as he cranked it. He pulled into the street, keeping his lights off. Laughing out loud, he headed home, eager for the satisfaction he would feel the next time *Solitude* was flown.

Then there would be one less obstacle between him and his prize—and one more victory to show who was really in control.

CHAPTER ONE

Solitude — the perfect name for the toy that defined Jake Stevens, not because he liked being alone. He didn't. He'd always found it better to be surrounded by the right kind of people, and Jake had a knack for collecting friends just like he collected brandy snifters from the cities he'd traveled to. But the only way to be completely autonomous was to be unattached. It was a credo Jake lived by, and it meant that he knew the value of his own solitude. At the top of the pyramid that was Jake's life, there was only one person — the one he smiled at in the mirror every morning. At thirty-nine, he was just where he'd wanted to be at this point in his life. Unfettered and financially fluid, he had the world by the tail, and today he was going to bag it and take it home.

Ignoring the doorman who greeted him, he trotted down the steps in front of the Biltmore. At the bottom of the steps, his red Porsche idled as the valet got out. "Hey, put the top down, will ya?" Jake called down.

The kid, who looked no more than eighteen, knew exactly how to do it, and as the top began to buzz back, Jake's attention was snatched away by the blonde on her way up the steps. She was college aged, probably twenty years his junior, but he'd never found that to be a problem. Tipping his sunglasses, he gave her that engaging grin that had always worked for him before.

She smiled back, as they always did, and slowed her step as he came toward her.

"I'm not usually this blunt, Ma'am, but I've learned over the years that if I let an opportunity slip by me, I sometimes never get it again. And you are, by far, the most beautiful woman I've laid eyes on since I pulled into St. Clair yesterday."

She laughed, as though she'd heard the line before, but it didn't seem to hurt his chances. "I'm Sarah," she said. "Are you staying in the hotel?"

"Yes," he said, "and if I had time, I'd turn around and escort you right back inside. But alas—" He threw his hand dramatically over his heart and sighed heavily as she laughed again. "I have to be somewhere—to look at a plane I'm thinking about buying." He waited a beat for her to be sufficiently impressed, and when her eyebrows lifted slightly, he went on. "Now, I don't want you to think I'm the kind of guy who hits on every woman he sees, but do you think, by any chance, you'd care to meet a lonely trans-planted Texan for drinks later? I can call you when I get back."

He knew he wasn't imagining the sparkle in her eye, for he'd seen it many times before. "I'm in room 323," she answered. "But if I'm not there, I'll probably be out by the pool."

The pool, he thought with a grin. *Perfect*. "I'll call as soon as I get back."

"You haven't told me your name yet."

"Oh, yeah," he said. "Jake. Jake Stevens."

But already he'd forgotten hers. The room number was all that really mattered. Waving, he trotted the rest of the way down the steps. Tossing a five-dollar bill at the valet, he slid behind the wheel.

Florida was great, he told himself as he pulled onto Highway 19. Opportunities everywhere he looked. It was pure luck that he'd gotten transferred here. He only wished he could spend less time house hunting and more time playing in the few days he had left before he had to report to work.

He pulled up to a stoplight and leaned his head back on the headrest, letting the morning rays of sunlight beat down on his face. The wind was picking up, haphazardly blowing his hair. *I should stop somewhere and get a haircut*, he thought, glancing into his mirror. But it didn't look so bad a little longer, and the women seemed to like it. Idly, he decided to wait.

The stoplight didn't change, and he started to get irritated. Traffic often made him feel out of control, and there was nothing he hated worse.

He glanced around at the billboards that dominated the four corners and saw one for his favorite cognac, another for a restaurant near Honeymoon Island, a third for the outlet mall, a fourth for a television station.

The light still hadn't changed, and he began to perspire. He flicked on the air conditioner, knowing that it would do little to combat the heat with the top down, but Jake had never been one to let logic interfere with his quest for comfort.

When the light flashed green, Jake stepped on the accelerator and flicked on the radio. The wind in his ears made it impossible to hear, so finally he turned it off and tried to concentrate instead on the new toy he was going to buy— a Piper Arrow PA 28. Just what he needed to make life complete.

Once he had it, he would finally have everything he wanted.

The wind was too strong for a leisurely afternoon test flight, and Lynda Barrett wished she'd scheduled it for another day ... another month ... another year. But this fellow Jake Stevens was her first potential buyer, and she had already delayed showing him the plane as long as she dared; she didn't have the luxury of waiting any longer. The maddening thing about listing something for sale is that, sooner or later, someone will buy it.

Lynda stood on the wing of the Piper, gently polishing the name she'd had painted on the side when she'd bought it two years ago. *Solitude.* This plane was her escape, her refuge from the pressures of her job as an attorney. She would rather have sold her home, her father's home, and everything else either of them owned than the plane.

But she had tried selling both houses, and there hadn't been any buyers. Now the only way she could see to get a start on paying off the enormous debts her father had bequeathed her was to sell her favorite possession—the only thing she had that anyone seemed to want to buy.

The wind picked up, blowing an empty paper cup across the tarmac. Her eyes followed it—until she saw Gordon Addison leaning against the wall of the hangar, smoking a cigarette. He was watching her the way he always did, with that narrow-eyed look that gave her chills. He hadn't spoken to her in weeks, not since she'd come up with her fifth excuse not to go out with him. He was the one thing about this airport she wouldn't miss when she sold her plane.

Moving to the other side of the wing so he couldn't see her so easily, she looked into the wind and ran her fingertips over the cold, smooth metal of the fuselage. She remembered the day she bought *Solitude*. It had meant that she'd finally risen above the humdrum existence of her parents—whose lives consisted of "Jeopardy" and macaroni-and-cheese. Lynda had had a plan—to have more, to do more, to *be* more. Buying the plane had meant that she had finally arrived.

As her love for the plane had grown, she had begun casting off friends, as though they exceeded the weight limit of the baggage she could carry. She had shaken off her hobbies, her clubs, and her church in order to free up more time to spend in the cockpit. The cockpit she was about to sell. Where would she anchor herself once the plane was gone?

Shaking off her quicksand depression, Lynda went back to polishing the plane. The prospective buyer would be here any minute, and she supposed she should be practicing some kind of sales pitch. She did need the money after all. But somewhere in the back of her mind, she knew she was still hoping some miracle would keep her from having to go through with the sale.

She heard the sound of a car and turned around. Across the tarmac, a red Porsche was weaving through the parked planes, as if the driver had a perfect right to drive wherever he pleased. Lynda stopped polishing and watched as he made his way toward her.

The man who got out was in his late thirties and sported a dark tan and designer clothes that mocked his attempt to look casual. He grinned up at her, a cocky grin that set her instantly on guard. "This isn't a parking lot," she called down.

"It's okay," he said. "I parked here yesterday when I looked at the plane, and nobody objected. I'm Jake Stevens."

The confidence with which he uttered his name riled her, and she resisted the urge to say, "Oh, *well*. Since you're Jake Stevens—"

Climbing down, she eyed him more closely. He was too good-looking, too self-assured, and probably had too much money. The combination made her dislike him instantly.

Grudgingly, she extended her hand. "I'm Lynda Barrett."

"I figured as much," he said. "Did Mike tell you I came yesterday?"

"Yes. He said you'd want to take a test flight today."

"I wanted to take one yesterday, but he had a problem with it."

"He runs the airport," she said, "but he doesn't own this plane. I do, and I was in court."

"So he said." He took off his Ray Bans and dropped them into his shirt pocket, as if by showing her his "mesmerizing" eyes he might soften her mood a bit. "No problem, though. Today's as good a day as any."

"Not really," she said, looking into the breeze. "The wind's a little stronger than I like."

"Not for me. I can handle it."

The ego behind his words made her grin slightly. "Of course you can. So, Lindbergh, any questions you wanted to ask about the plane?"

He cocked his head at her barb. "No, but I might have a few about its owner."

"Such as."

"Such as, where you get your attitude?"

"*My* attitude?" She breathed a laugh and shook her head, her comeback forming on the tip of her tongue. But something stopped her. *No need to make him angry*, she told herself. *Unfortunately, this is business.* Sighing, she took a stab at honesty. "Look, I guess I'm just having a little trouble with this. I'm not looking forward to selling my plane."

"I don't blame you." Walking under the Piper, he checked the wing flaps and glanced back at her. "I looked it over pretty well yesterday. You've really maintained it."

"I spend all my spare time taking care of it," she said. She watched him drain a little fuel from the wing sump and fought the proprietary urge to tell him to keep his hands off her plane. "Did Mike let you see the log books?"

"Yeah, and the maintenance records. He was able to answer most of my questions, but he didn't really know why you were selling it."

Lynda's stomach tightened. "Financial reasons."

15

"Your law practice isn't doing well?"

"My practice is fine, thank you."

Frowning, he turned back to her. "Excuse me for asking, but before I sink a wad into a plane like this, I need to know the real reason you want to sell."

"I told you the real reason."

"Okay, okay. Don't get so hot. Save it for something worthwhile."

It was his type that she hated she finally realized, and this guy fit every macho stereotype she could think of. "You're pretty sure of yourself, aren't you?"

"Sometimes." Grinning, he checked the engine sump and the oil, and Lynda watched, shaking her head at his arrogance.

The attitude, she thought. Her attitude was coming back again, filling her with bitterness, and somehow she had to fight it. Taking a deep breath, she tried to change the subject. "How long have you been flying?"

"About twenty years," he said. "Right now I fly a 747 for TSA Airlines."

Lynda raised her eyebrows. "Then why would you want your own plane? I'd think you'd be tired of flying when you aren't working."

Jake went to the propellers and ran his hands along the blades. "Flying for work and flying for pleasure are two different things. There's nothing like leaving the world behind and being up there all alone without anybody telling you where to go."

Lynda looked up at the sky and realized that, finally, they had found common ground. "It's a sanctuary," she said quietly. "If my church could blueprint that feeling, they'd pack the pews every Sunday."

He looked around the prop, eyeing her narrowly. "Oh, no. You're not one of those, are you?"

"Those what?"

"Those flower-selling, tract-passing, baloney-flinging religion junkies."

She couldn't decide whether to be offended or not. "Do you mean Christians?"

"Whatever they call themselves," he said, turning back to the plane. "I attract them, you know. They flock to me in airports like I'm wearing a sign that says, 'Try me. I'll believe anything.' "

"I've never sold flowers or passed out tracts or flung baloney, and you certainly don't attract me. At the moment, the only thing I'm trying to sell you is my plane."

Chuckling slightly, he touched the name painted on the side. "I like what you named it. *Solitude*. It fits me. I think I'll keep the name."

"You haven't even decided to buy it yet."

"No, but I'm really interested. It's the best I've found for the money."

"You'd better fly it first. It's a big step down from a 747 to a single engine."

"No kidding."

"You might not like it."

His grin returned. "You're trying to talk me out of it, aren't you?"

"No, of course not."

He stepped up onto the wing, opened the door, and turned back to her. "Come on, get in. Let's see what she can do."

Reluctantly Lynda followed him up and slipped into the seat next to him. She attributed the feeling of dread taking hold of her heart to her despair that she might have to surrender the plane today.

CHAPTER TWO

A m I making you nervous?" Jake glanced at her as he pitched the plane downward then pulled back up, like a Thunderbird performing for his fans.

"I always get nervous when my life is in the hands of a psychopath." Gripping the edge of her gray vinyl seat, she closed her eyes as he dove again. "You know, you won't get a good feel for the ride if you keep showboating."

He laughed and brought it back up. "I'd forgotten how much lighter this feels. I love the hands-on quality instead of everything being so automatic. The pilot is in complete control."

"I knew you were one of those control types."

He laughed. "Don't tell me you're not. You wouldn't own a plane like this if you didn't like being in control."

She looked out the window and saw the airport growing smaller below them. "I don't fly for control," she said quietly.

"Then why do you?"

"Because unless I'm in the company of an aspiring stunt pilot who asks a lot of questions, I can think up here. Reflect."

"So how long have you been hiding up here in your Piper?"

She shot him a look. "I've had the plane for two years if that's what you mean. The best two years of my life."

He chuckled. "You almost sound like you're talking about a husband."

"Oh, no. A plane can give a lot more pleasure than grief. Not like a husband at all."

"Those are the words of a bitter woman. You must be divorced."

His presumptions amazed her. "Actually, I've never been married. And I'm not bitter. Just smart." Her eyes trailed back out the window, and she wished he'd hurry and land so they could get this transaction over with.

"Me either," he said. "I try not to strap on anything I can live without."

Lynda laughed out loud, surprising him. "You've got to be kidding. You could live without that Porsche you drove up in or that Rolex on your wrist or that diamond cluster on your finger? Those are not the trappings of a man who likes to keep things simple."

"Hey, I never said I don't like a little self-indulgence now and then. Besides, we were talking about spouses, not possessions."

"We were talking about keeping things simple," she said. "I'm just pointing out your contradictions."

He was getting annoyed, and something about that pleased her. "It's not a contradiction to want a few material things. I'm a firm believer in going after whatever makes you happy."

"Is that what all those things do? Make you happy?"

"Don't I look like a happy guy?"

She smiled, unable to help herself. "But owning a plane would make you happier?"

"You got it, darlin'. It made you happy, didn't it?"

"Yeah," she whispered. "It did most of the time." That melancholy fell over her again, and she tried to steer her mind from imagining what life would be without *Solitude*.

"I'd like to close the deal as soon as possible," Jake said, cutting into her thoughts. "When we land, we can discuss the particulars."

She sighed. "I guess the sooner the better. Are you ready to land now?"

"Sure," he said. "I've seen what I need to see."

Taking the radio mike from its hook, she held it to her mouth. "St. Clair Unicom — Cherokee 1 – 0 – 1 – 2 Delta. We're ready to land, Mike."

Mike's voice crackled in their headphones. "All clear, Lynda. No traffic reported. Runway 4."

She glanced at Jake as he began to fly parallel to the right side of the runway. "I'll land, if you want me to."

19

"I've got it," he said.

She watched out the window as he boxed around the airport and began his descent, and her heart grew heavier. Absently, her fingertips stroked the soft gray cloth of the seats that were so comfortable to her, and she wondered if she'd ever find another sanctuary that was quite as fulfilling. Jake was getting a real bargain, and she was the big loser. She almost wished she hadn't cleaned the charcoal carpet last week or polished the instrument panel or vacuumed the cloth ceiling. All those things only contributed to the comfort and luxury of the quiet cabin. If it had been dirty or ragged or badly maintained, maybe he wouldn't have wanted it.

Jake reached for the lever to release the landing gear, and a short whirring sound followed as it started lowering. But the sound was too short, and Lynda shot a look at the instruments.

"Is there something wrong with these lights?" Jake asked.

Lynda checked the gear indicator lights. According to them, the landing gear hadn't gone down. She leaned up and grabbed the lever. Nothing happened.

"I heard them go down before," Jake said. "Didn't you hear it?"

"It didn't sound right," Lynda said. "Either they're jammed, or the light's not working. Pull up."

She waited as Jake aborted the landing and climbed again. "I'll check the circuit breaker," she said. "Keep trying the lever."

Jake tried again and failed, as Lynda pressed on the circuit breaker marked "gear."

"It seems okay," she said, maintaining her calm. "Let me pump it down manually."

Gripping the hand pump between the seats, she tried to pump it down by hand, but the light still wouldn't come on.

"Here, let me," he said, trying to move her hand.

"Something's wrong," she said, surrendering it. "The pump moves too easily, and nothing happens."

Jake tried it, his face growing tense. "It has to be a busted hose, or there'd be more resistance."

"No," she argued. "It can't be. It just can't."

But she couldn't think of anything else it could be, and as panic began to rise inside her, she tried it again.

There was nothing Mike Morgan hated worse than a hotdogger playing with a plane as though it were a paper kite. Aggravated, he watched out the window as the plane feigned a landing, then pulled up at the last minute.

It couldn't be Lynda flying, he told himself, sitting in his makeshift control tower that looked more like a concession booth. Lynda had too much respect for her plane. It had to be the arrogant guy who belonged to that red Porsche. Grabbing his microphone, he called up to the plane to put a stop to this.

"Cherokee 1 – 2 Delta—St. Clair Unicom. What's with the touch-and-go's, Lynda?"

He waited for an answer, and when he didn't get one, he pushed the button again. "Lynda? Do you read me?"

Finally, he heard her voice. "We're having a little problem with our landing gear, Mike. We're not sure whether it's down or not."

"Oh, no," he said to himself then glanced out at the plane circling overhead.

"Mike, we're going to do a flyby. Could you come out and see if the gear's down?"

Mike grabbed his binoculars with his left hand and pressed the button again with his right. "Affirmative, Lynda."

Then dashing through the glass doors, he tried to see just how much trouble they were really in.

Cherokee 1 – 2 Delta—St. Clair Unicom. You reading me, Lynda?"

"1 – 2 Delta." Bracing herself, Lynda looked over at Jake, whose temples glistened with perspiration. "How does it look, Mike?"

"Worse than we thought, guys. The landing gear is only partially down, and one looks like it's down further than the other."

Jake swore, and Lynda closed her eyes and tried to let the news sink in.

"We can't even do a smooth belly landing if it's *partially* down!" Jake said. "And if it's not locked all the way down, it could squirrel all over the place."

"Even if it's locked where it is, we'll land lopsided," she said. "We'll lose a wing and cartwheel."

Jake grabbed the microphone out of her hand. "Mike, could you see any oil?"

"I was just getting to that," Mike said. "It looks like there could be oil streaming down the belly behind the gear. Did you try to pump it manually?"

Lynda and Jake exchanged worried looks, and Lynda took the mike back. "We tried, Mike. It has to be a loose hose."

Jake snatched the microphone again. "Mike, we're gonna have to take our chances and land with what we've got."

"No!" Lynda shouted. "We could crash! My plane would be destroyed."

"Not to mention its passengers!" he shouted back at her. "But there isn't enough fuel for us to stay up here long enough for a miracle, so unless you've got any better ideas...."

Viciously, Lynda tried the hand pump again and then the automatic lever, as if the plane might have healed itself in the last few minutes.

Finally giving up, she took the mike back. "It won't go up *or* down, Mike. He's right. We don't have any choice."

"I'm so glad you agree," Jake said caustically.

Lynda ignored him.

"I don't see any alternative either, Lynda," Mike admitted. "This could be bad. The wind isn't gonna help any. This crosswind could be a nightmare."

"Yeah," she said, "and if the gear isn't down all the way, then our brakes aren't working, either. And the fire hazard...."

Jake jerked the mike back. "If we had a choice, Mike, we'd sure find another way. But we don't. Are you ready for us or not?"

"No, not yet," Mike said. "It'll take some preparation. Just stand by, and I'll get back to you."

Silence followed, and Jake set the microphone back on its hook and continued circling the airport.

For a moment, neither of them spoke.

It was the closest Lynda had ever been to death, yet she didn't feel the peace she had always thought she'd feel. She wasn't ready to die—not mentally, emotionally, or spiritually. Wasn't there supposed to be a warning so good-byes could be said, apologies made, and affairs put in order? She just wasn't supposed to take off into the sky on a morning test flight and then never come back down.

"I hope somebody moves my Porsche," Jake said, eyeing the small airport below them.

Again, Lynda was amazed. "We're about to crash, and all you care about is your car?"

His expression betrayed his growing anger. "You're the one who cared more about your plane surviving than the people in it."

"Hey, *I'm* in it. I'm not crazy about the prospect of death either!"

Wiping his forehead with the back of his sleeve, he said, "Look, we don't have time for this. We have to get ready, whether we like it or not. I'll land the plane. I have more experience with emergencies."

"You don't have experience with *this plane*, Lindbergh. The weight's different, and you don't have a feel for it. You might bring it down too hard, and with this crosswind—"

"How many real emergency landings have you ever made?" he cut in.

"None. But I know—"

"I've had two," he said. "*I'm* landing the plane."

"This is no time for ego!"

"You're right. It's not."

Livid, they stared at each other neither wanting to back down. Suddenly, the cabin seemed too small for both of them, and she wished she could put more space between them. If she could just breathe....

On the verge of tears, she said, "All right, maybe you *are* more experienced. You land it, and I'll cut off the engine and the fuel. We'll need to shut everything off before we touch down. This is gonna take both of us."

Cursing, Jake tried the pump again, his hands trembling. When it was obvious how hopeless it was, he sent another expletive flying and slammed his hand into the instrument panel. "Piece of trash! Don't you ever check your landing gear?"

"Of course I do," she said. "I've never had any problem with it at all! I just had an annual three months ago, and everything was fine."

"A pilot should know every inch of his plane!"

"I didn't notice *you* sticking your head up the wheel well on the preflight!"

"It's *your* plane." He wiped his forehead again. "Are you sure you weren't just trying to unload it on some poor soul before you had to foot some major repair bills?"

Her mouth fell open. "I didn't even want to sell it! If my father hadn't died and left me a mountain of debts, you wouldn't even be here!"

"Lucky me."

Again, thick silence filled the cabin, and she told herself she wouldn't cry. She couldn't do what had to be done if her eyes were blurry with tears. "Look, we have to try to get this plane down without either of us getting killed. Now, if we could just—"

"Cherokee 1 – 2 Delta," the radio cut in. "St. Clair Unicom."

Lynda took the microphone. "1 – 2 Delta. Go ahead, Mike."

"We're trying to clear the runway, but we need a little time to clear the tarmac, too, so no other planes are damaged. Just hang on for a few minutes. You have plenty of fuel, don't you?"

"Enough to blow us to kingdom come," Jake muttered.

She sighed and checked the gauge. "About forty minutes' worth."

"Well," Mike said, "it won't hurt to burn some of that off to cut down on the fire hazard. While we're waiting, is there anyone either of you would like for us to contact? Jake?"

Jake hesitated for a moment, racking his brain for someone who would care. The little blonde on the steps came to mind, but he only remembered her room number, not her name. He thought of his boss, but in case things came out all right, he was afraid of the conclusions the airline might draw about the crash landing.

Dismally, he realized that there really wasn't anyone.

"Jake?" Mike prompted. "Do you read me?"

Jake took the mike. "Nobody, okay? I don't want you to contact anybody."

He couldn't escape the long look Lynda gave him.

"Lynda?"

Jake handed the mike to her and saw the emotion pulling at her face. "Yes," she said quietly. "Contact Sally Crawford at

555 – 2312. Tell her to cancel all my appointments for this afternoon. But you don't have to do it now, Mike. Wait until … afterward, so she won't have to sweat this out."

Jake gaped at her. "Cancel your *appointments?*"

Her face turned rock hard, and she didn't answer him.

"Don't you have a mother or a lover or somebody?" he asked.

"No."

"So the closest person to you is your secretary? That's pretty pathetic."

Her face reddened. "Who do you think *you* are? At least I had somebody to call. What about *your* mother or a close friend or even an enemy or two? Surely you must have a couple of women somewhere who'd be interested in knowing you're about to buy the farm!"

His jaw popped. "Both of my parents are dead. And I'd rather admit there was no one than to hide behind some secretary and all those important appointments."

"If I wanted someone, I could have someone. There are plenty—" Her voice cracked, and she cut herself off, unable to go on. Tears came to her eyes, making her angrier, and she struggled to hold them back.

"But right now there's no one who cares that you're probably about to die. You're just as alone as I am."

"There are worse things than dying alone!" Lynda threw back at him.

"Are there?" His voice softened by degrees, and as he looked out the window at the activity on the tarmac below them, he said, "Right now it seems to me that the worst thing in the world is...."

"What?" she asked. "What is the worst thing in the world?"

"Dying with a total stranger."

The reality of that concept knocked the breath from her, and she fought the conflicting feelings assaulting her. As her first tears fell, they were both quiet, embroiled in battle with their own raging thoughts.

Her tears softened him, and finally, he let out a long, weary breath. "You're right, you know. There're at least three women who would like to see me burn."

"They probably have good reason," she whispered.

"Yeah, probably. I guess if you condemn a man for not wanting to tie himself to one woman for life, I deserve what I get."

"Life isn't really that long, though, is it?"

"Not lately," he said.

He looked out the window, searching the area around the airport. "If we could just find a pasture or something to land in. If we landed in the dirt, it would cut down on the fire hazard."

"The joys of flying in this part of Florida. Nothing but pavement and swamp. And the swamp has too many trees for a water landing."

"It might not be so bad if the gas tank weren't so low. I think I could get us down on the belly, maybe without cartwheeling, but the sparks could start a fire."

"Maybe they won't," she whispered with her last vestige of hope.

"Maybe not," Jake whispered. "I've still got a lot of living to do."

CHAPTER THREE

On the ground, Mike looked at the plane through his binoculars again, wishing for a miracle. But the landing gear was still unevenly dropped and only partially down. Dropping the binoculars around his neck, he waved an arm, directing the planes that were moving, one by one, from their parked positions on the tarmac. The red Porsche sat right in the way, and for a moment, he thought of driving it out to the middle of Runway 4 so that Jake would have to run over it himself. It would be poetic justice.

Then he quelled the thought and checked to see whether the keys were in the ignition. Waving to one of the men nearby, he said, "Get this car out of the way, will you?"

Sirens drew closer, and he ran to the end of the building and parted the growing crowd of spectators to direct the fire trucks onto the tarmac. Three of them whizzed past him, lights flashing. Then there were the ambulances — one, two, three, four — and he realized with a sinking stomach that they were preparing for additional casualties on the ground.

He started back to the planes taxiing out of the way and saw a van pull in behind him. It was a media van with the call letters *WTTV* on the side. The van slowed beside him, and a reporter he recognized from the six o'clock news jumped out. "We heard on the police radio that there's a plane about to crash." He pointed up to the plane circling overhead. "Is that it?"

"Stay back," Mike ordered as he kept walking. "Don't get any closer to the runway and move the van."

"Man, I need it right here."

"I'm telling you, when that plane hits the ground, it's liable to blow from here to Montana. Don't say I didn't warn you!"

"Have you been in contact with the pilots?" the reporter asked. But Mike didn't answer. He had too much work to do.

The trees beyond the airport were greener than Lynda thought they should be in September, probably because they'd had so much rain this summer. She wondered now why she hadn't noticed that stark, clear color before. Only now was she even aware that those trees existed. Of course, this landing was different. This time the plane might not stop until it reached them.

Between two lines of those trees, one on either side of the street leading to the small airport, she saw a convoy of vehicles that looked as small as toy cars heading to the gates. A shiver went through her. "Are those fire trucks?"

"And ambulances. Just waiting for us to hit bottom."

"Don't be so cynical. They're there to help us."

"There may not be anything left to help." He tore his eyes away from the small square airport and checked the gauges. Lynda followed his eyes and noted that they'd used up half of their fuel already.

"If you've already given up, maybe I should land the plane after all."

"No. If there's a chance of getting us out of this alive, I'm the one who can do it."

Disgusted, she gaped at him. "Has it ever occurred to you that you're not the final authority in all this?"

"No? Then who is?"

"Oh, that's right," she said. "You don't believe in God. You've got the world all figured out."

"I'm not into myths," he said. "I like facts. And what is there to figure out, really? You're born, you live, you die. End of story."

"It's *not* the end of the story," she said. "There's an afterlife."

He laughed then and shook his head. "Wouldn't that be convenient?"

She bristled. "Convenient?"

"Yeah. Tell yourself a little lie just before you crash, and maybe you'll feel better about giving it all up."

She opened her mouth to argue but changed her mind and wearily leaned back. "Believe what you want. You're not worth trying to convince."

The steady, muffled hum of the engine became the only sound in the cabin again, and their eyes strayed to the concrete square below them where mechanics, pilots, and staff ran up and down the tarmac. Half of the planes had been moved already, and the other half taxied out in a single stream of traffic, like toy planes strung together and dragged by a toddler. It looked orderly and peaceful from here, not at all like a rushed attempt to prepare for a tragedy.

The air seemed thinner now than she remembered it being before, and she longed to roll a window down as she would in a car. But even if that had been a reasonable thing to do at 10,000 feet, moving 100 miles per hour, the windows weren't built to budge. The vessel that had once been her refuge was now just a cage.

Jake seemed to be struggling with his own thoughts. Swallowing, he wiped his brow and glanced at her. "So how long since your father died?"

Wondering where that question had come from, Lynda reluctantly answered, "Three months."

"I'm sorry," he said quietly.

It was true that losing her father had been tough, but she couldn't say it was the death itself that had grieved her. Instead, it was the "what-might-have-been's" that had assaulted her when she'd buried him. The relationship they could have had. The one she had been too busy to maintain.

"You don't want to talk about it," he said quietly. "No problem. I'm just trying to get our minds off this."

She shook her head. "It's all right. I just can't think right now. It's so quiet up here—so *normal*. The engine's running like a charm; everything's intact. It's hard to believe that this landing is gonna do us in. But look at them down there. *They* know it. That's why they're hurrying around, getting ready for the worst case."

"Yeah," he said, "and none of them knows the first thing about us."

She turned back to him, and saw the first trace of vulnerability she'd seen. "Would it make any difference if they did?"

"There might be some comfort in knowing there was somebody down there who had a stake in whether we made it through this."

"It wouldn't help us land any smoother," she whispered.

"I don't know," he said. "It might."

Why his words frightened her, she wasn't sure. "Are you saying you'd take more care in the landing if you knew someone cared about you? That just because neither of us has close attachments, it doesn't *matter* if we crash?"

"No! I don't have a death wish."

"Well, that's the second time you've said something pretty negative about our landing. I'm starting to get really scared that you might just give up and let us die. Is that what you're saying?"

"Of course not! I don't *know* what I'm saying, okay? I just wish...." His voice trailed off, and he found it difficult to center his thoughts. "I mean, doesn't this make you feel ... something? Incomplete? Regret?"

A still, small voice reminded her what she knew—or what she had once known—about completion, about regret. The memories were vague from lack of use, and she couldn't share them with him for fear that he would mock her and throw the words back in her face.

"You *must* feel that way," he said. "I mean here you are in a busted plane called *Solitude*, telling your secretary to cancel your appointments. Not the makings of a full life."

The voice in her heart died, and she let her old, human voice speak instead. "You have a lot of room to talk."

"I know. Maybe I'm thinking that if I can figure you out, I can figure me out."

"Hey, there's nothing wrong with me. I'm a loner, okay? I have everything I need."

"Do you?" he asked.

"Yes. No surprises, no letdowns. No one to disappoint me."

"So you've eliminated the lows. But that also means there are no highs."

Those words might have been her own. But the ego part of her, the part that held pride to her breast like a shield, dismissed them. "That's why I fly."

"A woman who spends all her free time alone in an airplane strikes me as someone who's hiding from something."

"Oh, brother," she groaned. "You've got a lot of nerve, you know that? Driving up in your yup-mobile with your diamonds flashing and your arrogance dripping off you like cheap cologne—How dare you make any judgments about me?"

"I'm not. I'm making an observation."

Furious, she jerked the microphone off its hook. "Come in, Mike. This is Cherokee 1 – 2 Delta. I'm ready to land right now! Do you read me?"

Jake grabbed her arm. "What do you think you're doing?"

But Mike's answer came quickly. "Negative, Lynda. We're not ready."

"How long are you going to keep us up here?"

"Until we've taken every precaution! Do not land until I give you the go-ahead! Do you read me?"

Lynda wiped away another tear. "Loud and clear."

Slamming the radio down, she covered her face and told herself to calm down. She was letting this man dig at her in the painful, bruised places she'd been shielding for so long, and suddenly she wished she could just be alone to face her life—and her death.

"Look, I'm sorry," Jake said quietly. "I didn't mean to send you off the deep end."

"Just shut up, will you? You're not making this any easier. If you're so interested in figuring someone out, maybe you should do a little *self*-analysis. Why are *you* all alone in the world?"

He hesitated only a moment, and his voice was flat when he answered. "Simple. Because I'm a selfish pig."

"Now, there's an unexpected revelation. I guess fear of death brings out the truth."

"Too much maybe," he said sullenly. "Too late."

She let those words sink in and wondered if *she'd* gotten to the point of honesty yet. Had she missed the chances she'd had to face the truth? Would she get another chance?

That small voice prompted her again to tell him it wasn't too late, but the voice was growing more distant and easier to ignore.

"We're going to make it, you know," Jake said. "Together, we can do this. We're both experienced pilots, and neither of us wants to die."

She tried to imagine the plane landing carefully, easily, and without incident, but the possibility seemed too remote. "But neither of us has tried to land metal to pavement with no brakes in a crosswind."

31

"Talk about looking at the bright side," he muttered. He glanced at her. "You're shaking."

"So are you," she pointed out.

"I'm scared."

Lynda wasn't sure why those two matter-of-fact words, uttered by such a tough, hard man would shake her so, but she wilted and surrendered to her tears. "I'm scared, too," she whispered.

He reached over and took her hand, and something about that touch comforted her. Their eyes met, a moment of connection, where she thought she knew him, and he thought he knew her, a moment when they ceased to be strangers.

"Cherokee 1 – 2 Delta—St. Clair Unicom. Come in, Lynda."

Jake let go of her hand, and she grabbed the mike, bracing herself. "1 – 2 Delta. Go ahead, Mike. Are you ready for us?"

"Affirmative. You can land now, guys," Mike said softly. "Just watch that crosswind, and be careful. I wish I could offer you something in the way of advice, but you know what to do. I'll be praying for you guys down here."

Lynda swallowed and wiped her eyes. "Yeah. Thank you, Mike."

She put the radio back on its hook and looked at Jake, who was staring dully out the window. His face was empty, drained, and for a moment she thought he might cry too. She wished he would so that she could fully surrender to her own emotions and wilt outwardly the way she was wilting inside.

Finally, he looked at her, reached across to touch her face, and whispered, "Are you ready?"

"Yeah," she said. "You?"

"As ready as I'll ever be, I guess." He checked the gauges, then said, "Once we're on short final and know we've got the runway made, kill the engine and cut all the switches. And if you can, unlatch the door so we can get out fast."

In a gesture that surprised her, he leaned over and tested her seat belt then checked his own. "All right," he said. "Here goes."

The plane descended smoothly like any other craft coming in on any other day, but Mike knew that the moment it touched down the problems would begin. He eyed the rolling cameras and the reporter with his microphone in hand, waiting to get every gory frame.

The ambulances were in place, ready to speed to the scene, and the fire trucks were standing by. Mike felt a wave of dizziness and shook it away, telling himself this was no time for panic. There was too much that had to be done.

He brought the binoculars to his eyes as the plane narrowed the distance between the sky and the runway, and under his breath, he prayed for a miracle.

The plane touched down, sending a spray of sparks as it scraped down the runway—too fast, like a speedboat on an open sea. When it fishtailed, Mike dropped the binoculars.

For several seconds that stretched into eternity, the plane cartwheeled across the runway, rolling and sliding, breaking a wing here, losing the tail there, leaving pieces in its wake, until it finally rolled to a deadly halt on its side.

The ambulances and fire trucks launched across the runways. Stricken with dread and terror, Mike ran toward what was left of the plane.

CHAPTER FOUR

Across town in the law offices of Schilling, Martin and Barrett, Sally Crawford rushed to type the three motions that Lynda needed ready for court the next morning. As much as she managed to accomplish each day, it was clear to her that Lynda needed a second secretary. Sometimes things moved so fast that she had to run just to stay in place.

But it was tough convincing a workaholic that you were working too hard. As long as Sally's fingers flew across that keyboard, and the phone calls were answered, and the motions were filed, and the appointments were made, and the office ran smoothly, Lynda was happy.

She shouldn't complain, Sally admitted as she punched in the command to *print* then swiveled in her chair and began stacking the papers that had to be ready before the mail boy came around to empty the "out" baskets.

The phone buzzed; she picked it up. "Lynda Barrett's office."

"Sally, there's a Paige Varner here to see Lynda."

"Lynda's not in," Sally told the receptionist who intercepted visitors as they came in. "Take a message, and I'll have Lynda call her." Hanging up, she saw that the printer was finished, and she pulled out the pages.

The phone buzzed again. "Lynda Barrett's office."

"Sally, she says she's left messages, and Lynda hasn't called. She's pretty upset—"

Sally moaned. "All right. Send her back. I'll talk to her."

She hung up and sat for a moment, staring at the phone, wondering what excuse she'd use to cover for Lynda this time.

34

The plain, simple truth was that Paige Varner's was a *pro bono* case, and it wasn't exactly one of Lynda's top priorities.

She saw the elevator doors open, and Paige bolted off, clutching her three-year-old daughter, Brianna, on her hip. Paige's eyes were swollen and red as she cast Sally a frantic look and started toward her.

Sally got up to meet her. "Hello, Paige. Lynda's not here."

"I've *got* to talk to her," Paige said, starting to cry. "We've got to *do* something. He tried to kidnap Brianna!"

"Who?" Sally asked, leading her to a chair and making her sit down. Brianna's feet hit the floor, but Paige pulled her into her lap, unable to let her go.

"Her father," she said. "Do we have a court date yet? If we do, I can make plans to leave the state, so he won't know where we are—"

"Calm down," Sally said, stooping in front of her. "Now start over. Take a deep breath and tell me what happened."

Paige didn't want to take time to start over, but she tried. "Her day-care teacher called me at work and told me that Keith was there claiming that I told him to pick her up."

"Wait a minute. Don't you have a restraining order?"

"Yes!" Paige cried. "But it's *worthless!* We're not safe here! I have to talk to Lynda. If she can get us a court date, then I can get that over with and get out of town, before he takes her, or comes after me again, or—"

The phone rang, and Sally stood up reluctantly. "I'm sorry, Paige. I have to get that."

Paige covered her eyes and nodded.

Sally went back to her desk and grabbed the phone, praying it was Lynda. "Lynda Barrett's office."

"Is this Sally Crawford?"

Sally glanced at Paige. Brianna was wiping her mother's tears, and Paige was whispering to her. "Yes."

"This is Mac Lowery. I'm a mechanic at the St. Clair Airport. I'm afraid there's been an accident."

CHAPTER FIVE

For a moment, as the fog slowly cleared, Lynda lay still, trying to find some clarity to hang her thoughts on. The plane had hit belly to pavement, she remembered, and had slid for what had seemed like miles, breaking into fragments, crumpling, shattering, rolling—

Now the plane was on its side, and she hung sideways in her seat, still clamped by the seat belt that cut mercilessly into her shoulder and hipbones. Trying to get her head upright, wincing at the stab of pain in her ribs and the cracking pain in her head, she released the latch and slid from her seat against the back of the one next to her.

Pain seared through her, and she looked down to find the source of it. Shards of glass had lodged in her arm, her thigh, and her stomach. With bloody hands that seemed to belong to someone else, she tried to pull one out.

But then she saw him.

All clarity returned as she reached for Jake, still strapped into the bottom of his seat, which had broken off from its back. Twisted, unconscious, and soaked with blood, he lay limp under the bashed instrument panel.

"Jake!" Her voice sounded hollow and distant, as if it came from someone else as she tried to reach for him. "Jake, are you all right?"

But he didn't stir.

Panic shook her as the first hint of smoke reached her senses—then, with dim relief, she heard sirens. But they sounded too far away, and there was no time to wait!

Forcing herself to move despite her pain, she managed to free Jake from his seat belt then grabbed under his arms and, with all her might, slid him two feet back toward the door. Praying that it would open, she disengaged the latch. The door swung down, providing a hatch no more than a yard above the ground.

The smoke was growing thicker as the sirens came closer. Lynda half-fell out the opening. Then with every ounce of energy she could gather, pulled Jake behind her, ignoring her own fuzzy thoughts about his limpness and the blood soaking into her clothes.

The moment he dropped onto the pavement, she struggled to her feet beside the plane, grabbed his arms, and dragged him across the dirt as far away from the plane as she could before collapsing beside him.

She heard tires screeching and people yelling; suddenly she was aware of movement around her. Closing her eyes, she surrendered to the paramedics as they lifted her onto a gurney then ran with her like war medics taking her out of the line of fire. A vague protest formed in her mind that they should leave her and save Jake, but that thought evaporated as a loud, vacuum sound—*whoosh*—split the air.

She opened her eyes—her plane was engulfed in quiet flames that spread to cover the place where she and Jake had lain only moments before. *It should be loud,* she thought, *like a lightning bolt from God.* Instead, this explosion had been a quiet one, almost gentle, as it worked its violence on the plane.

As the paramedics hurried her along, she glimpsed another group of medics carrying Jake. He was still limp on the gurney, and blood glistened on that expensive shirt and those slacks that had been so perfectly creased such a short time ago. The paramedics set her down and, blocking her view, bent over her with stethoscopes and an IV. "No!" she cried, trying to move them out of her way. "Help him! He's bleeding!"

"So are you."

"No, take him first! Please!"

"He's in good hands," the lead paramedic said in a steady voice, trying to calm her. "*You're* my concern right now." He took her vitals, barking out numbers that meant little to her. Still, she strained to see around him. "Is he—is he—alive?"

They were busy attaching the IV, talking to each other over her, shouting and exchanging orders.

And then she saw the urgency on the faces of the other group of paramedics, and someone shouted, "Talk to him! He's going into shock!"

"Jake, can you hear me?" someone asked him. "Jake, you've got to hold on. We're getting you to the hospital."

"We're losing him!" one of the others shouted.

"Oh, no, God, please!" She lost sight of him as the EMTs crowded around him, desperately trying to bring him back. She saw someone bring the defibrillator, and heard the desperate counting and the "Clear!" then the shock that jolted his body.

She lost sight of him again as her paramedics loaded her into the ambulance, and she tried to sit up to see through the doors before they closed them. "Please! I've got to know if he's—"

But the doors shut, and the ambulance accelerated away.

Lynda didn't remember when she had lost consciousness, but when she woke, she was in a hospital room, the cold antiseptic smell stirring her back to life.

A woman she didn't know stood over her, shining a light in her eyes. "How are you feeling?"

Lynda squinted against the light and jerked her face away. "Am I in the hospital?"

"That's right," the woman said. "You just got out of surgery."

"Surgery?"

The woman nodded. "And judging by what you've been through, I'd say you're extremely lucky. You're scratched and cut up pretty good, and you broke a couple of ribs, but you're going to be fine." The woman patted her shoulder gently then said, "I'll go tell the doctor you're awake."

Lynda squeezed her eyes shut and tried to find some clarity. Images rushed through her mind: the plane hitting the ground; the horror of impact after impact; the sight of Jake strapped in his seat ...Jake drenched in blood ...Jake not responding....He was dead. It was her punishment, she told herself—although she wasn't sure at the moment what she was being punished for. A thick, smothering shroud of guilt draped itself over her.

Tears oozed from her eyes. She squeezed them shut and, under her breath, tried to bargain with God for Jake's life.

The door swung open. Two doctors came in, followed by the nurse, who rushed to Lynda's side when she saw her tears. "Lynda, you're going to be all right," one of the doctors said gently. "You had some internal bleeding, and we had to remove your spleen. I know it's been traumatic for you—but try to understand this: You're going to be okay. Please try to calm down."

Hiccuping her sobs, she reached up and grabbed the doctor's coat with her good hand. "Is he ... dead?"

"Is who dead?"

"Jake!" she shouted.

"Doctor, the other crash victim," the nurse said. "He was brought in with her."

The second doctor took her hand, and she gripped it with all the urgency she felt as he leaned over her. "I just left him, Lynda," he said. "He's still in surgery. His condition is critical, but—"

"He's alive?" she asked, almost sitting up. "Jake's alive?"

"We almost lost him," he said. "But we think he's going to pull through."

"Oh, thank God," she cried, wilting back down.

The doctor checked the monitors attached to her then whispered a few instructions to the nurse as Lynda tried to catch her breath. When she was able, she grabbed the doctor's coat again. "I want to see him. The minute he's out of surgery I need to see him."

"That won't be possible today," he said gently. "And even tomorrow, if he regains consciousness, he'll be in ICU. That means no visitors."

"Please," she said. "You can bend a few rules, can't you? Let me see him for five minutes. That's all."

The two doctors exchanged looks, and finally, one shrugged. "We'll see what we can do. No promises. But right now there are several people out in the waiting room anxious to see you. Are you up to any visitors?"

She covered her face with a hand and tried to stop her tears. "Uh, who's out there?"

The nurse pulled a pad from her pocket, flipped a few pages, and said, "Mike somebody. And Sally—she said she's your secretary.

And your pastor and a few people who said you used to go to their church...."

"Um, I'd like to talk to Mike first," she whispered.

"All right," the nurse said, "but just for a few minutes, okay? You don't realize how weak you are, but you will as soon as you start seeing people."

Lynda already felt too weak to talk, but there were things she needed to say to Mike. Things that couldn't wait.

CHAPTER SIX

T he police station smelled like stale cigarettes and three-day-old sweat, and the noise level was worse than the day-care center where Brianna spent each day. Paige bent and picked up the child, holding her close and felt that familiar surge of shame that she hadn't been able to shelter her from the ugly realities of life.

"It's okay, Brianna," she whispered, kissing the child's forehead. "We're going to get one of these policemen to help us."

"Are they putting Daddy in jail, Mommy?"

Paige hesitated. "I don't know, honey. We'll see. Do you want them to?"

"Yes," she whispered with timid honesty.

Paige made her way to the big desk where people waited in line to file complaints, trying to blink back the tears that threatened her eyes again.

A plane crash. It couldn't be real, yet it was. Lynda had been in a plane crash.

She closed her eyes and tried to fight off the abject terror that her lawyer could die — or might, in fact, already be dead. Sally had said that Lynda was still alive, but she'd been in such a panic that Paige wasn't sure it was true.

The person at the front of the line left the desk, and Paige counted the people in front of her. She was fourth in line. Any minute now it would be her turn, and someone would tell her what to do.

Brianna laid her head on Paige's shoulder, and Paige realized that the child hadn't had her nap today. She was tired. She should be home, safe in her own room, resting to a Barney tape, instead of waiting in a police station to find a way to keep her father from getting close to her.

Lynda had known ways and had made lots of promises, but Paige couldn't depend on her now. Those tears surfaced again, and she told herself that she should stop thinking so much of herself. Lynda's plane crash was a tragedy, but Paige could only deal with one tragedy at a time.

At last her turn came, and she tried to steady her voice as she faced the uniformed woman behind the desk. "My name's Paige Varner. I have a restraining order against my ex-husband, Keith Varner, but today he tried to take our daughter from her day care. I went to my lawyer first, but she was in an accident today...." Her voice trailed off, and she waited for a response.

The officer casually dropped her pencil and leaned forward, elbows on her desk. "Mrs. Varner, we can't arrest someone for violating a restraining order unless we witness the violation."

"What do you mean, witness it? Who has to witness it?"

"You're supposed to call the police when it happens, and when they arrive, they have to see him there. If he leaves, it's out of our hands."

Paige gripped Brianna tighter, incredulous. "But that's ridiculous! I wasn't there! The restraining order is supposed to keep him away from her, too."

"You should have had the teachers call 911. Next time, you need to call us as soon as he shows up, and if the officers get there while he's still there—"

"Next time?" Paige shouted. "There's not supposed to *be* a next time. You people are supposed to protect me from that!"

"We can only do what the law allows."

"Then what's the use in having a restraining order? He can still do anything he wants!"

"You do have recourse," the woman said, as if talking to a child. "You need to file a motion for order to show cause."

"A what?"

The woman sighed. "Mrs. Varner, did you say you have a lawyer?"

"Yes, but—" She stopped, pinched the bridge of her nose, and tried to temper her voice again. "I can't reach her right now.

And no one else will represent me because I—I don't have much money. Do I have to have a lawyer to do this?"

"It would help. Then a judge would review it and decide whether to arrest him or summon him back to court. But usually, if there was no violence involved, and if he didn't threaten you in any way, the judge doesn't opt for jail time."

"Threaten?" Paige asked. "You don't think it's threatening for him to show up at her school and tell her teacher that I told him to pick her up? Do we have to wait until he attacks one of us again or until he kidnaps her and takes her so far—"

"I'm just telling you your options, Ma'am. Now, if I were you, I'd contact my lawyer right away."

"But if there's no guarantee he'll even be put in jail...." Frustrated, she half turned away. "You don't know my husband. He'll just get madder and then come after me. And he's smart. He probably already knows that he can't be arrested unless he's caught. That's why he's getting so bold."

The woman behind the desk softened a little. "Look, I can give you the name of a shelter for battered women. We could get you in there tonight if you want."

Paige thought about that for a moment. Her mind was too muddled, and she couldn't think.

"Mommy, I want to go home," Brianna said.

"Just a minute, honey." Wiping her face, she tried to take a deep breath. "He knows where the shelter is. He told me that if I ever went there, he'd drag me out."

"But he *can't* know, Mrs. Varner. It's a very well-kept secret. He was probably just trying to scare you."

"You don't know him. He has ways of finding things out."

"Mrs. Varner, every woman in that shelter has an angry man looking for her. You just have to trust the staff to know how to handle these things."

"I can't trust anyone," Paige said dismally.

"Well, here's the number anyway if you change your mind." The officer handed Paige a piece of paper. "Good luck, Mrs. Varner."

But as Paige carried Brianna back to their car, she realized she was going to need a lot more than luck. What she really needed now was Lynda.

I have to tell you," Mike said as he approached Lynda's bed, "for a few minutes there I didn't think I was ever going to see that smile again." He pulled a chair up to her bed and sat down. "So how do you feel?"

"Like I've been spared," she whispered.

He leaned his elbows on his knees and rested his chin on his hand. "It *was* a miracle, you know. When I saw that plane hit the ground, I didn't see any way in the world either one of you would make it. Who could have believed you both would?"

"Jake's not even out of surgery yet, much less out of the woods."

"Yeah, but he has a lot of people praying for him out there."

"Really?" she asked, sitting partially up. "Who?"

"Some of the people here from your church."

"My church." Wearily, she wilted back down. "I'm surprised they remember me; it's been so long since I darkened the doorstep."

She looked at the man she had known for the last two years, the man with whom she had talked airplanes and flight reports and weather, the man who was as close a friend as she had. Only now did she realize how little they really knew about each other.

"Mike, I want to thank you."

"For what?"

"For offering to pray for us today," she whispered.

Tears came to his eyes, and he struggled to blink them back. "What else was I gonna do, Lynda?"

"Oh, I don't know. Stay busy. Throw up your hands. All I know is that I wasn't doing much praying up there. Yours are the ones that got answered."

As long as he was still breathing, Jake figured he was alive, even if he couldn't manage to open his eyes or move an inch or speak.

There was something in his mouth impeding his speech and something else holding his eyelids down.

Panic struck him, and he wanted to sit up, cry out, run away, but his body wouldn't cooperate.

He could hear quiet voices around him, a steady beeping of machinery, and he felt hands probing....

The crash, he thought. He had survived the crash.

Or had he?

Panic seized him, and he opened his mouth to cry out, but something in his throat choked him. Concentrating all his effort on the task of clearing his mouth, he lifted his hand— but he moved it only an inch or two before he felt something sting and someone laying it back down.

"Calm down, Jake," a soft voice said. "You're going to be okay. Just rest."

He struggled to open his eyes but failed. Once more he tried to cry out, but the voice was back again. "Don't try to talk, Jake. There's a tube in your throat. Tomorrow you can talk if you want."

But Jake's panic needed answers, and it needed answers now. He tried to formulate a question to ask but found that his mind was too fuzzy. Then the voices seemed to fade farther away, as numbness crept like mercy through his limbs.

And soon he forgot about those questions and surrendered instead to the darkness.

CHAPTER SEVEN

The rain began as Paige drove home from the police station, her brain reeling from the injustice of the system that left her entirely on her own. But it wasn't the first time she hadn't known where to turn.

She turned on her windshield wipers and tried to concentrate on the slippery road. The last thing she needed now was an accident. Lynda's was bad enough.

Then again, maybe a four-car crash on the highway was just what she should expect. Maybe she deserved all she'd been going through. Maybe, as Keith had said so many times, Paige was petty and selfish and stupid. Maybe she had brought all this misery on herself.

Lightning flashed, followed by a quick clap of thunder, and she touched Brianna's knee to reassure her. What did it really matter what Paige deserved, she argued. It was what Brianna deserved that mattered. Brianna deserved peace and she deserved safety and she deserved security and stability. She didn't deserve a father who could sing her a lullaby one minute and crack her mother's jaw the next.

The child was just drifting off to sleep as Paige turned onto their street and glanced ahead to her house halfway up the road. It would be good finally to get home, make Brianna a bowl of soup, and put her to bed for her nap.

Then she saw it: Keith's car in the driveway.

Slamming her foot on the accelerator, she flew past the house, skidded around the corner, and headed as far away from the neighborhood as she could.

Her breath came in gasps as she watched her rearview mirror for a sign of him. Terror clutched at her heart. Where could she go to be safe? Not home—he was there, sitting in her house, waiting for her.

Trembling, she pulled into a Walmart parking lot and groped for her purse. Grabbing out two quarters, she circled to a pay phone on the edge of the lot. Afraid to get out of the car, she inched as close as she could to the phone then rolled her window down. The rain poured in, soaking her arm as she reached for the receiver. Quickly she dialed 911.

"You've got to help me!" she cried when the dispatcher answered. "I have a restraining order against my ex-husband, but he's in my house waiting for me right now. You have to send an officer out immediately. They have to see him there!"

She rattled off the address, then restated the urgency. When she'd hung up, she tried to catch her breath.

She'd go back, she told herself. She'd go back to make sure they got him. If he was still there, maybe she'd go in and try to reason with him. Maybe that would hold him there until they came.

But what if it didn't? What if he took Brianna?

No. She couldn't risk it. Instead, she would drive by the house to make sure he was still there. Then she would watch from the corner, and when the police came, she could follow them into the driveway.

The rain pounded harder against the roof of the car, and the wind whipped more viciously, but Brianna stayed asleep as Paige, weeping softly, made her way back to the neighborhood and turned up her street. Holding her breath, she peered through the rain-blurred windshield to see if his car was still in her driveway.

He was gone.

Slamming the heel of her hand against her steering wheel, she cried harder. This was *hopeless!* He was out there somewhere, looking for her....

And the women's shelter would be the first place he'd look if she didn't come home. He'd told her more than once that he knew where all of them were, and if she ever went there, he'd go after her and make her sorry.

Leaving the street as fast as she could, she went back to the Walmart parking lot and dug through her wallet for money. She had thirty dollars and an ATM card. There might be fifty more in her account if her checkbook balance were right. That was enough for a hotel room, she told herself, trying to calm down. It would get her through until tomorrow.

She took a few deep breaths, trying to calm down, scanned the roads nearby to make sure he was nowhere in sight, and then pulled back into the street. *Don't even think about tomorrow right now*, she cautioned herself. *All you can deal with is one day at a time.*

CHAPTER EIGHT

The creak of her hospital room door woke Lynda from her shallow sleep. Squinting her eyes open, she watched the plump nurse come in, her nylons making a brushing sound as she walked and her white Reeboks squeaking on the floor. It was the same nurse who had attended to her the last time she'd awakened—Jill something—and Lynda watched her set down her tray of medications and flick on the dim light over Lynda's head.

"How are you feeling?" the nurse asked in a voice loud enough to wake the comatose patients on the floor above her. "Any pain?"

"Some," Lynda mumbled.

"Well, that's expected." Pulling a thermometer out of her pocket, she covered it with plastic and shoved it into Lynda's mouth. "If I had as many stitches in me as you have, I'd be hurting, too. The doctor said they pulled half the plane's windshield out of you." She took the thermometer, made a notation on Lynda's chart, then adjusted the IV. "We've given you something for pain, but if it's worn off, I can give you more."

Lynda moaned. "No wonder I've slept most of the day. No, I don't want any more." She watched the nurse wrap the blood pressure cuff around her arm. "Jill, do you know if Jake is out of surgery yet?"

Jill stared at her watch for a few seconds then slipped the cuff off again. "As a matter of fact, he is," she said, making another notation. "He's still critical, though. I don't have any of the details."

Lynda tried to sit up. "I want to see him."

"Sorry." The nurse gently pushed her back down. "He's still in ICU. No visitors."

49

"But I'm not a visitor. I was in that crash with him. It was my plane."

Jill snapped her chart shut and put it back in the pocket at the foot of Lynda's bed. "He isn't even conscious yet. Wait until tomorrow, and we'll see if we can get you permission to visit him. But not tonight, Lynda. Besides, you're still too weak to get out of bed."

"No, I feel fine. I just want to make sure he's all right."

"I'm sorry, Lynda. You'll just have to take our word for it tonight."

Lynda closed her eyes as the nurse left and tried in vain to steer her thoughts to something besides Jake's life. What weren't they telling her? Critical. What did that mean?

She tried to turn over, but a cut down her leg made it uncomfortable, so she shifted to her other side. The sheets were rough beneath her skin, and she wondered why they couldn't manage to get sheets that covered the whole bed, instead of those stupid half sheets that folded halfway down, overlapping another one that covered the end. It made changing the beds easier, she supposed, but that didn't help the patient's comfort any, especially when the patient was covered with cuts and scrapes. She longed for her own smooth sheets and the big bed she had shopped for a month to find.

She was so uncomfortable she might *never* fall back to sleep, and what good was lying here when Jake could be dying? If she could just see him, maybe she could relax tonight and let go of the guilt that was causing more pain than her broken ribs. If the only way to see him was to sneak through the halls and slip into ICU, she was willing to give it a try.

Making the decision almost as quickly as the thought came to her mind, she sat up and moved her feet over the side of the bed. The checkerboard floor was cold beneath her feet, and she felt a wave of vertigo as she sat up. Fighting it, she stood slowly. Her muscles strained, and she touched the place on her abdomen where her spleen had been removed. The pain in her head got worse, and she stood still a moment, waiting for the dizziness to pass.

Steadying herself with a hand against the brick wall, she put one foot in front of the other, stepping carefully until she reached the door. Already she felt soul weary, but she knew that ICU was just one floor up. If she could just get to the elevator....

Opening the door, she peered up the corridor. A visitor was going into another room, but she saw no one else. She closed the door behind her and took a barefoot step up the hall.

Miraculously, a wheelchair sat parked against the wall. Mumbling a "Thank you, Lord," she dropped into it. For a moment, she tried to catch her breath, but then, fearing she'd be caught if she didn't hurry, she grabbed the wheels and tried to push herself along.

Her left arm was stiff and sore, and pain stabbed through her ribs, making her perspire, but she pushed on nonetheless, passing the nurse's station without being noticed. She made it past the waiting room, where two or three people sat watching television, and breathed another "thank you" that none of them knew her.

Waiting anxiously beside the elevator, Lynda glanced up the hall. Nurse Jill stepped out into the hall from someone's room, and Lynda turned her head away. The elevator doors opened, and quickly she rolled on.

She pressed the button for the next floor up and waited, trying to fight the pain sending clouds circling through her head. The elevator stopped and she got off, careful to avoid the nurses clustered at the coffee pot near the elevator.

She was growing fatigued, and she pushed more slowly, wondering whether she'd made a mistake. But the doubts fled when she caught sight of the glass doors to the Intensive Care Unit.

A sign warned against unauthorized personnel entering ICU, and she knew that in the wheelchair she'd never get through that door and to Jake's bed. Taking a deep breath and bracing herself against the pain, she got to her feet.

Slowly, she opened the door and slipped inside.

A nurse was on the phone, and another one bent over a monitor. Stepping carefully, and battling the dizziness threatening her again, she made her way past them.

A little girl lay in an oxygen tent behind one curtain, and further down she saw an old man. She reached out to steady herself against the wall and checked a file on a door. Heather Nelson and then Lawrence Sims—

She froze as she came to the next room. Inside was a man with a bandaged face lying still on his bed, tubes and wires attaching him to the monitors and machines that hummed and beeped.

She searched for the name on the file on his door.

Jake Stevens.

A sob choked her, and she stumbled into the room. He was as still and pale as death. A bandage covered one eye and half his face, and large patches of skin were scraped from his arm, his hand....

"Jake?" she whispered.

He didn't stir. Muffling another sob, she stood over him, thinking how carefree and healthy he had looked this morning, driving up in his Porsche and irritating her with that lethal grin.

"Jake, I'm so sorry." Clutching the bed rail, she leaned over him. "I don't know how—"

"What are you doing here?"

The voice startled her, and she swung around and saw one of the nurses she'd seen outside, a black woman, standing in the doorway. "How did you get in here?"

"I—I had to see him," Lynda wept. "I had to."

Instantly, the nurse was at her side. "It's all right, child," she said, putting her arms around her and guiding her back to the door. "You're the lady who was in the crash with him, aren't you?"

Unable to speak, Lynda nodded her head.

"Honey, I'm so sorry," the nurse said, taking her to her wheelchair and lowering her into it. "But you shouldn't be out of your room. You should be in bed. Jake will still be here tomorrow."

"Will he?" Lynda asked, looking up at her. "He looks like—like he may not make it."

"Looks can be deceiving," the nurse said. "I don't know you, but I'd say you've probably looked better yourself."

"But he's still ... unconscious. What if he doesn't wake up? And what's wrong with his face? It's all bandaged."

"He was in a plane crash, darlin'. His face is the least of his problems."

Lynda grabbed the nurse's arm and started to stand, her face pleading for the truth. "Just tell me if—if he's expected to die."

The woman gently lowered her back to the chair. "I can't lie to you. It could go either way. But if he makes it through tonight, I'll feel a lot better about his chances tomorrow."

Finally leaning back, Lynda wailed into her hands.

"I'm gonna take you back to your room now, darlin', and tomorrow, if he wakes up, I'll make sure you get to see him. My name's Abby, and you can call me anytime tomorrow to get a report."

Lynda couldn't talk as the nurse rolled her back to the elevator.

CHAPTER NINE

Paige lay still as she heard a car door slam in front of her motel room. Footsteps passed her door, and then she heard the door to the next room open and a woman's shrill laughter.

It wasn't Keith. She turned onto her side and looked at her daughter, sleeping only in her underwear since they hadn't brought any extra clothes with them. The child slept soundly. Why not? She feared her father, but she didn't understand that her father was stalking them, threatening to take her from her mother and make her little life one nightmare after another, just as Paige's marriage had been.

What was he doing right now? Was he still waiting at her house, expecting Paige to breeze in and confront him? Or was he at his own apartment, devising another way of getting close to Brianna, inventing more lies about Paige's being an unfit mother, a child abuser, and a general danger to society?

"What am I gonna do?" she whispered to the darkness.

Brianna muttered a string of nonsense words under her breath. Turning on her side, Paige pulled her daughter against her. "It's okay, sweetheart," she said softly. "Mommy's here."

Brianna's breathing settled back into a peaceful rhythm, and Paige checked the clock. Only three hours before she had to be at work, she thought. What was she going to do with Brianna? She couldn't take her to day care again. Keith could come back and intimidate Brianna's teachers into handing her over. No, she couldn't take that chance. But she couldn't call in sick, either. She'd used up all her sick days earlier in the year when Keith had broken her arm and blackened both eyes. The shame of going to work like that had kept her home until makeup could disguise her bruises. But there were no sick days left.

There was no choice, she told herself. She would take Brianna to work with her. Brianna could sit on the floor and color as Paige typed; maybe if she explained it to her boss, he would understand. Maybe, just this once, fate would have a little mercy on her.

CHAPTER TEN

Someone had driven a stake through his temples, Jake thought as he opened the eye that wasn't bandaged. And if his pain was any indication, that someone had done the same through his cheekbone, his neck, down his arms, and across his shoulders.

Had some woman's angry boyfriend or husband beaten him to a pulp? Had he been in a car accident?

He opened his eye, and a cruel, blaring light forced him to close it. Confused, feeling the beginnings of panic, he squinted the eye open and tried again to orient himself. Before his eye was able to make out the room, his other senses detected the smell of iodine and alcohol, a soft beeping, and the electrical hum of machinery. Focusing, he saw the white walls of intensive care, the camera in the corner with which he was monitored, and the impressive machinery around his bed.

Yes, he thought through the haze in his brain. He'd been in an accident. But not a car crash.

A plane crash.

Catching his breath as the horror of his landing came back to him, he tried to sit up, but something held him down, and the pain stabbing through his face and head warned him not to try again.

His throat felt as if he'd swallowed a bucket of sand. He needed a drink, he thought desperately. He needed a drug. He needed to die.

"He's waking up!"

He looked up to see a pale, skinny nurse standing over him on one side, and a man with a stethoscope on the other.

"Jake, can you hear me?" the man asked in a voice so loud it thundered through his brain. "Jake, you're in the hospital."

No kidding, he thought, but when he tried to speak, his throat rebelled. The nurse set something cold against his lips, something wet—ice chips—and he opened his mouth gratefully and let the cold water ooze into his throat.

"How long?" he asked in a raspy whisper.

"Since the crash?" she asked. "Almost twenty-four hours. How do you feel?"

He thought of the worst hangover he'd ever had and decided it was a mere annoyance compared to this. "My head," he said, raising a lead-heavy hand to touch the bandage covering his eye.

"You have a gash down your face, Jake," the man said gently. "Your eye was pretty badly injured."

Jake looked up at him with horror. "My eye?"

"Yes. Do you have any feeling in your legs yet?"

His legs. There was no pain in his legs, he realized for the first time. They were numb. He tried to slide his leg up, to feel his toes, but it wouldn't move. Closing his eye, he wished he could block this out, that he could have stayed asleep, never to wake up and face the ways his body was failing him.

"Jake?"

"Tell me about my legs," he whispered, looking up at them with dread.

The doctor laid his hand on his shin. "Can you feel me touching you, Jake?"

"Yes!" he blurted, as if that proved that things weren't as bad as they seemed. "I feel pressure. Weight."

"That could be a good sign," he admitted weakly. "We need to run some tests." He started listing orders for the nurse, but Jake grabbed the sleeve of his coat and stopped him.

"What's broken?" he asked desperately. "My legs? My neck?"

It was obvious the doctor wasn't ready to be pinned down. "No broken bones, Jake, but you have deep lacerations in several places. The numbness is probably a blessing, considering the pain you might be feeling."

"I don't need any blessings like this," he bit out. "Besides, my head is enough to do me in."

"Well, if you need a stronger painkiller—"

"Yes," he cut in. "I need it."

"All right." But he didn't rush off for a hypodermic, as Jake had hoped. "Jake, your chart says you're new in town and no relatives have been notified. Is there anyone we could call for you?"

He thought of the one relative he still had, the one he'd woven stories about to make his past sound charmed, the one he had pretended was dead. "No," he said finally. "The last thing I need is people crying over me, waiting like vultures to see if the new me will have any resemblance to the old one."

"It wouldn't be like that, Jake," the nurse said. "You need the support of people who love you."

"I've never needed it before," he whispered as he closed his eye to dismiss them. "And I'm not about to start needing it now."

If you'd wanted a vacation, Lynda, all you had to do was say so." Sally Crawford pulled a chair up to Lynda's bed and set the bag she'd brought on the table in front of her. "I could use one, too, but you don't see me crashing a plane to get one."

Lynda was tired—her sleep last night had been restless and plagued with nightmares—but she managed to smile at her secretary. "Looks like I'm gonna get a longer vacation than I need. That blasted doctor said I have to stay out at least a month. Honestly, I feel like I'll be as good as new in a few days, but—"

"Lynda, you have injuries you can't even see. You have to let yourself recover. Besides, I'll be in the office taking care of the day-to-day stuff."

"But I have cases pending. Court dates...."

"Some of them can be postponed, and the ones that can't are going to be divided among the partners and associates. We went over all of them this morning. Your cases are in good hands."

Lynda sank back onto her pillow. "Well, I guess that's something."

"There's just one thing."

Lynda looked up. "What?"

"The Paige Varner case. No one wanted it."

"No one?" she asked.

"There's no money in it," Sally reminded her. "And it's a real shame because she came in yesterday all upset because her husband had shown up at her daughter's day care and tried to take her."

Lynda closed her eyes. "It's my fault. I've been putting her off."

"You've been busy. When you reach for a handout, you have to wait your turn."

That had, indeed, been her philosophy, Lynda admitted, but hearing it now, she didn't like the way it sounded. "She can't help not having any money. And that man. The restraining order obviously hasn't scared him at all. I was afraid it wouldn't. He's fearless. He'd *have* to be—he's suing *her* for custody, claiming *she's* the one who's abusive."

"She's anxious to get the case resolved so she can leave the state."

"I know. The judge has ordered her to stay in town until after court. Do you have her file with you?" Sally reached for her briefcase and pulled it out, and Lynda took it. "So nobody wanted her, huh?"

"I'll just tell her she'll have to find another attorney."

"No, she's tried." She studied the file for a moment, then glanced at Sally again. "Sally, am I really that mercenary?"

"How mercenary?" Sally asked, not following.

"So mercenary that I would push this case to the bottom of my priority list just because the hours I spent on it weren't billable?"

"Lynda, you did what anybody would do."

Lynda sighed and closed the file. "I'm keeping this case," she said. "I'll handle it."

"But Lynda!"

"It'll be all right," she said. "Just call Paige and tell her to come by to see me here."

Sally held back her protest, but her disapproval was apparent. "All right, Lynda. If you say so. I'm gonna go now. You look like you need some rest. A lot of it."

Lynda dropped the file onto the table next to her. "You think *I* look bad. You should see the other guy." But the words weren't said in humor, and that haunted look passed over her eyes again. "At least he's alive. I've been calling ICU every hour. As far as I know, he's still not awake, though."

"They're saying he may never walk again."

Lynda snapped a look back to Sally. Slowly, she sat up. "What? Where did you hear that?"

"On the news," Sally said. "Last night they did a report about the crash. Apparently he has a spinal cord injury, and he lost one eye."

Lynda brought her hands up to cover her face and sank back into her pillow. "Abby said his face was the least of his problems, but I didn't know...."

"All things considered, Lynda, he's lucky to be alive."

Lynda tried to take in a deep, cleansing breath and slid her hands down her face. "Yeah," she whispered. "I guess we have to look at it that way. I just don't understand."

"Understand what?"

"Why *I* wasn't hurt worse. My legs are fine. I only broke a couple of ribs and lost my spleen. He almost died, and it wasn't even his plane!"

"Lynda, stop beating yourself up. If you'd been hurt worse, do you think it would have taken away from his injuries?"

Sally didn't understand, Lynda thought dismally. Nobody could understand.

Sally seemed at a loss for anything else that would comfort her, so she opened Lynda's bag. "Well, anyway, I got you everything you wanted from home. If you need me to go back, I'll be happy to."

"No," she said, without even checking the bag's contents, "this should be enough. Thanks, Sally."

Sally slapped her thighs. "No problem. I'll get in touch with Paige as soon as I can. And you call if you need me. Everything will be back to normal in no time, okay?"

"Yeah," Lynda whispered, but as she watched Sally leave the room, she wasn't sure that normal would ever be good enough again.

Jake wished he'd stayed asleep.

And frankly, he didn't know why he hadn't. What was the use in waking up, just so he could listen to the doctor tell him again of the gash that had maimed his face and destroyed one eye? And that was just the beginning.

"Tell me about my back and my legs, Doctor. Tell me why I can't move."

Dr. Randall—a man in his mid-fifties who had more lines on his face than a street map of Tampa—leaned wearily over Jake's bed rail and seemed to consider his words carefully. This was going to be a tough one, Jake thought. When a doctor grew that thoughtful and hesitant about giving a prognosis, the most obvious question was, "How soon should I buy my burial plot?" But Jake feared the news might even be worse than death.

"You have lower lumbar compression, Jake, due to the impact of the crash, and that's led to a condition called spinal shock," the doctor said carefully. "It's caused paralysis in your legs. You can count yourself fortunate, though. If the compression had been higher, you wouldn't have use of your arms, either."

"So I'm supposed to breathe a sigh of relief because I'm a paraplegic and not a quadriplegic?"

The doctor accepted his cynicism with patience. "Let me finish, Jake. The paralysis could be temporary. You have a gash on your back, too, and a lot of swollen tissue. The steroids we're giving you are to keep the swelling down so it won't cause any more nerve damage. And until we get that swelling down, there's no way to tell how much of the damage is permanent."

Jake fought the furious tears burning his eyes. "Bottom line, Doc. Am I ever gonna walk again or not?"

Dr. Randall rubbed his eyes, leaving them red. "We can't know that for several days. Maybe longer."

"But what do you *think*?"

The truth seemed to take more out of the doctor than he had to give. "I don't know, Jake. We've been successful with a drug that we think regenerates the nerve cells, and we've started you on it today, in your IV. It all depends on the extent of the nerve damage. We just have to be patient and hope for the best. Meanwhile, you'll start working with the physical therapist and occupational therapist this morning to keep your joints and muscles working."

"I can't move," Jake scoffed. "How can I work my muscles or joints?"

"They'll do it for you. But Jake...." He touched Jake's arm, forcing him to look up at him. "As hard as your therapy is going to be, you have to cooperate. Those therapists are going to get you functioning as well as possible, but you have to work really hard. Harder than you've ever worked before."

"I don't want to work at being a functional invalid," Jake countered. "I'd rather just give it all up."

"Well, that's not one of your choices," Dr. Randall said, still kindly. "You flat-lined in the ambulance, but the paramedics brought you back. And later, when the worst part of this is behind you, you're going to be glad they did."

"They should have let me die," he said through dry, cracked lips. "I don't want to be here. I don't want to do this."

"No one ever does, Jake," the doctor told him. "But you're going to."

"What about *her*?" he asked. "The plane's owner. Did she make it?"

"Yes, she survived," Randall assured him.

"Is she paralyzed, too?"

The doctor seemed to know where this was going. "No. She broke some ribs, damaged her spleen, but she was lucky."

Jake's face reddened. "Terrific," he bit out. "And I'm lying flat on my back." Gritting his teeth, he slammed his fist on the bed. "It wasn't even my plane!"

"There'll be anger, Jake," the doctor said. "But you'll get through it. You'll need support. Call all of your family and friends to rally around you. Don't underestimate how much they can help."

Jake didn't respond, for the tears were blurring the one eye he had left, constricting his throat, making him so angry he could have killed someone if he'd just had a weapon.

Family, he scoffed bitterly. Friends.

Didn't the doctor realize that he didn't want anyone to see him like this?

Dr. Randall left him then with the monitors and machines humming in his room, with the IV dripping through a tube in his arm, with the nasogastric tube in his nose draining the bile that kept rising.

Who would have believed it when he'd gotten up yesterday morning, all enthusiasm and hope?

He wished he'd never decided to buy a plane of his own; he wished he'd never picked up the aviation magazine that had advertised the Piper in its classified ads; he wished he'd never met Lynda Barrett.

It seemed like a year ago that he came bouncing down the steps of the Biltmore, introducing himself to the blonde—now he couldn't even remember her room number—and riding off in his Porsche. He wondered whether anyone had contacted the manager of the Biltmore to get his stuff or called the moving company about storing his furniture. Was anyone watching his car?

But who? It wasn't as if he had anyone here he could call. He was new in town and completely alone. Flat on his back or not, he was on his own.

The thought sent rage spiraling up inside him, anger that he didn't know how to direct. Why had this happened to him? Why not her? *She* was the one who'd taken *him* up in a busted plane.

As if in answer to his thoughts, the nurse who'd been hovering over him all morning came to his door. "Jake, is it all right if Lynda Barrett visits you for just a minute? If you're not up to it, I'll send her away."

Jake looked at the door with his remaining good eye, welcoming the opportunity to feed his anger. "Yeah," he said bitterly. "Send her in. She might as well get a good look."

The nurse hesitated a moment, then disappeared. In a few moments, she was back, wheeling Lynda in a wheelchair. He gave her a once-over—she was stitched and bruised, too, but both eyes were intact, and her legs, crossed at the ankles, looked as healthy as his had looked yesterday.

"Hi, Jake," she whispered almost timidly. "How do you feel?"

He looked at the ceiling. "How do you think I feel?"

She took that gracefully. "Probably pretty bad." She watched as the nurse stepped out of the room to give them some privacy, then wheeled herself closer to the bed. "Jake, I'm so sorry."

"Not as sorry as I am."

She swept her eyes down his body, and they lingered on his legs. "We didn't know if you'd make it. I prayed all night that you would."

"What for? So I could lie here like a vegetable for the rest of my life?"

"I know how you must feel—"

"Do you?" he asked with exaggerated surprise. "Do you really? Tell me how you know how I feel, Lynda. Have you ever been paralyzed? Have you ever had the sight cut out of your eye? Have you had your face maimed beyond recognition? How do you know how I feel?"

She only gaped at him for a moment, and her fragile expression crumbled. "Okay, I don't know. But you survived, Jake. Just like I did. We both could have died in that crash, but we didn't."

He turned his head to look at her now. "Are you kidding me? I'm supposed to be happy that I'm useless as a human being instead of dead?" Disgusted, he looked at the ceiling again. "Why did you come in here anyway? What do you want?"

For a moment, she couldn't speak. "Just ... I just wanted to see if you were all right."

"Well, I'm not. Satisfied?"

It was clear that she hadn't expected this reaction from him, and he wondered if she'd expected them to bond from the trauma. Were they supposed to be best friends now and compare notes on what they remembered of the crash and eat lunch together and play cards? Didn't she realize that the very sight of her made him lament the day he'd laid eyes on her?

She covered her mouth and started to cry. "I guess I shouldn't have come. I'll go now."

"Yeah," he said. "You need to nurse those poor cracked ribs. I'd call the nurse, but I can't move."

At that, Lynda sprang to her feet. He watched her reach unsteadily for the rail, and with a look of furious determination made softer by the tears on her face, she grabbed the remote control with the nurse's call button from his bed table and thrust it into his hand. "That's one less thing you can feel sorry for yourself about," she said. Then, grabbing the handles of her chair, she walked carefully out of the room, pushing it in front of her.

Jake watched her go, his bitter anger at her for surviving intact fading as his indignation at her attitude grew.

Abby, the nurse who had found Lynda in Jake's room the night before, came upon her again, sitting in her wheelchair in the hall of ICU, weeping bitterly into her hands. Stooping in front of her, Abby tried to raise her face.

"Are you all right, child?"

Sucking back her sobs, Lynda looked up at her. "Jake just said some things—"

"He's hurtin', darlin'. Don't put any stock in what he says. When people hurt, they say all sorts of things."

But her assurance didn't help. This was bigger than words. "You want me to push you back to your room, honey?"

Lynda couldn't answer. "I went there to comfort him, and he just made me so mad—" She broke off and covered her face again. "I told him he felt sorry for himself. How could I *say* that?"

"You're human," Abby said. "Girl, I've been spit on, slapped, kicked, cursed, screamed at, puked on—and as much as I pride myself on keeping my cool, I have been known to say some nasty things, just because I'm human. You aren't even getting paid for listening to it. You can't expect to grit your teeth and smile through it. That takes something bigger than either one of us."

Reaching into her pocket, she pulled out a tissue, and Lynda wiped her eyes.

"You know where I go when I can't take much more, and I feel that old dark side of Abby taking over?"

"Where?"

"The chapel. It's on this floor. I'll take you there if you want me to, child. Maybe you'll find some peace there."

Lynda nodded. "Yes, that's where I need to go."

"Fine." Abby got to her feet and pushed her out of the ICU doors. "When I get off tonight, how 'bout I come by your room and wash your hair? I'll bet you're a pretty brunette when you don't look like you've lost a fight with a grizzly."

Lynda managed to smile under the tissue. "That would be great. I have trouble lifting my arms."

They reached the double doors to the small chapel, and Abby pushed her inside. The room was dimly lit with candles at the corners of the altar, and it was only big enough for three small pews on either side of the wide aisle.

Abby rolled her to the front and then in a more reverent voice, said, "There's a phone here at the back, honey. You call me when you're ready—extension 214—and I'll have someone come get you."

"Thank you," Lynda whispered.

Abby smiled, then closed the doors on her way out.

Lynda sat still for a moment, staring at the cross behind the small lectern and then behind that, at the stained glass window. A white dove was etched into the glass, flying down to the shoulder of a silhouette kneeling in a pool of water.

This is my son, in whom I am well pleased. God's words echoed through her mind, their very praise an indictment of her own actions.

Tears stung her eyes, and she sat before the altar, wishing to be judged, ready to be condemned. "I don't know what to say to him," she confessed aloud. "I don't even know what to say to you."

It had been too long since she'd had a serious heart-to-heart with God, too long since she'd sat in his presence. Now she felt her inadequacy like a verdict.

Awkwardly, she tried to thank him for her survival, but Jake's injuries limited her gratitude. And then she thought of the plane she had loved so much, destroyed in a matter of minutes, leaving her to face the solitude of her life without it.

As her own thoughts condemned her, she looked up to the window again.

... in whom I am well pleased ...

It was from the New Testament, she thought quickly, but she couldn't remember where. It had been too long since she'd read her Bible, and now she wasn't even sure where she'd put it.

But she didn't have to recall the reference to know what it meant to her.

God wasn't pleased with *her*. How could he be when she'd made a god of an airplane, an altar of her job, and an idol of her own ego? How could he smile on her when she'd spoken to a sick man the way she had today or when she'd ignored the needs of a poor battered wife who depended on her?

The truth was that she'd just quit caring. She hadn't cared about her relationship with God or her friends or her family. She hadn't cared about anything except her job and that plane. Not in a long time.

Like Peter after he'd denied Christ, she wept bitterly, brokenly, not expecting God to recognize or comfort her, not expecting his peace —

But suddenly it came.

Her tears slowed, her sobbing stopped, and she looked up at the dove on the window and felt his slow, warm, forgiving embrace welcoming her home.

Instead of remorse, she felt hope. Instead of shame, she felt purpose. It *wasn't* too late.

For a moment, she sat still in her wheelchair, her head bowed, her eyes closed. For the first time in she couldn't remember how long, she listened.

And God spoke.

In that still, small voice that could be so easily ignored, so quickly forgotten, so often dismissed as nothing more than an idle thought, he reminded her to whom she belonged.

And with that reminder came a flood of determination finally to do something about it.

But what?

She thought of Abby, offering to wash her hair after working a twelve-hour shift, because she couldn't lift her own arms. That was faith in action, wasn't it? It was giving of yourself when you got nothing back. It was stretching out of that comfort zone, even when you got cursed at.

The new Lynda would do better, she promised as she sat before that altar. She would stretch. She would grow.

And filled with a renewed spirit and a peace that gave her strength, she felt a sudden urgency to go back to her room and get started.

CHAPTER ELEVEN

She wasn't dead.

He had been there when the plane crashed. He'd been standing at the fence, watching like a curious spectator as the plane circled overhead and the ground crews scurried around in a panic. It had made the news on all three local channels and even got a mention on CNN.

He had watched as the plane descended at the end, had held his breath as it had spun. He'd seen both wings breaking off, metal flying, glass breaking—and he'd been sure that he'd succeeded, that it was impossible for anyone to survive that.

But the paramedics had moved too quickly, and when the plane had ignited, she was out of its range. He had watched, troubled, as the ambulances blared past him, carrying both passengers to the hospital.

Still, he'd seen the blood, and he had believed that the injuries would be too great, that she would die en route or on the operating table or later in her room.

But no. She was not only still alive, but she was also doing well. No lasting impairment. No permanent damage.

It was a failure. But it would not be repeated. Next time, she would not escape.

All he could do now was bide his time and wait until the right moment. It would come soon enough. And then his problems would be over.

Then he could finally get on with his life.

CHAPTER TWELVE

The orderly who came to get Lynda from the chapel had a cautious, compassionate demeanor, and Lynda wondered with some embarrassment if Abby had warned him of her emotional state. As he wheeled her toward the elevator, he made light conversation.

"It's gonna rain again today, looks like. And, of course, I left my umbrella in the car. Isn't that always where it is when you need it? But I don't get off till three. Maybe I'll miss the storm."

The elevator doors opened, and he wheeled her on. "Oh, I was supposed to tell you that there's somebody here to see you. She's down in the first-floor lobby."

"Who?" Lynda asked, straining her sore neck to look up at him.

"I didn't get her name," he said. The doors opened, and he rolled her off. "She couldn't come up because she has a kid with her. They won't let her past the first floor. I told her you would call down when you were back in your room."

Paige. Lynda grabbed the wheel to stop the chair and looked up at him. "I have to go down," she said. "I have to go see her."

"Are you sure you're up to it?" the orderly asked her. "You look tired."

"I'm fine," she said. "Really. It's important."

An alarm sounded, and two nurses bolted around the desk, running toward an emergency. "I can't take you," he said. "I have to help with this."

"It's okay. I can make it. Go ahead."

The orderly rushed off behind the nurses, and quickly Lynda rolled back onto the elevator, ignoring the pain in her ribs when she used her arms. One crowd of people on the cramped elevator commiserated about a grandfather and a heart attack; another couple at the back cried softly and whispered together. *Pain all around me*, Lynda thought. *Pain and desperation. How can I have floated through it for so long, not seeing any of it?*

The moment the doors opened, she saw Paige across the plush maroon-and-gray lobby and pushed toward her. She was sitting on the couch, rocking Brianna back and forth gently. Her clothes were rumpled and wrinkled, and her eyes were swollen, as if she hadn't slept in days.

"Paige?"

Paige looked up quickly. "Lynda!" She sprang to her feet and rushed to help her. "Oh, I didn't expect them to send you down here! I was going to call you when you got back to your room. Oh, I'm so glad you're alive! I didn't see how you'd survive, and when I called Sally today, and she told me—"

"It could have been so much worse," Lynda cut in, smiling at the child whose thumb had gravitated to her mouth at the sight of the bruised, cut-up woman wheeling toward her. "I'm really doing pretty well. How are you, Brianna?"

The little blonde girl took her thumb out of her mouth. "Fine. Did you hurt yourself?"

"Yes, a little. But I'll be better soon."

"Did you fall down?"

"Way down."

"Did it hurt?"

"Bad. But I'm okay."

"But you look ... terrible," Paige said. "I mean, not really terrible.... Just..."

"Like I've been in a plane crash? That's okay, Paige. I'm just happy to be alive."

Tears came to Paige's eyes, and she sank to the couch again. "I'm happy you are, too, Lynda. For really selfish reasons."

"What's wrong?"

Using her fingers, Paige combed her fine blonde hair back from her face and held it in a ponytail. "Keith was at my house when I went home last night," she blurted. "He was in there waiting. I saw his car in the driveway, and I kept going. I haven't been back."

70

"Did you call the police?"

She let the ponytail go, and her hair fell around her face again. "I called, but he was gone before they got there. I can't believe they have to catch him violating the order. Do they think he's stupid enough to be caught?"

"Where did you go, Paige?"

"To a motel. But I don't have much money left, and then this morning—" Her voice broke off, and she covered her mouth. Sensing her mother's despair, Brianna climbed onto Paige's lap and put her arms around her mother's neck to comfort her. The sweet gesture only made Paige wilt more.

Lynda pulled Brianna gently away. "Honey, see that book over there? Why don't you go get it and look at the pictures?"

"The Winnie the Pooh one or the Barney one?" Brianna asked.

"Barney," Lynda said.

The child considered that for a moment. "No, Pooh."

Lynda smiled faintly as Brianna gave her mother one last look, then scurried to the table with the books. Paige watched her every step of the way.

"Then what, Paige?" Lynda asked. "What happened this morning?"

"I couldn't take her back to day care, because he had been there yesterday. I was afraid he'd take her, Lynda, so I took her to work with me. And my boss came in and saw her, and he—he fired me."

"You lost your job?"

"Yes," she cried softly. "I might have all of forty dollars left to my name, and I'm afraid to go home." She looked at Lynda, her eyes pleading. For what, Lynda suspected even Paige didn't know.

Lynda took Paige's hand. "Sally told you that I'm keeping your case, didn't she?"

Paige nodded. "Yes."

"As soon as I get back to the room, I'll call her and get her to file a motion to get us before a judge so we can tell him Keith violated his order—"

"No," Paige cut in. "That won't do any good. It'll just make him mad."

"It doesn't matter, Paige. If he realizes he won't get away with it—"

"*If* they put him in jail, he'll get out in a couple of days. He'll come after me, Lynda. I'm afraid of him. All I want is my court date so we can get the custody hearing over with and have his visitation denied so I can take Brianna someplace where he'll never find us—"

A man walked past the place Brianna sat reading. Springing from her seat, Paige dashed to her daughter. "Brianna, honey, bring the book and sit by me."

"Okay." Brianna followed her mother back to the couch and climbed up next to her. Paige put her arm around her, as if only by touching the child could she be assured of her safety. Weary, Lynda realized that a court date could still be weeks away, and the woman had no livelihood and was living in terror. If Lynda hadn't left so much of her case to chance, it might have been over by now.

Lynda dropped her head into her hand, wrestling with the emotions she knew were on her face. "Paige, I hope you'll forgive me for letting you down."

"Letting me down?" Paige asked. "You haven't let me down. You're the only lawyer who would take me."

"No," Lynda said. "I *have* let you down. I could have pressed for a court date earlier. I could have paid more attention to your case."

Paige was silent for a moment, obviously confused about what to say.

"I want to make it up to you," Lynda whispered. "I've just been in the chapel, trying to sort things out, and I'm starting to see that I haven't been a very nice person."

Paige shook her head adamantly. "No, you're the greatest, Lynda. I don't know what I would have done without you."

"That's sweet," Lynda said, but she wasn't buying. "I want to help you for real this time. Somehow I feel like if I do, I'll be helping myself, too."

"But you *are* helping me."

"No," Lynda said. "Not really. But that can change. I want you to stay at my house."

Paige caught her breath. "No, I couldn't. Lynda, representing me for free is enough of an imposition."

"It's not an imposition. It's a favor," Lynda said. "Please, I want you to. My house is just sitting there, and Keith will never think to look for you there. I'll get Sally to get you some money out of my account, so you won't have to worry about your job *or* about Keith until we get into court."

Paige was stunned. "But that's too much, Lynda. You don't have to do this."

"Yes, I do," Lynda said. "Please, Paige."

"But why? I'm just a client. You hardly even know me."

Lynda paused and tried to find the right words. "Because your hair doesn't need washing."

Paige breathed a laugh. "What?"

"It's something I can do, Paige. Something besides sitting here and worrying about you. Please."

Paige stared at her for a moment as fresh tears came to her eyes. "I can't believe you'd do this."

"Then it's yes?"

Paige shrugged and looked down at her daughter. "Yes, I guess so."

"Then I'll go call Sally right now. She has a key, and she can let you into the house. There's food there, but she'll get you some money out of my account, so you can get anything else you need. Meanwhile, I'll make some phone calls. We'll get someone to go to your house and get your clothes and whatever else you need. Just don't tell anyone where you are. If anyone needs you, they can go through me or Sally." When Paige still didn't respond, she asked, "Does this sound all right to you?"

Paige surrendered and relaxed, her gratitude evident on her face. "Yes," she whispered. "Thank you."

As Lynda rode the elevator back up to her room to call Sally, she told herself that she should have offered Paige this kind of help weeks ago. It wouldn't have hurt her at all, and it would have made a world of difference in the young woman's life.

She only hoped she had the fortitude now to finish what she was starting.

Two hours later, Lynda was still on the phone when Sally came into her room. She whispered that she was on hold, and Sally set her hands on her plump hips and glared at her. "The nurse told me that she's calling the doctor to fink on you. She said you'd been either out of your room or on the phone all day. Lynda, if you don't stop this, you'll never recover."

Lynda put her hand over the receiver. "It takes my mind off my ribs. Did you get Paige situated?"

"Of course I did," she said. "I got her the money and gave her the key. I put them in one of the guest rooms, in case you ever get out of here. But at the rate you're working, that's not looking good. Who are you holding for?"

"Steve McRae."

"Keith's attorney? Oh, good. He ought to be a big help. He's the one trying to take that beautiful little girl away from her mother."

"He needs a warning," Lynda said. The Muzak on the phone stopped as someone picked it up, and Lynda raised a hand to silence Sally.

"Lynda?" the attorney asked in a voice that seemed a little too cordial.

"Yes, it's me," she said. "I need to talk to you about your client, Keith Varner."

"What a relief to hear your voice," he said. "I saw the crash on the news last night. I have to admit, I thought it would be a while before I'd hear from you again."

"Sorry," Lynda said in a saccharine voice. "No such luck. I am still in the hospital, which gives me all the time in the world to work on Paige Varner's case. And I called to tell you to warn your client that his harassment has got to stop."

"What harassment?"

"For starters, he tried to take Brianna from day care, despite the restraining order, and he broke into Paige's home—"

"Give me a break, Lynda," the man cut in, dropping the cordiality. "You know as well as I do that he has a key. It was his home."

"*Was* being the key word. She was granted possession of the house in their divorce, and the restraining order stated that he wasn't to come near it. And as for Brianna, until we see him in court, he isn't to go near her either."

"Put yourself in his place," the man said. "He hasn't seen his daughter in over a month."

"You're right. Not since he bashed her mother's head into the wall and knocked her out."

"Her word against his. He contends that *she* knocked *him* out when he was defending the child from one of Paige's rampages."

Lynda saw now what she was dealing with. "I'll have him arrested, Steve. If he comes near her again, I'll use every resource I have to get him locked up. Tell him."

The man sighed. "Anything else?"

"Yes. I'm going to appeal to the judge for a court date as soon as possible. I won't let you keep dragging this out."

"No need," the man said. "I got a date this afternoon. Despite what you might think, we're anxious to bring this to a head, too. It's October 14."

"That's six weeks away!" she said. "We need it earlier."

"Too bad. That's as early as we could get it."

She sank back onto her pillow and closed her eyes. "Six weeks is a long time, Steve. Tell your client that he'd better be on his best behavior during that time because I plan to pull out all the stops when we get into court."

"Good luck," he said. "You're gonna need it."

She heard the phone click in her ear, and slowly she dropped it back in its cradle and collapsed into her pillow.

"Good going," Sally said. "You told him." She looked at the color draining from Lynda's face and said, "Now will you get some rest? Paige and Brianna are safe, you have a court date, Keith's hand has been slapped—All is well with the world. Please, just get some rest before the nurses convince the doctor to sedate you."

"All right, Sally," she said, already feeling herself slipping away. "Maybe for a minute."

That night, true to her word, Abby came down from ICU with a cart made especially for washing hair and had Lynda lie down with her head over the small tub full of warm water. Gently, carefully, she washed Lynda's hair, methodically pulling more tiny chips of glass from her scalp as she did.

"It's a wonder you could sleep with all this glass in you and your hair all matted like this," she said. "Wasn't it hurtin' you?"

"Sure, it was," Lynda said. "But I thought the pain was just from the cuts." She closed her eyes as Abby poured more warm water over her head. "I thought they got all the glass out in surgery."

"No, child," Abby said. "It's hard to get it all, and the nurses don't have that kind of time when they're on duty. But we'll get every piece tonight if I have to work on it till my shift tomorrow."

Lynda opened her eyes and gazed up at the woman. "Why would you do this?"

Abby smiled. "Because it needs doin'. We're supposed to wash each other's feet, but I figure washin' hair is just as good."

The tear that rolled from Lynda's eye disappeared into the water Abby poured over her hair.

CHAPTER THIRTEEN

There was little relief for Jake in being moved out of ICU to a private room on the orthopedic floor. He was still flat on his back, unable to sit up or stand, unable to take care of his own bodily functions without help, and his hope of being released from this place was as dismal as his hope for the rest of his life.

But the Clinitron bed they laid him in gave him some degree of comfort. For one thing, it reduced the likelihood of bedsores. It felt something like a waterbed, except that air was continually pumping through it, making it conform to his shape and weight. And this room had a television so that he could keep remembering what normal people's lives were like while he contemplated what he'd do now that his would never be normal again. And he had a phone—a reminder that he had no one to call.

At least no one in Florida.

He looked at it, wondering whether anyone in Texas had heard of his accident. He doubted it. As far as they knew, he was living it up, as he'd always done. If they could see him now.

He picked up the phone and tried to remember the number of someone—anyone—who might care what had happened to him. What about Sheila—red, flowing hair, big green eyes. She'd been in love with him forever and had followed him around like a devoted puppy, even when he'd shunned her. He'd broken her heart, finally, and sent her on her way. But she would never get over him. She would want to know about this accident.

He dialed her number and waited as it rang, wondering what to say to her. Would she be glad to hear from him? Would she fly to Florida to visit him?

Quickly, he hung the phone back up. She might. He couldn't take that chance. He couldn't let her see him like this. *No* one could see him like this. Not yet. Not until the bandages came off and he could see how extensive the scarring was. Then he would decide.

Loneliness filled him like a disease, further darkening the black places in his heart. Jake Stevens wasn't used to being alone. What he wouldn't give for someone he *could* talk to without fearing how that person would see him.

And then he thought of that little truck stop in Slapout, Texas, where Doris waited tables each day, always naively hopeful that one of the truck drivers who came through would be the one to rescue her from her own loneliness and shame, make an honest woman of her, and provide her with the white picket fence and the little pink house that she had done nothing to earn on her own.

He wondered if she'd found her dream man yet among the regulars who came and went. He wondered if she'd been able to forgive him for running away from her himself, putting her behind him like forgotten garbage. Maybe she'd realized somewhere along the way that he'd had a life to make for himself and that he'd had to make it without letting her pull him down.

Maybe *she* would care that he lay here now, unable to run anymore.

He reached for the phone, called information, and got the number of the truck stop. With a trembling hand, he punched in the number.

"May I speak to Doris, please?"

On hold, he waited long, threatening moments, wanting to hang up. Finally, he heard her familiar voice, though it had grown raspier and deeper from cigarette smoke and booze.

"Yeah, hello?"

Jake swallowed, almost hanging up, but finally forced himself to speak.

"Mama? It's me. Jake."

Silence.

"Did you hear me, Mama?"

"I heard you," she said. "What do you want?"

If it was possible for his heart to fall further, it did. "I know it's been a long time. I've just been real busy, and—"

"Busy gettin' rich," she said. "I know why you haven't called. It's because you were afraid you'd have to let go of a few bucks if you talked to me. What made you call me now?"

He thought of telling her that he was lying in the hospital, that his charmed world hadn't been so charmed, that it had all come crashing down, that he didn't know if things would ever be the same. But something told him it wouldn't make any difference. He had never been there for her, though he could have been. Why did he expect her to be here for him now?

"Answer me, Jake. What do you want?"

"I just wanted to see how you were."

"Oh, I'm great," she rasped. "I just got a secondhand stove put in since mine has been out of commission for ten months. And my trailer is fallin' apart, but hey, at least it's a roof over my head. May not be a fancy condo like you've got ... "

He didn't know whether to offer her money or an apology, but that old anger that he'd nursed since childhood began to fill him again, keeping him from offering either.

"Look, I'm sorry I bothered you. You might as well get back to work."

"Yeah, I think I will. I can't afford to miss any tips. It's not like I have anybody to take up the slack if I can't pay my rent, is there?"

The click in his ear startled him, and for a moment, he held the phone to his ear as the dial tone hummed out its indifference. Then, as his face reddened, he hung up and lay glaring at the ceiling, trying hard to push the stark self-recriminations out of his mind. He'd been good at it before, but that was when he'd had life to keep him busy. There was always a party somewhere. Always a woman. Always a drink that could make him forget.

Until now.

He flung the telephone across the room, and it crashed with a final, protesting ring. There would be no parties now and no relief from his despair. But he didn't need his mother, and he didn't need his friends. They would all only let him down in the long run.

Mommy, is this gonna be our house?"

Paige smiled at her daughter, who sat on the floor playing with some of the blocks a police officer had gotten from their

79

house, along with most of their clothes. "No, sweetheart. We're just staying here for a while."

"Until that lady gets well?"

She left the spaghetti she was cooking and bent down to her daughter. "Maybe. I don't know how long we'll be here. But it's nice, isn't it? It's a lot better than that old motel room."

"But why can't we go home?"

"Because...." She lowered herself to the floor to put herself at eye level with the child and met her big, innocent eyes. There was so much Brianna didn't understand, and Paige didn't know how to explain it to her. How could she tell her that her father was a threat to them, that she feared for her life around him, that she feared for Brianna? "Because it has bugs," she said finally.

Brianna's face twisted. "Bugs? What kind of bugs?"

"The gross kind," Paige said. "A man's spraying so they'll go away, but it's gonna take a while."

"You mean spiders and stink bugs?"

Brianna might never want to go back into the house if she made it sound too horrible. "No. Roly-polies and grasshoppers. But this man is getting them out."

"Oh." Brianna got quiet, and Paige could almost see the wheels turning as the child imagined her bedroom full of roly-polies and grasshoppers. She hoped it didn't give her nightmares. She got up and went back to the spaghetti sauce simmering on the stove.

"Mommy?"

She looked back at Brianna.

"Can I keep just some of them? In a jar with holes in the top?"

She laughed out loud and realized it was the first time in weeks. "Yes, sweetheart. You sure can."

Jake, are you up to seeing that insurance guy?" Beth, Jake's nurse in orthopedics, asked him later that day. "I told him it was your first day in the private room and that you weren't up to seeing anybody, so if you don't want to, I'll nix it right now."

Jake looked irritably at her. "What insurance guy?"

"Something about the plane."

80

Jake had nothing better to do, and he'd grown so tired of being alone that he had actually been lying here wishing Lynda would come by. But after the way he'd treated her yesterday, he didn't really expect her back.

"Yeah, all right," he said. "Tell him to come in."

Beth disappeared, and Jake waited until a man in a dark suit came into his room and introduced himself as Rick Malone, investigator for the company that covered Lynda's plane.

"I just want to ask you a few questions," Malone said.

"About the crash?" Jake asked. "I would think the condition of the plane pretty much tells the whole story."

Malone consulted his notes, disregarding the comment. "Mr. Stevens, could you tell me if you or Miss Barrett did a preflight inspection of the plane?"

"Of course," Jake said. "I did it myself. I never fly without a preflight."

"And everything looked fine?"

"It looked perfect. And the day before I had really given the plane a once-over. I checked everything. I was thinking of buying it, you know. I wanted to make sure I wasn't missing anything. It was the best-maintained plane I'd ever seen for its age."

Malone plunked down, as if too tired to stand. "Is there anything you could tell me about Miss Barrett's behavior that day? Did she seem nervous, jumpy?"

Jake frowned. "What are you getting at?"

"I just want to know how she acted, Mr. Malone. Did she seem to behave normally?"

"How do I know if she was normal? It was the first time I'd met her. But yeah, I'd say she was pretty normal. She wasn't crazy about selling her plane. That was obvious."

"Did she suggest you test fly it alone? Or balk at going up with you?"

Jake thought for a moment. "No. She mentioned something about the crosswind, but I really don't think she would have let me go up alone."

"Did she mention her financial condition?"

Jake stared incredulously at him. "You don't think *Lynda* had anything to do with this."

Malone shifted in his seat. "We've been on the site since the crash yesterday," Malone said. "And we've found evidence that a hose was partially cut so the hydraulic pressure would pull it completely apart as soon as the landing gear was lowered."

Jake sat silently for a moment, trying to make sense of that. "It could have torn—"

"There's more. We've gone over all of the airport's security videos, and on the night before the crash, it caught someone tampering with that plane."

"Who?"

"We can't tell exactly," Malone said. "All we were able to make out was a penlight around the wheel well and the vague shape of someone under the plane. We can't rule out that the plane's owner might have set up the crash to collect the insurance."

Jake was getting angry. "Let me get this straight," he said. "You think she would sabotage her own plane and stage her own crash just to get the money when she could just as easily have sold it to me for full market value?"

"Maybe she didn't plan to fly with you," Malone said. "Or she didn't anticipate such a dangerous landing. After all, she did survive."

Jake gaped at him for a moment, unable to believe what he was hearing. "That is the most ludicrous thing I've ever heard. Lynda Barrett had nothing to do with that crash. She was as surprised as I was when the landing gear didn't go down. And she was scared to death. She could easily have *died* in that crash. What good would the insurance money have done her then?"

"All we know is that somebody did it."

"Then stop trying to pin this on her and find out who really did it and why." He struggled to sit up, but dropped down, defeated. "And when you do," he said through his teeth, "you tell me who they are. If it's the last thing I do, I'll make sure they pay."

CHAPTER FOURTEEN

I don't *believe* this." Lynda sat in a vinyl chair that hadn't been made for comfort, watching the parking lot below through her hospital room window as the insurance investigator cut between the cars. "He thought *I* had something to do with the crash."

"Don't sweat it," Mike said from where he sat by Lynda's bed. "Between Jake and me, we convinced him you didn't. But the question is, who did?"

She turned back to Mike, the light from outside casting a shadow on one side of her face. "Why would *any*body want to sabotage my plane, Mike? Wouldn't they know that the next time I flew it—?"

Mike only looked helplessly at her.

"That's it, isn't it? Someone was trying to kill me."

"Maybe. Maybe not. It could have been a random act."

"Were any of the other planes tampered with?"

"No. We've inspected all of them and checked back over the videotapes for anything out of the ordinary. It looks like it was just your plane."

She leaned back in the chair and looked out the window again. "How could I have made such an enemy and not known it?"

"I can't believe you did," Mike said. "Maybe it *was* random, Lynda. Random acts of violence happen all the time. People break into houses randomly, shoot at passing cars—"

"Some world we live in, huh?"

"You're right; it's not a pleasant thought—but it's better than thinking someone tried to kill you."

"What if they're still trying?" she whispered. She felt fear rising inside. "I mean, they failed, didn't they? What if they haven't given up?"

Mike got up and came to lean against the windowsill. "Think, Lynda. Is there anyone in your life who hates you enough to want to kill you?"

"Well, I didn't *know* there was, but obviously—"

"Not so obviously. I mean, yes, there's somebody out there who was trying to get his kicks, but that doesn't mean he's after you."

"Kicks?" she whispered. "Causing a plane crash gave him his kicks?"

"There's a lot of evil around us, Lynda. We don't have to let it consume us."

"What if we don't have a choice?" she whispered. "They're probably going to let me go home tomorrow. Am I gonna be a sitting duck? And what about Paige and Brianna? They're staying in my house."

"If he'd wanted *you*, whoever it is, he could have found you at home before, don't you think? That's what makes me think it's random."

Lynda shrugged, unconvinced.

"Anyway, the two cops who are working on it are planning to come by and talk to you today. If there *is* someone after you, they can get to the bottom of it." He leaned over and pressed a gentle kiss on her forehead and wiped a stray tear off her cheek. "It'll be okay."

"I just need some time alone to think about it, I guess."

"I'm going," he said. "But first, I want to tell you that the cops who are investigating this are Tony Danks and Larry Millsaps. Larry's a buddy of mine from church. I've known him for years. You can trust him."

She felt some comfort in that. "Thank you, Mike," she whispered.

The two people assigned to rehabilitate Jake—Allie Williams, a 120-pound dynamo who approached occupational therapy with a determination that rivaled Jake's determination to sink into depression, and Buzz Slater, a former paraplegic who'd become a physical therapist after learning to walk again himself—didn't seem to care that Jake's head was still on the verge of bursting with pain or that nausea was hiding just below the surface, waiting to assault him at any given moment. Since he awoke from the accident, their hands had been all over him, poking and prodding, flexing and massaging, despite his venomous verbal resistance.

Nothing he said daunted them, no insult offended them, at least not enough to make them leave him alone. Every two hours they came in and turned him over, massaged him, and bent him this way and that until finally he'd vowed to learn how to turn *himself* over just to get a little peace.

"That's not all you'll learn to do today," Allie said brightly as she wheeled a gurney into the room. "Today you're going to the tilt table in the rehab room. We're going to get you sitting up, so you can get out of bed."

That sounded easy enough, and Jake was almost hopeful as they wheeled him down the hallway, flat on his back to the big room where a dozen or more people like him worked—on mats, in a pool, on parallel bars, with walkers.

He didn't object when they transferred him to the flat table, but when they began strapping him down, he got worried. "What are the straps for?"

"To keep you from sliding off, Jake," Buzz said. "You've been flat for three days. We have to get you upright gradually. You may have some problems."

But Jake couldn't imagine ever having problems being upright. "Try me," he said.

They finished strapping him on then slowly began to tilt him up.

He felt a cold sweat prickling his skin; his head pounded. Though the table inched upward at a snail's pace, he grew increasingly dizzy, nauseous, weak....

"I'm gonna pass out!"

Instantly, they lowered him flat again.

"That's all right, Jake," Allie said. "You made it to thirteen degrees."

Jake looked at her. "That's all? Why did I react like that?"

"It's called orthostatic hypotension. You've been lying down for a while, so your circulation is weak. Your blood pressure drops when you're upright. We just have to keep trying it, getting a little higher each time, until you get through it. Ready to go again?"

He wanted to scream out that he wasn't, but instead he said, "No. I'm thirsty."

"We can give you some ice chips," Allie said, "but you won't be able to keep anything else down."

She put an ice chip in Jake's mouth, then allowed a few seconds for it to melt. "Ready now?"

Jake cursed as the table tilted again. As the blood drained to pool in his feet, the world threatened to turn black.

"Just get through this, Jake," Buzz said when he was flat again. "After this, we'll start you on traction."

Two hours later, they wheeled him back to his room in time for the bland lunch that awaited him, the lunch he couldn't eat. His skull felt as if it had intercepted the pain from all the places on his body that he couldn't feel. His stomach was empty but still threatened to turn on him, and the worst part was that for all his work, he'd only made it up to twenty degrees on the tilt table. At this rate, he'd be flat on his back for the rest of his life.

And the traction had been another nightmare. They had hooked him to the pulleys and turned the machine on, making it pull for twenty seconds, then release for five, then pull again....

Jake's hope as he endured the pain was that the pulleys would relieve the compression in his spine, free the nerves to function again, and bring the feeling back into his legs. But when the exercise was over, he was as numb from his hips down as he had been when he'd gotten here. It would take time, Buzz told him. Lots of time.

And time was something he had more than enough of. He had all the time in the world and absolutely nothing to do with it but endure more torture, more terror, more disappointment.

Yanking at the sheet the nurse had laid over him, he tried to fling it off the bed, but it was attached somewhere. Instead, he grabbed a glass of watery tea and hurled it across the room. It shattered and left a stain on the wall, but that did nothing to appease Jake's rage.

Lynda heard a crash as she reached the door of Jake's room. Stepping out of her wheelchair, she pushed the door open. A tray of food flew against the wall, and plates and food and a cup went crashing to the floor.

"Jake! What are you—?"

She ducked out of the way of the plastic pitcher.

Jake's face was red, and his bandage was wet with tears. Randomly, he reached for something else to throw. The phone book sailed across the room and then the tissue box. When he grabbed the phone he had already broken the other day and tried to yank off the cord, she dove for him.

"Stop it!" she cried, wrestling the phone from him and grabbing his flailing arms. "Jake, stop it!"

He fought for a moment more, and then, sobbing and cursing, finally gave up and let his arms fall across his face.

Lynda stood next to the bed, staring down at him, feeling helpless. Where were the people who loved this man? Where were the ones who could fight this battle with him? Was there really no one?

But there *was* someone, Lynda thought, succumbing to her own tears. *She* was here, and Jake needed her probably more than he'd ever needed anyone in his life.

She leaned over him and slid her hands to his shoulders. Somehow as he sobbed and shook and wailed, she got her arms around him, and suddenly he was clutching her like someone hanging from a cliff, about to fall to his death.

Maybe she was the only one who could pull him back.

He held her while he wept out his last ounces of strength while she cried against the bandage on his face.

"It's okay, Jake," she whispered. "I promise it's going to be all right."

But they were empty words. She could make no such promises.

When his grief had run out of strength for the moment, he loosened his arms.

Slowly, she let go of him.

He looked like a little boy in a broken man's body, she thought as she stroked his hair back from his damp forehead.

Tears still rolled slowly down his temple, but he was too exhausted to wipe them away.

She stroked his forehead until his wet eye finally closed, until she felt the last ounce of fight seep out of him, until she heard his breathing settle into a relaxed cadence.

When she was sure he was sleeping, she went to get someone to clean up the mess he'd made.

But she didn't leave him until someone from her floor came and forced her to.

For it was only now that she realized just how alone he was. As much as he might hate her, she was all he had.

CHAPTER FIFTEEN

He fingered the newspaper photo of the crashed plane, still amazed that anyone had survived. It should have been a sure thing. He'd snipped the hose with such precision, leaving it partially intact so that it wouldn't be noticed on the preflight. When the landing gear engaged, the pressure in the line was certain to tear it the rest of the way. The gear would go partially down without locking—a deadly combination of problems. They should have been the last ones she would ever encounter.

But Lynda Barrett had a way of getting around sure things.

He clenched his jaw in frustration as he picked up the phone and dialed the number he had memorized for the hospital. He'd gotten daily updates on her condition, posing as a reporter one day, an uncle the next, a deacon another. The nurses had been unusually forthcoming, probably because her injuries were so minor. She'd be going home soon, he'd been told. Now he just had to find out when.

He asked for the nurse's station on her floor then waited as he was transferred. After a few rings, someone answered.

"Third floor nurse's station. Sarah McNair speaking."

"Sarah!" he said as though he knew her. "How's it going?"

She hesitated, trying to place his voice. "Fine."

He grinned. He loved throwing people off guard.

"Listen, this is Bob Schilling, Lynda Barrett's law partner. I just tried calling her room, but the line was busy. I wonder if you can tell me yet if she's had any word on when she might be released."

"Uh ... just a second. I'll check."

He waited as she left the phone. She was back in just a moment. "I'm sorry, but there's no word yet. We may keep her a couple more days. Would you like for me to transfer you to her room?"

"No need. I'll drop by to see her this afternoon. You gave me what I needed for now. Thanks a lot, Sarah."

He hung up, frowning, and wondered whether he should make his move now, rather than waiting until she returned home.

But how?

He checked his watch. Three hours before he had to be at work. Time enough to pay the hospital a visit, check out the possibilities, and formulate a plan. If he played his cards right and caught her while she was sleeping, he might even be able to get into her room to see if she is on an IV. Maybe he could inject it with something—aspirin to thin her blood, maybe. Or he could grind up some of his blood-pressure pills. Maybe enough to make hers crash. Maybe this crash she wouldn't survive.

One way or another, he was going to get her out of his way. Lynda Barrett's luck was about to run out.

CHAPTER SIXTEEN

He knew they were cops the minute he spotted them. It was probably the sports coats that tipped him off, he thought; cops always wore coats to cover the guns strapped under their armpits. Or maybe it was the way they walked, with that quick, arrogant stride, as though they didn't exist on the same plane as everyone else. Then the radio blaring in their unmarked car confirmed it.

Were they here to talk to Lynda? he wondered. Had they realized yet that the crash was not an accident?

Curious, he sped up to join the two men where they waited for the elevator. Rubbing his hand over the slick hair he'd combed back, he tried to assess them over the frames of his glasses.

One of them, the dark-haired one who stood at least four inches above him, flashed him a smile. He hoped they'd never seen his picture before. The last thing he needed was to be identified before he even got to her room.

The elevator doors opened, and he followed them on.

"Which floor?" the blonde cop asked the other one.

"She's on three; he's on four. You want to talk to her first?"

"Might as well," he said, punching the button. "How about you? Where are you going?"

For a moment he didn't realize they were addressing him. "Uh . . . three."

"We may not be able to talk to him," the tall one said. "They're saying he's in pretty bad shape."

"We need to, man. Our hands are tied until we do."

The bell rang, and the number three flashed above them. The doors opened, and they all stepped off.

91

He looked both ways up the hall, as if trying to figure out which way to go. The two cops headed for the nurse's station. Taking out their badges, they flashed them to the first nurse they approached.

"Hi, Ma'am. I'm Larry Millsaps, St. Clair Police Department. This is my partner Tony Danks. Could you tell us Lynda Barrett's room number, please?"

He made a mental note of their names. He might need to know them later.

"Lynda's in 413. Down that hall and to the left."

"Thanks a lot." They started in the direction she was pointing.

He stepped into the waiting area and watched as they disappeared into her room.

What were they up to? Until now, the crash had been ruled an accident, at least according to the television. They couldn't know that someone had sabotaged the plane, could they? No—they were here for something else.

He eyed the room next to her; there was a name on the door. But the room on the other side of hers appeared to be empty. Checking behind him to make sure no one was watching, he went into the vacant room.

The bathroom door was on the side adjacent to Lynda's room. The door was closed. He remembered being in a hospital once that had rooms that adjoined through the bathroom, and carefully, he turned the knob.

The door opened quietly, and he peered in. Another door was on the other side. It must open into Lynda's room.

Grinning, he went in and pressed his ear against the door. He couldn't hear, so he hesitated a moment weighing the risk and then turned the knob.

The door opened silently, and he heard her voice.

Perfect. If he could get this close, he could wait until she was alone. Maybe he could wait until she slept, then put a pillow over her face. That way he wouldn't have to worry about IV's and blood thinners. He could take care of her with his bare hands and make sure that he did the job right this time.

Then, as quickly as the thought had come, he realized how absurd it was. The cops had seen him. If she were found smothered in her bed, wouldn't they consider everyone who'd been on the floor a suspect? Of course, they'd still have to find him and identify him, but it was too risky. When he finally took her out, he needed an alibi. He needed to be far enough away that they could never pin it on him.

For now, just listening was enough. Maybe he'd hear what he needed to hear.

CHAPTER SEVENTEEN

You're the pilot," Larry told Lynda as she sat up in bed, all bruised and scraped and stitched, like a mad scientist's experiment. "Maybe you can help us figure out what kind of person might know enough about planes to cut exactly the right hose."

Lynda shrugged. "A mechanic, I suppose. I'm not sure *I* would have even known which hose to cut."

Tony paced to the window and looked down on the parking lot. "What we're trying to determine is whether we're dealing with someone who's very familiar with planes or someone who didn't know what he was doing and just got lucky."

"Lucky, huh?" Lynda said in a dull, flat voice, and Larry wished Tony had chosen a better word.

"See, Lynda," Larry threw in, "it was difficult to determine if there was anything else tampered with, since the fire destroyed so much, but from what the NTSB can tell us, that was the only hose that was cut. It seems pretty deliberate. Calculated. Like someone who knew planes well had done it."

Lynda agreed. "It would have to be someone who's done a lot of work on airplanes."

Larry shot Tony a look. "So I guess that narrows down our hunt to someone with a background in aircraft mechanics or maintenance or maybe someone who had built planes."

"Did you interview all the guys who work at the airport?"

"We're in the process of doing it now. The problem is, we aren't having any luck finding anyone who has a vendetta against you."

Pulling her robe tighter around her, Lynda got out of bed and went to the dresser across the room. "I've been racking my brain since yesterday to think of anyone who might hate me. Maybe people whose cases I lost or didn't get along with or people I've been rude to." She let her voice trail off and tried to blink back the tears as she pulled a small notebook out of the drawer. Pulling out a piece of paper with a short list on it, she handed it to them. "These people wouldn't put me on their top-ten list of favorite people. But I can't see *any* of them doing something so deadly. I felt guilty even putting their names down."

"Anything would help at this point," Larry said, examining the list. "So who's this first guy?"

"Jack Gild. A client whose business was being sued, and I lost the case. He had to file bankruptcy, and he lost his home. He was really angry."

"What kind of business was it?"

"He repaired medical equipment. He was real mechanical, but I don't know if he knew about airplanes."

"What about this one? Doug Chastain?"

She sighed. "That was a client I dropped because he was so hard to get along with. I should have stuck it out, but I cut him loose before we went to trial, and it might have hurt his case."

"Did he make any threats?"

"No, not to my face. He really didn't seem like the violent type. He just had an attitude."

"What were his charges?"

"Arson. He and some friends got drunk and set a girl's yard on fire, just for kicks. Unfortunately, the house caught fire, too."

"How old is he?"

"Maybe twenty."

"What's he doing now?"

She shrugged. "I don't know. He served a little time, but I haven't kept up with him. And that third name, Gordon Addison. Well, I feel silly even putting it down. It's a pilot who's asked me out several times, but I didn't go. He has a tremendous ego, so I thought maybe...."

"That he might try to get even for his hurt pride?"

95

She winced. "Actually, it's ridiculous. Just mark him off. Talk about egos. I'm as bad as he is if I could imagine him being that torn up over my rejecting him."

"We'll just question him like we're questioning everybody. He won't know you gave us his name."

"All right." She sank back down on her bed. "This is the hardest thing I've ever done."

"It might save your life. Try to think of more names, Lynda. It's possible that your plane was picked randomly, that all of this had nothing to do with you specifically, but until we can determine that for sure, I think we have to assume it was someone going after you."

She went back to her bed and sat back on the pillows. "It's just so unbelievable."

"It always is when something like this happens."

"But who would want me dead?"

"Like he said," Tony suggested, "it may not be you at all. In fact, it's occurred to us that it could have been someone after Jake."

"But it wasn't his plane."

"Maybe someone knew he was looking at it. We're going to talk to him next."

Lynda's face changed. "I don't know if that's a good idea."

"Why not?"

"He's … having a real hard time. He's depressed. Really depressed. I don't know if he can take any pressure right now, especially if you're planting the seed in his mind that someone may have done this to him deliberately."

"It's a long shot," Larry said. "But we have to ask. Don't worry. We'll try to be sensitive. But sometimes it's helpful for someone in his position to have a chance to brainstorm with us. It gives them back a little control. If they know something's being done—"

"But nothing really *is* being done, is it?" she asked quietly. "I mean, you don't know who it is, so you can't do any more than I can."

"But we can keep digging until we reach the bottom," Larry told her. "And that's exactly what we intend to do."

Lynda stared into space for a while after they had left, wondering whether, indeed, someone wanted her or Jake dead and why. It was crazy. It was amazing. It was unlikely.

Yet it had happened.

She heard a knock and thought the detectives had forgotten something. "Come in."

Gordon Addison, one of the men whose names she had put on the list, stepped inside.

"Gordon!" she said, every muscle in her body tensing.

He smiled—which may have been, she realized, the first time she'd ever seen that expression on his face. "I didn't know if it was appropriate for me to come," he said stiffly. "But I wanted to bring you some flowers and tell you you're missed at the airport."

Her heartbeat accelerated as she took the flowers wrapped in tissue paper and tried to look grateful. "You shouldn't have, Gordon. But thanks. That's so sweet."

"How do you feel?"

"Better," she said. "I'm expecting to get out soon."

"Great. That's good news."

An awkward silence settled between them, and she looked down at the flowers, as if studying the petals.

"Well," he said, finally. "You look tired. I'll go. I just wanted to bring those by."

She swallowed. "Thank you. Really."

She watched as he left the room, and when the door closed behind him, she let out a deep breath and wilted back on her pillow. She should be ashamed, she thought. All he'd ever done to her was ask her out then act hurt because she wouldn't go. He wasn't a killer. Didn't the flowers prove that he was only trying to be nice?

But *someone* had tried to kill her. Someone who'd gotten into the airport. Someone who knew airplanes. Someone who had a vendetta. That made it hard to be anything less than suspicious of someone like Gordon, who met those criteria as well as anyone.

Finally, she picked up the phone, hoping she could catch Larry and Tony in Jake's room.

CHAPTER EIGHTEEN

Jake was so relieved to have visitors that forced his therapists to postpone his torture for an hour that he would have told the cops anything just to keep them there.

But for the life of him, he couldn't come up with the name of anyone who might want him dead.

"Think," Larry said. "You had looked at the plane the day before. Who knew about that?"

Jake shrugged. "Well, a few people. There's the first officer I fly with sometimes. We had a few drinks the night before while he was laid over. And there was the woman I met in a club that night ... and some of her friends. ..."

"Can you name them?"

He moaned. "The pilot is Frank Adkins. But as for the others, I can't even remember the name of the woman I was with. I'm not very good with names. Besides, why would someone who'd just met me want me dead?"

"You tell us," Tony said.

Jake was getting tired of this. "Nobody wants me dead, okay? It was *her* plane."

"Well, that's what we're thinking, too," Tony said. "But we just thought we'd try. If you think of anybody, maybe you could give us a call."

"Sure," Jake said, watching him set his card down on the bedside table. "If I come up with any valets I didn't tip enough or any gas-station attendants I might have offended, I'll let you guys know."

"And we might call you, if we think of any questions you might be able to answer."

"I'm not going anywhere," Jake assured them. "Look, you find that guy, okay? You find whoever it is and tell him what he did to me. He may not have wanted me dead, but you can sure bet that I'd love to see *him* dead. And if I ever get the chance—"

"We have to find him first," Tony said.

The door opened, and Abby stuck her head in. "Jake, Lynda was trying to call your room, darlin', but the phone wasn't working."

Jake glanced at it sitting cracked and lopsided on his table. "What did she want?"

Abby came in further. "Are you gentlemen from the police department?"

"Yes," Larry said.

"Well, she said to tell you that as soon as you left, one of the guys she put on her list visited her. Gordon somebody. He just left."

Tony and Larry looked at each other. "We'd better go," Tony said.

"Yeah." Larry patted Jake's arm and mumbled, "Take care."

Abby followed them out, and Jake watched the door close behind them then let out a labored breath. He wondered if the cops' questions had frightened Lynda. She was probably scared to death, and he couldn't really say he blamed her. He wondered if the guy who'd done this to them would really have the guts to show up here.

She'd given them a list, they'd said. Her paranoia about people she'd insulted, offended, or defeated almost amused him, but it really wasn't funny. She was struggling to think of people who had reason to be irritated with her since she couldn't think of anyone who hated her outright.

On the other hand, there were plenty of people who hated him. Women whose hearts he'd broken, men whose women he'd stolen, people he'd walked on, stepped on, kicked in the teeth—

Even his own mother.

He shoved the thought out of his mind.

Frustrated, he tried to sit up and move his legs, as if he could jump off the bed and run as fast as he could from his own thoughts, but they wouldn't budge. Finally, he gave up in a sweat and collapsed back into the pillows.

Why hadn't he just died?

Maybe it wasn't too late. Maybe if he just kept his eyes open for an opportunity, he would find a way to do just that.

If there was a hell for people like him, it couldn't be any worse than this.

Lynda saw the vacuous look in Jake's eye when she came to his room hours later. It was a haunting look, a look that spoke of defeat and self-loathing, that said he would throw the towel in if only he had a towel and knew where to throw it.

He seemed unwilling to look her in the eye now. She wondered if he were beating himself up for holding her and crying against her yesterday. He was probably surprised she had let him, after the way he had treated her. He had just finished throwing things at her, for pete's sake, as if doing her further harm could somehow relieve him of his own injuries.

But Jake Stevens didn't seem like the type to let anyone see him so unveiled, so vulnerable. And she could tell he didn't like it.

"Did you talk to Larry and Tony?" she asked.

"The cops? Yeah, I talked to them. Did they catch up with the guy who visited you?"

"I don't know," she said. "I never heard."

"They seem to know what they're doing. Maybe they'll find whoever did this. I just wish I could get out and look for him myself. You don't know how many times I've dreamed of getting my hands around his throat and showing him just what he did to me."

The words startled her, but then she realized that she had had the same fantasy. "I just want to know why he did it. What if we had died?"

She saw the raw pain growing more pronounced on his face. Covering his bandage with his wrist, he lay quietly for a moment. "Funny," he said finally. "I've been more concerned with the consequences of living."

He was back, she thought, that man who had been broken, vulnerable, and honest yesterday. Taking a chance, she reached down and touched his hand and moved it away from his face to make him look at her. "What do you mean?"

When he looked up, she knew the barrier was gone. This was Jake, the man so full of pain that he couldn't contain his grief or his rage, the man she liked more than the one he often pretended to be. "I mean if I'm paralyzed, I'll lose my pilot's license. Even in the best-case scenario—if my legs do start working again—I've still lost an eye. Which means I'm out of a job. There's disability, of course, or I could take a desk job. But TSA has a policy against keeping pilots who are damaged goods. And did I mention the fact that my face has a gash the size of the San Andreas Fault? The Elephant Man didn't have anything on me."

When she couldn't find the words to take his pain away, she squeezed his hand. And he squeezed back. It was something, she thought.

Trying to lighten the mood, she said, "No, but what's *really* wrong?"

He shot her a look that said she was crazy, but when he saw the grin in her eyes, he began to laugh softly. "Maybe I just need a hobby," he said facetiously.

"Sure," she teased. "You should take up woodworking or something."

"I'm actually thinking about taking up jogging. I hear there's a great running track on the roof of this building. And if running doesn't boost your spirits, you can always jump."

Her grin faded. "That's not funny."

His smile died as well. "No, it isn't. Don't mind me. I'm just fantasizing."

"You don't need to fantasize about suicide, Jake. That's not the answer."

She saw the mist welling in his eye as he looked away. "Then what is? The doctors told me I'll never take a step again. So tell me what good physical therapy will do me."

"None," she admitted, "if you go into it determined to fail. Besides, I know they've told you that there's a chance you could walk again. I've asked them myself."

"All right," Jake conceded. "A slim chance. A next-to-nothing chance. And judging by the way my legs are lying here like limbs on a corpse, I'd say the chances are even slimmer than that."

"And what odds would they have given either of us for surviving that crash? Probably none, Jake. And they sure wouldn't have bet on my being able to go home tomorrow, less than a week after the crash."

"They're letting you out?" he asked, his gears suddenly shifted.

She wondered at his choice of words. Did he consider this a prison? "Yes. Only because I have someone at home who can help me out."

"Yeah? Who's that?"

"A client of mine who needed a place to stay. But my point is that—"

"Well, if that's the criteria, I guess I'll grow old here."

She forgot what she was saying, and for a moment, just looked at him. "You're going to be all right, Jake. And if you need anything—I could go by your hotel room and bring you all your things. Or go to the store for you. I could sneak you in a hamburger...."

Jake looked up at the ceiling, his face expressionless. "Get off it, Lynda. You're gonna leave here without looking back, just like I'd do."

"No, I'm not," she said. "I'm going to visit you every day."

He moved his angry eyes back to her. "Why?"

"Because, I ... I want to."

He let go of her hand. "I don't need your pity," he said as his lips began to tremble. "And I don't need your visits. We hardly even know each other, and we sure don't owe each other anything."

"Jake, there's no way I'm going to forget that you're lying in here. And pity is the last thing I feel for you. I'm not the one moaning about how you'll never walk again and how you need to get to the roof so you can jump off."

"What if I don't want you to come?"

"Tough," she said. "I'm coming, anyway."

For a moment, he seemed at a loss for a reply. Finally, he muttered, "I'll believe it when I see it."

"Good."

There was a thick silence between them as they stared at each other, and finally his eyes softened infinitesimally. He reached for her hand again and held it in front of his face, as if examining it. "Are you sure it's safe for you to be at home?"

Instantly her courage deflated, and she felt like a broken, injured, frightened woman again. "I hope so. Mike seems convinced that no one's after me personally, that it was just some random act, that it could just as easily have been one of the other planes on the tarmac that night."

"And what do you think?"

She sighed. "I think I'll go along with his theory. I have to go on with my life, after all. And if there is someone after me, maybe having the police snoop around will deter him."

"Pretty optimistic, considering what you've been through."

"Yeah, well …" She looked down at their hands, clasped on his chest and felt a surge of warmth that there was someone who cared. "I'll be okay." Taking a deep breath, she redirected her thoughts. "Anyway, back to my offer. Do you want me to do anything for you when I get out?"

He considered that and realized there wasn't anyone else he could ask. And there were loose ends of his life to be tied up. Loose ends that he'd tried to handle by phone until now. "Yeah," he admitted finally. "There are a few things you could do once you get on the outside."

CHAPTER NINETEEN

The light assaulted Jake with jackhammer force as Allie, his occupational therapist, threw open his drapes the next morning.

"I like them closed," he muttered.

"Don't be silly. You can't lie here in the dark all day. You need sunlight to motivate you."

"Motivate me to do what? Roll over? I've gotten real good at that already."

"Nope," she said. "You're going to sit up today. We're gonna get you in a wheelchair if it kills you."

"It might," he said, getting angry. "We've only gotten to twenty degrees without me passing out or puking all over the place, remember?"

"Buzz is bringing a special wheelchair that reclines. We'll move you up as slowly as we need to. And to help with the circulation, I brought you these TEDS."

She held up a pair of stockings, and Jake moaned. "Forget it. I'm not wearing those. There's got to be a limit to the humiliation."

"Oh, yes, you are." She uncovered his legs and began to work a stocking over one foot. "And then we're going to wrap the legs tight with Ace bandages. It'll help you fight the orthostasis, so we can get you sitting up." As she spoke, she worked the tight stocking up his calf then propped his foot on her shoulder as she pulled it over his knee. "Tonight we're gonna start you on sequential compression stockings to keep the blood from pooling in your legs while you're asleep."

"If I could kick, I'd send you flying," he gritted as she got the stocking up his thigh.

"If you could kick, none of this would be necessary."

He lay on his back, miserable, as she fought the other stocking up then began wrapping both legs so tightly that he imagined his face turning red. He was almost glad he couldn't feel them.

"I have this theory about Mary Poppins," he told her through his teeth.

"Mary Poppins?"

"Yeah. You remind me of her. I hated her even when I was a kid. I've always thought she was a child abuser, leading those kids into all sorts of danger, introducing them to bums and no-accounts, playing with their heads. She was probably an occupational therapist before she was a nanny."

Allie looked undaunted. "Well, I did finish Torture 101 at the top of my class."

She finished wrapping just as Buzz came in followed by two orderlies, pushing a black monstrosity on two wheels.

"Hey, Jake," he said, just as cheerfully as Allie. "You ready to go for a ride?"

"You people are crazy. If I don't pass out in the first ten seconds—"

"When you start feeling faint, we'll lay you back for a few minutes," Buzz said. "This chair reclines to whatever angle we need. It'll be slow going, but we've got to get you sitting up before we can get on with serious therapy."

There was nothing he could do to stop them, so Jake braced himself as they surrounded his bed.

"All right now, on the count of three," Buzz said. "We're going to lift you carefully into the chair, lying flat. Our goal is just to get into it for a few minutes. Are you ready?"

Jake couldn't answer, but it was just as well. At the count of three, they lifted him into the chair.

Allie was all business now as she adjusted the recline of the chair and moved his foot rests to elevate his feet then carefully positioned them. Then she gave Buzz the signal to begin raising him up. "Easy, easy ... How do you feel, Jake?"

He couldn't find words to describe the agony of dizziness and nausea. Sweat dripping from his chin, he muttered, "Sick."

"He's pale. Let him down," she said, and they lowered him flat again.

"Imagine how bad it'll be when it's moving," he whispered.

"You'll get over it, Jake. Come on now. Let's try it again."

He groaned as they pulled him back up. "Talk about motivation," he said, breathing hard. "I'm starting to feel some. I'm wanting real bad to move these feet so I can ram them through your teeth."

Buzz suppressed his grin. "Well, we all have to have goals. But if it's any consolation, I've been there. I was in a bad car wreck when I was nineteen, and I had injuries real similar to yours." He held out his hands, as if he might burst into a shave-and-a-haircut routine. "And look at me now."

"Yeah, well, I'm not nineteen, and they told me I may never walk again."

"They told me that, too, man. But with hard work, I overcame it. That's why I went into physical therapy. I'm gonna do everything I can for you, too. Trust me. You do what we say, try really hard, and I promise you, if we don't have you walking within a few months, you'll at least be able to function within your disability."

Jake looked down at the wheelchair beneath him and realized for the first time that he truly was disabled now. He was one of those people he got impatient with in stores because they took up too much room in the aisles and slowed him down. He was one of those people who had to be boarded first on airplanes and needed special attention getting off. He was one of those people he had always looked at with an air of superiority, an air that said, "Sorry you're disabled, pal, but you're in my way."

Disabled. The word hung in his heart like a fish hook, and that familiar, fighting anger spread through him like an infectious disease.

"After we get you up higher," Allie said gently, "I can take you for a ride. You're probably ready to get out of this room on something besides a gurney, aren't you?"

He had seen a Stephen King movie once where a deranged nurse had wheeled her victim into walls, down stairs, and dumped him out into a heap on the floor when she was finished with him.

"No thanks," he muttered.

As if in punishment, they began raising him up again until his stomach churned.

By the time they had worked him up to forty-five degrees, Jake was exhausted.

"I—I think we damaged something," he grunted after they moved him back to his bed. "My head feels like it's about to burst."

"That's normal, Jake. At least now you know that you don't have to lie on your back all the time. You can sit up, and you can get out of bed. We may get you all the way up tomorrow. And before you know it, we can change you to a lighter-weight chair, and you can get in and out of it by yourself. After that, we may be able to send you home."

Home, Jake thought with a sinking heart. Where was that? He'd sold his condo in Houston, and everything he owned was here, except his car, which he couldn't drive. He didn't have a job, a place to live, or any friends to speak of.

And he might as well not have any family.

As Allie and Buzz left, he dropped his head back on the pillows. Home, he thought. What had once been such a given, such an expected element in his life was now something he didn't have. He was not only disabled, but he was also homeless. He didn't even want to think of all the biases he'd once had against homeless people.

He had no idea where home would be when he was released from here. At least he wouldn't be released for months and months. But that thought, his greatest comfort, was also his greatest fear.

CHAPTER TWENTY

You didn't have to come get me," Lynda told Paige the next morning when she met her in the lobby. "I could have had Sally bring me home."

"Well, that would be silly," Paige said. "Sally has plenty of work to do, and I'm just sitting there in your house."

Lynda looked down at the child sitting on the lobby floor, playing with a puzzle. She looked so safe today, so secure. "Paige," Lynda said with a heavy sigh, "we need to talk."

Paige's face took on a guarded look, and she started twisting her hair into a pony tail. "Okay."

Lynda sat down on the couch and glanced around, making sure no one could overhear. No one sat nearby. "Paige, they've found out that someone sabotaged my plane and caused my crash."

"How awful!" she said.

"Yeah, it's pretty awful," Lynda said. "But the really awful part is that this person might have been trying to kill me. We don't know."

Paige twisted her hair harder. "Do you know who it could be?"

Lynda shook her head dolefully. "I've thought and thought. But the bottom line is, if someone is out to get me, then anyone with me is also in danger."

Paige let her hair fall. "You want us to move out."

"No, that's not what I want. I just wanted you to know the danger. You have to know that living in my house might be putting you and Brianna in jeopardy."

Paige considered her child for a moment, then brought her gaze back to Lynda. "Are you scared?"

Lynda tried to find honest words to express what she felt. "I think . . . that maybe . . ." She failed and tried again. "I don't know. It could have been just a fluke that he picked my plane. But that's really just what I want to believe. If I'm wrong . . ."

Paige sat slowly back down on the couch, the look on her face telling Lynda that she couldn't take much more. "You don't need the stress of having us around anyway."

"I'd love to have you around, Paige. You know that's not it. And if you still want to stay, you can. You just had to know."

For a moment, she watched Paige's big blue eyes wrestle with the decision. Other visitors waited on the couches or milled through the lobby. The elevator bell kept ringing every few seconds, and on the intercom doctors were paged and codes were recited. In the corner across the room, a television was on, and a few children sat transfixed in front of it.

When Paige finally brought her eyes back to Lynda, Lynda fully expected Paige to thank her, then say that she would find another place to stay. But Lynda had underestimated the girl's desperation.

"Well, Lynda, I guess I see it like this. If I go home, I'm in absolute, inevitable danger. And if I stay with you, I may be in danger—but I may not. And since I don't see any other possibilities right now, I think Brianna and I will stay."

Lynda hadn't realized how much she had hoped Paige would say that until she heard the words. "Good," she said. "I'm glad." She reached out and squeezed Paige's hand. "We're in God's hands, Paige. I believe that. We're going to be all right."

And as they left the hospital, Lynda believed it more than ever.

CHAPTER TWENTY-ONE

oday. She was going home today. Thanking the nurse who'd given him the information, he hung up the phone, leaned back, and laughed.

So much for patience. He didn't have to wait even one more day.

But he had a lot of work to do if he was going to take care of things tonight. He'd heard every word that she'd said to the police that day in her hospital room, and the knowledge empowered him, even while it created a new urgency. He had to do this quickly before they managed to stop him.

Grabbing his car keys, he dashed out of his apartment, his spirits higher and more hopeful than they had been since the day of the crash.

CHAPTER TWENTY-TWO

The airport looked just the same as it had the morning of the crash, and as Paige pulled her car into a parking place facing the fence—and beyond that, the runway—Lynda found herself reliving that morning. It had been windy, like this, and she remembered thinking she should have postponed the test flight. If only she had. But that wouldn't have helped, would it? The crash would have happened anyway the next time she took the plane up, and she might not have survived the landing if she'd been alone.

"Are you all right?" Paige asked quietly.

Lynda shook herself out of her reverie. "Yeah. Fine. It's just kind of weird, coming here after what happened."

Paige crossed her arms over the steering wheel. "Is it really necessary? I mean, I'm sure Jake's car is fine."

"I just have to get his hotel key out of it," she said. "And I want to get Mike to move it someplace where Jake doesn't have to worry about it."

Paige checked the back seat where Brianna was sound asleep in her car seat, and she patted Lynda's hand. "You go on in and do what you need to. I don't want to wake her up. Take your time, okay?"

"Okay." Wincing against the pain in her ribs when she twisted, Lynda got out of the car and went inside.

The small airport was just as she remembered: the blue couches forming a square in the middle of the floor; the line of vending machines against one wall; the posters of exotic places; the rest rooms; the tall desk that looked like a concession stand but was really Mike's version of a control tower.

Mike sat there now, sipping on coffee and going over paperwork. He looked up when she started toward him.

"Lynda!" Spilling his coffee, he blotted it up quickly then came around the desk to meet her. "What in the world are you doing here?"

She hugged him, careful not to test her ribs, and he led her to a seat and made her sit down. "They sprang me this morning."

"You should have called me," he said. "I would have picked you up. Are you okay? Do you need a wheelchair? I have three."

She couldn't help being amused. "Mike, relax. I'm fine. I may look like Frankenstein's daughter, but I'm really okay."

"But you aren't supposed to drive this soon after your surgery, are you? And shouldn't you be at home—?"

She touched his arm to stem his rambling. "I didn't drive. I have a friend out in the car waiting for me. I just came to make some arrangements about Jake's car and get some things out of it for him."

"Oh. Well, okay. I have it parked in the hangar."

Getting to her feet, she tried to look stronger than she was. "Do you have the keys?"

"Yeah. He left them in the ignition that day. I locked it up and put the keys in my safe." He hurried around behind the desk and unlocked the safe.

"Here they are." He handed them to her. "I'll walk out to the hangar with you."

"No," she said. "It's okay. You need to stay here. Who knows? Somebody's landing gear might fail."

He hesitated then looked at the controls behind his desk and realized she was right. "All right," he said. "Are you sure you'll be all right?"

"I'll be great."

She pushed through the glass door of the airport, and the wind immediately whipped her hair into her face. Shoving it back, she peered across the concrete to runway 4. She wasn't sure exactly where her plane had ended up—the crash was such a blur to her now—but she remembered waking up and seeing Jake crushed and twisted and bleeding, and she remembered sliding him to the door....

112

Shivering, she started to the hangar.

It was open, as it usually was this time of day, and planes sat lined up, waiting to be flown. There was a big space where she had occasionally parked *Solitude*, and tears came to her eyes. But she reminded herself that she hadn't come here to mourn, and she blinked the tears away. She had things to take care of.

She saw the red Porsche parked at the back of *Solitude's* empty space, and slowly she started toward it.

"Lynda? How are you doing?"

She looked up; one of the mechanics was standing on the wing of a plane. "Hi, Mac. I'm great."

"You sure look a lot better than I expected you would after I saw that plane hit."

She smiled. "It'll take a lot more than a little ole plane crash to get me down."

He laughed. "It's good to have you back."

But her smile faded. She wasn't back. Not really.

She went to Jake's car and unlocked the door, but as she did, she heard footsteps behind her. She turned and saw Gordon Addison.

Though she waved, a shiver went through her again; quickly, she got into the car and locked it shut. Trembling, she looked back at him through the windshield, wondering whether he knew she had given his name to the police or whether they'd caught him leaving the hospital and interrogated him about why he'd come. He was standing half in the shadow of his plane, staring at her as if surprised to see her. That look frightened her, and she found it hard to breathe. She had to calm down. He probably wasn't the one who'd done this to her, and she had no reason to be frightened. Besides, there were witnesses all around them here in the hangar — mechanics and maintenance people, other pilots — and he couldn't do anything to her here.

When he disappeared behind his plane, she calmed down. He wasn't going to approach her. She was just being paranoid.

She tried to relax in the sleek interior of Jake's car, smelling the spearmint scent of the gum he kept on the dashboard. Opening his glove compartment, she found the hotel key just where he'd told her it would be. She pulled it out, along with the hairbrush he kept there, the sunglasses, and the ID tag that identified him as a TSA employee.

Putting them into the bag she'd brought with her, she looked around for anything else he might like to have. There was an aviation magazine on the passenger's seat—probably the same one in which he'd seen her classified ad—and she stuffed it into the bag to throw away. She flipped down the visor over the driver's seat and saw his checkbook. Slipping it out of the pocket that held it, she dropped it into the bag, and looked around for anything else. Only the gum, she thought, and he might like that.

She got out, opened the small trunk, and saw some of the bigger items he'd put there during his move—things he'd decided to bring to Florida himself rather than turning them over to the movers since he might need them before he found a place to live—and she took out what she thought she could carry and made a mental note to ask Mike to unload the other things and take them to Jake. The more personal items he had around him, the better he would feel.

Taking one last inventory, she reached for the trunk, wincing at the pain in her ribs, and closed it.

She jumped, startled—Gordon Addison stood leaning against the car, staring at her with his arms crossed. "You scared me, Gordon."

"What did you tell the police?" he asked.

She swallowed and looked toward the plane where Mac had been working. He was gone.

"What do you mean?" she asked, starting to back away.

He stayed where he was. "They came here this morning asking all kinds of questions. Where I was the night before the crash, what my relationship with you is, why I came to the hospital yesterday—"

"Well, they interviewed everybody here. They weren't singling you out."

He pushed away from the car then, the frown on his face revealing a deeper anger than she could hear in his voice. "I want to know what you told them."

"I told them something about everybody here, Gordon. Not just you." Again, she searched around for Mac or one of the other mechanics, and though she could hear some of them on the other side of the hangar, none was in sight.

"If you think I had anything to do with that crash—"

"Of course not," she cut in. "What reason would you possibly have?"

As if he turned that question over in his mind, he left it unanswered.

Lynda started to walk away. She half expected him to catch up with her, grab her, and stop her, but as she stepped out into the wind again, she turned back. He hadn't moved from where he was standing, and he was watching her.

With more energy than she could spare, she walked faster until she was all the way to Paige's car.

Later that night after Paige had cooked her the best meal she'd had since her mother died, Lynda walked outside to sit on the massive deck attached to the back of her house. The cool night air felt good on her face as she lay on a white wicker chaise lounge chair and gazed up into the stars. Somewhere, under these same stars, an enemy lurked with deadly intention. God knew who it was.

Maybe it wasn't Gordon Addison at all, she thought. Maybe it was some kid caught in a game, and now that he'd seen the results of his actions, he was remorseful and repentant. Maybe it *was* just an accident.

Or maybe not.

But the face of Gordon Addison, angry and pensive, staring at her in the hangar today still chilled her.

Across the deck, a cricket chirped, and she could hear the sound of the leaves in the oak tree whispering over her head. The breeze had grown cooler while she was in the hospital, but she knew it wouldn't stay that way for long. Soon the temperature would rise, and it would feel like summer again. Summer didn't let go easily in Florida.

The back door opened, spilling light out, and Paige looked startled. "Oh, I'm sorry. I didn't know you were out here. I was just going to take the garbage out, but I'll do it later."

"No, it's all right," Lynda said. "I was just thinking."

Paige set the garbage bag in the vinyl can next to the deck and took a step toward the chair. "Really, if you want to be alone ..."

"Sit down, Paige," she whispered. "Brianna's asleep, everything's put away—you deserve to rest."

"Oh, I'm not tired. Really. I love doing household things. And I'm so thankful that you've given us a place to stay."

"You don't have to wait on me hand and foot just because you're grateful. I think I'm getting a lot more out of this deal than you are."

Paige was quiet for a moment. "I just want you to see that I'm . . . decent. I don't want you to think I'm just trash."

"Why would I think that?"

Paige had trouble meeting her eyes. "I don't know. That's what people think about women who have to hide from their ex-husbands. Things like this don't happen to 'nice people.' "

Lynda touched her hand and made her meet her eyes. "I've *never* thought you were trash, Paige. If anyone is, it's me, for not giving your case the priority it deserved."

"Well, why would you? I couldn't pay—"

"That doesn't matter," Lynda said. "You needed help, and I just became another problem."

Paige walked out to the railing of the deck and leaned back against it. She sighed and rubbed her eyes wearily. "Sometimes, I look back on the dreams I had growing up and all the promises I made myself, and I can't figure out how I got into all this."

"What promises, Paige?"

Paige turned her back to Lynda and looked out over the night. "Promises that I'd have a different kind of life when I grew up." She laughed softly, but there was no joy in the sound. "You know, the picket-fence promises. The ones about the knight in shining armor who would protect me instead of threatening me."

Lynda tried to listen beyond Paige's words. "Paige, did you come from an abusive home?"

Paige was silent for a while, and Lynda wondered if she'd heard her at all. When she finally spoke again, her evasion told Lynda what Paige couldn't. "Keith seemed like just the kind of man I needed. Strong and smart—have I told you that he has a genius IQ?"

The turn in the conversation surprised Lynda, but she tried to follow it. "Really?"

"Yeah. But he still keeps failing. He's a computer whiz, but he has trouble keeping a job because of his temper. I think he expected to really be somebody. But his IQ hasn't helped him much. That only adds to all that anger boiling inside him. I really don't think he means to let his temper blow up the way it does. He's just so used to being in control. Every time I leave him, it just sends him into a rage."

"You've left him before?"

Paige turned back. "Yeah, a few times."

Lynda sat up. "And you went back?"

Paige turned to the night again. "He convinced me to, every time. Told me how sorry he was, that he'd change, that he'd never lay a finger on me again. He really did love me, Lynda. I know he did. And I worried about him. Nobody understands him like I do."

Lynda got up then and went to stand beside Paige. She turned Paige to face her and saw Paige's tears. "You sound like you still love him."

Paige shrugged. "I just get so mixed up. Sometimes I hate him, and sometimes...."

"But he hurt you, Paige. He hurt Brianna. How could you find any rationale for that?"

"He never means to, Lynda. It just ... happens."

Lynda tried hard to keep her expression from revealing her amazement — or her judgment. "Paige, abusive husbands kill their wives all the time. They kill their children."

"I know that," she said. "That's why I'm here. That's why we're divorced. I'm just trying to explain to you why I'm in this position. I'm not stupid, you know. Things happen to people sometimes that are out of their control."

"I know that more than anyone." She reached out to stroke Paige's hair and wished she had the wisdom that Paige needed right now. "But Paige, you did what you had to do to protect yourself and your daughter. It took a lot of courage, but you did it. Don't back down now."

"I'm not," she said adamantly. "Besides, Brianna's scared to death of him. Whenever I get weak and think of going back, I remember that."

Lynda stared at her, wanting to blurt out that she was crazy if she'd even considered going back to Keith, that she needed to go to counseling and get help, and that she needed to step back and start looking at things realistically.

But then she realized that Paige didn't need to be condemned right now. She needed patience and understanding. And she needed someone she could count on. Maybe that was the reason God had forced Lynda to rearrange her priorities: so that she'd be here for Paige. Not as a judge but as a friend.

She only hoped she had the grace to put friendship ahead of her own personal biases.

CHAPTER TWENTY-THREE

The five-gallon bug sprayer was perfect for the job. He screwed off the top, pulled the sprayer cord out, and dropped in the funnel he'd brought. Then, careful not to spill any, he poured the gasoline out of the can with the "J.R.'s Auto Repair" logo on the side.

That should be enough gas, he thought, checking his watch. It was after midnight. Lynda should be asleep by now since it was her first day home from the hospital. She was probably zonked out, what with those internal injuries and those painful broken ribs. She should thank him for putting her out of her misery.

He loaded the bug sprayer and the empty gas can into his car and drove across town to Lynda's house; he had located it days ago by simply looking up the address in the phone book. Turning down the exclusive street lined with groomed palm trees and extravagant homes, he did a drive-by, checking out the lights in the neighbors' houses, making sure there were no late-night walkers, no dogs liable to bark, no policemen staked out in parked cars.

He slowed when he reached Lynda's house, a two story Tudor style that reminded him of a miniature castle, and he thought how ironic that she had that whole house to herself when there were entire families living out of cars. She deserved whatever he gave her.

And it looked like the perfect night. No lights had been left on. The garage door was closed, and even the porch light was off. It would be easy to steal through the shadows and do what he had to do.

He drove the car around the block and parked at a vacant lot he'd found earlier. Quietly, he got out, pulled the empty gas can and the sprayer full of gasoline out with him, and cut through the trees separating the yards.

Her backyard was the third from the vacant lot. He slipped into her yard and saw the deck that would be the first to ignite. Quietly, he laid the empty gas can in the grass, close enough to the house to be found later but far enough away to escape harm. Stealing closer to the house, he began pumping the trigger on the sprayer and doused the side of the deck with gas.

The fumes reached his nostrils, satisfying him, and when he finished the deck, he ran a stream along the walls of the house, then turned up the side between the house and the garage, and kept spraying.

He sprayed until he ran out of fuel, and still there was no sign that Lynda had awakened. It was all falling perfectly into place.

Reaching into his pocket, he pulled out the matches he'd brought. All he had to do now was light it.

And then his problems would go up in flames.

CHAPTER TWENTY-FOUR

Across the street, Curtis McMillan, an eighty-year-old retired judge, awoke from a sound sleep. It happened more and more often these days, this middle-of-the-night wake-up call, when he knew that going back to sleep would be next to impossible.

Careful not to wake Lizzie, who didn't have that problem and had slept like a baby since he'd met her his senior year of high school, he reached for his robe and slippers and padded into the kitchen.

Without turning on the light, he got a glass out of the cabinet and scuffed to the sink for water. Next to the sink were his glasses; shoving them on with his free hand, he brought the glass of water to his lips.

His eyes focused on the night outside the window and the shadows of windblown trees dancing on Lynda Barrett's house across the street. Poor woman, he thought. Bless her soul. He hoped she was recovering quickly and would be home soon. The crash was such a tragedy.

He set the glass down and started to head toward the den to see if any late-night movies worth watching were on, but as he turned, a movement outside caught his eye.

It was different from the shadows of trees. It moved more deliberately, more methodically, and he cupped his hands on the glass and peered out more earnestly.

It was a prowler, he thought, someone trying to break into Lynda's house.

His heart began pounding, as if he'd climbed that flight of stairs at the courthouse, and calling out, "Lizzie!" he reached for the phone.

He heard his wife stirring as he punched out 911. Just as the dispatcher answered, the perimeter of the house went up in flames, draping the walls like neon paint.

And he couldn't see the prowler any more.

By now, Lizzie was in the kitchen, and the dispatcher was waiting.

"It's a fire at 422 West Evan Street," Curtis blurted, and Lizzie looked quickly out the window and threw her hand over her mouth. "It's arson," he said. "I saw a prowler, and then it went up in flames."

"Oh, Curtis!" Lizzie shouted.

"It's okay," he said then to both the dispatcher and his wife. "Thank God nobody's home."

Lynda rested more soundly that night than she had since her plane crashed, tucked in her own bed on the second floor of her own home. The soft percale sheets on her queen-sized bed were a wonderful contrast to the hospital sheets, and as she snuggled down under her Laura Ashley comforter, she felt welcomed by the items around her she had grown to love: the antique furniture she had collected a piece at a time, the finely crafted vases with silk flower arrangements, the oriental rug on her hardwood floor, the small baskets of potpourri scattered around the room, and her favorite art hung in strategic places on her papered walls.

She had worked hard for these comforts, and as she slipped into the depths of sleep, she had a sweet contentment that all would be well.

But sometime just after midnight, a whining sound outside startled her. Disoriented, she sat up, looking around, hearing it more clearly. A siren ... no, two or three sirens, right here on her street. She scrambled out of bed, but the moment her feet touched the floor she felt the heat and caught the faint smell of smoke.

"Paige!" Grabbing the pillow from her bed and holding it to her face, she ran down the hall to the guest bedroom where mother and daughter slept. "Paige, get up! There's a fire!"

Paige sat up and rubbed her eyes. "What?"

"The house is on fire! Get Brianna!"

As though a light had come on in her brain, Paige grabbed the child and began to cough. The smoke was more dense on this side of the house; Lynda was choking on it as well. Grabbing another pillow and wrestling it out of its case, she tossed the case at Paige. "Here, cover Brianna's face with this!"

"The floor's hot!" Paige shouted, and Brianna started to cry.

"We've got to get out!" Lynda cried as Paige followed her into the hall.

Lynda reached the top of the stairs in a half-dozen frantic strides then immediately jumped back; long, reaching flames were climbing the carpeted stairs and lapping against the wall. "We'll have to go out the window!" she shouted, pushing them toward the other end of the second floor. "Hurry, before the floor collapses!"

Two of the windows they passed were engulfed in flames from the outside, but at the far end of the house, the flames hadn't yet taken hold. Lynda threw open the window. "Climb out there on the roof. Hurry!"

Brianna's screams went up two octaves as she saw the flames licking their way up the side of the house. But holding her tightly, with the pillowcase pressed over the child's face, Paige climbed out and ran to the edge of the roof. Lynda followed her, ignoring the pain shooting through her ribs, pulling at her stitches, but she couldn't fight the dizziness beginning to take hold.

"How will we get down?" Paige screamed.

Only then did Lynda see the flashing lights of three fire trucks in front of her house. Someone shouted, "There's someone on the roof!"

In seconds, a ladder had been elevated to lift them down, out of the grasping hands of the flames.

They hadn't even reached the ground when the roof they'd been standing on caved in.

And so did Lynda. Covering her face in horror, she got off of the ladder and slid down to sit in the dirt, watching through her fingers as her house and everything she owned surrendered to the fire.

Brianna's wailing only echoed what was in Lynda's own heart as paramedics rushed to examine them. Lynda was just too tired and too stunned to express it herself.

"I'm so sorry, Lynda," a voice said above her as the paramedics put her on oxygen. She looked up into the troubled eyes of Curtis McMillan from across the street, who stood over her in his slippers and robe. "I didn't know you were home! I thought you were still in the hospital—I should have checked. I should have called."

She pulled the oxygen mask away from her face. "What are you talking about?"

"I woke up around midnight and happened to look out the window. I saw him start the fire, so I called the police, but I told them you weren't in there. I didn't know—"

"Wait a minute," she said. "You saw someone start the fire?"

"Yes," he said. "I thought it was a prowler at first. He was sneaking around your house, and the minute I had 911 on the phone, I saw him light it. The house went up in flames, but I didn't even check to see if you were in there."

"Did he go *into* the house, Judge?" she asked in a shocked whisper.

"I didn't see it if he did. But he must have doused it with gas because the fire caught instantly and circled the house—"

The paramedics were checking her vitals, prodding under her clothes, checking her incisions and her ribs. Impatiently, she shoved them away and got to her feet. "Judge, did you see his face? The color of his hair?"

The old man shook his head with distraught frustration. "He was more or less just a shadow. I only saw him for a second."

Smoke fell like a cloud around them as the flames devoured her house. Waving it away so she could breathe, she grabbed the old judge's arm. "I have to talk to the police," she told the frustrated paramedics. "I'm fine, really. Just let me go."

"But you probably need to go to the hospital! You need to be examined at least!" one of them said.

"In a minute," she said.

Lynda pulled the judge toward one of the trucks to find someone in authority. But as she did, she saw a car approaching, and Tony Danks and Larry Millsaps got out.

Still pulling the judge behind her, she met them at the car. "It was *arson!*" she blurted before they could even get out. "This is Judge Curtis McMillan, my neighbor. He saw the man who did it."

Larry shook the man's hand then somberly studied the house. "Thank God you got out."

124

"Only because he called." Lynda's face glowed with the orange reflection of the inferno as she gazed back at it. "He called 911. The sirens woke me up." Turning back to Larry, she said, "It's official now. Someone's trying to kill me."

Larry opened his arms and she collapsed against him, crying out her rage and terror as everything she loved burned down behind her.

CHAPTER TWENTY-FIVE

S o what's next?" Lynda's voice was weary as she looked across Curtis's kitchen table to the two detectives who had spent the last hour questioning the old couple.

"We follow up on the leads we've got until we apprehend the right person," Tony said.

"You don't *have* any leads," she said in a hoarse voice. "You don't really have a clue who he is, do you?"

Larry leaned forward on the table, meeting her eyes directly. "Here's what we know, Lynda. It's probably a man, between five feet eight and five feet ten, around 180 pounds. We know that he has at least a working knowledge of airplanes—"

"And we have the gas can he used with the name of an auto repair shop on it, even though he didn't leave any fingerprints."

"And you know he wants me dead."

"Yes," Tony admitted. "That does seem to be his goal. Now all we have to do is find someone with a motive. We still need your help for that."

But Lynda couldn't help. Wearily, she got up and went to the same window through which Curtis had seen her house catch fire, and she peered at the smoldering pile of rubble that had once been such a source of pride. Next to the pile the garage still stood, unscathed except for the black scars from the fire that had just begun to penetrate the structure when the fire trucks arrived. Lizzie, who had been tending to a fresh pot of coffee, slid her arm around Lynda. "It'll be all right, honey. These young men aren't going to let anything happen to you."

Lynda didn't respond. Instead, she ambled into the living room where Paige and Brianna sat in a rocking chair. Brianna was asleep, and Paige's smoke-stained face looked numb with shock as she leaned her chin against her daughter's head and stared blankly in front of her.

"Well, I guess the thing to do now is figure out where we're going to go," Lynda said. "At least our cars survived."

"I was just thinking how glad I am that *we* did," Paige whispered, bringing her dull eyes back to Lynda's.

Lynda shook her head, feeling gently — and, she was sure, unintentionally — reproved. What were her lost treasures compared to her life? And Brianna's? "You're right. Once again for some reason, God spared us."

Lizzie squeezed Lynda's shoulder again. "Honey, I've already made up the guest rooms for you. You're going to stay here tonight, all three of you."

"No, Lizzie. That's sweet of you, but I can't do that."

"Why not?"

Her face reddened, and she hugged herself as a shiver ran through her. "Someone's trying to kill me," she said. "I'm not safe. And if I'm in your house, *you're* not safe. I shouldn't even be here now."

Lizzie's eyes drifted to her husband's. Curtis took the baton. "Lynda, don't you think you're safe enough tonight? I mean, he wouldn't dare come back, and besides, how would he know you were here?"

"It's okay," she said, waving off the questions. "I've got an idea. I still have my father's house on the other side of town. I've been trying to sell it, but I'll just have to live there until I can rebuild. It should be safe. Only a few people even know I have that house. If I don't tell anyone where I am ..." She met Paige's eyes, and saw the despair on her face, the indecision. "Paige, I know you won't want to come with me, but I can give you some money so you can get by until he's caught. You could stay here or get a hotel—"

As if she'd spent the last hour holding them back with a paper-thin wall of resolve, Paige's eyes filled with tears. "Maybe I should just take my chances and go home."

"No," Lynda insisted. "You can't. Paige, we've come this far. Don't let this make you drop your guard."

Paige pinched the bridge of her nose and tried to steady her voice. "I can't keep taking your money, Lynda. I've got to start handling things myself."

"Not until after we go to court, you don't." Lynda stooped in front of her, making Paige meet her eyes. "I know this was traumatic tonight, but don't give up just because some lunatic is out to get me. That has nothing to do with you."

Larry, who had been jotting notes on a pad, looked up at Paige. "What do you mean, take your chances? What's the risk in going home?"

"My ex-husband." Paige swallowed, and a tear dropped from her cheek onto the top of Brianna's head. "He's abusive, and he's suing me for custody of Brianna. Lynda's representing me."

"She's not safe at home," Lynda cut in. "Despite our restraining order, he's tried to take Brianna, and he's broken into her house. That's why she's staying with me."

"I see." Frowning, he got up and paced across the kitchen. "And you don't have anyone else you can stay with?"

Paige shook her head. "My family is in Arizona. But the judge ordered me to stay in town until this court thing is settled."

Tony frowned and stared thoughtfully at Paige, as though flipping through possibilities in his mind. But it was Larry who had the solution. "Listen, Lynda, what if I guaranteed that we'll have someone guarding your father's house, at least for the next couple of days? That way Paige and Brianna could go with you, and you could feel safe. If it isn't common knowledge that you have that house, chances are you'd be okay there anyway."

Lynda was skeptical. "Larry, I know how the police department works. They're not going to waste a man guarding me twenty-four hours a day."

"I'll take care of it," Larry promised. "Even if Tony and I have to take turns on our off-hours, I know I can at least get them to agree to somebody the rest of the time."

Lynda glanced at Tony, who was gaping at Larry, but Larry ignored him. "You both need protecting. You might as well be in the same place so we can kill two birds with one stone."

Lynda smirked. "Somehow that cliché isn't very comforting to me right now."

"Sorry," Larry smiled. "So what do you say?"

Lynda turned her worried eyes back to Paige. "Paige, this is up to you. I can't ask you to put your life and your daughter's life in jeopardy to stay with me."

The turmoil on Paige's face told Lynda what a struggle this was. Then Paige wiped her eyes and settled her troubled gaze on Lynda. "Who'll take care of you if I'm not there? I promised. You just got out of the hospital. The doctor said—"

"Paige, I'll be fine. For heaven's sake, I just scaled the roof and got out of a burning house. I can take care of myself. I've done it for a long time."

Paige dropped her head back on the chair. "This nightmare just keeps getting worse."

They waited for her decision, not prodding her, and finally, she took a deep breath and tried to steady her voice. "I guess we'll stay in a hotel. But ... I swear I'll pay you back someday, Lynda. I know it's hard to believe, but—"

"It's not hard to believe, Paige. But I don't care about the money right now. That's not important."

"I feel like I'm letting you down or taking advantage of you, and you've been so nice to me."

Stooping down in front of the rocking chair, Lynda stroked Brianna's sleeping head. "You aren't letting me down, Paige," she said softly. "You're protecting your daughter. I think you've made the right decision. And when they catch this guy, you can stay with me again."

Paige turned her worried face to Tony and Larry. "Do you promise you'll guard her? You won't let anything happen to her?"

"I promise," Larry said. "And we'll take you to the motel tonight to make sure you get there safely."

Tony didn't look too happy about all the promises Larry was making on his behalf, but he didn't argue.

Lynda's father's house sat at the end of a dead-end street; a thickly wooded area separated it from the other two houses back up the road. Looking out the living room window, Lynda realized that she'd never thought of her parents' house in terms of safety before. She had only seen it as too small, too old, too mundane for an up-and-coming young lawyer.

The furniture was worn and faded, hopelessly outdated. From the rickety rocker in the corner to the recliner that had provided the only comfort her father had been able to find in his last days, she had been ashamed of it all.

Now it was all she had.

And coming here from a position of vulnerability and fear, she found some comfort in that it was so secluded and so familiar.

Larry touched her shoulder, and she jumped. "Sorry," she said, embarrassed. "I guess I'm a little jumpy."

"Can't say I blame you." Stepping closer to the window, he peered out. "Well, one thing's for sure. No cars will be coming here by accident. If anyone comes this far up the street, they're looking for something."

Lynda glanced across the street; in the moonlight, she saw only one edge of the empty car backed into the wooded lot where Larry would be spending the rest of the night.

Turning away from the window, she looked back over the stale-smelling house she hadn't walked into in weeks. "It's pretty dusty in here. No wonder it hasn't sold."

Larry looked around. "It's homey. I like it."

"I used to hate it," she said pensively. "I couldn't wait to get away from here. My folks turned the garage into a little apartment for me when I started college since we couldn't afford for me to live on campus. It was a little more freedom, but I still felt so trapped here."

For a moment, she let melancholy creep in as she surveyed the living room where her parents used to spend so much time — her mother crocheting, her father reading the paper and watching "Jeopardy" at the same time, each occasionally blurting out an answer that often was right. The standing joke around the house was that someday her father's ship would come in by way of a stint on "Jeopardy," where he was certain to win. But he'd never made it.

Shaking off her thoughts, she sank wearily onto the gold-and-green plaid couch.

"Where's the linen closet?" Larry asked.

She gave him a questioning look. "At the end of the hall. Why?"

"I'm going to make a bed up for you," he said. "I don't think you want to sleep on a bare mattress."

"No, I can do it," she said, getting up. "Really."

"Sit down," he ordered gently. "I've had broken ribs before. And you're not in any shape to be up at this hour, much less dressing beds. Now, which bedroom do you want?"

She looked toward the hall for a moment, trying to decide. "The guest room. I don't think I can sleep in my father's room yet."

"How long has he been ...?" The word fell off, and Lynda took a deep breath.

"Just three months."

"I'm sorry," Larry said. "Looks like a run of bad times for you."

"It could be worse," she whispered. "I thought it was bad luck that I hadn't sold this house, but now I see that God was saving it for me."

"No subtlety there, huh?"

Remembering what Mike had told her about Larry being a believer, she smiled as he left the room, and she heard him in the guest room, shaking out sheets and blankets, stepping around the bed. Was changing beds a part of his job description?

After a few minutes, he came out. "All done. You get some sleep now, and I'll be right out there in my car. No one's gonna get past me, so just relax. And tomorrow, I'll take you to the doctor to get checked out, just to make sure you didn't hurt yourself getting out of the house."

"I'm fine," she assured him, "but I need to go by the hospital anyway. I need to visit Jake."

"Then you can do both." He picked up the cellular phone he'd made her bring in from her car. "Now since you don't have a phone hooked up here, use this if you need to call anyone. I've got one in my car, too, and I've punched my number in here already. If you need me, all you have to do is punch the memory button and the number 1."

"Okay," she said, taking the phone. "Thanks."

He looked reluctant to leave her, and she knew it was because she looked so fragile. Lifting her chin and trying to look a little tougher, she said, "You don't have to worry about me, Larry. I'm really fine."

He sat down across from her, fixing his soft, green eyes on her. "You know, Lynda, you've survived two really narrow brushes with death in the last few days. You've seen two pretty obvious miracles, so maybe we'll get a couple more to help you out."

Lynda sighed. "I'm starting to wonder."

"About what?"

She swallowed, knowing that the thoughts raging through her mind bordered on blasphemy. "I just … sometimes wonder if God's really working in this. I mean … it's just all so bizarre. Why is he letting this person do these things to me? Is he trying to teach me something, or is he just turning his head, or is it Satan?"

"I personally don't like to attribute a whole lot to Satan," Larry said. "I believe God is in control. And he's working on this. I can tell."

She got up, trying not to cry, and turned her back to him. "Then why doesn't he just strike this person dead and keep him from terrorizing me anymore?"

"Because God doesn't work that way," Larry said. "If he did, Tony and I would be out of a job."

Lynda tried to laugh, but it didn't come easily. Taking a deep breath, she turned back around. "Thank you for watching over me, Larry. I feel better knowing you're out there."

"No problem," he said, getting up. "Call if you need me."

Lynda could only nod mutely as he went out the door and locked her in.

Across town, in a hotel room that was nicer — because Lynda had insisted on it — than the cheap motel Paige had stayed in just days before, Paige lay next to her sleeping daughter and stared up at the ceiling.

She heard the elevator ring, and her stomach tightened as she listened to the doors open and the footsteps in the hallway and then a door opening halfway down the hall. Relieved, she let out her breath.

Too many noises, she thought. Too many strange people around her. Too many reasons to be afraid.

She got up, went to the window, and peeked out between the crack in the curtains. Down in the parking lot, a trucker with a cigarette in his mouth walked around his eighteen wheeler, a huge rig that took up the whole back edge of the lot.

Everyone was suspect. Anyone could have set that fire. Anyone could have almost killed her and Lynda and Brianna tonight.

It was ironic that she had been staying with Lynda only to get out of danger in the first place.

Helpless, she dropped down onto the bed and closed her eyes against the tears assaulting her. How was she ever going to find peace in her life again? Would she spend the rest of her life running with Brianna, relying on the kindness of others? Even if she proved that Keith's allegations about her being an unfit mother were a lie and was allowed to keep custody of Brianna, wouldn't she still have to fear him for the rest of her life? Wouldn't he be able to track her down wherever she went?

Seeking comfort, she mouthed a clichéd prayer that she feared fell on deaf ears. "God, if you're listening—please help us."

Brianna jerked, and her face twisted in her sleep. As she muttered something incoherent, Paige began stroking her daughter's forehead. Was she dreaming about fire? Or about her father? Or was it some new nightmare, the next one, that her little mind was working through?

"It isn't fair," Paige whispered, not certain if she still addressed God or the black space around her. "She's too little to fear for her life. She's just a baby."

Brianna rolled over, found her mother, and snuggled in next to her.

And as Paige held her closely, that powerful maternal love that could fix boo-boos and scare away monsters washed over her, and she knew that whatever happened—whatever she had to do—she would protect her daughter.

CHAPTER TWENTY-SIX

Still flat on his back, Jake stared mindlessly at the television screen as Harry Smith interviewed someone in Washington about a bill being debated in the Senate. It didn't affect him, he thought, touching the bandage on his eye that had been changed this morning. Nothing affected him any more—he didn't have a job or a home or a life. He might as well not even exist for all the hope he had.

CBS broke for a commercial. After a detergent ad, the local news came on for an update. He reached for the remote control to change the channel as the anchor told about a fire in the exclusive Willow Heights area last night.

"*Police suspect arson. The home belonged to local attorney Lynda Barrett, who—*"

Jake dropped the remote control and tried to raise himself up. Dizziness assaulted him, and he dropped back down, straining to listen.

"*—was involved in the plane crash at St. Clair Airport earlier this week. Sources told Channel 16 News that there is evidence that the crash was the result of foul play, and that this may have been a second attempt on Barrett's life. Barrett and two houseguests escaped the fire, but we have no word yet on whether they sustained any injuries.*"

Amazed, Jake groped for the buzzer to ring for his nurse. In moments, she was in the doorway. "What is it, Jake?

"Do you have Lynda's number?" he asked.

"No, but I can look it up."

"You can't look it up!" he threw back. "Her house burnt down last night! Do you have her number at work?"

"Her house burnt down? Are you sure?"

"I saw it on the news," he said, breathing hard. "Was she—was she brought in here last night?"

"Well … I don't know. I can go check." She walked further into the room and peered at the television screen. "Do you think somebody's really trying to kill her?"

"Without a doubt," Jake said. "Just—get me a phone book. And a phone that works. I'll pay for the one I broke. And see if anybody knows anything."

The nurse hurried in, pulled the phone book from the drawer in Jake's table, and handed it to him. "Who are you calling?"

"Her office. Maybe her secretary can tell me where she is."

"I'll go see if she's checked in here," she said, scurrying out of the room.

CHAPTER TWENTY-SEVEN

Curtis McMillan sat at his kitchen window, looking across at the neighbors clustering in Lynda's yard, marveling at how thoroughly, and how quickly, the fire had destroyed her home. He had watched all morning, trying to remember exactly what he'd seen, so that some detail that could help the police might come back to him. But there were no details. It had been too dark and had happened too fast.

He saw a car drive by, slow down in front of the skeleton of the house, then pull over on the side of the road. Curtis wondered if he was another reporter — there had been so many around early this morning. But as he got out, he saw that he didn't carry a camera or a notepad, and for a moment, he just stood and looked at the structure, as if stricken by what had happened. Then, slowly, he headed toward one of the clusters of neighbors.

"You should come away from that window, Curtis," Lizzie said. "You're getting obsessed with it."

Curtis glanced back at her over his shoulder. She was knitting — something for Brianna, he suspected. She had really taken to that little girl last night.

"It's not obsession, Lizzie," he said. "It's just that I don't remember when there's been this much excitement around here. People coming and going ... Investigators, fire inspectors, reporters ..."

His eyes strayed out the window again, and he saw that the man was questioning the neighbors, and one of them was pointing toward the McMillan's house. Was he asking who had reported the fire? Or something about Lynda?

136

The man started to cross the street toward his house, and Curtis stood up. Something about his walk looked familiar ... and he was the right size ... but he couldn't swear it wasn't just his imagination groping for the culprit, trying to make up for what he hadn't seen last night. But in all his years on the bench, he'd had many cases where the perpetrator of a crime had been caught returning to the scene. Could this be ... ?

The doorbell rang, and Lizzie jumped up. "I'll get it. Probably another reporter."

But Curtis didn't think so. He went to stand behind her, and she opened the door slightly. "Yes?"

The man flashed a smile that made Curtis uncomfortable. "Excuse me, but I'm John Hampton, a close friend and coworker of Paige Varner, the woman who was staying with Lynda Barrett. I saw her and her daughter on the news this morning—that they were in the fire. I wanted to check on them, and one of the neighbors told me you might know where I could reach them."

Lizzie stiffened and started to close the door. "I'm sorry. I don't know where they are."

"Well, you must have heard them discussing it last night. Didn't they mention anybody they could stay with?"

Lizzie stepped aside, and Curtis came to the door. "Paige and Brianna are fine," he said. "No one was hurt."

"Well—are they still with Lynda?"

"I wouldn't know," he said. "Who did you say you are?"

"John Hampton, sir." He reached out and shook the old man's hand. "Don't you know where either of them is?"

"I'm afraid I can't help you." Curtis started to close the door, and the man backed away.

"All right," he said. "Well—thanks, anyway."

He backed down the steps, but Lizzie and Curtis kept staring at him through the narrowing opening in the door.

Lizzie closed it all the way and locked it. "Get the tag number, Lizzie," Curtis said as he headed for the phone.

Lizzie rushed to the window and squinting, whispered the numbers out loud as the man drove off down the street. Then, quickly, she scribbled them down. "Do you think he's the one you saw last night?"

"I can't say," Curtis told her, dialing the police station. "All I know is he's the right size. He could be the one. We'll just let the police decide."

Larry's eyes felt like sand by ten o'clock that morning, and he hoped his third cup of coffee would finally clear his fatigue. He poured it into the styrofoam cup, then went back to the table where Tony sat with their captain, going over the few things they did have on the Lynda Barrett case.

"I'll make sure she has a round-the-clock watch for at least a few days, but I can't do it indefinitely, guys. We just don't have enough manpower."

Larry pulled up a chair and sat down, rubbing his eyes. "Well, maybe he'll slip up soon."

The door opened, and one of the uniformed officers stuck his head in. "Call for you guys. It's Judge McMillan. Says he has a lead on the Barrett case."

Larry slid his chair back. "That's Curtis. He's our eyewitness," he told the captain. "I'll take it."

He closed the door behind him and went out to his desk. Picking up the phone, he said, "Millsaps, here. Whatcha got, Judge?"

"A man was just by here looking for Paige and Lynda," Curtis said. "He said his name is John Hampton, and he insisted that he had to know how to reach them. Now I may be jumping to conclusions, but I thought you—"

"You didn't tell him anything, did you?"

"No, of course not."

"John Hampton, huh?" Larry asked, jotting down the name. "Can you give me a description?"

"About five-eight, 180 pounds," Curtis said. "He may be just what he said he was, of course—a concerned friend—but one can never be sure. Lizzie got his license number just in case."

Larry sat back hard in his chair, smiling. "Tell her if I were there I'd kiss her. What's the number?" He wrote it down. "Thanks, Judge. If he comes back, you call me. Meanwhile, we'll find out who this sucker is, and if he's involved, you can bet we'll pick him up."

He hung up, tore off the page with the license number, and turned to the computer on his desk. "Lucy, go in there and get Tony," he said, punching the numbers onto the keyboard to start a search. "Tell him I may have something."

He waited a few seconds as the computer searched, and just as the license number surfaced, Tony reached Larry's desk.

"What is it?"

"A guy showed up at Judge McMillan's house, looking for Paige and Lynda. They got his tag number."

He watched as the information scrolled down the screen then finally stopped on a name. "Well, he lied about his name. That's a bad sign."

"Who is it?" Tony asked, leaning on the desk.

"Says the car belongs to Keith A. Varner."

"Varner. Isn't that Paige's name?"

"Yep." Punching a command on the keyboard, Larry started a cross-search for any information he could find on the man. "That's her exhusband, all right. We show a restraining order against him."

"But that doesn't make sense," Tony said. "Paige wasn't anywhere near that plane. And last night their daughter was with her. Would he deliberately burn down a house with his child in it?"

"He would if he's a nut case." Larry pressed the button for a printout, then tore it out of his printer. "Happens all the time. I say we pick him up."

"For what?" Tony asked.

"For questioning. We can't prove he was there when the house burned, but we can at least find out where he was and why he's looking for Paige when he's not supposed to go near her."

"All right," Tony said. "Let's go."

CHAPTER TWENTY-EIGHT

Keith Varner wasn't used to being told what to do, and when Larry and Tony found him sleeping in his apartment and insisted that he come with them for questioning, he hadn't taken it well. Now he sat in the interrogation room waiting for his lawyer, trying to be a little more cooperative since he was beginning to see that he had no choice.

"I was looking for my little girl," Keith told Larry. "There's no law against that, is there?"

"No, but there's a law against arson, pal."

"I told you I was at work last night. Ask anybody."

"We did. We found out that you work alone on the bank's computer system. You're not that closely supervised. You could have left at any time and come back."

Keith dropped his face helplessly into his palm. "What would you guys do? You're sitting at home watching the news on television; you hear about some fire, and all of a sudden you see your only child right in the middle of the whole thing." He looked up at them. "I freaked, okay? I didn't care about that stupid restraining order. I just cared that my Brianna was okay. And I *still* haven't found out if she is."

"She's fine," Larry said. "And your concern is moving, especially considering that her mother feels the need to hide from you to protect that same child."

"Give me a break!" Keith shouted, slapping the table and springing to his feet. "It's the oldest trick in the book. There's probably a restraining order and an abuse accusation for every custody case that's brought to court. You guys have been around. You know how things work!"

Tony glanced at the notes he'd found in Paige's and Keith's files. "Says here that Paige called just the other day because you had broken into her home. She also alleged that you tried to take the child from her school."

Keith sat back down and leaned forward, fixing his eyes on theirs as if they could understand. "I just had to know she was okay. I wanted to see her, make sure she was clean, didn't have any bruises, that sort of thing. Paige may come across as a sweet, mousy little thing, but she can be violent when you cross her, and she tends to be real selfish. She's neglected my daughter before. And if I broke into her house, why didn't I get arrested?"

Neither Larry nor Tony made any response.

"It's her word against mine. You won't show one violation of that restraining order against me. Look in the file. Do you see one?"

"That just means the police department didn't catch you in the act."

He leaned his elbows on the table. "As I recall, you're innocent until proven guilty. I'm telling you, boys, this is a war. She'll stop at nothing to keep me from getting custody, so she's going around staging crises to make her look like the victim. She deserves an Oscar."

The door burst open, and Keith's lawyer, a spit-and-polish yuppie who'd been too successful for his own—or anyone else's—good, rushed into the room. "What's going on here, gentlemen?"

Larry shot Tony a look that said the production was about to begin. He'd never liked Steve McRae, first because he was a smart aleck who thought he had all the answers and expected everyone else to acknowledge it, and second, because he'd gotten too many criminals off on technicalities, after the police department had spent hours of legwork making an arrest. With a bored, markedly unimpressed expression, Larry muttered, "We were just questioning your client about his whereabouts last night."

"They think I torched the lawyer's house," Keith said, like a kid telling his mommy of all the wrongs done against him. "Can you believe that? I wouldn't be surprised if Paige gave them the idea herself. Great strategy. Make me out to be the culprit, and it'll still be in the judge's head by the time we have the hearing."

McRae set his briefcase down on the desk but didn't sit. "Is my client under arrest?"

Larry glanced at Tony, knowing there wasn't cause. His restraining order didn't prohibit him from going to the site of a burned-down house, and as far as they could document, he hadn't gone near Paige or Brianna. At least not today. "Not at this time, no."

"Then I'd suggest you release him immediately, gentlemen."

"We could get a warrant. Search his house. Lock him up."

"Not without evidence," his attorney said. "And unless I've read the report wrong, the only evidence you have is that he asked one of the neighbors where his daughter is. Am I missing something?"

Larry rolled his eyes and breathed a heavy sigh.

"He fits the description of the arsonist," Tony said. "We have a witness, you know."

"No way," Keith said.

All eyes in the room turned back to him. "What's that?" Larry asked.

What Larry had at first thought was fear instantly became indignation. "I said, *no way*. Did someone tell you they saw *me* there last night? Could they pick me out in a lineup? Could they describe what I was wearing?"

Neither of the cops answered, and after a moment, McRae began to chuckle. "You know, if you guys would stop wasting time bringing in innocent fathers, you might get a little police work done. Now, if you're finished with him ... "

Tony swept his hand in a be-my-guest gesture, indicating that Keith was free to go. Keith got up and with a mocking grin, extended his hand to Larry for a facetious handshake. Larry made no move to take his hand. "It's been fun, guys."

"Hasn't it, though?" Larry muttered.

Keith headed for the door. Still within hearing range of the two cops, he said, "If somebody's really trying to kill that woman, and Paige is still staying with her, that means she's putting my daughter into direct, unnecessary danger. Isn't there something I can do about that before this guy tries again?"

"There sure is," McRae told him. "We'll go back to my office now and put our heads together."

Larry waited until the men were gone, then glanced back at Tony. "I think he's lying."

Tony shook his head. "I don't see it, Larry. He could just be a father who cares about his little girl."

"His wife is hiding from him. Doesn't that tell you something?"

"It tells me that both their stories are convincing, and either one could be a lie. When custody of a child is involved, sometimes the parents take desperate measures. You know that."

"Sometimes they will," Larry agreed. "Even to the point of killing her lawyer?"

"Why her lawyer?" Tony asked. "Why not Paige herself?"

"He almost did, last night."

"Well, the crash had nothing to do with Paige. Your theory is kind of scattering all over the place, Larry. I say we get back to the facts. Stick to what we know for sure."

"All we know for sure," Larry said, "is that there was a crash and a fire, and Lynda almost died in both of them. And that if we don't do something soon, chances are, there's going to be another attempt."

"Then let's get out there and find the guy," Tony said.

143

CHAPTER TWENTY-NINE

The physical strain of the night before had taken its toll on Lynda as had the stark loneliness. Outside, a policeman whom she hadn't met guarded her house in Larry's place. Fighting soreness and fatigue, she got up and went to the washer to drop in the pajamas she had worn here last night, the only clothes she had escaped with. Today, she wore an old T-shirt of her father's and a ragged pair of her old jeans that she'd found in one of the closets.

She wondered what Paige and Brianna were going to do for clothes. Mrs. McMillan had given Paige a housedress to wear last night, but it wasn't something Paige would want to be seen wearing in public. And Brianna had nothing but the big T-shirt she'd worn to bed last night for pajamas.

Larry had left a note under Lynda's door before he'd left that morning with the phone number and room number of the hotel where Paige was staying. Now Lynda dialed the hotel, hoping she'd catch Paige there.

"Hello?" Paige's voice was soft, tentative.

"Paige? It's just me."

"Lynda!" she said, breathing more freely. "How are you feeling?"

"A little tired and a little sore. But very much alive."

"Yeah, me, too. I keep trying to be thankful."

"I was thinking," Lynda said. "We all need clothes. Do you think it would be too much trouble for you to take my credit card this afternoon and buy us all something to wear?"

"I'll be glad to go shop for you, but we're fine," Paige said. "Really. We don't need anything—"

"Come on, Paige," Lynda insisted. "Everything was burned. You can't wear the same thing every day for the rest of your life."

"But it isn't your responsibility to pay for replacements. I can go to the Salvation Army or something."

Lynda moved her phone to the other ear, as if that would help her make her point more clearly. "My house was insured, Paige. I'll get compensated for it. Please. I want you to buy enough clothes for several days for both of you. Socks, underwear, shoes, clothes—everything."

Paige still wouldn't budge. "I still have some things at my own house."

"Not enough. Admit it, Paige. Most of your clothes were at my house."

Paige hesitated. "Okay. I guess they were."

"Come on. Let me do this. Help me assuage some of this guilt."

"Guilt? What do you have to feel guilt for?"

"Everything," she insisted. "Don't make me recite the list. Just buy some clothes."

"All right," Paige said with a chuckle. "Maybe just a few things."

Lynda smiled weakly. "Good."

"So what time are you due for your doctor's appointment?"

"Three o'clock," Lynda said. "They said Larry or Tony will take me." She breathed a soft, sad laugh. "Isn't this amazing? I'm practically trapped here in this house that I've been trying desperately to get rid of and can't go anywhere without police protection." Her voice broke off, and tears filled her eyes. Her voice betrayed her despair as she whispered, "Who would have ever thought I'd be in this position?"

"It's gonna be okay," Paige said, too quickly and without conviction.

And as Lynda surrendered to the emotions she'd been storing up, she realized how ironic it was that this woman whom she had vowed to comfort and protect was now comforting her instead.

An hour later from the offices of Schilling, Martin, and Barrett, Sally Crawford dialed the number of Lynda's cellular phone.

"Hello?"

"You're not going to believe this," Sally blurted. "Are you ready?"

Lynda hesitated, and Sally realized with a tinge of guilt that Lynda couldn't take many more surprises. "What is it?" she asked in a hoarse, hollow voice.

"Keith Varner just filed a motion with the court to get temporary custody of Brianna pending the hearing"

"What? That's ludicrous! He's wasting his time."

"I don't know," Sally said. "He's basing it on the fire last night, Lynda. He saw Brianna and Paige on the television coverage, and now he's saying that Paige has put Brianna in jeopardy."

"You've got to be kidding."

Sally wagged her head, as though Lynda could see her. "The hearing's tomorrow. If you're not up to meeting him in court, maybe Bill or Andy can fill in."

"No," she said quickly. "I'll be there."

"Are you sure, Lynda?"

"Dead sure," she said. "Call me back if you need me. I'm keeping the cellular close by."

"Are you sure you don't want to tell me where you are, Lynda? I could do some shopping for you, or whatever. You know you can trust me."

"Of course I do. But knowing could put you in danger," Lynda told her. "It's best if no one knows. Besides, I'm not sure the office phone isn't bugged. If you need to give me something, I'll meet you somewhere. And be careful, okay? This lunatic might follow anyone who knows me, hoping they'll lead him to me. I don't want you getting caught in the crossfire."

"Reassuring thought," Sally said. "Maybe I need to get a gun. So have there been any leads yet?"

"None that I know of." She paused. "Sally, you're the one who has to deal with the tempers of all the irate clients. Have there been any angry enough to kill me?"

"Not even close. Most of your clients are pretty happy."

"Well, one of them isn't. Would you do me a favor and pull up a list of all the cases I lost in the past—say, three years? Or even cases I may have won but didn't win big. You know, low awards, that sort of thing."

"Will do," Sally said. "I'll call you as soon as I get it. Hey, Lynda, take it easy, okay? You sound really tired."

"What can I say? It's been a rough week."

"Are you sure you're all right?"

"Well, I'm safe. I'm being guarded twenty-four hours a day, at least for a while."

Sally heard a doorbell ring on Lynda's end.

"Sally, I've got to go. Somebody's here."

The phone clicked, and Sally hung up, hoping that whoever stood at Lynda's door wasn't bringing more trouble.

Lynda saw Larry Millsaps through the peephole in the front door and let him in. "I thought it must be you. I'm almost ready to go."

"No hurry." Larry came in and closed the door behind him.

"Sorry about the outfit," she said, slipping on a pair of sandals. "I found these shoes in my old closet. They must be ten years old. And the clothes are my father's. All I had when I got here were the pajamas I was wearing."

"You look fine. Uh—before we go ... can I talk to you for a minute?"

Lynda stopped what she was doing and braced herself. "Sure. What is it, Larry?"

He looked dead tired, and Lynda realized he hadn't slept all night. "I thought you should know that Keith Varner was caught hanging around your house today, asking questions about where Paige and Brianna are. Apparently, he saw them both on the news."

"Oh, no."

"Judge McMillan called and reported it, and we picked Keith up for questioning. We had to consider the possibility that he could have set the fire."

"Keith? But that still wouldn't explain the crash—Paige wasn't anywhere near it," Lynda said quickly. "And besides, why would he try to kill his own daughter?"

"Good question," Larry said. "One that probably lets him off the hook. His answers were reasonable when we got right down to it."

"You let him go, didn't you?"

"Had to. That hotshot lawyer of his rode in on his white horse, and we didn't really have any evidence against him. And it's possible that he *was* just trying to make sure his kid was all right."

"You didn't tell him where they are."

"No, of course not. We didn't give him a clue."

Lynda pulled out a chair and slowly fell into it. "He's assuming she's still with me."

"How do you know?"

"Because I was just on the phone with Sally, and she told me that his lawyer has filed a motion for a temporary hearing to get custody of Brianna pending the final hearing. He thinks she's in danger."

Larry plopped into a chair and rubbed the stubbled jaw that was in desperate need of a shave. "I thought this might happen. He was already talking about it when he left."

"He won't get her," Lynda assured him. "I'll be there myself. I have all of Paige's medical records already, showing fractures and injuries that he caused. Oh, if only formal charges could have been filed against him for violating his restraining order, so I'd have something concrete to mention in court."

"Sorry. So far, all he's guilty of is looking for his daughter. We can't arrest him for that. Chances are that's all he's done."

Lynda shook her head. "Except beat and terrorize his wife. I don't know how much more Paige can take." Lynda took a deep breath and tried to think like a lawyer. "Part of this is probably his attempt to draw her out or make me tell in court where she is. If he accuses her of putting Brianna in danger by staying with me, then he thinks I have to tell him where she is to prove she's not. But it won't work. I know every judge in this town. If I tell them she's not staying with me, they'll believe me."

"Problem is, McRae knows them, too." Larry gestured to the phone. "You want to call Paige and break the news before we go? I can talk to her if she has any questions."

"She's not there," Lynda said glumly. "I asked her to do a little shopping for us. I'll take the phone with me. She's supposed to call when she gets back to the room."

148

CHAPTER THIRTY

Jake had tried all day long to reach Lynda or find out how she was, but the people at her office had been deliberately vague. Though he could understand their caution, he had been desperate for information.

Now she stood before him, keeping her promise to visit him even though she was on the tail end of her second trauma in a week—a fact that moved him more than he cared to admit. She looked pale and bruised and weak, but she was, nevertheless, one of the most beautiful sights he'd ever seen.

But it wouldn't do to tell her that, so he hid his feelings behind flippancy. "You look worse than I do," he said.

"Thanks." She walked closer to the bed and leaned on the rail to look down at him.

"Sit down, Lynda," he said quietly. "You don't need to stand for my benefit. I can see you fine if you sit."

Acquiescing, she pulled a chair across the floor and sat down. Her eyes were tired and dejected, and he longed to see in them the fiery spirit he had grown accustomed to.

Without thinking, he reached out and took her hand. Closing her eyes, she brought his hand to her face and squeezed it. For an instant, it made him feel needed, as if his existence gave her strength, as if he had some purpose other than lying flat in this bed. "You're in trouble, Lynda," he whispered.

"Tell me about it."

He could see from her eyes that she wasn't taking this lightly. "What did the doctor say?"

149

"He said not to do any more leaping from two-story buildings for a while."

"I'm serious."

She smiled. "I'm okay. Just tired and sore. He told me to get plenty of rest and try not to exert myself."

"So, what are you doing in here?"

She closed her other hand over his and looked down at it. "Visiting a friend."

He wanted to tell her how much he appreciated it, how it changed his day, but something inside him kept him from saying it.

"Have they found out who did this? Do they have any promising leads?"

"They're working hard on it," she said. "I guess I can't complain."

"But it could happen again. Are they protecting you?"

"Yes," she said. "Twenty-four hours a day. Larry's right outside."

As if to take the focus off her, she stood and leaned on his bed rail again. "So how are *you* doing?"

"Not so good today," he said. "I've had visions of you wasting away somewhere from smoke inhalation or living in some homeless shelter or making yourself an open target for some insane sniper."

He could see that his concern pleased her. "I should have called," she said. "I guess I didn't realize it was all over the news."

He grinned. "That's okay. My phone was kind of broken anyway, remember? They replaced it today."

She laughed softly, and he joined her as his eyes swept over her. It felt good having her so close, and he wondered if it were Lynda Barrett he was growing attached to or just the idea of having anyone he could touch.

To be honest, he really couldn't say.

"So how was physical therapy today?" she asked.

"Oh, peachy," he said. "My therapists are a laugh a minute. We're still working on getting me upright."

"You have to start somewhere, Jake."

He breathed a laugh. "What's the point?"

She thought about that for a second. "Don't you want to sit up?"

He shrugged. "I'm just trying to be realistic. It's such a simple thing, but when I try it, my system goes haywire." He fixed his eyes on the ceiling. "I'm trying to accept. That's what the shrink told me to do."

"You're not being realistic *or* accepting," she argued gently. "Realistically, you've got your whole life ahead of you. All you can do is work with what you have and make it the best it can be. And pray. Hard. I've been praying for you, Jake."

"No offense, Lynda, but if there is a God, it doesn't look like he's on your side."

Instead of the fight he expected, she wilted. The defeated look that crossed her face startled him, and he hated himself for putting it there. Lowering herself back into her chair, she said, "Maybe you're right."

He frowned. "So you're backing down from your beliefs now?"

She shook her head, and he saw the tears reddening her eyes. "No," she said. "I'm not backing down. I guess I'm just confused. Is God really dealing with me through all this? Maybe it's just a really loud wake-up call."

She saw the emotion cross his face, and finally, he whispered, "I'm sorry, Lynda. I didn't mean to upset you. I was just trying to rile you—to see some of that famous Barrett passion in your face again."

She kept those haunted eyes on him for a moment, but finally, the humor in what he'd said seeped in, and a rueful grin returned to her face. "I'm still going to pray for you, Jake. I'm going to pray that you'll stop being a jerk."

He smiled.

"I'm also going to pray for your therapy," she said. "Maybe if you get more mobile, you'll have a better disposition."

"Don't waste your time praying for me," he said. "I've got this under control."

"Is that why you can't sit up?" she asked. "Is it better to keep telling yourself that you'll never walk?"

That question irritated him, but she didn't seem to care. He let go of her hand. "Do you think I *want* to lie here like this?"

"No, I don't," she said, standing up again. "So don't do it. Work hard and do what the therapists tell you, and stop thinking how this is the end of your life. Start thinking of it as a beginning."

"The beginning of *what?*"

"The beginning of your learning how to be a human being." When he gave her a surprised look, she went on. "You know, you weren't my idea of a terrific guy when you had functioning legs and a flawless face."

"So you think being paralyzed is going to build character?" he asked, growing angrier. "Hey, I didn't need to have my world ripped out from under me to know how to be a human being."

She looked regretful. Setting her elbow on his rail, she dropped her forehead into her palm. "I'm sorry, Jake. I need to learn how to keep my mouth shut. I really didn't come here to lambaste you." She slid her hand down her face and lifted her brows as she gazed at him over her fingertips. "I was really just trying to get that famous Stevens passion back in your eyes."

He didn't find that amusing, as she had. For a moment, he was quiet, focusing his eye on the ceiling to keep from meeting hers. When he spoke again, his voice was lower. "I'm not a charity case. I don't even know why you're here. Tell the truth," he said glumly. "They hired you to give me an aerobic workout, didn't they? You come in here, get my blood boiling, then leave. It's probably covered under my health insurance."

"Right," she said with a wink. "It's all a clever conspiracy. And they wanted to find a lawyer to get your blood boiling because we're so good at it."

He smiled now. "I thought so."

"Oh, I almost forgot," she said. "I went by your hotel on the way home yesterday and got all your stuff and paid your bill and checked you out. Luckily, your things were still in my trunk when the fire hit. The garage was all that was left standing. Larry Millsaps left the boxes at the nurse's station since I'm not supposed to carry anything heavy. They'll be bringing them in later. Maybe you'll feel better having your own things."

"I don't know," he said. "I was getting kind of attached to these air-conditioned gowns." He smiled and squeezed her hand. "I appreciate your doing that for me. What about my car?

"It's been parked at the airport since the crash," she said. "It's just fine, locked in the hangar until you're ready to move it."

"Terrific," he said. "I hope it's safer than your plane was."

"We'll move it wherever you want."

Jake looked at her, his eye soft, searching. "Do you feel guilty about the accident or what? Why are you doing all this for me?"

"Because I care about you," she admitted with great effort.

"Why? You hardly know me, and what you knew before the accident, you didn't even like."

"I see a lot of potential there," she said with a coy smile.

He didn't find that amusing. "Well, I hate to disappoint you, Lynda, but crippled and half-blind, the only potential I'm likely to reach is the potential for suicide."

Her face changed. "That's the second time you've mentioned that, Jake. You don't mean it, and when you say it, I feel just as threatened as I felt after the fire last night."

"Why would that be a threat to you?" he asked.

"Because I've started getting attached to you, Jake, and I don't let go of my friends that easily." Tears came to her eyes, and she blinked them back. "I had you figured for a guy with at least a little bit of integrity," she said quietly. "The guy who landed my plane wasn't a coward."

"The guy who *crashed* your plane did what he had to do. But don't worry. It's not like I have a gun under my pillow or a knife in the drawer. I can't get out of bed to hurl myself out the window, and I don't have free access to the drugs they're giving me. I'm trapped here for now."

"If I can go out there and fight for my life, Jake, you can do it in here. And if you think I'm going to sympathize with your fantasy to rig up a noose, then you need to call a neurologist because you have brain damage, too."

Someone knocked on the door, but Jake only kept staring at her, his own misty eye taking seriously the fire he had restored to hers.

He heard the door open. "Sorry to interrupt. How are you, Jake?"

Finally breaking the lock he had on her eyes, Jake saw Larry and nodded.

"I'm gonna have to take you on home, Lynda," Larry said. "Tony has a suspect in custody. He thinks he might be the one who's been after you. I have to get to the station to question him."

"Really?" Lynda wiped her eyes. "Who is it?"

"One of the guys on your list," he said. "Doug Chastain."

"Doug?" she asked. "But—what evidence is there?"

Jake frowned. "Who is this guy?"

Larry checked the notes he'd jotted when Tony had called. "He's a mechanic who lives in the area, and he already has one prior arson conviction. We traced the gas can we found back to where he works."

"You're kidding," Lynda said.

Larry tried to hurry her to the door. "This might be the guy, Lynda."

Her face suddenly hopeful, she turned back to Jake. "I'll be back tomorrow, Jake," she said. "And I'll call you tonight and let you know what they come up with. That is, if you don't break your phone between now and then."

He nodded again but didn't speak until she was almost out the door. "Hey, Lynda? Be careful, okay?"

"You, too."

Jake got her meaning. He only wished he had a choice.

CHAPTER THIRTY-ONE

B race yourself," Tony told Larry as he rushed into the precinct. "He's in an even worse mood than he was when we interviewed him yesterday. He got a tad bit offended when I told him he was under arrest."

Larry watched the twenty-year-old kid through the one-way glass. Yesterday, when they'd interviewed him at home, Larry had been suspicious, but he'd talked himself out of considering the kid a suspect since he had no experience with airplanes. It was feasible that he could have started the fire, but could he have rigged the crash in such an expert way? "What have you got on him?"

"Besides his prior arson conviction and his mechanic experience and the gas can we found with the name of his employer on it, we found gas stains in the carpet in his trunk. Fresh ones. You could still smell the fumes. And his alibi is weak."

Larry stepped closer to the glass. There was a tattoo of a bald eagle covering most of Doug's upper arm, and his hair was doused with mousse and spiked to stand straight up on his head. He wore a black T-shirt with the sleeves rolled up to his shoulders and a general expression of readiness to curse the next cop who crossed him.

"So what's his alibi?"

"Says he was at home. No witnesses."

They opened the door, and the kid burst out of his seat. "You might as well let me out of here," he spat out. "I didn't do it."

Larry gave him a long, considering look as the kid sneered back at him. Finally, he reached across the table to shake his hand. "I'm Larry Millsaps," he said, then withdrew his hand when the kid rejected it. "Why don't you calm down, Doug? My partner here can be a little gruff sometimes, but I just want to ask you a few questions."

"I already answered the main one," the kid said. "I didn't do it!"

"Didn't do what?"

"I didn't set her house on fire! They keep asking me if I had a grudge against her, if I was in the area last night, if I was near the airport when that crash happened—I'm telling you morons, I've never even been *down* that street, and I wouldn't know how to get to that airport. I was sitting at home last night. Reading."

Larry's eyebrows lifted. Somehow he couldn't picture this kid reading. "Reading what?"

The kid threw up his hands. "What is it? You don't think I can read?"

"You don't look like the type who stays at home and reads."

"Yeah? Well, you don't look like the type who gets out of work by pinning crimes on innocent people." He sat back and cocked his head arrogantly. "I was reading *Hamlet*. You got a problem with that?"

"Yeah? Who wrote it?"

"You tell me," the kid challenged. "You're the one with all the answers. What do you do? Go down the list of ex-cons in the area and assign one of them to each crime that comes down?"

"We found a gas can that belongs to your employer," Tony said less patiently.

"Yeah? Well, maybe *he* did it! Were my fingerprints on it?"

Neither Tony nor Larry answered, but they both knew that no fingerprints had been found on the gas can. The arsonist must have been wearing gloves.

"How do you explain the gas stains in your trunk?" Larry asked.

Doug mouthed a curse. "I mow yards on weekends, okay? I always take extra gas in case I run out. I'd have been more careful not to spill some if I'd known somebody was gonna be sniffing around trying to pin something on me."

"What do you carry it in?"

He looked from Larry to Tony then back again. "In a can, okay? Probably a J.R.'s Auto Repair can. We have them all over the shop. People stop by and borrow them all the time. Lots of people have them."

Larry only watched him as he rambled, giving him enough rope to hang himself.

The kid realized what was going on and crossed his arms obstinately. Flopping back into his chair, he said, "I'm not talking anymore without a lawyer."

"Do you have one?"

"Sure, man," he said facetiously. "Got one on retainer."

"You don't have one, do you?"

"So appoint one," the kid said through his teeth. "Only don't appoint that witch whose house burnt down because she'll string me along and dump me at the last minute. Besides, there's somebody out there still trying to kill her. I don't want to be around her."

Tony shot Larry a telling look, and Larry nodded.

The door opened, and one of the officers stuck his head in. "Tony, can I see you a minute?"

Larry watched his partner leave the room then turned back to the kid. "I'll have an attorney appointed, but he won't do you any good if you're not telling the truth."

"You don't want the truth, man. You want a scapegoat."

The door opened again, and Tony stepped back in. "I just got an interesting bit of information." He pulled out a chair and set his foot on it. Leaning on his knee, he looked down at the kid. "Seems somebody you work with called your house three times last night, and you weren't home."

"So I didn't feel like talking," Doug said, his face reddening. "I'm taking a night class at the college, and I had to read *Hamlet*. I swear. You can call and check. Search my house. You'll find my Shakespeare book."

Tony shot Larry a skeptical look.

Doug slammed his hand on the table. "Hey, man, last time I checked, it wasn't a crime to unplug your phone!"

"No, it isn't. And neither is going to the Monroe Street Lounge, where several people saw you earlier last night."

Larry breathed an incredulous laugh. "Still want to stick to your story about being at home reading?"

157

"You asked me where I was when the fire started. I was at home. So I had a few drinks earlier. That's no crime either."

"And it just slipped your mind?"

For a moment, Doug sat still, his face a study in belligerence and hatred, but finally, he leaned forward and clasped his hands in front of his face. "Go ahead and get that lawyer," he said. "I'm not saying another blasted word."

CHAPTER THIRTY-TWO

The radio news blared in the background as Keith Varner checked out the suit he would wear in court tomorrow. He would look like a competent businessman when he faced the judge, he thought, and Paige would play the role of a stringy-haired waif about to have a nervous breakdown. And the law-yer—he chuckled for a moment at the thought that she was going to appear in court to represent Paige. When he'd seen her on the news after the fire, she'd looked like someone who'd been beaten up. He could just see the judge's reaction to her propping her-self up in the courtroom—complete with bruises and scrapes and the stitches that held her together—fighting for Paige. Her very presence would be all the argument he needed that she herself was in danger and, therefore, Brianna was in danger. By tomorrow night, he'd have Brianna at home.

He went into the empty bedroom in his apartment, kicked aside the piles of dirty laundry, and considered where he would put the child's bed. There, in the corner. Once the judge awarded him temporary custody, he'd ask him if he could get her bed from her home. That way she'd be comfortable with him. He just hoped she didn't cry all night like the last time he had her.

But that he blamed on Paige. She had filled the child's head full of lies, and until he got that woman out of his daughter's life, he would never get Brianna to bond with him. He had so many plans for them. She would learn to be dependent on him, to obey and respect him, to need him....

He went back into his small den, knocked the newspapers out of his chair and onto the floor, and flicked on the television.

Maybe there was another hint about where they were. Maybe they'd have something about the sheriff department's pitiful hunt for the arsonist.

He listened through two murders, a rally for a local politician, a mail fraud scam that had been uncovered.

"—and in other news, an arrest was made today in the Lynda Barrett case—"

He leaned forward and turned it up, watching carefully as the film clip showed the mechanic being led through the precinct in handcuffs. Flopping back on his couch, Keith began to laugh. It was perfect. They were off his trail. They were hanging it on that poor bozo he'd heard Lynda name that day in her hospital room. It had been easy to find him, and using the gas can to lead them to where Chastain worked was ingenious. Now Lynda Barrett had a false sense of security. He loved it.

Now there would be another chance, he thought with a smile. If he didn't convince the judge to give him Brianna tomorrow, he could still make sure he got Lynda Barrett out of the way before the real hearing. It would take a host of angels to keep her alive the next time.

CHAPTER THIRTY-THREE

The telephone rang, and Lynda pulled it out of her jeans pocket, which was baggy enough to carry several small appliances. "Hello?"

"I hope I didn't wake you."

It was Paige, and Lynda smiled at the sound of her voice. The house was getting awfully quiet. She abandoned the stack of books she'd been sorting through in the closet and sat down on the closest chair. "I just woke up a few minutes ago, and I've been sorting through some things to see if my dad left a Bible somewhere."

"Any luck?"

"No. I know he had one, though. He used to wave it at me all the time."

She could hear Paige's soft laughter. "I'll go buy you one if you want."

Lynda sighed. "No, that's okay. I'll get one the next time Larry or Tony takes me somewhere."

"Well, it doesn't look like that'll be necessary any more. The guy they picked up? Looks like he's the one."

Lynda caught her breath. "Really? How do you know?"

"They called me a little while ago. Larry said you were tired when he brought you home and were probably sleeping, so he asked me to give you a couple of hours and then tell you. They shot his alibi to pieces, found gas stains in his car—it's him, Lynda. We're home free."

Lynda leaned back in the chair. "No more guards? No more surprises?"

161

"Nope. They called the guard back to the precinct over an hour ago. Look out the window."

Lynda got up and pulled the curtain back. For the first time since she'd come here last night, there was no one watching her from across the street. A chill went through her, and she had the fleeting sensation of standing on the edge of a cliff, leaning, leaning, with nothing to catch her when she fell. "They're gone."

"That's right. You don't need them now."

Lynda allowed the news to sink in for a moment. "I knew he didn't like me when I resigned from his case, but I didn't think he'd come back to kill me."

"Well, at least he's behind bars. And we can come and go as we please. The only thing we have to fear is this hearing tomorrow."

Lynda pushed aside her uneasiness and tried instead to concentrate on tomorrow. "This is perfect, Paige. Keith's motion is based on your putting Brianna in danger by being with me. That whole premise has just been shot into a million pieces. Once I tell the judge that I'm not in danger any longer, his theory is shot. And then I'll tell the court that your whereabouts are confidential due to Keith's threats and leave it at that. In fact, if you want to check out of the hotel right now, you can come here. It's probably okay now."

"I don't know," Paige said. "He's assuming I'm still with you."

"But he doesn't know where I am."

"I told you, Lynda. He's smart. He figures out ways to get information."

"He's not *that* smart. He's just conditioned you to think so. But even if he did find out, he's not as likely to hassle you knowing I'm here as he might be if you were alone. I mean, I'm the one who's going to pull out all the stops when we finally get to trial. He won't want to give me any more ammunition to throw at him."

Paige hesitated. "Even if you're right, I still think I should stay here tonight. If for some reason the judge asks you point blank if I'm staying with you, you can say no."

Lynda sighed. "You're right, I guess. But how about tomorrow?"

"Are you sure you want us there?"

She heard the smile in Lynda's voice. "Of course I want you. I need company. I'm at my wit's end."

"Okay, then," she said. "Tomorrow. And about that Bible. Why don't I buy you one and bring it when I bring all the clothes I got for you?"

"Where's Brianna?"

"Watching Barney. It's almost over."

Lynda looked down at the junk she'd begun sorting through. "Paige, if you would do that, it would be such a lifesaver. Use the credit card I gave you last night. I'll call the store and find out what translations they have and tell them what I want. Just ask the clerk when you get there. By the way, do you have one?"

"A Bible? Well ... somewhere ... at home."

"Buy yourself one, too," she said. "On me. A little thank-you for taking such good care of me. And get Brianna something, too."

"Lynda, you don't have to do that."

"Yes, I do," Lynda whispered. "And you have to let me."

A few minutes later Lynda dialed her office number. "Do me a favor," she told Sally. "Go back a couple of years and dig up Doug Chastain's file. I need to refresh my memory about his case."

"I heard they'd arrested him," Sally said. "Thank goodness. You want me to bring it to you along with the other papers I need to give you for tomorrow?"

"Yeah," she said. "We can meet this afternoon."

"Are you going to tell me where you are yet?"

Lynda considered it a moment and realized she didn't yet feel safe enough to tell anyone where she was. "No, I'll just meet you somewhere. Call me on my cellular phone before you leave work today."

"Are you supposed to be driving?" Sally asked.

Lynda hesitated. "Well ... no. But it can't be helped."

"Yes, it can. I can bring them to you."

"Just humor me," Lynda said. "I'll get over it. It'll sink in eventually that I'm not being hunted."

"All right," Sally said with resignation. "Do you want to come to the office?"

"No. I don't think I'm up to seeing everybody yet. How about the Jackson Street Post Office? Then I can just have Paige meet me there too with some stuff she's picking up."

Sally let out a ragged breath. "All right. But I'll be so glad when all this is over."

"You think *you* will."

Paige drove up just as Lynda finished signing some papers Sally needed her to sign. Saying good-bye to her secretary, she got out of her car and got into Paige's.

Paige handed her the Bible, still in its box. "They were expensive," she said. "You should have just ordered me a paperback one."

"I wanted you to have that one," she said. "Did they put your name on it like I told them?"

Paige opened her box and took out her leather-bound Bible. Running her hand across the name engraved in gold, she said, "Yeah, they sure did." Her eyes were misty when she looked up at Lynda. "That may be the sweetest thing anybody's ever bought me."

"Well, make it worthwhile. Read it."

Paige leaned over and planted a kiss on Lynda's cheek. "You're a real friend."

"I'm trying," she said. "But I've got a lot of catching up to do."

CHAPTER THIRTY-FOUR

"A re you sure you should be here today, Lynda?" Judge Albert Stacey set his elbows on the conference table, assessing her with deep concern. Keith and his lawyer sat on one side of the table, and Lynda sat alone on the other.

She tried to smile, but it was difficult. The long walk through the building had been tiring, and she'd encountered several bouts with dizziness since she'd been here. Everywhere she went, people stared, especially those who knew her. She hadn't even tried to hide the bruises and scrapes on her face. "I feel fine, your honor. And I had to be here today. This motion Mr. McRae is filing is ridiculous and a waste of the court's time."

The judge turned to Keith's lawyer. "Well, I've reviewed the motion, and my understanding is that your client is concerned about the safety of this child since she was involved in the fire at Miss Barrett's the other night. Am I reading that correctly?"

"Yes, Judge. Mr. Varner feels that his ex-wife has deliberately risked the child's life by staying in the same home with Miss Barrett, even after so many attempts have been made on her life."

"Excuse me," Lynda cut in. "Be specific, please. How many attempts?"

McRae sat back in his chair with a look that said she was walking proof of his case. "You tell us."

Rather than telling him anything, she addressed the judge. "Your honor, there were two attempts made on my life. The first was the plane crash I was involved in last week, and the second was, obviously, the fire two nights ago. Paige was staying in my house while I was in the hospital, primarily because she became convinced that the restraining order she had filed against Mr. Varner was not going to stop him from breaking into her home or trying to remove their child from school. At that time no one realized that anyone was after me. It wasn't until after the fire the first night I was home that we realized that."

The judge turned back to McRae. "So what's the problem exactly? How did Mrs. Varner endanger her daughter's life? Are you saying *she* started the fire or knew it was going to happen?"

"Of course not, your honor."

Keith couldn't stay quiet any longer. "I'm saying that for all I know she's still staying with her, even though she's aware that someone's out to get her."

"Your honor," Lynda said, calling his attention back to her side of the table. "May I?"

He gestured for her to go ahead with her explanations, and she took a deep breath. "First of all, I can assure you that Paige Varner and Brianna are safe and that they have been in no danger—except perhaps from Mr. Varner—since the fire. In fact, they're here in the building as we speak but chose not to come into the hearing because she feared the child would be traumatized by seeing her father."

"Oh, for crying out—"

The judge's stern look silenced Keith, who gave a disgusted look at the ceiling, as if calling on some unknown entity in the plaster to come to his aid.

"Secondly," Lynda went on, "the police have a suspect in custody. They captured him yesterday, and he's in jail awaiting his own hearing."

"Really?" the judge asked, eyebrows raised. "Well, I know that's good news for you."

"Extremely good news, your honor."

Keith rolled his eyes. "So a guy was arrested. He could get out on bond within the week if he's the right guy in the first place. How can I be assured that my child is safe?"

Lynda answered the question for him. "Your honor, I can assure you that it's my priority to keep those two safe as well. In fact, that's why theirs is the only case I've kept since my accident and why I came here, against doctor's orders, to make sure the rights of Mrs. Varner and her daughter are adequately protected."

Judge Stacey studied the motion in front of him, and McRae seized the moment of silence to speak up. "Judge, my client is also concerned with the mother's neglect of the child, her inability to support that child, and her past abuses. Mrs. Varner has lost her job and left her home, and my client worries about her mental stability and her capacity to provide Brianna with what she needs. He's concerned about their whereabouts, as I'm sure you would be if your own children disappeared."

"Well, your honor, I can answer that as well," Lynda spoke up. "For the duration of this crisis—and it is a crisis, sir, whenever a battered wife goes into hiding—I am helping my client and her daughter financially. I won't allow them to go without. For the time being, I've recommended that she remain in hiding."

The judge sat back in his chair. "Well, I'm satisfied that the child is in capable hands and that she's being cared for. As for the allegations of neglect and abuse on either side of this case, that remains to be proven in the appropriate hearing. That's not what this hearing is about. I hereby rule that the child shall remain with her mother until the trial."

Keith cursed, and his lawyer grabbed his arm, trying to shut him up, but he burst out of his chair and started for the door.

Lynda waited until he was gone then turned back to the judge with a little smile, knowing he made note of the volatile temper. She hoped he was the judge assigned to the custody hearing. "Thank you, your honor."

Patting her hand, he got to his feet. "Quite impressive that you would come to court in your condition, Lynda. It speaks to your conviction that the child is in the right place." He leaned over the table and whispered, "And I trust you."

"I appreciate that, sir. Would you like to confer with Mrs. Varner?"

"No, that won't be necessary."

She watched him disappear through the door that led to his chambers and picking up the few papers she'd been able to carry in with her, she went back to the conference room where she'd left Paige.

Paige jumped when the door opened then wilted with relief when she saw it was Lynda.

"What happened?"

"We won," Lynda said. "I told you."

"Oh, thank God." She drew Brianna into a crushing hug. "Where is he? Is he still in the building?"

"No, he's gone. He rushed out cussing and ranting. I'm glad you weren't there."

"Me, too." Propping her chin on Brianna's head, she said, "Are you sure we can win next time, Lynda? He's not going to pull a fast one on us and trip us up, is he? He's always been able to do that with me."

The worry in Paige's eyes touched Lynda. "He won't trip me up, Paige. I'll have so much against him, he won't know what hit him. We'll get everyone who's ever seen him lose his temper into that courtroom. I'll have documentation of every trip to the emergency room, every neighbor who heard him yelling through the walls, every call to 911. I won't leave anything to chance."

Paige's lips trembled as she took it all in. "It's Brianna's life at stake here," she whispered, "but if I have to trust anyone to fight for it, I trust you."

CHAPTER THIRTY-FIVE

Keith cruised through the courthouse parking garage, looking for Paige's white car. He found it on the third level.

He stopped his car right behind it. The door-lock buttons were down, he could see. He glanced around to see whether there was anyone nearby who might see him when he got out.

Someone was pulling into an empty space a few cars down. And two people across the aisle stood talking beside one of their cars.

He took a piece of paper off the seat next to him, folded it to look like a note, and got out the switchblade he carried in his pocket. Leaving his car idling, he stepped out and glanced at the others in the garage. He still hadn't been noticed.

He set the blank note under her windshield wiper, so it would look as if that was his purpose then pretended to drop his keys. Bending over, he opened his switchblade then slashed her front tire. Still stooped, he went to the back one and stabbed it, too.

He drove around until he found a parking place on the other side of that level from which he'd be able to see her come to her car.

It would take more than a judge to keep him from being with his daughter.

CHAPTER THIRTY-SIX

Paige held Brianna's hand as they stepped off the elevator into the parking garage. Trying to remember where she had parked her car, she let her eyes sweep over the colors until she came to the white Chevette parked across the garage.

The car parked next to hers began to pull out as she approached, leaving the space next to her car empty. Her step slowed—through that open space, she saw that both tires on that side of her car were flat.

She froze.

She heard a car start across the garage and caught a glimpse of pastel blue pulling out—the color of Keith's car.

Her heart stopped and she dropped her purse, spilling out her car keys, a lipstick, some change. Abandoning it, she grabbed Brianna and bolted back toward the elevator.

Brianna started to cry, but over the child's sobs Paige heard tires screeching. The elevator was taking too long. She scanned the area for a door to the stairway. Quickly, she headed toward it and shoved it open. It clanged shut behind her as she tore down the stairs.

Above her, just beyond the door, she heard a car door slam and footsteps running. The door above her opened, and she heard the click of shoes taking the steps faster than she could move.

Her foot slipped, and she stumbled, skinning her shin against the metal railing. Brianna's screams went up an octave. Reaching out to grab the rail with her free hand, Paige steadied herself and took the next flight down.

As if she only now realized what they were running from, Brianna's shrieks grew more piercing, reverberating through the stairwell. Her little arms tightened desperately around her mother's neck. Struggling to breathe, Paige threw herself at a door on one of the landings.

But just as her fingers grazed the handle, Keith grabbed her shirt and flung her against the wall. He reached for Brianna, but the child fought and struggled and screamed. Bracing herself against the wall, Paige kicked him with all her might.

He fell back, cursing, then rallied and grabbed her hair. He jerked her off-balance, trying to get his arm between her and the child. Then he shoved her back and kicked her feet out from under her. Losing her grip on the child, Paige fell back, stumbling down four stairs and landing on her back.

"Mommmmmeeee!" The child's terror rang through the stairwell, echoing off the walls. Keith grabbed her, and she bit his arm and kicked him with her sharp little shoe. He recoiled long enough for her to reach her mother again and attach herself in another strangling grip.

Suddenly the door one flight below them burst open. Startled, Keith let them go and took a step backward, then turned and fled back up the steps.

"Help me!" Paige cried, stumbling down the stairs. She fell into the building and collapsed as a crowd formed around her, Brianna still screaming at the top of her lungs, clinging for dear life to her mother.

It took twenty minutes to quiet the child's screaming, but she trembled for the next two hours as Lynda and Larry sat with Paige and Brianna, trying to calm them both.

"I searched the whole garage and all around the courthouse, Paige," Larry said. "He's gone."

"Can't you—can't you arrest him?"

"We have to find him first."

"What if he finds *me* first?" Paige shouted. "Who would have ever thought he'd try to snatch her out of my hands right here at the courthouse?"

"He's getting desperate," Lynda said. "He's liable to do anything."

"He'll go to every hotel in the city until he finds my car—if I can manage to drive it again after what he did to my tires. He'll find us. I know he will."

"No, he won't," Lynda said through her teeth. "You're coming home with me. I'll send someone to change the tires, and we'll get your car later. But you don't need to be alone."

"What's happening to us?" Paige cried, sopping her tears with a wadded tissue. "Everywhere I turn, there's danger. How am I ever going to protect her? Feel her. She's still shaking."

Lynda laid her hands on the child and felt the shiver. "She must have been pretty scared when she saw him."

"Well, what do you expect? To have him burst out of nowhere like that and start grabbing her—What is he trying to do to her? Doesn't he realize that a child shouldn't ever have to be that afraid?"

Lynda stroked back Paige's hair where it was matted to her wet face. "It's going to be okay, Paige. Come on. Larry's following us home now."

Wearily, Paige got up, shifted Brianna more securely to her hip, and with a troubled, miserable expression, regarded Larry. "You have a gun, don't you?"

"Of course I have a gun. I'm a cop."

"But—you would use it if you had to, wouldn't you?"

"That's my job, Paige. Don't worry. I'm not going to let anything happen to you."

Her face was pale as they started out of the room. "Larry, do you think I should get a gun?"

Lynda watched Larry's face, for she had wondered the same thing herself. "No, Paige, I don't. Too many accidents happen. Too many people rely on them when their tempers flare. Too many people die because there was a gun too readily available. And I sure don't recommend it with a child in the house."

"That's what I thought you'd say." But as they walked to Larry's unmarked car, Paige whispered to Lynda, "If I had the money, I'd buy one anyway. And the next time Keith sprang up out of nowhere, I'd be ready."

Larry was quiet later that day as he and Tony prowled St. Clair in their unmarked car, working on a cocaine case that they were close to breaking. The sheriff's department was too small for any of its detectives to specialize in one area, so Larry didn't know from one week to the next what kind of crime he'd be assigned to.

It gave the job some diversity, which he supposed was a plus. But the minus was that they slapped a file closed so quickly the moment they had someone booked that he was never able to get a sense of closure.

"What's on your mind?" Tony asked, glancing over at him as he drove.

He shrugged. "I don't know. I was just thinking about that Doug Chastain kid. Did I tell you we found a Shakespeare book in his apartment?"

"Three times. Why is that bothering you so?"

He sighed. "I didn't say it was bothering me. I just stated a fact. He really is enrolled in night school. And his phone *was* unplugged."

Tony rubbed his chin in disbelief. "So you think a guy who reads *Hamlet* can't burn down a house? Is this another one of your bleeding-heart theories?"

"No," Larry returned. "But I don't want to assume somebody's guilty just because he has an attitude and a weird haircut. Especially when his alibi could be true."

"*Part* of his alibi. The other part was a lie. And what about his mechanic skills and the gas stains and the arson conviction and the gas can? You think some Shakespeare book clears up all that evidence?"

"No, I don't." He took in a deep breath and shifted in his seat. "I just feel uneasy about things. Like maybe we closed the case too fast."

"We have an assignment board full of unsolved cases, Larry. Neither one of us has time to dwell on long shots."

"Well, I'd feel better if we could pick up Keith Varner again. Slap an assault charge on him."

"There are deputies working on it, buddy."

Larry was quiet for a few moments. "You just should have seen how scared they were today. The little kid and Paige. Even Lynda. I wish there was something definitive we could do."

Tony only chuckled. "Lighten up, pal. They'll be fine."

CHAPTER THIRTY-SEVEN

Paige tucked her sleeping child into bed in the master bedroom then pulled back the curtain and peered out the front window. The street was dark, and she wasn't sure she would even know if someone sat out there, watching, waiting. What if Keith had discovered where they were? What if he were just biding his time, waiting until her guard was down to pounce again and snatch Brianna from her hands?

She was getting crazy, she told herself, but she wished the police would go back to guarding the house again. But police never guarded battered, frightened mothers or abused children. They didn't consider the threats wrathful husbands made to be as serious as attempted murder. Paige didn't see the difference.

Sighing, she closed the curtain and went through the living room to the back door. Through the window, she saw Lynda sitting on the patio with her head resting against the back of her chair, staring up into the stars.

Quietly, she opened the door and stepped outside. "Lynda, are you okay?"

Lynda offered a weak smile. "I'm fine, Paige. Sit down."

"I don't know." Crossing her arms, Paige gazed across the yard to the woods behind the fence. "I feel too vulnerable out here. I think I'd rather stay closed up inside."

"I felt that way at first, too. But I love sitting outside at night, and I decided not to let Doug Chastain take that away from me. You shouldn't let Keith."

"All right." Still watching the shadows beyond the yard, Paige took the padded swing across from Lynda and began to move gently back and forth. "I've been so jumpy today since the run-in with him. It feels good to relax."

"It does, doesn't it?"

Crickets chirped in the yard, signaling that fall was approaching, and Lynda smiled. "Those crickets remind me of college."

"College? Why? Did you study them?"

Lynda laughed. "Crickets? No. But every fall, the library seemed to be full of them. Especially at night. I'd be there studying, and those crickets would be chirping as loud as you could imagine, and I'd look for them so I could throw them outside. I don't know why they bothered me so much."

Paige closed her eyes against the cool breeze whispering through her hair. "I always meant to go to college. When I married Keith, he promised I could. But every time I brought it up, he nipped it in the bud."

"Well, maybe you could try it now."

Paige shook her head. "No, I'd never make it through. I'm not smart enough."

"Smart enough?" Lynda asked. "Paige, you have as much upstairs as anyone I know."

Paige didn't seem to buy it. "Besides, now I have to worry about making ends meet. It's not easy supporting a child alone. The whole time we've been divorced, I haven't gotten one penny of child support from Keith. But I don't really want it. I don't want him having anything at all to do with Brianna." Hugging herself, Paige scanned the fence.

"I think God's with you on this, Paige."

Paige chuckled softly. "Oh, really? Why?"

"Call it deductive reasoning. You've come through more narrow escapes than I have. You do believe in God, don't you?"

Paige sighed. "I guess so. I wish I had as much faith as you."

"Where do you get the idea that I have more than you?"

Paige considered that for a moment. "Well, you live a real decent life, Lynda. You're a good example. Like you really believe."

"Why?" Lynda asked honestly. "Because I don't have a criminal record, I only let a curse word fly when I'm really mad, my name is on a church roster, and I have a pro-life sticker on my bumper? Is that my example?"

"No," Paige said. "Because you took Brianna and me in, and you gave us money, and clothes...."

Lynda sighed. "That's nothing, Paige. With my income, I should be ashamed for all I *haven't* done."

Paige was amazed. "Lynda, you just don't know. Other people aren't like that. Even family."

Lynda grew quiet for a moment, and Paige diverted her eyes, knowing she'd said too much.

"Paige, you never talk much about your family. Why?"

"Not much to tell," she said without conviction. "They live in Arizona."

"But have you contacted them to tell them what's going on? Do they know you're in trouble?"

"Oh, Lynda. They don't care."

Lynda sat up straighter. "Don't care? How do you know?"

Paige blinked back the tears pushing into her eyes. "Lynda, you have to know my mother. She's lived with my father for thirty years, and no matter how bad things get, she believes in sticking it out. No matter who gets hurt."

Lynda sat quietly, weighing the implications of what Paige had just said and decided to take a chance. "Paige, were you abused when you were a child?"

Paige looked into the trees for a moment, struggling to keep her face free of emotion, but it wasn't easy, and finally, she covered her face with a hand and squeezed her eyes shut, but the tears pressed out anyway. "I won't let Brianna live that way," she whispered. "I'm not like my mother. I can't turn my head, and I can't keep bouncing back."

Lynda moved across to sit on the swing next to Paige, reached out for her, and pulled her into a hug, and Paige laid her head against Lynda's shoulder and wept like a child.

"Is that why you married Keith? To get away from home?"

She nodded. "He ended up being so much like my father. I thought his temper was just normal because that's the way things always were at home, too. But it's not normal, is it?"

"No," Lynda said. "It's not normal. It's criminal."

Paige wept for a moment longer until she heard Brianna crying through the door she'd left open, and sucking in a deep breath, she got to her feet. "Brianna's crying," she said quickly, wiping her face. "I guess I'll go lie down with her." Paige could see the helplessness on Lynda's face, and she wished she hadn't burdened her with this. "Good night, Lynda."

"Good night."

Paige hurried into the master bedroom where Brianna, in the throes of a dream, cried out in her sleep. Lying down beside her, Paige stroked her face and comforted her. "Shhh. Mommy's here. Nothing's going to hurt you."

As she held her, she felt the terror seeping out of her.

For a while, she lay still in the dark, thinking about the fears that plagued her daughter, and that stalked her as well. They were real fears—fear for her life, fear of losing her child, fear of harm coming to either of them. She had never expected to live in such fear once she left her father's home.

Despair settled into her heart like a slow-moving disease, but as she drifted toward sleep, she thought she heard a voice: "*Shhh. I'm here. Nothing's going to hurt you.*"

And even as she sank into sleep, she realized that the voice, the promise, and the feeling of peace warming through her felt as tangible as that little girl curled up against her chest.

CHAPTER THIRTY-EIGHT

The crowd in the bar where Keith had decided to brood was thinning out, and men and women had begun to couple off with a frenzied desperation, as if going home alone was tantamount to social suicide.

But it wasn't his reputation that worried Keith tonight; rather, it was that he'd driven into the parking lot of his apartment building today to see three sheriff's cars. He didn't have to be Einstein to figure out that they were looking for him.

Never one to linger too long when trouble was brewing, Keith had turned his car around before they could spot him and had headed to this obscure bar across town where people knew him only by his first name.

He'd been drinking for hours, and his head had begun to throb. He needed to lie down somewhere.

Sliding off the bar stool he'd been propped on for the past several hours, he stumbled toward the door, catching the chairs as he passed to steady himself. He heard laughter outside as he fell out into the night and saw a couple of intoxicated men pawing at a woman who cackled loudly enough to wake the dead. Though they weren't looking at him, he suspected that the laughter was directed at him anyway, and he set his eyes on his car and concentrated on getting to it.

Again, laughter erupted behind him, and he swung around, letting a string of expletives tear from his mouth. One of the men cursed back at him and started toward him, and Keith opened his car door and fell behind the wheel.

179

He heard the man's fist hit his trunk, and groping to get his key into the ignition, he started the car. The man was banging on it now, and the woman's abrasive laughter split the night again.

Cursing because his hands were so maddeningly slow to cooperate, he got the car into gear and took off through the dirt.

Looking in his rearview mirror, he saw the man shouting obscenities at him. Keith rolled down his window and yelled back, "You can't touch me! I'm invincible!"

But that invincibility was meaningless if he couldn't prove it to someone. He wished he knew where Paige was tonight, so he could burst into her house, jerk her out of bed, and remind her who the man of the family is. He would show her what all her whining and running had gotten her. He would teach her how to show a little respect.

The idea became more attractive to him as he wove and zigzagged through town, heading toward the neighborhood where he had lived with her. Maybe she and Brianna were home. Maybe she had run out of money and been forced to go home, and he could walk in and surprise her....

The street was dark, and he chuckled under his breath and tried to focus his blurry vision on the house as he got closer. There were no lights on and no cars in the garage. Blast it all, she wasn't home. She was still hiding.

He thought about pulling into the driveway and going in, just to rest for a few minutes until his head quit hurting. But that voice inside his head that remained the slightest bit rational reminded him that a world of trouble would fall on him if he were caught here after what had happened today. No, he had to keep driving. He had to go home.

He ran over a corner curb making the turn off her street and felt his car bounce and screech as he accelerated. His eyes were growing heavy, and his head was hammering, but somehow he kept driving.

By rote he made his way home and pulled into his parking lot, making a cursory inspection through his blurred vision; he saw no squad cars. Satisfied, he pulled into a space. They'd forgotten about him by now, he thought with relief. That was the thing about the St. Clair Sheriff's Department. If you weren't there the first time they looked for you, chances were, they wouldn't be back. Not on a stupid charge like approaching his wife at the courthouse.

His parking job was crooked, but at least he didn't hit the car next to him. He cut off the engine and got out, stumbling toward his apartment while he searched his key chain for the apartment key.

When he heard a car door slam, he didn't bother to look. His head hurt too badly, and he had to find that key—

"Police! Hold it right there! You're under arrest!"

Keith cursed again and turned around, his hands limp at his sides as he glared at Larry Millsaps, who held a gun on him as if he'd just caught him robbing a bank. "You gotta be kiddin'."

Larry came up behind him and threw him against a car next to him, which wasn't difficult since he could barely stand as it was.

"What're the charges?"

"Assault, contempt of court, and whatever else we can hang on you."

Jerking him up, Larry threw him into the back seat of the unmarked car as he read him his rights, and Keith decided that he didn't care where Larry took him or for what reason, as long as there was a place there to lay his head.

There was no outside light to indicate that it was morning, but the sounds of echoing doors and yelling men sliced through Keith's brain with machete force. His head still pounded, but forcing himself to open his eyes, he looked around and tried to orient himself.

And then he remembered that he was in jail.

The reason escaped him, however, and clutching his head, he sat up on the side of his cot and tried to think. Had he gotten into a fight last night? Had they pulled him over for drunk driving? Had it been for driving by Paige's house?

Paige. It was something about Paige. The haze over his brain seemed to clear as he recalled the incident in the parking garage yesterday when he'd tried to take Brianna. What had Paige told them?

Fury rose up inside him, intense enough to propel him to the cell bars. "Hey!" he shouted up the corridor. "Hey! I want to talk to my lawyer!"

An inmate several cells down yelled for him to shut up, but he turned up the volume a few decibels. "I want a lawyer, do you hear me? I have the right to a lawyer!"

He heard someone coming then, a linebacker in a guard's uniform, and he backed a few steps away from the bars. "Are you gonna let me call my lawyer?"

The man leveled hateful, bloodshot eyes on him as he stuck the key in the lock and opened the door. "Come on, Varner."

Keith hesitated. "Are you—am I gonna call my lawyer now?"

The man smirked. "What do you think? That I'm gonna smash your face in as soon as you step over this line?"

Keith didn't like the question, so he offered no answer.

The man's grin faded. "Get out here, Varner. You're wasting my time."

He felt nauseous as he stepped out of the cell, and the guard escorted him to the telephone.

Two hours later, standing in front of a judge who might or might not let him out on bail, Keith did as he was told and let his lawyer do the talking.

"It was all a misunderstanding, your honor. My client and his ex-wife are in the middle of a custody dispute. She's tried pinning things on him before to stack the deck in her favor, but this takes the cake."

The judge didn't seem all that interested. "Says here that he vandalized her car, assaulted her, and tried to take the child against the orders of the court. Is that or is it not true?"

"No, your honor," McRae said. "All that happened is that they happened to be parked on the same level in the parking garage. He hadn't seen his child in over a month, and when he saw them coming across the garage, he was overcome with the desire to see her and approached her. He never dreamed she would interpret it as a threat right there in the courthouse parking lot."

The judge propped his chin in his hand, as if he'd heard it all a million times and didn't know if he could stay awake for one more.

"His ex-wife saw him and assuming incorrectly that he planned to take the child, took off running down the stairs. Unfortunately, she slipped and fell on the way down, and when my client heard her scream, he went to see if she was all right. She milked the incident for everything it was worth, your honor, and made it look as if he had assaulted her, which couldn't be farther from the truth. Judge, I ask that you drop these charges so that we won't waste any more of your time."

The judge studied the paperwork on his desk. "Is his ex-wife in the courtroom?"

McRae made a helpless gesture. "We weren't able to reach her or her attorney. My guess is that they are reluctant to stand before you with such a blatant lie."

The judge assessed Keith, who was tired and unshaven. "I'm divorced, myself, Mr. Varner, and I know how difficult it is to be without your children. But your ex-wife must have a restraining order for a reason."

"I told you, Judge. She's stacking her deck so she'll win permanent custody."

The judge rubbed his head, as if he nursed a headache of his own and then in a half-audible voice, said, "All right then. I'll give him the benefit of the doubt." He leaned forward then and pointed a finger at Keith. "But I won't do it again. If I see you back in this courtroom for any reason, Mr. Varner, you'll go to jail. Do you understand me?"

"Yes sir."

"All right." Banging the gavel, he moved on to the next case.

Trying to look humble and sincere, Keith left the courtroom. But inside he was dancing; he'd gotten away with it again.

His lawyer brooded as he drove him home, which aggravated Keith. He wasn't in the mood for this silent treatment. His head still hurt, and he wanted to take something and go to bed for a few hours before he had to go to work. When they reached Keith's apartment building, Keith started to get out.

"Hey, Keith," McRae said, stopping him. "No more antics, huh? You almost ruined your case."

"I didn't do anything," Keith said.

McRae breathed a disbelieving laugh. "This is me you're talking to. I know what you did, and it was stupid. And if you do anything like it again, you're going to have to find yourself a new lawyer."

"Okay, so it was stupid. I lost my head."

"Don't lose it again."

Keith got out then leaned back in the door. "Relax. It's going to be all right. We'll still win the case. Paige won't be able to fight back much longer."

McRae frowned back at him. "What do you mean by that?"

"Just that you should trust me," Keith said. "I've got this under control."

CHAPTER THIRTY-NINE

The maddening thing about having his own clothes in his room was that Jake couldn't put them on. Allie had told him that he'd have to be sitting upright before he could learn to dress himself, and even though she'd offered to do it for him, he'd declined. He liked the gowns, he told her. She believed him — which just proved how naive she was.

The truth was that he couldn't stand the thought of a woman doing something so personal as dressing him. Already Jake had little dignity left. The things they had to do for him were things he'd always taken for granted. Now he'd never take anything for granted again.

That morning they had put him in that monstrosity of a wheelchair again, and he'd persuaded them to leave him in it; the longer he sat upright, the easier it would become. He was up to sixty degrees now, and he was determined to conquer this particular obstacle. But it was taking too much time.

Rolling carefully toward the closet, he tried to reach a coat hanger, but it was just out of reach. Looking around in the closet where the nurses had put all of the things Lynda had gotten out of his hotel room, he found a tennis racket. Carefully, he slipped it into the triangle of the hanger and lifted it off the rod.

He dropped the racket then bent the hanger into a straight piece of wire with a hook at one end, and slipped it into the waistband of his sweat pants. If he could just hook that waistband over his foot and work it up to the point where his arms could reach, maybe he could actually get them on.

He broke out in a sweat as he maneuvered the pants with the hanger, trying to hook them over, missing, then trying again. The waistband of the sweat pants kept collapsing when it hit his feet, and the hanger offered little control, but he kept trying.

And trying.

And trying.

But it was too difficult, and finally, he gave up and flung both the pants and the hanger across the room. Slamming his hands down on the wheelchair armrests, he let out a raging curse.

A knock sounded on the door, and he cursed again, hoping it wasn't Lynda. It was bad enough that she saw him as a helpless invalid, but he didn't relish the idea of her catching him in this stupid chair, reclined back the way he was, wearing that degrading hospital gown that covered only his thighs, revealing the stupid stockings and Ace bandages wrapped the length of his legs.

The door opened, and Mike, the guy from the airport, stuck his head in. "Hey, Jake. Is it a bad time?"

Jake breathed a sigh of relief. "No, come on in."

Mike stepped tentatively into the room, wearing the same look of awkwardness most people did when they saw him. "I thought I'd come by and see how you are doing."

"Terrific," Jake said, throwing up his hands. "I'm great. How are you?"

Mike went to the chair across from Jake and started to turn it around but saw the sweat pants lying at the foot of it. Bending down, he picked them up. "You want me to hang these up for you?"

Jake swallowed. "You can throw them out the window for all I care."

Mike's eyebrows rose. "Tired of them?"

Jake laughed sarcastically. "Yeah, that's it. I'm sick of them."

Mike sat down and was quiet for a moment, and Jake knew he wasn't making it easy on him. "Thought you might want some of your stuff," Mike said, holding out a box of Jake's things that were in the trunk of his car. Lynda thought you might want it, but I thought I'd make sure. If you don't need any of it, I could just put it back."

Jake considered it for a moment, wishing that he had some means of taking care of these things himself. "Uh, just put it back in the trunk. It's okay."

"All right," Mike said. "You know, it's really good to see you sitting up."

Jake gave a dry laugh. "Not all the way up."

"You're getting there."

"Maybe."

Mike shifted. "When I think how close you came to going up in that plane's explosion — I still don't know how she got you out."

Jake frowned. "How who got me out?"

"Lynda," Mike said. "The plane was on its side, and you were strapped into your seat. Somehow, she unfastened you and pulled you through the door then dragged you away, even before we could get there. The plane went up seconds later."

"She did that? With broken ribs, spleen damage, and cuts all over her? How?"

Mike smiled. "I guess somebody was helping her. Maybe there was a reason you weren't supposed to die."

Jake couldn't exactly swallow that. "Well, if you think of one, you let me know. Right now, I'm not looking toward some great purpose. All I want to do is get my pants on."

Mike looked down at the sweat pants he was holding. "These? Hey, man, I could help you with these." He got up and came to stand at Jake's feet, but Jake shook his head.

"No, that's all right. I don't need them."

"But you'll feel a hundred times better if you don't have to wear that gown. No offense man, but I don't think that's your look."

Jake grinned, then eyed the pants again. "If you could just get them over my feet and up to where I can reach them — "

"No problem." Mike slipped the pants over Jake's feet and slid them up his legs. As soon as Jake could reach them, Mike let him take over.

It took some effort, but Jake worked them under his hips and all the way up.

"Would you look at that?" Jake asked. "I look almost normal now."

Mike went to the closet. "Which shirt do you want?"

"Give me that Far Side T-shirt," Jake said, pulling the gown off over his head and tossing it to the bottom of the closet.

Mike handed him the shirt, and Jake pulled it on and tucked it in.

He looked down at himself and smiled. "Man, that feels better."

"It sure looks better," Mike said.

Jake looked up at Mike, gratitude in his eyes. "I owe you one, buddy."

"Well, then, we may as well run up the tab. I can come by tonight and help you change again if you want. Or drop by on my way to work in the morning."

"No need," Jake said. "I'll ask my PT. He just wasn't here this morning, and my OT is a woman. I think I'll be fine. Either that, or I won't take these off again."

Mike laughed and relaxed back in his chair, feeling like he knew Jake better already.

CHAPTER FORTY

I can't believe my eyes," Lynda said later that day. "You're sitting up and dressed and everything."

Jake looked up at her from his wheelchair by the window, trying not to look quite so glad that she was here. "Yeah, but let me tell you. It's no picnic."

Lynda took the chair across from him. "When did this happen?"

"This morning. I got up to sixty degrees, so they left me here. I threw my usual tantrum, called them names, and threatened lawsuits, but they left me anyway."

He could see that she wasn't sure if he was kidding or not. "Don't you want to sit up?" she asked.

He shrugged. "It's not as simple as that, Lynda. Sitting up is a major ordeal. If I ever get all the way up, I'll never take it for granted again."

Her face softened. "I'm sorry, Jake. I didn't mean to be insensitive."

Now he felt like a heel. "It's okay. Actually, I asked them to leave me in the chair. I wanted to look out the window."

Lynda peered out at the parking lot below them. "So how is it?"

"Makes me feel more like a prisoner, frankly," he said quietly. "I'm stuck in here, and there's a whole world still out there."

"A whole bunch of cars, anyway. Oh, look. Is that a red Porsche parked over there? It looks just like yours."

Jake struggled upward to see it. "Where?"

"In that last row, off by itself."

189

Jake spotted it, and his face changed. "Yeah, it does look like mine. What do you know?"

"Me?" she asked with a grin. "Nothing. I don't know anything."

He looked up at her, his eye narrowing and saw her teasing grin. "Lynda, that wouldn't be mine —"

She nodded slowly. "I had Mike move it today. He said he came in and saw you."

Jake gazed hungrily down at the car. "He didn't tell me he brought my Porsche."

"It's a surprise," she said. "We were going to wait until you could see it out the window, but here you are."

His smile faded, and a look of longing came over his face — not for the car but for the life he'd had when he could drive it.

Lynda looked down at his chair. "Does this thing roll easily?"

"It's supposed to," he said.

"Then how about if I take you for a walk? We can go say hello to the car."

Jake grinned. "I'd like that. But what about your ribs? You're not supposed to push anything heavy, are you?"

"I'm doing a lot better," she said. "I'm getting my strength back. Don't worry."

"I don't want you hurting yourself for me, Lynda."

"Would I do that?"

"Of course you would. You already have."

"What does that mean?"

Jake's look was soft as he met her eyes. "Mike told me how you pulled me out of the plane. Nobody told me. I don't know how I thought I'd gotten out, but it never occurred to me that you'd done it."

"You would have done the same thing for me."

She started pushing him toward the door, and he mulled those words over. *Would* he have done the same thing? If she had been unconscious and he'd been the one awake, would he have risked his life to take the time to save her?

He doubted it. And if he *had,* he no doubt would have told her about it the moment she came to. He didn't like doing things he didn't get credit for.

But she'd done it and then hadn't mentioned it; she probably counted her heroism as such a natural thing that it hadn't occurred to her to tell him.

Shaking off the thoughts, he tried to be flip again. "So—has anybody tried to kill you today?"

She smiled. "Not today. I think it's all over now that they have Doug locked up. I'm starting to relax a little."

"So you feel pretty sure he did it?"

She was quiet for a moment. "Well—I still find it hard to believe. I mean, it's just weird that he would try something like that after all this time. But I guess things fester. Who knows what prison was like for him? Maybe he spent the whole time plotting his revenge on me."

As she spoke, she pushed him down the long hall and onto the elevator then to the first floor and through the courtyard where patients were scattered about under trees and strolled down sidewalks while the Florida sun shone down warmly and the autumn breeze cooled.

"How do you feel?" she asked after a moment.

Jake was smiling. "Fine," he said. "I'm feeling just fine."

"We can go back in any time you want."

"Not yet," he said. "I really do want to see my car."

She pushed him out onto the parking lot and through the rows of cars. He closed his eyes and let the sun beat down on his face and thought how good it was to be out of that controlled, air-conditioned environment.

When he opened his eyes again, he saw his car. Slowly, he smiled. "Not a scratch on it."

"No, it looks pretty good, for a Porsche."

He laughed as they got closer, and he touched the fender with featherlight fingers, as if greeting a cherished lover. "Man, what I wouldn't give to sit in it again."

Lynda's smile faded. "Well—I could go try to find an orderly who'd be willing to lift you in."

Jake shook his head. "No. I can't sit all the way up, remember? I'll save it for later."

The look she gave him was sweet and surprised. "Jake? Do you realize that's the first positive thing I've heard you say?"

"That I can't sit up?"

"No, that you'll save it for later. You know you're getting better, don't you?"

He sighed. "I guess so. I'm just not very optimistic about how much better I can get." He rolled to the window of the car, peered in at the plush, sleek seats that used to feel so natural beneath him. "Thanks for bringing it here, Lynda. It made the effort of sitting up worth it."

"Good," she said. "I'll leave it here for a while, so you can look out and see it any time you want."

He smiled. "That'll be good."

She wheeled him back to the courtyard where other patients and family members milled around. They found a shady place under a tree, and she sat down on a bench opposite him. Jake relaxed and looked up at the sky. It was cobalt blue, cloudless, a perfect day for flying. He wondered if he'd ever be able to experience that feeling again.

"Do you miss flying?" he asked her.

She nodded. "Yeah. I miss it pretty bad."

"What are you gonna do about your plane? Get another one?"

"No. I was going to sell that one, remember?"

He brought his gaze back to her. "But you loved it so much."

"Maybe too much. Anyway, I've kind of reconciled myself to giving it up for a while."

"What a waste," he said, his gaze returning to the sky. "You can fly and don't want to while I'd give my right arm to fly—and can't."

Lynda followed his gaze to the sky.

"They replaced me, you know," he went on. "I got flowers from my boss at TSA. I called him to thank him, and he said that he'd had to find a replacement. He said they were looking into a supervisory job on the ground if I wanted it, but I told him no thanks."

"Well, couldn't you at least consider it?"

"Right now, I'm not up to considering anything. I don't want to take a desk job, and I don't want to be on disability, and I don't want to be grounded for the rest of my life."

192

"You can get a medical waiver to fly with one eye, Jake, if you get use of your legs back. Maybe you can't fly for TSA, but you'll be able to fly again someday."

"But I loved my job." His voice caught, and he let out a heavy breath. "I guess I thought that maybe ... by some miracle ..." His words fell off, and she saw the tears gather in his eye as he shook the thought away.

After a moment, as if one dread reminded him of another, he spoke again. "We're having the unveiling Monday."

"What unveiling?"

He pointed to the bandage on his face. "The bandages. They're taking them off for good."

"Jake, that's wonderful."

Those tears seemed to well deeper. "Is it? I have a gash that goes through my eye to my cheekbone, Lynda. It was bad enough to blind me. I don't even know how many stitches I have. Do you honestly think I'm looking forward to seeing myself?"

"It'll be okay. You have good doctors."

"It doesn't matter how good they are if I have only one eye and a mug that would terrify children." He looked away, as though doing so could divert her attention from his tears. "You know, I was a good-looking guy. Women liked me. It was my greatest strength."

"I guess that's a matter of opinion."

"What? You didn't think I was good-looking?" he asked skeptically.

"Oh, there is no question that you were. But that wasn't your greatest strength. It never is. Maybe you needed to stop relying on your looks so you could find what you're really made of."

He felt his face reddening. "In other words, I was arrogant about my looks, so I needed to lose my face? Is that what you're saying?"

"No. What I am saying is that looks are just temporary, anyway. Don't you think it's time you go deeper into yourself to discover other strengths?"

"Wow," he said. "What did the doctor do? Ask you to prepare me for looking like the Elephant Man? Did he tell you to teach me to be beautiful on the inside?"

"No. Your face is going to be fine, Jake. You lost an eye. But you can still see. You're not blind."

"I'm blind enough to lose my job even if I get my legs back! What am I gonna do for a living?"

"Not everyone who works in the airline industry is a pilot, Jake—there are other positions, even at TSA. And if that doesn't appeal to you, you'll find something, Jake! You're an intelligent man. It's going to be all right."

Her reassurances seemed to make him angrier, and he looked off into the trees and shook his head dolefully. "Sometimes I wish I could have your kind of naivete."

"I'm not naive," she said. "In fact, I think I'm pretty savvy." She touched his hand, and he recoiled. "Jake, look at me."

He moved his disgusted gaze back to her. "What?"

"You're scared, but it'll be all right. In fact, I'll be here when they take the bandages off if you want. Do you want me to be here?"

He breathed a sarcastic laugh. "Yeah. You can give me another pep talk like this one after I see myself. You always make me feel so much better."

"I'm sorry, Jake," she said. "I haven't been trying to depress you, really. Do you want me there?"

His shoulders wilted, and he rubbed his forehead. "Yeah, I guess so," he said quietly. "I'll probably need somebody in my corner."

"Okay, I'll be here. And you'll see. You're probably even better looking now than you were before."

"Yeah," he said, not believing a word. "The scar will give me character, right?"

"Right. I happen to really like men with scars."

"Yeah, sure," he said. "I didn't notice any scars on that detective friend of yours."

She frowned. "Who, Larry?"

"Yeah, *Larry*."

For a moment, she stared at him blankly, and he hated himself for sounding like a jealous lover. He wasn't jealous. He was just ... curious. "So you two are getting pretty close, aren't you?"

She seemed to struggle with the smile creeping across her face. "There's something about having a maniac trying to kill you that makes you depend on the detective on the case. Call me crazy. I don't think I'll be seeing that much of him now, though, since they caught the guy."

She couldn't tell if Jake accepted that or not or if he even wanted to. Finally she stood up. "Are you ready to go back in?"

"Yeah," he said. "I have a hot date with Oprah. Can't miss that."

"Do you want me to bring you some books Monday? Or a radio? Or a hamburger?"

"Why don't we get these bandages off first, and then I'll decide if I have an appetite."

She looked down at him, wishing for the right words. "Are you that scared, Jake?"

He thought for a moment then said honestly, "Scareder than I was when we were about to crash. On Monday, I might just hit bottom."

CHAPTER FORTY-ONE

Wearing his shaded glasses and a fake mustache with his hair moussed back, Keith pulled into the parking lot outside the Schilling Building where Lynda worked and slowly drove through it, searching for her car. If only he could find it, he could wait for her to come out then follow her to wherever she was staying now. He could get her out of the picture once and for all and find Paige and Brianna in the bargain.

But her car wasn't there. It wasn't going to happen today. He tried not to let it discourage him.

But the clock was ticking, and recent developments hadn't helped his case any. If he knew Lynda Barrett, she'd find some way to use his arrest against him in court, even though he'd gotten off. She was slick that way. That's why she was dangerous. He never should have shown up that day at Brianna's school, but after the crash, he'd felt so sure he wouldn't meet with any resistance. If Paige didn't have a lawyer to run to, she would start feeling defeated and give in.

He'd always made her give in before. All those visits to the emergency room when he'd convinced her to tell the doctors that she had fallen down the stairs or been in a car accident or a dozen other creative stories he'd come up with, she had always complied.

Until Brianna had gotten hurt.

That, he admitted now, was his biggest mistake, but it wasn't as if it was all his fault. They'd been arguing, he and Paige, and she'd mouthed off to him, forcing him to crack her with a backhand across the face. Brianna had started crying—that loud, shrill, eardrum-piercing screaming that drove him up the wall—and someone *had* to shut her up.

It was his duty as a father to teach her to control herself.

But, as usual, Paige had gone off the deep end. And Lynda Barrett had empowered her to leave him, once and for all, and take his little girl.

But if he could get rid of Lynda now, he knew he could reason with Paige again. She *knew* he was a better parent. He made more money and could give Brianna nicer things. He could teach her self-control, teach her right from wrong. He could discipline her much more effectively than Paige, who let her run wild most of the time. And he was certain that he loved her more.

All he had to do was catch up with Lynda. She would have to report to work sooner or later, and when she did, he would be waiting. What he would do then he wasn't sure, but he knew something would come to him.

For a while, he drove around town—as he did every day before he reported to work—looking through parking lots of hotels and apartments, driving through neighborhoods and parks, looking for Paige's or Lynda's car, searching for his daughter's tawny head among the children at playgrounds.

He had even called Lynda's secretary, pretending he was an insurance investigator looking for her, but the woman wouldn't tell him a thing. When he'd asked her when she expected Lynda to return to work, she'd said maybe another week or two, possibly sooner.

He thought as he drove: What *would* he do when he finally caught up with her? She had escaped the crash and the fire, so this time his attack needed to be swift and vicious. And certain.

A bomb.

A slow smile came to his face as he flipped through the possibilities. It was easier to buy dynamite than a gun, and he knew enough about engines to rig it to her car. All he needed was a few ingredients and a window of time to plant it in the right place. Then it would be all over.

Turning the car around, he headed for the interstate. He'd have to buy the dynamite out of town, so the cops couldn't trace it to him after the fact. While he was at it, he should probably get a gun, too. Then if he discovered where they were all staying before Lynda returned to work, he could try one more time to get her out of the way.

One more time was all he would need.

CHAPTER FORTY-TWO

The big church that had once been like a home to Lynda was still warm and welcoming, but in many ways she felt like the Prodigal Son, covered with mud and pig slop, starving and remorseful as she returned to her Father's house.

At her side was Paige, holding Brianna on her hip, looking a little awkward and nervous as they stepped through the side door of the church and entered the hallway where the Sunday school classes were.

Paige's step slowed, and Lynda saw the trepidation on her face. "I hate to leave her. I know this sounds crazy, but what if somehow Keith found out we were coming? Or sees our car here? He's smart, Lynda. What if he comes to her class and takes her?"

Lynda knew she couldn't promise that nothing would happen, not when Paige had encountered so many surprises already. "I really wanted you to come to the adult class with me, Paige," said Lynda, "but I understand your fear and wanting to stay with Brianna."

"I think it's more important right now for *her* to be in Sunday school," Paige said. "Do you think they'd let me stay with her? I could help with the other kids."

She had half-expected Paige to flee back home. This idea was at least better than that. "I'm sure it'll be all right," she said. "They always need help in the preschool area." She followed the signs to the class for three-year-olds and looked inside. A few children were already there, playing with blocks, coloring, and banging on the piano in the corner of the room. Lynda didn't know the teacher, and sadly she realized that a whole new group of people had become family members in the church in her absence. Maybe it wasn't even her family any more.

The teacher welcomed Brianna with delight and immediately interested her in some Play-Doh, and Lynda waited as Paige explained that she didn't want to leave her.

The teacher embraced Paige as an answered prayer. "My assistant just had a baby, and I didn't know how I was going to handle the class today. Come on over here, and you can help me get the glue out for the projects."

Satisfied that Paige was welcome, Lynda left the room and drifted back up the hallway, wondering if her class was still meeting in the same place. Despair and humility fell over her as she went up the hall, against the crowd beginning to get thicker and realized that the few people she did recognize didn't notice her.

And then she saw Brother Tommy, the pastor who'd once had such faith in her, the man who'd come to visit her in the hospital, who'd started a prayer vigil for her the moment he'd heard of the crash.

Like the Prodigal Son, she was transformed by the joy in his eyes, and he cut through the crowd, arms outstretched to meet her.

"It's so good to see you, Lynda." He hugged her carefully, as if he feared breaking her. "I've been waiting for you to come back."

Sadly, she looked around her. "I don't even know anyone any more."

"Sure you do," he said. "Come on. I'll go with you to your class. They'll be glad to see how their prayers have been answered."

The class met in the same place it had for years, and by the time the hour was over, Lynda felt accepted back into the family. When she met Paige and Brianna outside the sanctuary before the worship service, she felt so full of God's Spirit that she had no doubt some of it would spill over onto Paige.

CHAPTER FORTY·THREE

Across St. Clair, Keith Varner worked at his kitchen table with the background noise of a broadcast church service filling the dead air in his apartment. He had all the ingredients laid out on the table in front of him: fuse wires, needle-nose pliers, ten pounds of Power Prime Dynamite, a blasting cap—everything he would need to blow Lynda to kingdom come.

All he would need was a few minutes under her car, and he could tape the bomb to her gas tank, wire it to the starter, and then get back and wait.

He could see it now. The explosion, the fire, the ambulances that would get there too late, and the media reports. And then he'd get a call from his lawyer saying that the court date had been postponed until Paige was able to find another lawyer. Only she wouldn't be able to get another lawyer because she had no money, and then she'd have to make a choice: either go into court to represent herself or give Brianna to him without a fight. And if she chose to represent herself, it would be a joke. Paige was not an articulate person, and she froze whenever she had to speak in front of a crowd. She would stutter and stammer and hem and haw, but she wouldn't make her case as clearly as he and his attorney would. It wouldn't take anything for the judge to rule that Keith was the better parent to have custody of his daughter. It was practically a done deal.

All he had to do was make sure that—once he caught up with Lynda Barrett—she would be taken out of the picture once and for all. And if he could get her when she was parked in her office parking lot, maybe she would have Paige's file and all of the evidence against him in her briefcase. That, too, would go up in flames.

He heard the choir on television singing the "Hallelujah Chorus," and with a round of laughter, he joined in.

He had an awful lot to be thankful for.

CHAPTER FORTY-FOUR

Jake was sitting upright in bed when Lynda got there on Monday morning, and she stopped and smiled at him before coming all the way into the room. "You look like sitting up comes more naturally now, Jake," she said. "Are the nausea and dizziness gone?"

"Yes, thanks to those two sadistic slave drivers who wouldn't let me rest until I was upright." He grinned slightly then and added, "Actually, I'm pretty thankful for them."

"So am I."

She came further into the room and set down the bag of magazines and books she'd brought him. "So have you heard from the doctor yet?"

His grin faded. "I'm told he's in the building, but he hasn't made it by yet." He breathed a sardonic laugh. "Amazing. Getting this bandage off seems like a matter of life and death to me, and to him it's just routine."

"It's going to be all right, Jake. I know it is. Have they prepared you at all? I mean, you've seen yourself when they changed the bandages, haven't you?"

"They wouldn't let me. The hospital shrink convinced the doctor that I couldn't handle it. When they took my eye out after the crash, they put in an implant and attached it to the muscles. They told me it doesn't look like an eye at all. In fact, they said it looks like the inside of my mouth. Talk about bloodshot."

Lynda stepped closer to the bed, realizing that this might be more grim than she'd expected. "I guess I figured they had already put an artificial eye in."

"No, they can't do that for another three weeks or so. Most of the swelling has to go down. Plus, they have to make the eye. The guy who makes them and installs them is coming by this morning, too, to fill me in on the gory details."

"The guy who makes them puts them in?" she asked, cringing. "Is he a doctor?"

"Nope. An optician."

"An optician in the operating room?"

"Apparently there's no surgery involved," he said. He glanced up at her and noted the dour expression on her face. "Hey, if you don't want to stay, I understand. In fact, I'm not too thrilled about anybody seeing this but me."

"I'm staying," she said firmly. "You're going to need somebody here. It's just—I didn't realize they did it that way."

Groping for something to get both their minds off the dread, she glanced at the untouched breakfast tray beside his bed. "Aren't you going to eat?"

He shook his head. "Can't. I don't have much appetite today."

"But Jake, you're losing so much weight."

"And you think that'll detract from my good looks?" he asked sarcastically.

"Well, it won't help your therapy. You need your strength."

"I can't eat," he bit out. "Period. So give it a rest."

"Fine."

He reached over to his bed table and pulled out the mirror he shaved with. As he gazed into it, Lynda realized that the bandage allowed him to imagine his eye still intact and his scars perfectly healed. After it came off, however, there would be no imagining.

"Did you know I was in a calendar once?" he asked quietly.

"A calendar? What kind?"

"It was a calendar that the Chamber of Commerce in Houston put together—Houston's eligible bachelors. I was August. For a couple of years, people recognized me wherever I went. I had women lined up. I even got fan mail."

She wasn't impressed. "And are you better for the experience?"

He thought for a moment. "All I know is I didn't have a scar down my face, and my baby blues were intact. Small things, I know, but they meant a lot to me."

The catch in his voice reminded her how hypercritical it was for her to pass judgment on his vanity, when she had lost so little in comparison. "They're not small things, Jake," she whispered. "It's got to be a trauma. But you know, don't you, that no matter what your face looks like under that bandage, they can do plastic surgery? They're doing great things now. And artificial eyes look real."

"Yeah," he whispered without conviction. "I keep telling myself that."

She was about to name all the celebrities she knew who'd had false eyes when the door opened, cutting off her thoughts.

"Good morning, Jake," the doctor said, coming into the room followed by an entourage of others. "Are you ready to get that bandage off?"

"Ready as I'll ever be."

"Great." The doctor was too cheerful, and Lynda wished he would make this a little easier, acknowledge Jake's suffering, offer him reassurances. As the doctor approached, she started to step away from the bed, but Jake caught her hand.

"No. Stay here."

"Okay," she said.

The doctor sat on the edge of the bed and got the scissors out of his pocket. "Jake, I'd like you to meet Dan Cirillo. He's the one who's going to be making your eye."

Jake shook his hand.

"Have they explained to you that you shouldn't be shocked when you see your eye, Jake?" Dan asked.

"Yeah, they warned me."

"It's not going to be pretty, but we'll put a patch over it until we can put a prosthesis in. After that, you'll be almost as good as new."

"Unless TSA has changed its policy about pilots having vision in both eyes, I won't be good as new." Turning back to the doctor, he said, "Let's get this over with."

Lynda held her breath as the doctor began to work the tape off Jake's face. She felt his hand tightening, and she squeezed back, wishing there were more she could do.

The doctor got the tape off and slowly began to peel the gauze away from Jake's face.

She saw the gash down his eyebrow, the black, blood-caked stitches that had been cleaned and sterilized with yellow iodine whenever the bandage had been changed. Now it was clear just how deep the gash on his face had been, deep enough to require several layers of stitches, and deep enough to destroy his eye.

"Yes, that's healing nicely," the doctor said in a pleasant voice as he worked the bandage further down. "When I saw that gash originally, I didn't know how well we'd be able to repair it. But this looks very nice."

But Lynda knew Jake's heart was going to be broken. The doctor uncovered his damaged eye, and she saw the small scar down the center of his eyelid, where it had been severed.

"Can you open that eye now, Jake?"

Jake opened it slowly, and it came only halfway up. In the socket was a pinkish-clear implant that looked nothing like an eye.

Perspiration beaded on her temples, and she tried to fight the tears threatening her. She couldn't cry. Whatever she did, she had to be positive. She had to smile.

The rest of the bandage peeled down easily, and finally, the doctor rolled it up and handed it to a nurse. Then, leaning in, he examined the gash. "Let me take these stitches out before I let you have a look," he said, reaching for another pair of scissors the nurse handed him. As he snipped, he kept talking. "The healing looks good, Jake. If you opt for plastic surgery later on, after it all heals, you can do a lot to get rid of this scar. For now, though, it looks like you lost a bad fight."

He finished snipping the stitches, pulled them out, and then cleaned the scar. "What do you think, guys?" the doctor asked. "Better than we expected?"

The others in the room concurred with scripted enthusiasm, but Lynda was silent.

The doctor got up, and Dan took his place to examine the eyelid.

Jake's hand still clung to hers.

"Most of this swelling should be gone in a couple of weeks, Jake. When that happens, you can come by my office, and we'll make you a new eye."

Jake looked up at him. "Come by your office? Will I be out by then?"

"Oh, you'll be going home in a few days, Jake," the doctor said as he made a notation on his chart. "You're doing fine. You're sitting up now, so there's no reason we should keep you here. You'll have to come back every day for therapy, of course, but there's no reason you have to stay here."

Ambivalence was written all over Jake's face. "Doc, I can hardly get around in that chair. Do you really think I'm capable of going home and taking care of myself?"

"Dr. Randall seems to think so, and he's ordered Allie to start concentrating on that a lot in the next few days," he said. "And we certainly don't mean to send you home alone. You'll need someone with you at first, to help you, and of course, you can't drive yourself back and forth to the hospital for therapy."

Lynda saw the emotional struggle on his face.

"So this is it?" Jake said. "You're accepting that I am like I am for good? You're not going to give me any more hope of getting better—or any more help?"

"There's plenty of hope, Jake, and we'll be helping you every day. We haven't given up on you."

She saw how desperately he struggled not to let go of his tenuous emotions, and finally, he looked up at Dan again. "So is this eye gonna wander all over the place? Are people going to know which eye not to look at when they talk to me?"

"It shouldn't," he said. "Artificial eyes have come a long way, Jake. They tend to move pretty well, especially if the initial surgery is done right. It looks like this was."

"*Pretty* well?"

"They satisfy most people who have them," he said. "But there are some methods to get more precise movement with the other eye. Most people don't think they need them after they see how well the eye moves, but for people who are on television, or say, models, we might go that extra mile and install a peg in the back of the eye that helps kick it around. Either way, the eye is going to be very similar to your other one. Most people won't realize you have a prosthesis."

Jake wasn't buying any of it, and Lynda had to admit that she wasn't either.

"So—are you ready to see?" the doctor asked.

Jake let go of her hand and took the mirror the doctor offered him. Slowly, he brought it to his face.

For a moment, he showed no expression as he saw the scar cutting down his face, the still-swollen socket where his eye used to be, the red conformer in the place of his eyeball, the black-and-blue bruising covering his forehead and most of his cheek.

"Not bad, huh?" the doctor asked.

Jake couldn't speak.

"It's not finished, Jake," Lynda whispered. "You have to give it time."

She saw the tear forming in his swollen eye, and felt some relief that he could still make tears. His face began to redden, and she realized that he was about to break down. She turned back to the doctor and the others. "Can you give him a little time alone?"

"Sure," the doctor said, patting his leg. "Jake, you give us a call if you have any problems. Lynda, here's the eye patch. It's easy to put on. Ring for a nurse if you have any problems with it."

Jake stayed silent as they left and kept staring blankly into the mirror.

"Do you want me to go, too, Jake?"

He didn't answer her, but his face grew redder, and he began to tremble.

"Jake?"

His face twisted, and his knuckles turned white as he gripped the mirror's handle. Suddenly, he hurled it across the room. It crashed against the wall.

"Stop it, Jake!" Lynda shouted.

But he didn't stop, and when he reached out and turned over the table beside his bed sending a cup of water, a plastic pitcher, a box of tissues, and the telephone crashing onto the floor, she covered her ears. "Jake, I know you're upset, but—"

His face still raging red, he scooted to the side of his bed, pushed his legs off, and acted as though he would stand on them and walk out on sheer anger.

"Jake, stop it!" she said, trying to hold him back, but he shook her away. "You know you can't do that! Jake, you'll fall!"

Gritting his teeth, he tried with all his might to stand on his feet, but they only hung there limply, brushing the floor without life.

The rolling tray of food sat next to his bed, and he swung his arm and sent it toppling over, too, his breakfast spilling onto the floor with a crash that reverberated throughout the room. Righting it, Lynda began to cry. Finally, she swung around to him, her hands in fists at her side. "Who cares about your stupid face!" she screamed.

He froze then and brought his tormented gaze up to her, staring at her with greater, deeper pain than she'd ever seen in anyone. Catching her breath, she cried, "It's not what matters, Jake! There's so much more to you!"

"That's easy for you to say," he said through his teeth. "Your face was only bruised!"

"And yours has a scar! It's not the end of the world, Jake! Your face has nothing to do with who you are!"

"Get out of my room," he said, trying to pull his legs back up. She reached over to help him, but he pushed her away again. "Just get out!"

Muffling her sobs, she ran from the room, not knowing what to do, where to go, how to help. For now, any help she offered was futile. Jake was hitting bottom, and there was nothing she could do to pull him back up. Not now. Not yet.

Instead of going home, Lynda found refuge in the prayer room and prayed that Jake's heart, so freshly broken, would start to seek God's face, instead of his own.

Jake couldn't remember weeping as hard as he wept that day. Now he knew the meaning of "gnashing of teeth." His teeth were gnashing, his heart was bleeding, and he didn't know where to turn.

No one could comfort him. No one. He would never be comforted again.

He wept over his distorted face and the legs that refused to move and his life that had been so prosperous and busy and content before. He wept over his loneliness, his isolation, despite how self-inflicted it was. And he wept over having no place to go even though he would be released in a few days. Where would he go when he couldn't even walk, and his face might frighten strangers? Was there a halfway house for maimed invalids?

Not for the first time he wished he'd died in the crash.

Jake Stevens, who always had so much control over his life, who was unfettered and uncommitted, who had all the money he needed, and who won friends and influenced women wherever he went, was now broken, alone, and homeless.

And there was no hope.

From the depths of his despair, from some place he didn't know existed inside of him, he cried out to God in fury. *I don't even know if you're up there, God, but I need a miracle.*

Did God hear him? He didn't know. But in that faithless moment of brokenness when he'd been sure that he was talking to thin air, he decided to believe that God had indeed heard him. He had no other choice.

CHAPTER FORTY-FIVE

Jake wore the patch the next day, even though he was despondent and still refused to eat. He put forth little effort in therapy. He had determined that he was going to die even if it took every ounce of the strength he had remaining. Nothing mattered any more.

When Lynda knocked on his door, he was surprised. After yesterday, he had expected never to see her again. "What are you doing here?" he asked.

She stayed in the doorway, leaning against the wall. "I wanted to see how you are. I worried about you all night."

"I'm still here," he said. He swallowed and struggled with the apology on the tip of his tongue. "I figured I scared you off yesterday. Thought you wouldn't come back."

She started slowly toward him. "I never even considered staying away," she said. "You're not going to run me off just because you have a bad day."

"All my days are bad," he said.

She came to his bedside where he was sitting up. "You know, the way you reacted yesterday wasn't surprising. I might have done the same thing."

"Would you?" he asked sarcastically but without much fervor. "I would have thought you'd take it real philosophically. It's just a face, they're just legs, it was just my life."

"No," she said. "I wouldn't have felt that way at all. I'd be as mad as you were. I might not have the strength you had to throw things and knock things over, but I'd have been just as mad. You know, for somebody who has to stay in one spot, you sure did a lot of damage."

"Yeah," he said without humor. "Funny how much strength you can come up with when you don't care anymore."

"You do care, Jake. You know you do."

He fixed his sight on the ceiling. "Nope. That's where you're wrong."

Crossing her arms as if warding off his chill, she got up and stepped closer to the bed. "Well, anyway—I kind of like that patch. It gives you an air of mystery."

He kept staring at the ceiling. A tear fell to his cheek and rolled to his chin. "I'm gonna give little kids nightmares and old ladies heart attacks everywhere I go."

"No, you're not, Jake. They'll be fascinated, especially when you tell them the scar is the result of a plane crash."

He met her eyes directly for the first time that day. "Do you think the artificial eye is going to look just like mine?"

"I think so, Jake. They said it would."

"How can it?" he asked helplessly.

"I don't know how, but it can. Trust them."

He wiped the tear off his face and looked at the ceiling again. "I wonder if this is as good as it gets."

"Of course not. There are still several layers of stitches in there. There's a lot of swelling." She reached out and touched his injured cheek with her fingertips. "It'll go down," she whispered. "When these bruises clear, you'll see."

He took in a deep breath and caught her hand in his fist. Another tear dropped out, and he whispered, "No one back home would even recognize me. Not even my mother."

Lynda was confused. "Didn't you say your parents had both died?"

He let go of her hand then and covered his face, and a sob overtook him, then another, and another, until he wilted against her.

She sat next to him on the bed and held him, and she felt his arms closing around her, felt the despair, the loneliness, and the regrets wash out of him as he wept.

"I have a mother," he whispered. "I lie about her. But I have one."

"Jake, why haven't you told me? She should be here. I would have called her."

"She wouldn't have come," he said with certainty. "There's a lot of bad blood between us. She hates me."

"She can't hate you," Lynda said. "Mothers don't hate their sons."

"They do when their sons go years without seeing them, pretend they don't exist, and are too stingy to give a dime to help them out." He caught another sob, and his body shook with the force of it.

She pulled back to search his face. "But, Jake …"

"I'm being punished," he said, pointing to his injured face. "That's what all this is about. Before the crash, there was a lot of ugliness inside of me. Now I'm wearing it on the outside, too."

Lynda just held him tighter.

"I'll call your mother for you, Jake," she offered softly. "I'll talk to her. Does she know you're here?"

He shook his head. "She doesn't know anything about the crash. As far as she knows, I'm still living high, looking good, and trying to forget where I came from."

Someday she wanted to know just where that was, where Jake Stevens came from, but for now she was more concerned with where he was right now.

"Don't call her," he said. "I've got enough scars to last me a lifetime. I don't need any more."

"You need your mother, Jake. I'd give anything if mine were still alive and could be here with me one more time. There's so much I'd say to her."

"She *won't come*, Lynda."

"She needs to have the chance to decide that for herself."

"Fine, then," he said. "Call her. You'll see. She's the only Doris Stevens in Slapout, Texas. Just don't get your hopes up. Her tongue can slice right through you."

"I've survived worse," she whispered. "And so have you."

He crumpled in tears again and breathing a deep sob, shook his head viciously. "No, I haven't. I haven't survived. Not at all."

And as they clung to each other, Lynda searched for a way to make Jake see that it wasn't the end, it wasn't the worst, and he wasn't alone.

She would be here for him no matter how bad things got because in a strange way that she wasn't able to understand just yet, his despair had become her own. And she was determined to find a way to change it into joy.

May I speak to Doris Stevens?"

The woman who had answered the phone didn't respond but just put the phone down, and Lynda hoped that she had gone to get Jake's mother. It hadn't been easy to track her down. First Lynda had called information, only to find that they didn't have a listing for Doris Stevens, so she had tried the Slapout post office. The postal clerk knew Doris and had explained that she was listed in the phone book under her initials, H. D. Stevens. Graciously, she gave Lynda the number then told her to try Grady's Truck Stop if she wasn't home. That was where Doris worked, she said.

Now she waited, listening to the noise of the crowd in the background, and hoping that Doris would be able to hear her. She had practiced all the way home from the hospital what she would say, but now that the moment had come, she had forgotten all of it.

"Hello?"

Lynda's heart skipped a beat. "Is this Doris Stevens?"

"Yeah, who wants to know?"

"My name is Lynda Barrett. I live in St. Clair, Florida. Ms. Stevens, I've gotten to know your son, Jake. He's here and—"

"Whatever he's done, I had nothin' to do with it."

Lynda hesitated. "Ms. Stevens, why do you think he's done anything?"

"Because he's got a heart of ice, that's why. I ain't seen the man in eight years. He got to be a big-shot pilot, and now he's ashamed of me. Well, you know what? I don't care. I'm ashamed of him, too."

This was harder than Lynda had imagined. "Ms. Stevens, Jake's been in an accident. A plane crash."

"What?"

The voice came through louder, clearer now, and she imagined the woman clutching the phone tighter. "That's right. About three weeks ago."

"Three weeks?" She hesitated, and then in a softer voice said, "That's about when he called me. He didn't tell me nothin' about no plane crash."

Lynda didn't know what to say to that. Why would Jake have called her and not told her that he was lying in the hospital? "He was injured badly, Ms. Stevens. He has a bad back injury that has caused paralysis in his legs."

"He can't walk?"

"No. There is a possibility that the paralysis will go away, though. They think when the swelling goes down, the feeling may come back. But there's no guarantee. And he also had a severe cut to his face and lost an eye."

Doris muttered an expletive then asked in a wobbly voice, "So what do you want from me?"

The question took Lynda by surprise. "Nothing. I just thought you'd want to know that your son is in the hospital in a lot of pain. Ms. Stevens, he's absolutely alone. He apparently doesn't know many people here—"

"What is he doin' there, anyway? I thought he lived in Houston."

She couldn't believe that Jake hadn't told his mother he was moving. "He was in the process of moving here when this happened. Ms. Stevens—he needs you."

She laughed then, a bitter, cold laugh. "Oh, yeah? Well, where was he when I needed him? Huh?"

"I don't know."

"Yeah, well, neither do I. Is there a lawsuit involved here? Is he suin' somebody?"

Until now, the thought had never occurred to her that Jake could sue her. Deciding against telling her that it was her plane and that she had been in the same crash, she said, "No, not that I know of."

"Then there's no money involved?"

"No. I haven't heard him suggest suing, at all."

"Then there's no need in my comin', is there?"

She didn't want to believe that Jake's mother was mercenary enough to see dollar signs in Jake's accident, so she chose to believe that it was a question of how she would finance the trip. "Uh—if you don't have the money, I'd be happy to send you a plane ticket."

The woman hesitated. "I wouldn't have a place to stay."

"I'd pay for your hotel, too," she said. "Will you come, Ms. Stevens?"

Again a pause. "What's the weather like there this time of year?"

"It's fine. Nice."

"Nice enough to go to the beach?"

She closed her eyes. Surely she wasn't looking at this as an opportunity to take a free vacation. "I don't know, Ms. Stevens."

"How close are you to Disney World?"

Reality began closing in on her. "I would think your time would be spent with Jake. Don't you care about his condition?"

"Let me tell you something," the woman spat back. "I raised that ingrate by myself with no help from anybody. I was there for him until the day he skipped town without lookin' back. When I was strugglin' and needed a hand, he wasn't there for me. So now, when he can't walk and can't see, I'm supposed to welcome him back with open arms so I can wait on him hand and foot? What's in it for me?"

For a moment, Lynda was quiet. "Maybe the knowledge that you did everything you could for your son?"

"I already did that," she said. "I don't owe him nothin' more."

Slowly Lynda set the phone back in its cradle and rested her face on her palm. No wonder he had lied about his mother. No wonder he hadn't visited her. Their relationship was an endless cycle of blame and selfishness and anger, a cycle that Lynda wasn't wise enough to break.

But what would she tell Jake? That his mother wouldn't come unless there was a monetary settlement involved or a trip to Disney World or nice weather for sunbathing?

How could a mother have such contempt for her son?

"Are you crying, Miss Lynda?"

Lynda turned around and saw Brianna standing in the doorway, looking up at her with big, curious eyes.

"Come here."

Brianna came slowly toward her. "Why are you crying?"

"Because somebody just made me real sad." She pulled Brianna into her lap, and the child kept gazing at her.

216

"Did somebody hit you?"

"No."

"Did they try to take you?"

She realized then that Brianna was going down the list of things that made her sad, and Lynda felt a twofold rush of sorrow. Closing her eyes against the tears, she dropped her face to Brianna's crown. "No, Brianna, no one tried to take me. I'm sad for someone else."

"So they won't have to be?" she asked, as if trying to understand this new concept of surrogate sorrow.

She smiled. "Something like that."

Brianna laid her head against Lynda's chest, as if she knew that sitting still might be of some comfort to her, and finally, she looked up at her again. "Do you like to color?"

Lynda smiled. "Yeah. Yeah, I do."

Brianna slid out of her lap. "Come on, then."

And Lynda realized that the child's simple therapy might be just what she needed right now.

CHAPTER FORTY-SIX

It felt like a burning, tingling sensation, just on the outside of his big toe. Nothing to get excited about.

But Jake got excited anyway. He jerked the sheets off his legs and peered down at his feet.

He'd been so exhausted when he'd gotten back from rehab today—where they'd forced him to work despite his indifference—that he had almost forgotten the scar and his eye. Maybe now he was just imagining the sensation. Maybe he just wanted to feel it so badly.

But it felt real, and his surprise gave birth to a fragile hope.

He started to call the nurse but changed his mind. What if he told the nurses, and they assured him it was just a side effect from the traction they'd had him on in the rehab room? What if he found out that it was nothing?

He focused all his concentration and every ounce of his energy into that big toe, willing it to move. But it lay still, dead, not getting the messages his brain was sending.

Was this no different than the pressure he felt when he was touched or pulled? Was it without meaning?

He heard Lynda's familiar rat-tat-a-tat-tat knock on the door and called, "Come in."

She came into the room all cheer and sunshine, and he debated whether to tell her what he felt.

"Hi," she said.

"Hi." He kept staring at his foot.

"How'd your rehab go today?"

"Good."

She followed his gaze to his toe. "What are you looking at, Jake?"

He didn't answer for a moment then finally looked up at her. "My toe," he said. "I've been feeling some pain in it. Kind of a burning."

She caught her breath and with wide eyes, went to stand at the foot of his bed. Touching the toes on both feet, she asked, "Can you feel this?"

His eyes grew wider. "Just on that toe. But I feel you touching that toe!"

She was trying to hold back her excitement, just as he was. "Have you tried to move it?"

"I was trying," he said. "It hasn't budged."

"Well, try again. Come on, Jake. Move it."

Silence fell over the room as he found his concentration again, and as though he could telekinetically move the toe, he stared down at it.

"Was that a twitch?" she asked finally. "I thought I saw a twitch!"

Jake wasn't sure. He tried again, and this time the toe moved an eighth of an inch.

"You did it!" Lynda cried, jumping up and slinging a fist through the air. "Oh, Jake, you moved it!"

He started to laugh, and she ran around the bed and hugged him.

"Call somebody before I forget how," he said.

With trembling hands, she found the button that called for the nurse.

It was definitely cause for celebration, Dr. Randall said when he finally made it to the hospital to examine Jake. It might mean that Jake could get his legs back.

But for all his newfound hope, Jake couldn't escape the doctor's qualifier that it didn't mean he'd get all his feeling back, or get movement in his leg or the rest of his foot. But this was something.

Torn between exhilaration and frustration, he asked Lynda to take him out of the hospital.

Glad to be asked for anything, she wheeled him outside where night had already descended, and the stars lit up the sky with a magnificent brilliance. Jake leaned his head back and looked up, taking it all in.

Lynda had gotten quiet, and he could see that something was on her mind. Maybe there was something she didn't want to tell him. When they got to a small park near the hospital, she locked his wheels and sat down on a bench facing him.

He met her eyes squarely. "What's wrong, Lynda?"

"Nothing. Why do you think something's wrong?"

"I could read it in your mood swings today," he said. "As happy as we got, something kept bringing you down."

He studied her face for a moment. "She won't come, will she?"

Lynda couldn't deny it. "No."

He took in a deep, ragged breath. "It's okay," he said, trying not to look crestfallen. "I told you it would be that way. What did she say?"

He saw the turmoil on her face and realized that it must be bad, too bad for her to relate to him. He almost wished he hadn't asked. "She's just ... busy right now."

Jake looked into the breeze and thought about the last time he'd seen his mother. He wondered if she had changed, or if the years of hard work, cigarette smoke, and nights spent in the truck stop flirting with the patrons had aged her. "When you told her about my injuries ... What did she say?"

"She was shocked," Lynda said. "She said you had called her since the crash, and you didn't say anything about it."

"She didn't seem all that receptive." He could see by her face that she knew what he meant. "There's a lot of water under our bridge, Lynda," he went on. "I haven't been proud of where I came from, and I haven't been particularly proud of her. I've said and done some hateful things. She has a reason for hating me."

As he spoke, he felt exposed, open, as transparent as he'd ever been in his life. But Lynda had already seen farther into him than anyone else ever had. "I think you're changing, Jake."

He breathed a laugh. "Oh, yeah? You think so?"

She smiled. "I don't think the old Jake would ever have admitted guilt."

"Well, I've had a lot of time to think about it over the last few weeks."

Her smile faded. "Have you been thinking about going home, Jake?"

He averted his eyes again and studied the trunk of the tree next to him. "Home where? I've thought of going back to Texas to finish my therapy there. There are people there I could probably stay with. That is, if they aren't too repulsed by me. I haven't even told them I've been hurt."

She wasn't sure why that disappointed her. "Is that what you want to do?" she asked.

He sighed. "I don't know. It honestly feels like I'm somebody else now. Like the Jake Stevens they all knew is dead. And here I am in his useless shell, trying to figure out who I am now. And nothing against all my friends, but most of them are kind of—self-centered. I can't see them wanting to help out an invalid."

"You're not an invalid," she said. "You're just in transition. You need time."

Something about that sweet declaration made his heart soften, and he smiled at her. She leaned forward, her big, round eyes drilling into his, and he wondered how she had managed to make him risk more honesty with her than he'd ever risked with anyone else. Even himself.

"I had an idea," she said. "But I don't know how you'll feel about it."

"What?"

She averted her eyes and studied her hands. "I've been staying at my father's house, and there's a garage apartment there that used to be mine. It's got a small kitchen, a refrigerator, and a bathroom, and it's pretty comfortable." She made herself meet his gaze. "I was thinking that ... maybe when they release you ... you could stay there. I could take care of all your meals, transport you back and forth to the hospital for your therapy every day, and help you in whatever way you needed. But you'd still have your privacy."

A lump the size of Wyoming formed in his throat, and he gaped at her, not believing that he'd heard her right. "I couldn't, Lynda. That's too much of an imposition. You're recovering, too. The last thing you need is somebody like me in your way."

"You won't be in the way. You'd have your own place. You won't have to worry about rent or food or anything for a while. I have someone else staying with me, a client of mine and her daughter. She's hiding from her abusive ex-husband until we can get into court. Between his shenanigans and the stuff that's already happened to me, we're both a little paranoid. It might be nice to have a man around the house."

The word "man" shook him, for he hadn't thought of himself as a man in a long time. "Not that I'd be of any use if anything happened," he said. "I guess I could run over somebody in my wheelchair, but it's not like I can defend you."

She smirked. "I don't know, Jake. You were pretty dangerous the other day. If you had something to throw—"

He took it as it was intended and chuckled softly.

"Besides, we don't need defending," she said. "Her ex doesn't know where we are, and the guy who was after me is still in jail. Your presence will just lend a little stability."

She didn't mean it, he thought. She was just saying that to make him feel needed, but he had to admit he appreciated it. She was giving him the option of keeping his dignity, his masculinity. She was offering him a home, temporary though it might be.

It was better than any other option he had.

She saw his reticence. "Come on, Jake. Say yes if for no other reason than to appease my conscience. It was my plane that crashed. Let me make it up to you as much as I can."

Tears came to his eyes, and he struggled to hold them back. "You don't have to buy my forgiveness," he whispered after a moment.

"That's not what I'm doing," she said. "The truth is neither your feet nor your hair needs washing, so I can do this instead."

"What?"

She smiled. "Never mind. Just say yes."

He sighed. "You're going to regret it."

"No," she said with a smile. "I don't think I will."

CHAPTER FORTY·SEVEN

The sound of his heels echoed through the old, musty judicial building as Keith checked the sign on each door, looking for the county clerk's office. He was tired of waiting. He'd spent most of several days watching the parking lot at Lynda's law firm, but she hadn't been there yet. Then he'd tried to get her forwarding address by sending something to her old address with a note to the post office to return it with her new one. But the address they had returned was to a post office box. He had even tried staking out the post office, but he hadn't been able to be there all the time, and if she'd checked her box, he'd missed her.

But he wasn't stupid. He had resources, and he knew how to use them. And he was going to start with public records. It had been worth the drive to St. Petersburg where the county records were kept, and though he didn't know what he was looking for, he was sure he'd know when he found it. His goal for now was to find every public record that existed on Lynda or her family. Something there would have to give him a clue.

He found the office and went into the dimly lit room that looked as if it could use a good electrician to update the wiring. A young couple was there getting a marriage license. Smirking, he leaned on the counter and thought of telling the poor guy to save his fifteen bucks and run like the wind. But the kid was young—too young to be reasoned with, old enough to make mistakes that would ruin his life. Just like Keith had been when he and Paige had stood there, giggling like this couple and anticipating the life they were planning together.

But that was before he'd learned what a shrew she was.

Now, on the battleground of their marriage, his daughter had become the spoils. Didn't Paige realize what her obstinance was going to cost her? Didn't she understand that when he got through with her, she'd have nothing left? Least of all Brianna.

The couple blushed over their finished license, and Keith flashed them a saccharine, congratulatory smile then winked at the lady behind the desk. "Cute kids," he said as they left the room.

"Yes, they are," she said. "I hope everything works out for them."

"I'm sure it will," he said. "We've been married for ten years now, and we're as happy as the day we came in here to get our license."

"Oh, that's nice."

"Yes. Course, I realize that not everybody is as lucky as I am, but we work at it, you know? Teamwork. It's the only way."

He could have sworn her eyes were twinkling as she smiled up at him. "That's so rare these days. Frankly, I worry about every couple that comes in here. I pray for them."

"Good for you," he said. "Good for you."

She cleared off the papers she'd had them sign and stuck them in the appropriate bins. "Now, what can I do for you?"

"I need to look up some public records."

"All right," she said, grabbing a form out of another bin. "Just fill this out, and I'll show you how to find them. What exactly are you looking for? A person or a property?"

"A person, but that might lead me to real estate."

"That's fine. And what is the last name of the person you're looking for?"

He almost gave her Lynda's last name then realized that there had been too much publicity about the attempts on her life. "Barnett," he said finally. "Frank Barnett."

"All right," she said, taking the form back and checking the fake signature. "Just follow me. We have A through J in this room."

She took him to a huge room full of volumes of public records for Pinellas County and led him to a computer where she showed him how to find the name of the person he was looking for, see the list of documents the county had on that person, and determine what volume the record was in.

He thanked her profusely then waited as she left him alone.

The moment he typed in Lynda's name, two listings came up. Quickly he jotted down where to find her birth certificate and the documents pertaining to her property. There was no record of a marriage license or a divorce or any judgments against her or any other documents.

Leaving the computer, he found the book with her birth certificate and flipped through it until he found her name. There she was.

As if he'd found some crucial bit of information, he stared down at it with a smile and quickly jotted down both parents' names and her birthdate in case he ever needed it.

The documents on her house would be useless now; the house was burned, so she wouldn't be going back. He went back to the computer and typed in her mother's name.

A list of records emerged, and he jotted down the number of the book that had records on her property. He scanned the list again, looking for anything else he could use and saw her death certificate.

Dead end, he thought, clearing the screen.

He punched in her father's name. Again, he jotted down property book and came across another death certificate.

Frustrated, he sat back in the chair.

All right, he told himself, *don't give up yet. There's got to be something here.*

Looking down at his note paper, he noticed a connection. One of the numbers on the list of Lynda's properties matched the book number for the property on both of Lynda's parents. Had she inherited their home? If so, it surely wasn't the one that had burned down — that one had been far too new and expensive.

He flew to that book, pulled it out, and shuffled through the pages until he came to what he was looking for — A house on the other side of town, bought forty years ago; ownership had been transferred to Lynda three months ago upon the death of her father!

He banged his fist on the table then waved it over his head in exhilaration. This was it! It had to be. She was staying in her father's home, and he had found her! Paige and Brianna were probably there with her!

He slammed the book shut but didn't bother to put it back. Quickly, he went back to the computer, cleared the screen so no one would link him to her, and headed out without another word to the clerk.

CHAPTER FORTY-EIGHT

It had been months since the garage apartment had even been opened and years since it had been used for more than storage. With Paige's help, Lynda cleaned all of the junk out of it then set about scrubbing. A thick layer of dust had settled over every piece of furniture, and the bedspread and sheets and curtains all smelled musty. She gathered them all up to wash while Paige vacuumed the mattress and couch, the recliner, and the carpet, which really didn't look so bad considering how old it was.

"Does this Jake person know about me?" Paige asked in a slightly troubled voice as she worked.

"Yes. I told him last night."

"Mmmm." She coiled the cord on the vacuum cleaner then got her bucket from Brianna, who was sitting in the empty bathtub, "scrubbing it" with a dry brush. "So you say he's paralyzed? He can't walk?"

"No, he can't. What's the matter, Paige?"

Paige shrugged. "I don't know." She started to say something, stopped then tried again.

"What is it, Paige? What's on your mind?"

Paige leaned back against a wall and looked down at her feet. "I was thinking. Maybe it's time we went on home."

"Home? Are you serious?"

"Well, yeah. I mean, Jake's coming, and you won't be alone any more."

"But Paige, what about Keith?"

Paige thought that over for a moment. "He's probably cooled down by now. His rages don't usually last that long. He's probably feeling real bad about what he did, and when he gets like that—sorry and all—he can be okay. Maybe I don't have to be afraid of him."

Lynda wanted to scream at her that she was being stupid, but if her time with Jake had taught her anything, it was that she had to learn diplomacy. "Paige, if you go back home and have any contact with him at all, it could ruin our case. And it could get you killed."

When Paige covered her face with her hand, Lynda stepped closer. Removing Paige's hand and making the young woman look at her, she said, "Paige, what's really wrong?"

"I don't know. Maybe I'm just homesick. And with Jake coming—I don't know; I'm just not very comfortable around men."

"But you weren't uncomfortable with Larry or Tony."

"I didn't have to be *alone* with them much. Besides, I knew they were protecting me."

"Well, think of Jake as protecting you, too. And you're not really going to be alone with him. I'll be here."

"Yeah, but you'll be going back to work soon." She caught herself and tried to rally. "I'm sorry. You're helping me, so you have every right to help him, too. It's awfully nice of you. I'm sure he needs help. I'll get over it."

"But will you get over it here or at home?"

Paige met Lynda's eyes, and Lynda saw the struggle there. "You'd hate me if I went back home, wouldn't you?"

"No, Paige, but I think *you* would hate you."

"But I'm not considering taking him back. Not at all. I just miss things being familiar."

Lynda sat down and studied the carpet for a moment, trying to find the right words. "Paige, familiarity has a lot of power. That's why you went back to Keith all those times before. It probably had a lot to do with familiarity, didn't it?"

Paige nodded.

"And if you let familiarity cause you to put yourself in danger again, don't you think that when—not if, but when—Keith shows up, he'll be able to convince you one way or another to take him back for that same familiarity?"

"Maybe, but—"

"Paige, he might take Brianna this time and go so far that you'd never see her again. The court date isn't that far off. He's bound to be getting desperate."

Paige's face changed, and she glanced into the bathroom at Brianna, who was singing the theme from "Barney." When she looked back at Lynda, she whispered, "You're right. Absolutely."

Lynda got up and faced Paige head on. "Paige, Jake's paralyzed. Why would you be worried about what he might do?"

"That's the crazy part. I know he won't hurt me if he's your friend, and I know he couldn't if he wanted to. But—men are so unpredictable to me. I never knew what to expect with Keith. Just when I thought I had all my bases covered, he'd show me that I didn't."

"You have them covered now, Paige. Right?"

Her sigh suggested she wasn't sure. "Maybe being around Jake is what I need now. Maybe he'll restore my faith in men."

Lynda wished she could say that was possible, but she wasn't so sure. "Well—he's a little scary-looking right now. He has a patch over his eye and a big scar down his cheek, and he's not the most pleasant person to be around because he's so angry about his injuries. But I've watched him change since I met him. In big ways. And he's going to keep changing. He'll have to if he's going to make it. But he'd never hurt you or Brianna. More likely, he'll keep absolutely to himself, and you won't see him at all except to take him meals."

Paige regarded Brianna, still sitting in the empty bathtub. "I guess I should realize how lucky I am," she said. "I have my legs, both eyes, and I have Brianna." She smiled and turned back to Lynda. "And I have you. So does he. Because of that, I promise to make him feel welcome here."

"Thank you, Paige. I knew I could count on you."

CHAPTER FORTY-NINE

Keith knew better than to drive down her street; it looked like a dead end. Instead, he parked his car a couple of blocks away in a small church parking lot and walked into the thick woods that lined one side of the street, except where it had been cleared for houses. There were only about three houses on the street, two right at the entrance and one secluded down at the dead end. He worked his way quietly through the woods, trying not to be seen.

There was someone outside at the first house he passed, a man working in the garden, so he assumed that wasn't the house. He crept forward until he had a clear view across the street and read the numbers on the opposite house. That wasn't it, either.

So it must be the one at the far end of the street. He stole through the trees and came up to the cyclone fence that defined the property. But there was no sign of any of them. He needed to get around front to see if he could identify one of their cars.

He was just about to risk stepping out of the woods when the back door opened. Keith froze.

He saw his little girl bounce out, and his heart melted.

It had been so long since he'd seen Brianna happy. The last few times she'd been screaming her lungs out, after all those ideas Paige had put into her head about him. But once he got her, he would manage to erase those ideas and turn them back on Paige. Then Brianna would be just as happy with him as she was now without him.

He trembled with anticipation as she walked out into the yard, talking to her doll as she went, and he poised himself to act the moment she came close enough. He could reach over the fence, grab her, and have her out of here before Paige even knew she was gone.

He wished he'd brought some candy or something to keep her quiet until they got away.

But then Paige came out with a broom and started sweeping the back porch. That was her, always cleaning, as if she couldn't stand to sit still.

Well—too bad. He would grab Brianna anyway, whether Paige saw or not. Maybe he could get out of there before she could get to the phone—

No. That was ludicrous. He'd be arrested before he got his car started. And he'd probably wind up in jail. This time, McRae would probably wash his hands of him, and he wouldn't have an advocate in court, and that lady lawyer would convince the judge that he was dangerous.

Quietly, he sat down on the ground behind a bush and watched, waiting for Paige to go back in and for Brianna to come near the fence. His only hope was to take her when Paige wasn't watching, so he'd have a head start in getting away.

But that wasn't going to happen today.

Paige said something to the child, and Brianna turned and frolicked in behind her mother. The door closed.

He didn't move. Maybe they would come back out. Maybe Brianna would stray out here alone....

He heard another door close, one he couldn't see from this position and then a car door. In seconds, he heard the car in the driveway starting.

They were leaving!

Jumping up, he ran through the trees back toward his car parked at the little church, hoping to catch up with them and follow them. But by the time he was behind the wheel, they were nowhere in sight.

Cursing his luck, he slammed his hand against the wheel. Didn't it always happen this way? Fate just kept working against him.

But it wouldn't forever. Sooner or later, something had to give. He thought of the possibilities, now that he knew where they were living. He couldn't set this house on fire because Brianna might be hurt. And if he installed the car bomb here, Brianna might be in the car or nearby when it blew up. No, he couldn't do anything that might put her in danger again. But he could watch the house; he could follow Lynda and, when she got to where she was going, fix a little surprise in her car. Or, if he kept watching, sooner or later Paige would take her eyes off Brianna and he could grab her. Either way, when the chance came, he would be there.

Time was running out, and he was getting anxious. But he was several steps ahead of the game already.

And he intended to win.

CHAPTER FIFTY

The morning Jake was to be released Lynda gave the garage apartment one final inspection. It was clean now, and she'd moved things around to accommodate his wheelchair. While the room wasn't as luxurious as he was probably used to, it was certainly better than a hospital room. She sat down in her father's recliner, which she'd asked Larry to move out here for Jake, and looked around at the small rooms her father had so lovingly built for her.

She had never forgotten the ribbon-cutting ceremony her parents had had for her the day she'd moved into the room. Her father had made a little speech in which he told her that while this room signified her independence from her parents, its proximity to the house symbolized that no matter how independent she grew or how far away she moved, she would always belong to them. Always.

As she sat here now, breathing the familiar scents and absorbing the warm colors and textures, she missed her parents. As much as she'd wanted to believe she was independent when she'd moved into this room, she had been far from it. Her parents had helped her to take her first leap out of the nest gracefully. They had made it easy for her, until she'd learned to fly on her own.

In many ways, Jake was like she had been then. She would have to teach him that he could be independent and that he could make it on his own. But she also wanted to teach him who he belonged to. And she surprised herself—she who had been so long without darkening the doorway of a church—with the fervency of her desire that Jake understand this.

She bowed her head and whispered a heartfelt prayer that this room would be blessed and that God would change Jake here. Then she got out the Bible she had bought especially for him and slipped it into the drawer of the end table beside the recliner. She wouldn't mention it; he would have to discover it for himself. She only hoped she would be able to help him understand the truth of its message.

She couldn't preach to him or force him. All she could do was pray for him.

Jake's life—both physical and spiritual—was in God's hands.

Allie walked beside Jake's wheelchair as he left the hospital, letting him push the wheels to move it along. He couldn't believe they were sending him home like this, still unable to walk. Oh, Allie had taught him how to function well enough in day-to-day activities, and now that he could sit all the way up and had this smaller, more maneuverable chair, he was much more capable. But he still didn't like it. Hospitals are supposed to heal people, not teach them how to cope with their brokenness.

But the alternative—*staying* in the hospital—was worse. He'd rather be going away somewhere, even if it wasn't home.

Lynda had brought the car to the front entrance. She had dressed up for the occasion, he saw, and had pulled her hair up in a loose chignon. He wondered why she'd bothered.

"Do you need help getting in, Jake?" she asked.

He wasn't sure whether he did or not but decided not to accept it anyway. "I can do it," he said, sidling his chair up to the open car door.

"You can do it, Jake," Allie said, not offering a hand to help. "Just use your arms and your stomach."

He could feel them all holding their breath as he got his arms into position then slid his body onto the car seat.

As if he'd just completed some Olympic feat, they all congratulated him. He felt like a toddler who'd just gone to the potty by himself, and the idea of such pathetic enthusiasm worsened his mood.

Lynda closed his door and got into the driver's side, but Allie came to his window. Jake lowered it.

"Just because you're going home doesn't mean you can neglect your therapy, Jake. I want you back here at nine tomorrow, and Lynda can just plan to leave you for six hours or so. We'll see if we can get some more of your toes to burn."

He smiled in spite of himself; he liked the sound of that. "I'll be here."

And as they drove away from the hospital, Jake wasn't sure whether to consider it a beginning or an ending. To him, it seemed as though he left the old Jake back there in the morgue, and he didn't yet know who the new Jake was.

CHAPTER FIFTY-ONE

A butterfly lit on Keith's shoulder, and he waved it away and peered between two bushes to the yard where Brianna played. Paige had set up a little tea party for her, and she had all her dolls in attendance. He smiled as she talked aloud to her friends and herself like a little princess to her courtiers.

But as always, Paige was right there, hovering over her. Calculating the distance to his car, which he'd parked on the closest street behind Lynda's house through the woods, he tried to decide whether he should chance jumping the fence and grabbing Brianna. Sweat broke out on his forehead, and he wiped it on his sleeve. He would have the advantage of surprise. Paige would probably be stunned long enough for him to get Brianna. It would probably take less than ten seconds to get back over the fence and maybe another thirty to get back to his car. By the time Paige stopped screaming and got to the phone, he would have blended into the cars on the main road a mile or so away.

The butterfly flitted across the fence and lit in some wild-flowers growing in an old, untended garden. Keith watched Brianna laughing with one of her dolls and then pouring more invisible tea and offering it a cup.

He heard a car pull up in the front, and his heartbeat accelerated. "Lynda's home," Paige said as she got up. "I'll be in front, okay, Brianna?"

Brianna nodded indifferently as Paige went around between the garage and the house, and a slow smile came to Keith's lips. Was Brianna really alone?

He straightened and stepped through the bushes, watching his child with hungry, anxious eyes. He watched the butterfly flit over to the table where she sat.

"Mommy, it's a butterfly!" she said, her voice soft so that she wouldn't frighten it away.

It fluttered off, and Brianna got up and followed it. It lit in a piece of grass, and she bent over, trying to coax it onto her finger, but it flew a little further. As if it were in cahoots with Keith, it led her closer, closer, closer to the fence until she was almost close enough to reach.

Keith stepped into her view and touched the fence, whispering, "Brianna."

She looked up at him, stunned. The butterfly flew away.

His heart hammered, and his hands shook; there was so little time before Paige came back.

"Come closer, honey," he whispered, leaning over the fence. "Come give Daddy a kiss."

Her bottom lip began to tremble, and she backed away, farther out of his reach.

"Brianna, I said to come here," he said more firmly. "Now."

She started to cry and looked around for her mother, who was nowhere in sight.

He was getting angry now. This wasn't working out like he'd planned. Gritting his teeth, he whispered, "Brianna, I told you to come here right now! I'm your daddy!"

He started to lunge over the fence, but Brianna screamed and lit out across the yard.

Cursing, Keith realized he'd gone too far; he'd never catch her before she made it to the front yard. Afraid of being caught, he tore back through the woods to his car.

Lynda had just gotten Jake into the apartment and introduced him to Paige when they heard the scream.

Paige dashed outside and found Brianna almost to the garage apartment already, shrieking.

"What is it, honey? What's wrong?"

"Daddy! Daddy! He's gonna take me!" she screamed.

Paige stepped back into the doorway, looking helplessly at Lynda. "No, honey. Daddy can't get you here."

"It's him!" Brianna screamed.

"It's me, isn't it?" Jake asked. "She saw me coming in, and I scared her."

Paige wasn't sure. "Honey, that's not Daddy. That's a nice man named Jake. Remember I told you he was going to live here? Remember we got the room fixed up for him?"

Hiccuping her sobs, Brianna refused to look up.

Paige looked apologetically at Jake. "She's — terrified of men. If you knew her father you'd know why. I'm so sorry."

"It's all right," he said. "I make a pretty scary first impression."

"I'll take her in," Paige said and quickly hurried back toward the house.

The silence in their wake was palpable, and Lynda turned back to Jake, trying to find the words that would make him feel less like an intruder. "Not exactly the welcome I had planned for you. I'm sorry, Jake."

He tried to take it philosophically. "Hey, I told you I'd frighten little kids. It's no surprise. Look, if this is gonna be a problem, they were here first."

"It'll be all right," Lynda assured him. "She's just been through an awful lot lately. Her father tried to fight her out of Paige's arms at the courthouse just a few days ago. It was terrifying to her. It's not the way you look, Jake; it's the fact that you're a man."

But Jake wasn't buying it. "It's okay, Lynda. Really, I can handle this."

She sighed. "We're having dinner at seven. Paige has been doing the cooking. She made a special dinner just for you."

"Maybe I'd better just eat here."

"Out of the question. You have to have dinner with us tonight."

"It might spoil your appetite," he said sardonically. "That is, if it doesn't send the kid into hysterics again."

"She'll be all right," Lynda said. "Come on. We all need to get used to each other."

"Bet you never dreamed you'd have a houseful of wounded souls, did you?"

238

"Recovering souls," she amended with a smile. "And I couldn't be happier to have all of you here. It's about time I had someone besides my secretary in my life." It seemed like so long ago that they'd had the argument in the plane about the emptiness in both their lives, but Jake remembered and smiled slightly.

She went to the portable intercom she had bought just for him. "I haven't had the phones hooked up yet. I'll get someone here eventually, I guess. I'm just a little jumpy about having strangers here. Anyway, if you need anything, just press this button, and I'll hear you in the house."

"I won't need anything."

"Well, the kitchen's stocked, the refrigerator's full, there are towels in the bathroom.... Oh, and I had some special rails put into the tub, so you shouldn't have any trouble getting in. I can't think of anything else."

"It's real comfortable, Lynda," he said softly. "Thank you."

Her smile was genuine. "I'll see you at seven, Jake. And if you don't show up, I'm coming after you."

Brianna was still crying when Lynda went back into the house. Paige held her close and rocked her, but the child hadn't calmed down at all. "Is she all right?" Lynda asked.

"She's scared to death," Paige said. "She's shaking worse than she was at the courthouse."

Lynda sat down next to them and stroked the tiny child's hair. "Do you think it was Jake?"

"I don't know, Lynda. I think she must have caught a glimpse of him after he got out of the car. She probably thought he was Keith for a split second, and it freaked her out."

"Brianna, were you afraid of that man we were with?"

Brianna hiccuped another sob. "It was Daddy."

"No, honey," Lynda said. "That was Jake. And he might look a little scary with that patch over his eye and that wheel chair, but he's a really nice man. You're going to like him."

But Brianna was still trembling and crying softly, and Paige tried to loosen the child's clutch so she could see her face. "Honey,

239

you didn't finish your tea party. Do you want to go out and get your dolls?"

"No!" Terror twisted the child's face, and she threw her arms more tightly around Paige's neck. "Daddy's there!"

Paige sighed with frustration and glanced at Lynda. "No, he's not, sweetheart. That's just Jake, and we have to be nice to him because he needs our help."

But the child couldn't be convinced. "I'll go out and get her dolls, Paige," Lynda said. "She'll be all right. She just has to get to know him."

"Yeah," Paige said, though her voice lacked conviction. "Look, we'll give it a try, but if she goes off the deep end when he comes over for dinner tonight, I think I'll just take her to McDonald's or something."

"Of course," Lynda said. "I don't want her to be afraid."

She went outside, feeling more despondent than she had hoped to feel on Jake's homecoming day. She gathered up the dolls then dropped down wearily on the porch swing with her arms full.

What was she going to do? The last thing Jake needed was for someone to be afraid of him, reinforcing the fears he had of being too repulsive to go out in public.

And the last thing Brianna needed was more terror in her life. They had all been through enough. Lynda just wondered when the ripples of all this tragedy would finally settle down.

In the apartment, Jake rolled around in his chair, unpacking the few belongings he'd brought with him from the hospital. Lynda had already brought over most of his things in the past few days, and they had been all neatly put away.

Quietly, he opened each drawer in the big room, exploring the contents, taking mental inventory of where she'd put his socks, his shirts, his underwear. Then he came to the end table with the Bible.

He smiled as if he had expected as much but closed the drawer without taking it out.

He rolled to the window and looked out at the driveway, to the red Porsche that Lynda had moved here from the hospital just yesterday. It had been well protected; there wasn't a scratch on it.

Rolling to the door, he went outside, hoping the child wasn't anywhere near a window; he didn't want to frighten her again. But he needed to get to his car, to smell the leather of the seats, feel the wheel in his hands....

He rolled down the driveway, opened the driver's door, and aligned his chair so that he could pull himself into the seat.

It felt different than he remembered—cramped, tight, but he put his hands on the wheel nonetheless and imagined himself driving through town that day he'd gone to the airport. He'd been on top of the world. He hadn't realized then how far he had to fall.

But it wasn't the car that was different now. *He* was different.

And now he couldn't drive this car. He might never be able to again. Even if he could by some miracle have it redesigned so that a paraplegic could drive it by hand, it wasn't big enough to fit his wheelchair into. Besides that, it was a look-at-me car, a car that screamed that an eligible bachelor was inside, looking for a good time.

He didn't want anyone to look at him now, and he didn't feel so eligible any more, and he had more important things on his mind lately than having a good time.

Like an old girlfriend who didn't fit into his life anymore, the car felt uncomfortable, awkward, useless.

Grief washed over him, grief at the things he was leaving behind. The car, the job, the fast friends, the money ...

And what was left of him was something he couldn't quite relate to, something he couldn't quite identify.

"If I'd known I was going to be left with just my character," he whispered to no one, "I'd have worked harder at building some."

But there was none there, at least none that he could put his finger on. He was helpless and hopeless and heartless. And he didn't want to be any of those things.

Cursing, he pulled himself out of the car and back into the chair, slammed the door, and went back inside.

He should count his blessings, he told himself sardonically. At least he *had* a Porsche, even if he couldn't drive it. And a house-ful of great furniture, even though it was in storage and he had no place to put it. And a little black book full of names of women he couldn't call.

His anger faded as his despair grew, and he found himself grasping for the real positives, the ones that might add up to just a little bit of hope.

He was able to sit up.

He could still see out of one eye.

He could move his toe.

He had a temporary place to live.

Little things. But they were all he had. And he'd better get used to them, he thought, for he would probably never have the big things again.

CHAPTER FIFTY-TWO

When Brianna had cried herself to sleep, Paige laid her down on the couch and went to help Lynda prepare dinner. She watched as Lynda bustled around nervously, looking distraught, too preoccupied to notice Paige's help. Whenever Lynda passed the kitchen window, which looked out toward the garage apartment, she peered out, as if to catch a glimpse of Jake.

"What's wrong, Lynda?" Paige asked finally.

"Nothing," Lynda said. "Why do you think something's wrong?"

"Well, you've been awfully preoccupied."

Lynda stopped what she was doing and looked out the window again. "I saw him go out to his car and get into it," she whispered.

Paige frowned. "He can't drive—can he?"

"No. He just went out and sat in it for a while. You'd have had to know him before to understand. He loved that car. When we were in that plane knowing we were about to crash, he was actually worried about who would take care of his car."

"You were going to crash, and he was worried about his *car*?"

"Yeah. And it was so sad to watch him roll out there just to sit in it. Maybe I shouldn't have brought the car here."

Paige didn't know what to say. It seemed so silly to her to grieve over a car when there was so much else to mourn. "So—do you think he'll come over at seven?"

"I don't know," Lynda said. "I hope so. He needs to be around people."

"But the thing with Brianna—I wouldn't blame him if he stayed locked in there forever after that. That was so embarrassing."

"I still don't understand it," Lynda said. "I mean, he has that scar and everything, but it's not that bad."

"That's because you're used to it," Paige cut in. "We're not. It's the whole picture. The scar, the patch, the wheelchair. It's going to take some time."

"But he's still a man. Inside he's just like you and me. Just because of a scar on his face—"

"You're right," Paige said. "Absolutely right. But this isn't a rational thing. It kind of took me by surprise, and it obviously jolted Brianna. I'm ashamed of myself for saying that, Lynda, but I'm going to get over it. I'm sure once I get to know him I won't even notice those things."

Weary from the emotional toll the day had taken on her, Lynda sighed and dropped into a chair. "Maybe when he gets his artificial eye it'll be easier."

"Oh," Paige said, "I'm sure I'll get used to him before that."

"I mean other people," Lynda said. "I want him to be able to go out in public—to the store, to a movie, to church—without people staring at him." But Lynda knew that if it were up to Jake, he might not ever count himself healed enough to blend normally with the public.

"Does he go to your church?" Paige asked.

"No. In fact, I just met him the day of the crash."

"*Really?* All this time I thought the two of you had known each other forever. I mean, the way you kept visiting him, and the way you took him in—"

"No. He's all alone. He doesn't have anybody. You know, almost dying with somebody is quite an intimate experience. It bonds you somehow."

"Yeah." Paige smiled. "I've had that experience myself."

Lynda realized that she referred to the fire, and she smiled. "Yeah, you have, haven't you? Then you understand. I can't help caring about Jake. Even if he's totally opposite from me, and he's belligerent and moody." She went to stir the pot on the stove and then wiped her hands on a towel. "I have a theory about Jake. I think maybe God is refining him."

"What does that mean?"

"Do you know how they used to refine silver?" Lynda asked.

Paige laughed. "No, not that I recall."

"Well, I heard it in Sunday school a long time ago. The silversmith hammered the silver into little pieces and then melted them. And he stayed with it the whole time, making sure it wasn't damaged in the fire. But as the silver melted, the impure metals rose to the top. He removed it from the fire, scraped off the impurities, and saw a blurry image of himself in the silver. Then he put it back on the fire and did the whole thing again. He did it seven times, each time scraping off another layer of impurities, until he saw his clear reflection in the silver. God does that with us, too."

"Scrapes off the impurities?"

"Yes. But he also puts us through the fire. What you're going through with Keith is your fire, Paige. And what I'm going through. And what Jake's going through."

Paige tried to follow. "So you think he's making these things happen so he can get the impurities out of us?"

"Maybe he didn't *make* them happen, but he's using them," Lynda said. "And with each trial, we get stronger and purer. And he sees more of his reflection in us."

"But people don't always get closer to God when they suffer."

"True," Lynda said. "Sometimes we cling to those impurities, and we're impossible to refine. But I think God keeps working on us. And sometimes he has to take everything we've got to make us notice him."

Paige was quiet for a moment, and finally she looked up at Lynda. "Is that what you think he's done with Jake?"

Her eyes drifted to the window again. "I think that's what he's done with *me*," she whispered. "Whatever he's doing with Jake, that's between Jake and God. All I know is that whether God caused or allowed the crash to happen, it happened, and here we all are in this house together. And I don't think it's an accident."

Jake struggled to get himself into the tub and onto the bench that Lynda had left there for him so that he could take a shower. But once he got there and turned on the water, pleasure burst through him. He hadn't had a private shower since he'd gone into the hospital. An orderly had taken him into one in a wheelchair every day for the last couple of weeks, and he'd felt degraded and embarrassed to let a stranger help him with such intimate needs. Now he was on his own, and as difficult as it was, it was worth the effort.

Getting out, his hand slipped on the rail and he fell, but he quickly pulled himself back up into his chair. He could do this, he told himself. He could take care of himself. He didn't need nurses and aides and orderlies to wait on him hand and foot.

He rolled back into the bedroom and gathered his clothes from the drawer. Allie had been working with him to teach him to dress himself, but it was still difficult getting pants legs up, and putting the socks on was almost too much. He looked around, wondering where Lynda had put his Birkenstocks.

And then he felt it.

That burning sensation again, spreading *throughout* his toes and down the bottom of his foot!

He wiggled the toe that he'd managed to move the other day then concentrated on moving the other ones. For a moment, they resisted and just lay there, motionless. But he kept trying, kept focusing, kept watching—

His little toe twitched.

"Yes!" he shouted, feeling as if he could leap out of the chair and dance a jig on the coffee table. He moved the toe again and then with great effort, managed to bend the middle three toes slightly.

Tears welled in his eyes, and he looked up at the ceiling. "Thank you," he whispered brokenly. "Thank you."

He couldn't bear to put shoes on those feet, for he wanted to show Lynda what he could do. He glanced at the clock—almost seven. She probably wouldn't mind if he barged in a little early.

Humming a tune, he finished getting ready. Leaving his feet bare, he rolled out across the patio to one of the back doors of the house.

Lynda had seen him burst out of his apartment and race in his wheelchair across the concrete, and now, before she had even made it to the door, he was banging urgently.

She threw it open and saw the joy on his face. "I moved them," he said. "The other toes. I moved all of them. Look!"

She caught her breath and looked down at his bare feet and saw the infinitesimal twitch of his toes. A small movement but as significant as kicking the winning field goal in the Super Bowl. "Oh, Jake!" she said, throwing her arms around him. "Paige, come look! He's moving his toes!"

Paige came to the door and looked down at them, not sure what it meant. "Does this mean you'll be able to walk again?"

"It might," Lynda said.

"I'll walk," Jake told her. "I know I will. I'm gonna throw myself into my rehab and work with everything I've got."

"Do you have feeling in your other foot?" Paige asked.

"Not yet. But I will."

It was one of the first purely positive things Lynda had ever heard from Jake, so she didn't dash his hopes by reminding him that there were still no guarantees.

He came into the kitchen and closed his eyes as he breathed deeply of the smell of the turkey baking in the oven, the home-made dressing baking beside it, and the vegetables on the stove. "And to think I didn't believe in heaven. It was right here in this kitchen all along."

Lynda smiled. "Heaven smells a lot better than this," she said. "But I think you're gonna like it." She stirred the peas then turned back to him. "How are you doing over there? Is everything going all right?"

"I've hit a few rough spots," he said. "But all in all, it's good to be free of that hospital." He looked down at his toes again, wiggled them slightly and then threw his head back and laughed. "I can't believe this. I never thought I'd feel anything there again."

He saw Paige's face change from amusement to concern as she looked past him to the doorway, and quickly he followed her gaze. Brianna stood there, clutching her blankie to her cheek and looking sleepily into the kitchen.

For a moment, they all held their breath as she assessed Jake. "Who are you?" Brianna asked calmly.

He glanced up at Paige then back at the child. "I'm Jake," he said in as calm a voice as he could. He extended his hand gently, as if coaxing a deer to eat out of it. "Who are you?"

"Brianna," she said, taking his hand and shaking it. As she stepped closer, she regarded the patch on his eye. "Are you a pirate?"

He laughed. "No. I just hurt my eye, and I have to wear this until it gets better."

"Like a Band-Aid?"

Lynda smiled; Paige just looked confused.

"What is this?" Brianna asked, touching the wheel on his chair.

"It's a wheelchair," he said. "I hurt my legs, too, and I can't walk. So I ride around in this."

Brianna's eyes lit up. "Is it fun?"

He smiled. "Well—"

"Can I ride?"

He looked up at Paige, surprised, and a slow smile came to his face. "Well, sure." Patting his leg, he said, "Hop up."

Brianna climbed onto his lap, and he began to roll her around in circles. She giggled as if she had a new toy then looked up at him and pointed to the scar. "How'd you get your boo-boo?"

He stopped and looked at Lynda again, his smile fading. "I had a real bad cut."

"I have a Band-Aid if it hurts. A Garfield one."

He smiled down at her. "It's not so bad."

"Can we ride some more?"

It was as if he'd been validated, accepted by the world and by life; he did not, after all, repulse this little child. As he rode her into the living room, Lynda looked back at Paige.

"Well, what do you think of that?"

Paige shook her head. "Weird."

"Well, I'm grateful. Children are so resilient."

"And so unpredictable," Paige whispered. "I don't get it. She was petrified this afternoon."

"Well, maybe the nap did it. Maybe she was just irritable when she saw him, and he took her by surprise."

"Guess so," Paige said. "But I never would have dreamed she'd warm up to him this fast." She watched, flabbergasted, as he tipped the chair back, almost making Brianna fall out, and she clutched him tightly and giggled with delight.

That night, Lynda led Jake out onto the patio as Paige put Brianna to bed, and they sat side by side, looking out over the yard.

"I told you you weren't repulsive," she said with a smile.

"That sure was one quick turnaround. I'll never understand children."

"Who knows what set her off today? It doesn't really matter now, though." She caught him looking down at his foot, wiggling the toes again. "I think you've gotten more movement just in the last few hours."

"I have," he said. "And unless I'm imagining it, I'm starting to feel that burning on the bottom of my other foot."

"Really?" she asked. "Jake, maybe the swelling's going down. Maybe the traction's helping. Maybe—" Her voice trailed off as she saw him look distractedly out across the yard and rub his top lip with his finger. "What's wrong?"

"Do you think I'm getting my hopes up too high? I mean, it's such a little bit of feeling."

"It has to start somewhere."

"But what if it doesn't go any further? What if—"

"Hey—I was just starting to enjoy the positive, upbeat Jake. Give yourself a chance to be happy before you start knocking yourself down again."

His smile returned like a gift, and he started to laugh quietly. "Who would have thought?"

"What?"

"That day when I looked at your plane, who would have ever thought that we'd be sitting here, actually friends?"

"I sure didn't."

He raised his eyebrows. "Was I that bad?"

"Pretty bad," she admitted. "I knew your type."

"Yeah, well, you were probably right." He looked up at the stars sprinkled across the sky. "Do you think I'll ever look normal again?"

She smiled. "When you get your eye, Jake, you'll probably start knocking the ladies dead again. I dread it, actually. I hate to see you revert to your old self."

"My old self seems a long way away," he said softly. "I don't know if I'll ever find him again."

CHAPTER FIFTY-THREE

Keith was glad there were no street lights on this deadend street; the darkness gave him the perfect cover. Ever since he'd left Brianna that afternoon, he'd been watching his back, waiting for a uniformed car to squeal up behind him, lights flashing.

Why it hadn't happened he wasn't sure, but he knew he didn't have much more time. The court date was fast approaching, and with every day that passed, Lynda Barrett would find more and more evidence against him. Already she had all of the medical reports, and she probably had records of all of Paige's calls to the police. And McRae had warned him that she was getting depositions from neighbors who claimed to have witnessed things. The idiots ought to mind their own business instead of sticking their noses into things they didn't understand.

He was getting desperate either to take Lynda out or grab Brianna and run. Either way would bring about the same result. All he wanted was his daughter.

He crept closer to the house and saw the cars in the driveway: a red Porsche that he recognized as belonging to that paralyzed pilot who was still in the hospital, Lynda's BMW, and Paige's old Chevette with new, unslashed tires. He smiled and laughed softly as he slipped his knife from his pocket. Releasing the blade, he started toward the car to slash the tires again — then caught himself. Not a good idea. If he didn't manage to get Brianna tonight, Paige would know he'd been here. As much as he'd like for her to know she hadn't bested him, he couldn't take that chance yet.

She'd figure that out for herself anyway—when he disappeared with Brianna.

He stole through the front yard, glancing from one window to another. All of the curtains were drawn, but he saw a light on in two of the rooms. One of them, he guessed, was the living room, but the other, dimmer one, probably came from a bedroom.

Knowing that Brianna always slept with a nightlight, he stole toward it and checked the screen to see if it was locked. It was, but it was plastic screen—easy enough to cut if he could be sure he wouldn't be heard. He wondered if the window was locked. From here, it looked as if it was.

The idea of cutting a section out of the glass big enough to slip his hand through and unlock the window was quickly discarded; the section he cut would likely fall in and shatter on the floor. No, he couldn't do anything that stupid.

Quietly he made his way to the front door, tested the knob, and found it locked. Not giving up, he went around to the side of the house, saw the garage apartment, and wondered whether it was empty. Maybe he could hide in there until he had the chance to catch Brianna.

He pulled a silver fingernail file from his pocket, preparing to try to pick the lock.

Voices.

He froze.

They were coming from the back patio just around the corner of the house. Two voices. A man's and a woman's.

For a moment he couldn't breathe, and he stood motionless like a bobcat caught in headlights, trying to decide which way to go.

Finally, he slipped around the garage apartment into the woods surrounding the fence. Once hidden by the bushes and shadows of the trees, he tried to figure out who was outside. But it was too dark; he could barely see the two forms on the patio. They were talking quietly. The woman was Lynda, he thought. Brianna must be inside, then.

But this man, whoever he is, certainly changed the equation a bit. Is he one of those cops who'd picked him up, here because Brianna had told them he'd been here today? Were they setting a trap for him?

Panic gripped him. Turning, he jogged silently back through the woods and came out on the block behind Lynda's house. Hurrying back to his car, he flipped through all the possibilities.

But by the time he'd settled in behind the wheel, he'd decided that he was just being paranoid. After all, even though he hadn't gone home today, they could have caught up with him at work if they'd been after him. Still, he'd better stay away for a few days, just until the heat died down.

Work, he grimaced, checking his watch. He had to get back before someone noticed he was gone. He needed to keep this job — at least until one way or another he managed to get Brianna. Then he could quit and flee the state before Paige caught up with them.

He would show her. He would show all of them. And somehow he'd make Paige sorry she'd ever filed those divorce papers.

CHAPTER FIFTY FOUR

I've got to get to the hospital fast!" Skidding his chair across the kitchen floor, Jake grabbed Lynda's purse and keys off of the table. "My left foot is burning!"

If not for the look of unadulterated joy on his face, Lynda would have been alarmed. "Jake, slow down. I'm coming."

"Didn't you hear me?" he asked. "The *other* foot. It's burning!"

She caught her breath and grabbed his chair, stopping him halfway down the driveway. He turned back to her impatiently. "Are you telling me that you have feeling in *both* feet now?" she asked.

"Yes!" he said. "Now come on! I want to get to the hospital."

Laughing, she grabbed her keys from him and ran to get into her car. By the time she'd started the engine, he was already inside, folding up his chair and slipping it in behind his seat. "Jake, do you think this means—"

"You bet it does. I'm gonna walk."

"But—are you sure?"

When he met her gaze, she realized how good hope looked on him. "As sure as I can be. I'm gonna walk, Lynda. I know it."

She was quiet as they drove to the rehab wing of the hospital, possibilities flitting through her mind. As they drove, she prayed that he wouldn't be disappointed, that his hopes wouldn't be shattered, that this new burning sensation did indeed mean that something was happening. Something permanent.

She got out of the car to help him when they reached the hospital, and when he was in his chair, he checked his watch. "You want me to give you a call when I'm finished?"

"That'll be fine," she said. "Do you think it'll be several hours?"

He nodded with certainty. "I'm gonna work today until either I stand on these feet or collapse trying."

"Jake, don't push it. You've come a long way. There's no need to get impatient now."

"Don't worry about it," he said with a grin and started inside. She caught up to him. "Don't you want me to take you in?"

"Nope," he said. "I can take it from here."

She stopped and watched him moving farther away from her. "Don't do anything stupid, okay?"

"Like what?"

"Like — throwing away your chair or something. You're going to give this time, aren't you?"

"As little as possible," he said.

She got back into the car and sat at the wheel for a moment, praying with all her heart that his expectations weren't in vain.

But Jake wasn't known for his patience or for his emotional resilience in the face of disappointment.

Buzz and Allie were pleased with the new sensations in his feet, but as Jake might have expected, his doctor was a little more reserved. "We've got to be patient, Jake," he said. "Don't expect too much too soon."

"But can't I expect anything at all, Doc? I mean, this all means *something*, doesn't it?"

Dr. Randall could have made a killing as a poker player, for his expression never betrayed a thought. "Well — your swelling has probably gone down significantly, which would help with the spinal shock. And the traction is, no doubt, helping with the compression. There's certainly cause for hope, Jake. But I have to emphasize that there are no guarantees."

"Give me odds, Doc. What are the chances that I'll walk again?"

The doctor wasn't about to go that far. "I can't do that, Jake. If I gave you terrific odds, and this is as much feeling as you ever get back, you'd never forgive me."

"But if you were inclined to give me odds, you're saying they'd be terrific?"

The doctor laughed. "I didn't say that."

"But they *are* terrific, aren't they?"

"They're hopeful, Jake. They're better than they were when you came in. But there still are no guarantees."

"Yeah, well, I can live with that," Jake said. "I've been through enough in the last few weeks to know that nothing comes with guarantees. Not life, not health, nothing. In fact, *you* could walk out of here right now and meet with a terrible accident and never walk again. So essentially, you and I have the same guarantee."

Dr. Randall smirked. "Thank you, Jake, for pointing that out to me. I appreciate it."

"No problem. I give as good as I get."

Dr. Randall laughed again and patted Jake's leg. Jake thought he felt it.

"Allie and Buzz are putting you in the pool today. It should be a nice change of pace."

"What will that do?" Jake asked. "Increase circulation? Help with motor coordination?"

"Well, it does a number of things. Today you'll just float and do some resistance exercises with your arms. The lack of gravity sometimes makes it easier for people to stand when they're ready, but you're not ready for that yet. We'll just take it a step at a time."

But Jake decided he *was* ready. When they took him to the pool and moved him from the chair into a harness seat that would lift him mechanically and lower him into the water by a chain, he saw the parallel bars in the pool and immediately knew what they were there for. People used them to balance ... to stand ...

To walk.

The water felt like liquid heaven, and as he slid into it, he let his upper body relax. Allie helped him float then ordered him to push his arms against the water.

She stood waist deep, and he tried to determine where the water would have come on him. He was six-two, and she was only five-seven or so. If it came halfway up her ribcage, it was probably waist deep for him.

He kept at the arm exercises the doctor had told him about for as long as he could but didn't want to tire himself out. He would need his arm muscles when he stood. "Can we go to the parallel bars?" he asked Allie finally.

Grinning, she shot Buzz a look. "Jake, we were just going to float today."

"Come on, Allie. Just let me see what my feet will do without gravity."

"I say we take him over there," Buzz said.

Allie's grin grew more mischievous. "Truth is, I have been wondering just how much function you might have in those feet."

"Then let's go."

They helped him over to the bars, and Jake grabbed one on each side of him. The weight of his legs made them float to the bottom, and for the first time since the accident, he was in a standing position, upright, his height towering above Allie and even above Buzz.

"Can you feel your feet touching the bottom?" Allie asked.

He barely felt the smooth bottom of the pool and looked down at his limp legs. "Sort of."

"Now, see if you can let your weight rest on your legs. Use your gluteus," Buzz said. "That's the trick. You have to hold your torso up with your glutes."

He felt his face reddening as he put every ounce of concentration he had into tightening his gluteals, and he looked down at his body. His legs weren't taking the weight, and his stomach was trying to arch outward. He tightened more and felt his body aligning more normally, but it was still only his arms that held him up. His legs were useless.

But Allie and Buzz didn't see the futility of it, and he saw that they were pleased by the smiles on their faces as they checked the alignment of his legs and feet to his torso.

"This is good, Jake," Buzz said, standing in front of him. "Real good. You have the muscular strength to stand, even if your legs aren't cooperating."

"What good are the muscles if I can't use them to do what I want?"

"You *will* be able to get them to do what you want, Jake. It's happening a little at a time, but we're seeing a lot of progress. So are you, and you know it."

He let his arms relax a little, and his body collapsed into the water. Allie caught him.

Defeated, he let her pull him into a float, but he feared the weight of his disappointment would drown him completely. And he almost didn't care if it did.

Something was wrong. It wasn't like Brianna not to want to go outside. But since the day Jake had moved in and Brianna had run in screaming that her daddy was trying to get her, she had absolutely refused to set foot through the back door, with or without her mother. Paige was getting frustrated; they'd been too cooped up in the house, and she wanted Brianna to get some fresh air.

"Honey, why can't we go out there? I'll be right there with you. There's a fence and everything. Nothing's going to happen to you."

Brianna's bottom lip puckered out, and she looked worriedly through the door. "No, Mommy. I don't want to."

"But why? Just tell Mommy why."

"Daddy's out there."

"He's not, honey. He doesn't even know where we are. How could he be out there?"

Brianna shrugged, but she didn't accept Paige's logic. Paige realized that regardless of what had originally triggered it, Brianna's fear was real, not imaginary, and she couldn't dismiss it. Stooping in front of her daughter, she got to eye level with her. "Brianna, tell Mommy why you think Daddy is out there."

"Because he is," she said, and big tears filled her eyes. "He's waiting for me."

"How could he be?"

The question confused the child, and she didn't answer, just wiped her eyes and smeared the tears across her temples.

"That day you thought you saw Daddy, it was Jake. He scared you, and you thought he was your daddy. But it wasn't him."

"Yes, it was," Brianna said. "I was chasing the butterfly, and he told me to come with him."

"The butterfly?"

"No, Daddy!" Brianna was getting upset now, and Paige pulled her into a hug.

"It's okay, honey. We don't have to go out. You don't have to cry."

257

Brianna hiccuped a sob and nodded her head, as though that would be fine with her.

But Paige couldn't understand what the problem was, and later that afternoon as Brianna napped, Paige stepped out into the backyard and looked around at the perimeter of the fence. There was nothing but woods that backed up to the fence and no trails. No one would be there by accident. If there had been someone there, he would have been there deliberately.

Had Brianna really seen someone?

She wanted to dismiss the possibility, as she had so quickly done when it had first come up, but she realized now that Brianna had never really demonstrated a fear of Jake except for that first meeting. And she wasn't entirely sure that Brianna had even seen Jake at that point.

Had Brianna been trying to tell her something all along, something that she had refused to believe?

She looked through the trees again, shivering with the sense that she was being watched, that someone was out there. Someone dangerous.

Had Keith found them? Had he approached Brianna in the back yard?

Starting to tremble, she backed into the house. Quickly, she bolted the door then ran to the front and checked the lock. In the master bedroom, she locked the door that opened to the patio.

By the time she was back in the kitchen, she heard a car door. Lynda was back with Jake.

Breathing a huge sigh of relief, she rushed outside.

Jake was getting into his wheelchair with a hang-dog look on his face, and Lynda was decidedly sober, too. But Paige hardly noticed.

"Thank goodness you're both home."

"What is it?" Lynda asked.

"Keith," she said breathlessly. "You know how Brianna keeps insisting that her father is in the backyard?"

Lynda waited for Jake to move away from the car door then closed it. "Yeah."

"Maybe he was."

Lynda stopped cold. "You think Keith was back there? When? How?"

"I don't know," she said. "But I'm scared. What if Brianna wasn't imagining it? What if he really was back there? I mean, she's obviously terrified of something, and it isn't Jake because she warmed right up to him that night. But she still won't go outside."

Lynda stood still, thinking for a moment. "Maybe we ought to give Larry a call."

Jake pulled the house key out of his pocket and quietly opened his apartment door.

"Jake?" Paige asked before he could go in.

He looked back at her over his shoulder. "Yeah?"

"Would you mind ... coming into the house for a while? Just for security. Until we hear from Larry? I'd feel better if there were a man around."

He looked stunned by the request. "Who are you worried about? Me or you?"

She didn't understand the question and glanced at Lynda for help. "I'm just scared, Jake. I was hoping—"

"So you think I need a couple of women to protect me?"

She looked stricken. "No. I wanted you to protect us."

"Nice try," he said, rolling over the threshold and pivoting at the door. "But I think I'll stay here."

He closed the door hard, and Paige jumped. "What's wrong with him?"

Lynda sighed. "He had these grand delusions of walking today, I think. It didn't happen. He's really depressed."

"But I really meant it, Lynda. I'd feel better with a man in the house. Why did he twist what I was saying?"

"Because he truly doesn't feel that he can offer us any protection. In his own mind, he's useless, so he thinks he's useless to everyone else, too."

"Oh, for heaven's sake." As if she had no more time to dwell on Jake's problems, Paige headed inside. "I need to go in and check on Brianna."

Lynda gave Jake's door one last glance then followed her in. "I'll call Larry," she said.

CHAPTER FIFTY·FIVE

Keith knew better than to come back, especially in the daytime, but the obsession that kept him from sleeping, eating, or thinking drove him to take chances.

In the three days since he'd tried to grab her, Brianna's face had haunted him day and night: the fear in her eyes when she'd spotted him; the way she'd backed away; the shrill scream that had startled him and sent him running through the woods....

She'd been brainwashed, and he had to put a stop to it. He couldn't allow her mother to poison her mind against her own father. It would take some time to get those thoughts out of her mind and win back her trust. But once he had her in his possession, he would have all the time in the world. He would tell her that Paige was dead, that she'd been in a car wreck or something. She'd get over it quickly; kids are like that. Resilient.

He moved quietly through the trees, again approaching the fence around Lynda's house. He had to be bolder if he was going to succeed. He hadn't gotten many breaks lately. Even his lawyer was turning against him.

He took his usual place, sitting on the ground against a tree, hidden behind two bushes, between which he had a clear view of the back door. He still seethed from the call he'd gotten from McRae that day, asking him whether he'd found where Paige was staying and whether he'd approached the child without permission.

"I don't *need* permission," Keith had said. "She's my kid. I'm her father, and no judge is ever going to tell me I can't see her."

"Does that mean you did show up at their place and threaten the kid?" McRae asked.

"How would I know where they're staying?"

McRae had thought about that for a moment. "You're a smart man, Keith. Did you or didn't you find them?"

He'd been amused at McRae's assessment of him; he always enjoyed it when people found out this night-shift employee had some brains. For a moment, he'd entertained the thought of telling him how he'd found Lynda's house, but then he realized that it wouldn't pay to brag. McRae was liable to resign from the case, and then where would he be?

So he'd lied and told McRae that he didn't have a clue where they were, but that if some guy had approached his daughter, he wanted the police to find out who it was. He'd even suggested filing another motion for temporary custody since she still seemed to be in danger, but McRae had rejected it. Court was only two weeks away, he said. He wasn't going back before the judge on Keith's behalf until the trial.

But Keith could see the writing on the wall. McRae was pulling back, losing faith in him. If Keith couldn't depend on him anymore, then he couldn't depend on the justice system to get Brianna. He could only count on himself.

And in just two weeks he would have to go into court and face Lynda Barrett. Unless something happened to her in the meantime.

So he was back here, waiting for a glimpse of Brianna, praying for another chance to grab her. This time he wouldn't botch it.

And if he couldn't reach Brianna, then he'd bide his time until he caught Lynda leaving and rush to his car to follow her.

He heard the side door open; he got to his feet, still crouched low, and moved until he could see who was coming out. It was Lynda, all dressed up, as though she was going to church, but she was alone.

Perfect. He took off through the trees. If he could make it to his car and follow her, he could plant his little surprise under her gas tank while her car was in the church parking lot. Talk about hellfire and brimstone.

Laughing breathlessly, he fired up his car and drove up the block and around the corner. He pulled over and waited.

261

Today was the day. Lynda would be taken out, Paige would be homeless and without representation, and his court case would be in the bag. Piece of cake. Even McRae would have to give him credit for working things out.

He saw the car come to the end of the street, stop, and then turn right. He waited until it was far enough away so she couldn't see him. Then he began to follow.

CHAPTER FIFTY-SIX

I thought you were going to invite Jake," Paige said as Lynda turned the corner.

"I did. Last night and again this morning. He wasn't interested."

"He should go anyway," Paige said. "After all you're doing for him ..."

Lynda looked at her thoughtfully. "Is that why you're coming with me? Because you feel you owe me something?"

Paige looked embarrassed, as though she'd just stuck her foot in her mouth. "No, of course not. I told you, I need to get Brianna back in church. You've made it easier. It's not always so easy to walk into a new church by yourself."

Lynda wasn't sure she believed her. "I didn't mean to strongarm you into going with me or to make you feel guilty if you didn't. It's just that what they teach there is the most important thing in the world." She glanced into the rearview mirror as she merged into the next lane. "I just wish Jake would have come. He needs to hear that message more than anything."

Paige didn't respond, and Lynda wondered whether she agreed.

They pulled into the parking lot of the church, waiting behind a few cars looking for parking places as cars from the earlier service left. Three security guards in the parking lot helped to direct traffic. She glanced in her rearview mirror again to see if she was holding anyone up.

A pale blue car slowed at the entrance to the parking lot, hesitated, and then drove on. The car looked familiar, but many of the cars here looked familiar.

They parked and went into the church, and again, Paige opted to stay in Brianna's class with her. She was starting to learn where everything was and what was expected of her, and the teacher seemed glad to see her.

As she went to her class, Lynda hoped that Paige would also seize the chance to be ministered to. She wasn't sure that the foundation of Paige's faith was any stronger than Jake's was.

CHAPTER FIFTY-SEVEN

Outside, Keith circled the church, trying to decide what to do. He had seen Paige and Brianna in the car with Lynda, so he could forget about the bomb, at least for today. He wanted Lynda dead, and if Paige had to go, too, the more the merrier. But he didn't want his little girl to die.

Besides, even after the traffic died down, the security guards remained in the parking lot like sentinels guarding the cars.

Continuing past the church, he pulled into an empty space in the parking lot of a closed jewelry store. For a moment, he just sat and thought, trying to sort out the possibilities.

Brianna was in that church somewhere now. Probably since she was a visitor and the teachers didn't know the family, no one would protest if her own father showed up to get her.

On the other hand, if she went into hysterics and started screaming like she had the other day, they would call the police. And this time there would be witnesses.

Still, there was no harm in going in to check things out. Then he could make a plan. He reached into the glove compartment for the fake mustache and thick glasses he'd used the day he bought the dynamite. Then, walking at a brisk pace as though he knew where he was going, he went in the back door of the church, hoping to avoid the Christian "welcome wagon" that always seemed to be on the lookout for visitors.

He ducked into a men's room at the end of the hall and wet his hair so he could comb it back. It wasn't him anymore, he thought, looking into the mirror. It was someone else — someone who couldn't be identified.

He went back into the hallway. There seemed to be classrooms further down the hall. He saw the babies through a glass window in the nursery nearby. The kids seemed to get older as he walked on until finally, he came to the three-year-olds' room.

He passed the door quickly without looking in for fear of startling Brianna if she saw him. But then he turned back and peered in from the side.

He saw his little girl working a puzzle at a table near the door. His heart began to race.

Just a few steps away, he thought. All he would have to do is wait till the teacher had her back to him, take a few steps inside the door, and grab Brianna before she had the chance to scream. He could have her in his car before anyone noticed she was gone.

He stepped closer, trying to see inside to where the teacher was. He saw two of them, and they both had their backs to him. It was perfect.

"I'm finished!" Brianna said, popping the last piece into the puzzle. "Mommy, come look."

He jumped back, startled, as the teachers turned around. One of them was Paige.

What was she doing here? Didn't they have classes for adults? Did they let just anybody teach these children?

His heart sank, and he quickly found the closest door and jogged back to his car.

When he got in, he hit his steering wheel and let out a loud curse.

Today wasn't going to be the day after all, he thought, cranking his engine and screeching away. But tomorrow had to be. Time was running out.

CHAPTER FIFTY-EIGHT

If there was a bright side to a boring Sunday, it was that Paige had cooked a meal fit for a prince. Jake sat quietly at the table, reminded of his days as a child when one of his friends—Jimmy Anderson—used to go to church every Sunday then come home and eat a big, sit-down meal with his parents. Jake had envied him. Doris always used Sunday mornings to catch up on her sleep, and then they feasted on sandwiches or canned ravioli on paper plates. At the time, Jake had believed that it was the meal he envied, but now he realized that it had been more than that—it was the good mood everyone seemed to bring home from church, the structure of having a reason to get all dressed up, and the camaraderie of sitting down together at the table. He'd shared that meal with the Andersons a time or two when he'd shown up to play at exactly the right moment, but when Doris had found out, she'd forbidden him to go anymore.

"They look down their noses at us," she had said. "And when you eat with them, it's like saying that your own mother won't feed you. You can eat at home if you're hungry."

Well, his mother couldn't stop him now.

But the conversation today was awkward, and he could see that Lynda was struggling to pull him out of his melancholy. He admired her for the attempt; he just wasn't sure that anyone could do it. Even though he'd spent the night wallowing in depression, he'd still hoped that when he woke this morning, he'd have more feeling in his feet and legs than he'd had yesterday. But he'd been disappointed again.

"Brianna likes her Sunday School class," Paige said. "Don't you, Brianna?"

267

Brianna nodded and finished her mouthful of potatoes. "Are we going back tonight?"

Paige gave Lynda a questioning look.

"If you want to," Lynda said. "I'm going, and I'd love for you to go with me."

"Can we go every day?"

Paige laughed. "No, honey. They don't have it every day."

Brianna looked perplexed at that.

"So what did they teach you in there?" Jake asked for the sake of conversation.

"About Jesus making people well." Her eyes brightened, and she began to get excited. "And there was this guy like you, Jake, and he couldn't walk, only they didn't have wheelchairs then—"

"She asked," Paige interjected with a smile.

"But he was lying down by the beautiful gate, the man was—"

"The name of the gate was Beautiful," Paige clarified.

"And you know what happened?"

"What?" Jake asked, getting uncomfortable.

"Some of Jesus' friends came and told the man to stand up, only he couldn't stand up, but they took his hand like this—" She slid down from her chair and went to take Jake's hand to demonstrate. "And he said—what did he say, Mommy?"

"Rise and walk," Paige said.

"Yeah!" Brianna said. "He said, 'Rise and walk,' and you know what the man did?"

Jake withdrew his hand and took a deep breath. He didn't want to know what the man had done. He didn't care because it had nothing to do with him. But the child waited beside him, bursting with excitement, and he knew she wouldn't back down until he took the bait. "What?"

"He got right up, and he could walk!"

Jake glanced at Lynda, who was smiling proudly at the child's enthusiasm, and he wondered if they'd rehearsed it in the car. He didn't like being talked about behind his back, and in his opinion, the story they'd chosen was particularly cruel. He didn't appreciate it.

"That story is in Acts, isn't it? And who gave him the power to do that, Brianna?" Lynda prompted.

"Jesus!" she said. "Jake, why don't you do it?" When he didn't answer, she shook his arm. "Jake?"

"I heard you," he said, staring down at his food. "I heard every word." He looked up at Lynda and Paige. "Nice try. If I recall, there are stories in there about people's eyes being gouged out, too. You want to lay one of those on me?"

"Jake, come on," Lynda said. "We didn't plan this."

Jerking his napkin out of his lap, he threw it on the table and started to back out of his place.

"Jake, what's a matter?" Brianna asked in her high-pitched voice.

"Nothing's the matter," he said, glaring at Lynda again. "You know, it's reprehensible to use a child to deal a low blow like that."

Lynda's face showed the full force of her anger. "Oh, right. Riding home in the car today, I asked Paige what we could do to really twist the knife in you. We came up with that story, and Paige said, 'I know! Let's use Brianna!' It was a clever plan, Jake, only you're too smart for us."

Confused at the exchange, Brianna sat back down, still looking at Jake, and said softly, "I asked Jesus to make you walk. Didn't I, Mommy?"

Paige put a protective arm around her daughter. "Yes, honey. You sure did." Her voice hardened, and she leered at Jake. "She told the whole class about you, Jake, and we all prayed for you. I don't know how you can turn this into some kind of conspiracy."

A host of emotions did battle on his face. "I don't need your prayers."

"Well, you're getting them anyway," Lynda said. "Powerful ones. Jesus said that children's angels always see the face of God." She looked at Brianna. "That means that God listens extra carefully to the prayers of children."

Jake, too, looked at the baffled child staring up at him with those big, questioning eyes.

"If that's the case," he said, "then where was God when her dad was abusing her? If God's paying special attention to the children, why do so many of them have to suffer?"

And Lynda knew that they weren't just talking about Brianna any more. They were talking about Jake.

Trying with all her might to fight her anger instead of Jake, she lowered herself back into her chair. "God got her out of there, didn't he? He used her mother to protect her."

"Why didn't he protect her before anything ever happened?"

She hesitated. "I don't know. There's a lot of evil in this world, Jake. God didn't cause it. And we don't know how he's working in suffering children's lives. We don't even know how he's working in our lives."

"Then you're contradicting yourself again, Lynda. Out of one side of your mouth, you tell me this beautiful idea about children having angels with access to God. And out of the other side, you say that it really doesn't make that much difference because God can't protect us from evil."

"I didn't say that he couldn't. God can do anything."

"Oh, I see. He just won't."

Paige's hand came down hard on the table, startling them all. "That's not what she said, Jake, and you know it!"

"It *is* what she said."

Lynda started to speak, but Paige stopped her. "You have a lot of nerve, you know that?" she said. "All she's done is take care of you, be a friend to you, feed you, give you a place to live — and you still keep throwing her kindness back in her face!"

"Paige, it's all right," Lynda said quietly.

"No, it isn't!" she said. "And as for God, he *has* protected Brianna. He's protected me, too. He gave us Lynda, and a place to live, and a means to get away from Keith. And he even made it so I didn't have to worry about money or a job or anything while I'm waiting to go to court. And I know he's going to take care of that, too. I know because he's taken care of everything else." Tears choked her, and she stopped, trying to steady her voice. "You know, you're not just blind in that one eye. You're blind in both eyes if you can't see that God is providing for you, too. If he didn't care, you'd still be in the hospital right now, and everybody would be trying to figure out what to do with you!"

Brianna started to cry. Picking her up and hugging her close, Paige went on. "Or worse. You could be just like you were before the accident, walking around on two good legs with two good eyes, worshiping that Porsche of yours and in all your vanity and arrogance, be even more blind and crippled than you are now!"

Lynda collapsed back into her chair and covered her face, uttering a silent prayer that whatever happened, the outcome of this wouldn't be as bad as she anticipated.

Paige stormed from the room, carrying Brianna, and silence fell over them as Jake sat motionless in his wheelchair, avoiding Lynda's eyes.

She rubbed her hands down her face and looked at him over her fingertips. "Jake, I'm sorry."

He started rolling his chair toward the door. "I think I'd better go now."

"But you didn't finish eating."

"I'm not hungry," he said quietly and left the house.

B ack in his room, Jake pulled himself onto the bed and lay flat, looking up at the ceiling. Tears rolled down his temples, and he wondered why he felt as if he were drowning in that waist-deep pool with legs that served only as cement weights to pull him under. Why did he try to pull everyone else down with him?

Restless, he sat up, wiped his face, and pushed his legs over the side of the bed. His eyes strayed to the drawer in the table beside his chair where she'd put that Bible. He pulled it out and began flipping through it.

Acts, she'd said. He found the book then turned the pages, looking at the topic headings for the one about the crippled man being healed. He was almost surprised when he found it.

He began to read the third chapter aloud:

One day Peter and John were going up to the temple at the time of prayer—at three in the afternoon.

Now a man crippled from birth was being carried to the temple gate called Beautiful, where he was put every day to beg from those going into the temple courts.

When he saw Peter and John about to enter, he asked them for money.

271

Peter looked straight at him, as did John. Then Peter said, "Look at us!"

So the man gave them his attention, expecting to get something from them.

Then Peter said, "Silver or gold I do not have, but what I have I give you. In the name of Jesus Christ of Nazareth, walk."

Taking him by the right hand, he helped him up, and instantly the man's feet and ankles became strong.

He jumped to his feet and began to walk. Then he went with them into the temple courts, walking and jumping, and praising God. When all the people saw him walking and praising God, they recognized him as the same man who used to sit begging at the temple gate called Beautiful, and they were filled with wonder and amazement at what had happened to him.

Jake stopped reading as tears dropped onto the pages of the Bible, and he wondered why that passage affected him so. It was just a story. But it was *his* story. He could have been the man who'd "been put" at the gate to beg. In many ways, he was "put" here to beg from Lynda for the food and the shelter he needed. His pain was the same as that of the man who was so desperate, so alone that he had to cry out to everyone who passed to help him.

Funny how quickly pride could vanish when you were desperate.

His eyes strayed out the window to that red Porsche sitting like an indictment in the driveway, and he knew that Paige was right. In some ways, he had been just as crippled before the accident as he was now. He clenched his teeth. He'd rather be figuratively crippled than physically crippled any day.

He looked back at the Bible. Why had Peter and John cared about the man? Why hadn't they just stepped over him and forgotten him? Why hadn't they averted their eyes? Why hadn't they just thrown money at him?

He didn't know the answer, any more than he knew why Lynda had helped him. And Paige was right. He continually threw her kindness back in her face. It was a hobby, challenging her beliefs, but he'd learned already that he wasn't going to shake them. Lynda knew what she believed. He, on the other hand, didn't have a clue.

But as the afternoon passed, he continued to read. Maybe he would find out.

When someone knocked on his door two hours later, he'd already finished the entire book of Acts and had turned back to Matthew. But he didn't want Lynda to know it yet. Closing the book, he stuck it back into the drawer then went to answer the door.

Paige stood there, her arms crossed in front of her, and she gave a stab at smiling. "Hi."

"Hi," he said.

She swallowed and looked down at her hands. "I just came to tell you I'm sorry. I shouldn't have blown up at you like that."

"Yes, you should have," he said. "You were absolutely right, and it needed to be said. I owe you an apology."

For a moment, she seemed unsure if he was mocking her. "Really?"

"Really," he said. "It's all right, Paige."

She laughed softly. "And I was so nervous about coming over here. I figured you'd never speak to me again, but I wanted you to come for supper. It's just leftovers, but you liked what we had today. It was cut a little short, but—"

"I'll be there," he said. "Is Brianna up?"

"Yeah," she said. "She just woke up from her nap."

"Maybe I'll come over in a little while and play with her. Let her know I'm not a total jerk. Maybe thank her for praying for me."

"She'd like that."

He closed the door and sat for a moment, surprised at how good it felt to make someone smile.

Maybe the day wasn't turning out so badly after all.

CHAPTER FIFTY-NINE

The burning had spread partially up Jake's calves by the next morning. Allie and Buzz didn't want to put him in the pool again so soon, but when he managed to move one foot at the ankle, they gave in to his pleading.

Determined that he would stand this time, he moved between the parallel bars, got his feet into place, and tightened his gluteals.

"That's good," Allie said. "Real good."

"Just watch the knees," Buzz told him. "Keep the stomach from bowing out. Easy now."

Focusing hard, Jake got his knees to lock. It took a moment for him to realize that he was standing. He looked up at them with something close to terror in his eyes.

"I'm doing it. I'm standing!"

He would have paid money for the look on Allie's face as she realized that he really was.

"Buzz, he is. He's standing!"

"All right, Jake. Let's see how long you can do it."

Already he felt the energy seeping out of him, and he knew he couldn't hold the position for long. "I feel so heavy," he said. "And wobbly." He looked up at the joy in both their faces. "But this is the beginning, isn't it? I'm gonna walk again."

"Looks like it, man," Buzz said. "I'd bet money on it."

His PT's confidence was what Jake had waited weeks to hear, but now that he had, exhaustion kicked in, and he deflated like a balloon losing its air.

"That's okay," Allie assured him. "You were up for about thirty seconds. That's great."

"But you're sure it means I'll walk."

"It means you'll be able to get around on your legs. You might need crutches or a cane or walker, but—"

"No," Jake cut in. "I'm going to walk on my own. You'll see. It's gonna happen."

No one tried to dampen that enthusiasm as he worked toward doing that for the rest of the day.

Jake decided not to tell Lynda about his progress; he wanted to surprise her when he took his first steps. When the doctor declared that Jake's eye was healed enough to have his prosthesis put in, he decided not to tell her about that, too. It would be more rewarding to see the surprise on her face. After she dropped him off at the hospital for therapy, he got Buzz to drive him to the optical center where he'd be fitted for his eye.

He was mildly surprised as he wheeled himself into the shop with hundreds of pairs of glasses on the walls and posters that advertised contact lenses. "I thought this place would seem more—medical," he told the receptionist. "I didn't know you could pick up an eye like you'd get a pair of lenses."

"Well, there's a little more to it," she said, pushing his chair into the back room where Dan Cirillo, the optician, waited. "But probably not as much as you'd imagined."

He wasn't expecting to have the eye made while he waited, but that was Dan's intention. After they'd taken the impression of his socket, Jake waited for the wax model of his eye to be made, and sat in front of the optician and allowed him to use his other eye as a model while he painted a little disk to match Jake's iris. When that was done, the wax model was ready to try on, and Dan checked its fit.

Jake thought it odd that he couldn't feel it. Pulling it back out as easily as he would a contact lens, Dan said, "Okay—go on back to therapy for a few hours, and by the time you're done, your eye should be ready."

Buzz brought Jake back that afternoon, and Dan greeted him with a plastic, painted model. "So what do you think?" he asked.

Jake cringed. "No way. That's not gonna look normal."

"Wait and see."

Dan put the eye in, then tested the movement. "It's perfect," he said. "It moves right along with your other one. I think you're really gonna be happy with this."

He handed Jake a mirror, and bracing himself, Jake brought it to his face. The eye looked identical to his other one, and he felt a rising sense of relief that the man in the mirror looked more like the Jake he used to know than he had since the crash.

He blinked, testing it and then moved his eyes back and forth to see how it felt.

"What do you think?"

Jake's smile spoke volumes. "I think I'm amazed."

Jake wasn't wearing his patch when Lynda picked him up that afternoon, and she gaped at him as he got into the car. "Jake, why didn't you tell me?"

His grin almost split his face. "I wanted to surprise you."

She couldn't stop staring. "Look at me. I can't even tell which eye is false. It looks just like your other one!"

Still grinning, he leaned over and planted a quick kiss on her lips. The look on her face told him she was stunned, and he began to laugh. "It's back. The old mesmerizing charm. I hypnotized you with my baby blues, didn't I?"

"Well, I—"

He kissed her again. "See? I've still got it."

Shaking her head, she started to laugh. "It's like a whole personality change."

"It's hope, darlin'," he said, leaning back in his seat. "Just pure, colorful hope. I might just wind up with a life after all, now that I don't make people cringe when they look at me."

Still laughing, she started the car. "So are there any other surprises?"

"You mean, am I gonna lay one on you again? I don't know," he teased. "If I were you, I'd keep my guard up."

He enjoyed the pink color that faded across her cheekbones as she drove and realized what a joy it would be when she finally did learn of the other surprise he hadn't told her. He had stood outside the pool this afternoon on both feet without holding his weight up with his arms. He was ready to walk, he thought. It was just a matter of time. In a very few days, maybe he'd be able to walk out to the car when Lynda came to get him. The look on her face would almost make all the misery he'd gone through worth it.

CHAPTER SIXTY

When Lynda announced that she was going back to work on the following Monday to prepare for Paige's deposition a few days later, Paige was concerned. Lynda still had yellow bruises on her cheekbone and forehead, and last night Paige had caught a glimpse of Lynda dressing. Black bruises still colored her ribcage, and Paige could only imagine the pain that Lynda had been suffering without complaining since the crash.

"You know, I could go with you and help you," Paige said as she worked on getting breakfast ready, so at least Lynda wouldn't have to leave on an empty stomach. "I could bring Brianna something to occupy her, and—"

"Paige, what do you think I have Sally for? She can help me."

"I'm just worried about you. It's too soon to be going back."

"The doctor said it's all right. Besides, we go to court in two weeks. I have to be ready."

"But you could prepare for the deposition at home. Why do you have to go in?"

"There are things I can do better there, Paige. I want to document every infraction Keith has ever had in his life, and I need to be there to get it all put together the way the judge likes it. McRae's had some run-ins with this judge, which may play in our favor as long as I don't do anything to neutralize that advantage, so I'm going to do everything I can to please him in court. I have to contact all of the witnesses and meet with them. With time running out, I can't afford not to be on top of this."

Paige felt like a heel for being the cause of this.

"But are you sure you feel up to it?"

"I'll be fine, Paige."

"All right," Paige said, giving up.

"Will you be all right here with Jake?"

"Yeah," Paige said. "I don't know what it is, but his mood seems to be changing lately. I think we'll get along fine."

CHAPTER SIXTY ONE

F inally!" Keith whispered to himself when he saw Lynda's car pull into her parking space beside her office building. He had figured that she'd probably be back to work today since it was Monday and she had to prepare for the hearing. He'd been sitting in his car across the street for a couple of hours already, waiting for her to make her appearance. His homemade bomb, wrapped in a leather pouch, sat on the seat next to him.

He had already decided that her personal space was in the perfect location—far enough to the side of the building that the security guard couldn't see it easily. Besides, as Keith had noticed for the past two hours, the guard stayed in his little office inside the building most of the time, watching television and talking on the phone. Keith could slip under her car, plant his package, and rig some wires, and the guard would never know. He could do it quickly; he'd been practicing.

Then all it would take was one turn of the key.... Keith made an exploding noise and then laughed as Lynda got out of her car and headed into the building.

He waited until she'd had enough time to get on the elevator then grabbed his package and got out of his car. The security guard was nowhere in sight. Looking down and walking fast, as if he knew exactly where he was going, he reached her car, looked around casually to make sure no one was watching and then got down on the ground and slid under it.

On his back, he unwrapped the bomb, pulled the duct tape out of his front pocket, and peeled off a long piece. He tore it off with his teeth, taped it to the gas tank, and then peeled off some more. When the bomb was taped securely enough to stay put, he inched forward on his shoulder blades and wired the bomb to the starter.

The guard still hadn't resurfaced when Keith stood up slowly beside the car. He hurried to the sidewalk, then slowed to a leisurely pace and cut across the street to his own car again.

Should he get out of the area or stick around and watch? The temptation was too great. He got back into his car, got comfortable, and prepared to wait as long as he needed to see the result of his planning and cleverness.

CHAPTER SIXTY-TWO

The wall of noise that assaulted Lynda when she got off the elevator startled her into a near coronary—until she realized that it was just her co-workers shouting "Surprise!"

Pressing her hand over her heart, she stepped back onto the elevator, and Sally grabbed the doors to stop them from closing. "It's a welcome back, Lynda!"

Lynda covered her mouth then and started to laugh, allowing Sally to pull her into the circle of her friends and associates. "You guys wouldn't do that if you knew how many surprises I've had in the last few weeks!"

Barraged with welcomes and pats on the back, she let them sweep her to the staff lounge where they had donuts and drinks and a "Welcome Back, Lynda" cake.

When the celebration was over and she wound up back in her office with Sally, she settled back in her chair and relaxed. "Gosh, it's good to be back."

"We're just so glad you're alive," Sally told her.

Lynda pulled Sally into a tight hug. "You've been a life-saver, holding down the fort the way you have. I really appreciate it."

Sally took a deep breath. "Well, it'll be nice helping you get caught up. I'll admit, it's been a little hard juggling everything. Are you ready to dive into this mess?"

Lynda looked over the stacks of mail, messages, and papers on her desk. "I really need to get some things done on Paige's case first. Then we'll tackle the stack."

"All right." Sally shuffled the papers around and pulled out her pen and notepad. "Shoot."

And as Lynda started doing what she did best, she felt as if the world were realigning itself, and things were on their way to getting back to normal.

Jake helped Paige with the breakfast dishes as Brianna sat on a stool at the sink, "washing" the plates but getting more suds on herself than she did on the dishes.

He'd been quiet ever since Paige had told him that Lynda had gone to work today, but he couldn't pinpoint what bothered him about it the most. That she might not be physically ready to dive back into work yet? That she hadn't told him? That she wouldn't be the one to drive him to the hospital for therapy today? Or was it simply that she wasn't here, and he missed her?

"As soon as you're ready to go, I'll change Brianna's clothes and take you," Paige said.

Jake shrugged. "No hurry. Buzz and Allie don't expect me today until ten o'clock." He rolled his chair up to Brianna's stool and asked, "Why don't you and I go outside and get some fresh air, Brianna?"

Brianna's little smile faded, and she shook her head and kept scrubbing a plate. "No."

Paige stopped what she was doing and shot Jake a look.

"Why not?" Jake asked.

"Cause." It was a simple answer, but in Brianna's mind, it probably covered it all.

"Cause why?"

"Daddy might come."

"She just insists that he's been out there," Paige said quickly. "That day you got here, when she started screaming, I thought she was just mixed up. That she thought you were her daddy ..."

"But she sure wasn't afraid of me later."

"Yeah, that's been bothering me, too." She walked to the back door and peered out the window into the back yard. "Maybe he really was here."

To Jake, that seemed unlikely. Why would anyone take that chance? It would be crazy, coming here and talking to Brianna. If he were caught, it would show everyone, including the judge, that Keith lacked any kind of judgment, that he was willing to break the law, and that he was unpredictable — and dangerous. "Hey, Brianna, what if I go out there with you?" he asked. "Your mom and I want some fresh air. We could all go. Nobody's gonna take you with all of us out there."

From her stool, Brianna looked down at him then thoughtfully considered her mother. When her eyes moved back to Jake, she said in her borderline baby voice, "You won't leave me? Even if he comes, you won't let him get me?"

"Of course not," Jake said. "But your mom will never let him get you, either."

"He's strong," she said matter-of-factly as she slipped off the stool. "He can push her down."

As Brianna scurried through the house to find her shoes, Jake and Paige exchanged troubled looks.

In seconds, Brianna reappeared with her shoes.

Paige's eyebrows rose. "Are we going out?"

"Only if Jake comes."

"I'm coming, kiddo." But as Brianna put on her shoes, he looked up at Paige and asked, "Why would that make her feel safer?"

"Because you're a man," Paige said. "I guess she thinks Keith is more of a threat to me than he is to you."

As Jake let that sink in, Brianna ran to get her dolls. They followed her out the door, then watched as her gaze gravitated to the back corner of the yard. Timidly, she took a few steps into the grass.

Paige followed her gaze to the area beyond the fence where it would be easy for anyone to hide.

"What's on the other side of those woods?" Jake asked behind her.

"A street with a few houses." She glanced back at him. "You think he was here, too, don't you?"

"I don't know, Paige."

Feeling sick, Paige settled onto the swing as Brianna set her babies around the picnic table and began talking to herself.

"I can't believe this," Paige whispered. "When I married him, I thought he was a dream come true. I thought he was my escape. But three days after we got married, his temper exploded, and I found out I'd just traded one nightmare for another."

"Did he hit you that soon?"

"No. If he had, I probably would have left. But he broke things and yelled a lot. I started trying to walk on eggshells just to keep from setting him off. But it's like he doesn't think straight. There is no reasoning with him. Keith has a whole different way of viewing the world than most people."

"So why did you stay with him?"

She considered that for a moment. "You have to understand him. He had been this brilliant kid raised in foster homes with no one who ever really got that involved with him. He had never had anyone of his own or anyone he could trust, and I had this stupid idea that if I just proved myself to him he'd settle down."

"When did he start hitting you?"

"When I was five months pregnant with Brianna." Her eyes filled, and she blinked back the tears. "And there I was with this little baby on the way ... and my only real option was to go back to my family — which wasn't an option at all. Besides, I wanted Brianna to have a father. And I wanted to give her a home. I kept thinking that once he saw her, he'd love her so much that he'd change. If not for me, for her."

"Did you ever leave him before now?"

"Sure I did," she said. "Several times. But he always talked me into coming back. You have to understand; we were in the military. He wasn't home half the time, so I told myself that I could manage the times he was. When I'd leave him, we'd be stuck in some town where I had no friends, no help." She swallowed. "I owe a lot to Lynda. If she hadn't been willing to take my case and give me advice, I don't know if I would have had the courage to leave him for good, even after he hurt Brianna. I don't know why it's so hard for me to stick to my guns."

Jake's eyes strayed to the child playing at the table then scanned the trees on the perimeter of the yard. "Did you say he was in the military?"

"Yes. The Navy."

"No wonder he was gone so much."

"Yeah. He'd be out on that aircraft carrier for weeks at a time. I wouldn't even hear from him. It was so peaceful."

"Aircraft carrier?" Jake cut in. "What did he do?"

"He was an aircraft mechanic," she said. "On the ships, they—"

"Wait a minute." Jake stopped her and sat straighter. "Did you say he was an *aircraft* mechanic?"

"Yes. He..." Her voice trailed off as she saw his reaction, and she realized what he was thinking.

"Does Lynda know this?"

"Well, she knows he was in the Navy. I don't think she ever asked what he did there. Jake, you don't think—"

"Paige, was Keith ever a suspect in the plane crash?"

Paige gaped at him. "I don't know. But anyway, they caught the guy who did that."

True, Jake thought, they had. Yet he couldn't dismiss the uneasy feeling that had gripped him. "I'm just saying—what if they were wrong? What if they got the wrong guy? I mean, if Keith knows airplanes, he would know exactly what to do to sabotage Lynda's plane. The cops may have overlooked it because you don't think of airplanes when you think of the Navy."

"But why would he do that? To get Brianna, he would have to get *me* out of the way, not Lynda—and I wasn't anywhere near Lynda that day." She thought back to the day that had erupted so horribly, starting the bizarre chain of events that had brought her to where she was now. "As a matter of fact, he went to the day care that morning trying to get Brianna. That's when this whole thing started."

"Doesn't that seem coincidental? That Lynda and I crashed the same morning that he started aggressively trying to take Brianna? Whoever sabotaged our plane did it the night before the crash. He could have been anticipating that Lynda would be out of the way, so that when he kidnapped Brianna, you'd have no one to help you."

Paige's face slowly drained of its color. "No, it can't be. Keith would do a lot of things. Sinister, mean things. But I can't believe he'd kill somebody."

"When they questioned him about the fire, you thought he could, didn't you?"

She got up, unable to sit still. "No. I mean yes. I was con-fused, but—Brianna was in that house. Of course, he didn't know that at the time." She turned back to Jake. "Keith *can't* be the one. He can't be. Because if he is, then the guy they've got locked up is the wrong guy. And Keith is still loose."

"Waiting to hit again."

The thought chilled her. Rushing across the grass, she picked Brianna up. "Come on, honey. We're going in." Abandoning the dolls, she took her into the house.

"Mommy, I want to play!"

"No, honey." She stepped back as Jake followed them in. Then she let Brianna down, closed the door, and bolted it. "We have to come in now."

"Paige, I think it's okay if she plays—"

"No!" Paige ran her trembling hands through her hair. "Bri-anna said he was here, and he was, Jake. He found out where we are, and he's been watching us! He's going to do something! I have to stop him!"

He watched her run frantically around the house, looking for something. Brianna stood watching her, not moving, and her thumb gravitated to her mouth. "Lynda took the cellular phone, didn't she? We haven't gotten a phone hooked up yet, Jake. Can I use the one in your car?"

"Sure," he said. "Who are you calling?"

She was out the door before he could get an answer. Pulling Brianna onto his lap, he rolled out after her.

She was already in the car dialing. After a moment's wait, she said in a shaky voice, "This is Paige Varner. I need to speak to Larry Millsaps, please." She closed her eyes and shook her head, apparently not liking the answer she received. "Then I'll speak to Tony Danks. Well, when will they be back? Do you know how I can reach them?"

She wilted and covered her face. "No, they can't call me back. Look, this is an emergency. Tell them to come to Lynda Barrett's house as soon as possible. And tell them I think they've got the wrong guy!"

Hanging up, she breathed a quick sob. "I'm going there."

"Where?"

"To the police department. I'm going to wait there until they get back. We're not safe here, Jake. You come with me."

"No," he said. "I'll stay in case Lynda comes home."

"Oh, no!" Paige wailed. "*She's* in danger, too. If he would mess up her plane and burn down her house, he'll do anything. If she's at work, she's a sitting duck. He knows where to find her!"

"All right," Jake said, trying to calm her. "I'll stay here and call her, and you take Brianna and go to the police station. Don't worry. I'll make sure Lynda's careful, and Tony and Larry will take care of the rest."

Sucking in a deep breath and wiping her face, she carried Brianna to her car.

Jake was dialing Lynda's office before Paige was out of the driveway, but the receptionist put him on hold for what seemed an eternity. When she came back, she told him that Lynda's line was busy. Would he like to hold, call back, or leave a message?

"Let me try her secretary," he said.

"Her line's busy, too. But she could call you back."

"Look, have her call me, but tell her it's an emergency. Tell her not to move until she talks to me. Did you get that?"

"Yes, sir."

"I mean it. This is very serious. Tell her to call me on my car phone at this number. Do you have a pen?"

He rattled off the number, and the woman jotted it down. "I'll give her the message, Mr. Stevens."

Jake cut the phone off and sat still a moment, wondering whether Paige had overreacted, and whether his own concern had caused her to. If this were all just a wild tangent....

Somehow, he didn't think it was.

He sat beside his car for twenty minutes or so, waiting for Lynda to call him back, and finally he dialed the number again.

"She's in a meeting, Mr. Stevens," the receptionist said. "I gave her the message, but—"

"Did she see it, or did you just put it on her desk?"

"Well—I gave it to Sally and told her it was urgent. But she was already in the meeting."

"How could she be in a meeting if she was on the phone before?"

"I guess she hung up and went before I could get back there."

He wanted to reach through the phone and throttle the woman. "Look, I don't *care* if she's in a meeting. Get her out."

"I can't do that, sir. It's a partners' meeting, and I've been given instructions to—"

"Then transfer me to Sally!"

He waited as he was put on hold, realizing what Paige must have gone through all those months before she was one of Lynda's priorities.

"Lynda Barrett's office."

It was Sally, and he breathed a sigh of relief. "Sally, this is Jake Stevens."

"Jake, I got your message. What's going on?"

"It's a long story. Is there any way you can get Lynda out of that meeting for an emergency?"

"Well, I suppose I could, but—"

"Then do it! Tell her to call me ASAP! I'm sitting out here by my car so I can take the call. Here's the number."

When he hung up, he waited, his heart racing. If only he could do something besides sit. If he could just get into this car and drive to her office.

Minutes ticked by, but the phone didn't ring. And he had no intention of going inside until it did.

Lynda couldn't have been more relieved when Sally got her out of the meeting. The sheer act of sitting still was making her ache all over, and her head throbbed from all the questions her partners and associates kept flinging at her about the cases they had taken over for her. And it was all time she could have spent working on Paige's case or catching up on her correspondence.

Sally gave her a once-over as she came out, laden down with papers. "Are you feeling okay? You look pale."

"I'm a little tired. What's wrong?"

"I got you out because Jake has been calling. He says it's an emergency. You'd better call him. He's waiting at his car. Here's the number."

Frowning, she took it. "Did he say what's wrong?"

"Nope."

289

"Okay, I'll call him," she said, heading for her office. "Hold all my calls."

She hurried into her office and dialed the number. Jake answered on the first ring.

"Hello?"

"Jake, it's Lynda. What's going on?"

"Lynda, Paige and I were talking, and we hit on something I think you should know about."

"What?"

"Did you know that Keith Varner used to be an aircraft mechanic?"

She caught her breath. "No he wasn't!"

"Yes, he was. In the Navy," he said. "He worked on airplanes on an aircraft carrier."

"Are you sure?"

"Dead sure. Paige said it herself."

There was a moment of silence, and finally, Lynda blew out an unsteady breath. "Jake, they had him. After the fire and again after the assault. They had him twice, but they let him go. It was him all the time."

"Yeah. Some poor guy is sitting in the slammer right now for something he didn't do, and this lunatic is still out there. Probably waiting for another opportunity. Or at least we have to assume for your safety as well as Paige's and Brianna's, that that's true."

She felt dizzy, and for a moment, she considered asking him to hold while she splashed cold water on her face.

"Where's Paige? How's she taking this?"

"The way you might expect, just short of hysterical. She decided to take Brianna and go to the sheriff's department to talk to Larry and Tony."

"Good. That was smart."

"But I'm worried about you."

She swallowed and reached for her car keys. "Frankly, *I'm* worried about me. Look, I'm coming home. I'm not feeling that terrific anyway. I'll just call it a day."

The relief was clear in Jake's voice. "All right. I'll see you soon. Lynda?"

"Yeah."

"Be careful, huh?"

She sat for a moment after he'd hung up, trying to organize her thoughts. She wasn't going to panic.

Picking up the phone, she buzzed Sally's desk. "Sally, would you get me all those files I need to look at for Paige's case? I'm going home, and I'll take those with me."

"Sure thing."

She looked up the number of the police station, dialed it, and asked for either of the two detectives.

Neither Larry nor Tony was in, and they couldn't be reached.

As she sank back into her chair, Sally breezed in with the files. "Lynda, are you sure you're all right?"

"Yeah. Sally, Jake's just run across some information that makes him think Keith Varner caused our crash and that he burned down my house."

Sally's eyes widened. "Paige's husband?"

"Yeah. And to tell you the truth, I think he's right. It all makes sense." She was trembling as she got to her feet. "I'm going home, but if Larry or Tony calls, tell one or both of them to call me on the cellular phone. I have to talk to them."

"Okay."

Lynda reached for the stack of files that contained the depositions from all the witnesses, all the emergency-room reports, and all the police complaints and stories from neighbors. But Sally put out a hand to stop her.

"This is too heavy for you," she said. "Give me the keys, and I'll go drop them in the car for you so you won't have to carry them."

Lynda managed a smile. "That would be great." She tossed her the keys. "I have a few other things I need to do before I leave."

"I'll be right back," Sally said and flitted out of the room.

Lynda sat and thought for a moment then decided not to wait for Larry and Tony. She would go straight to the DA, even before going home to Jake. Picking up the phone, she dialed the district attorney's number and told him she was coming right over.

Preoccupied, she got on the elevator and rode it down, hoping to intercept Sally in the parking lot.

The security guard was waiting just outside the elevator door when she got off.

"Sally said she'd bring your car up to the door, Miss Barrett, so you wouldn't have to walk."

Lynda smiled wanly. "That was sweet of her. All I wanted her to—"

A sound like the end of the world shook the building, breaking out the front windows and knocking her to her knees. The security guard threw himself against her, covering her from the flying glass with his body.

"No!" she screamed as she hit the floor, but it was too late. She'd already seen the glow that bathed the parking lot in a weird, unearthly light and the smoke that billowed across the lot as if shot from a hose. She knew without the slightest doubt that a car in the parking lot had just exploded.

And she knew without looking whose car it was.

292

S truggling to her feet, Lynda crunched across the shattered glass and through the ruined door toward the flames, but the security guard caught up to her on the sidewalk.

"You have to stay back!" he shouted.

"But Sally's in there!" She tried to push him away, but he held her more tightly, and finally, the fight turned to mourning as she collapsed into his arms, covering her face with her hands, watching through her fingers as the flames devoured the car.

Already a crowd was spilling out of the building, and she heard sirens.

"They've got to get her out!" she cried.

But the guard wouldn't let her go. "She's dead, Miss Barrett. There's no way she could have survived that."

Lynda shook free of him again. "But it was my car! It was meant for me!"

She collapsed on the ground and immediately friends surrounded her as the parking lot filled with emergency vehicles.

P aige paced the floor at the police precinct, waiting for Larry or Tony to come back in or call. She couldn't just stay here, she told herself. Keith was still loose out there. He could try to hurt Lynda or even Jake again. He could burn the house down — or worse.

Grabbing Brianna from the dirty floor where she'd been looking at a book, she went back to the precinct desk and tapped the arm of the uniformed deputy who had helped her earlier. "I have to go," she said. "Please tell Tony or Larry when they come in that Keith Varner is the one who's been after Lynda Barrett. Please. They have to arrest him."

The man had already checked Paige's situation out in the computer. He knew that she'd complained about her ex several times. He also knew they were embroiled in a custody battle, and he'd seen enough to know that such spouses would do whatever it took to discredit the other. He jotted down the note disinterestedly then slipped it in a stack. "They'll get the message."

Paige could see that he wasn't counting it as urgent. "I'm telling you if you don't do something, somebody might die. He's out there."

"Call us if anything comes up," he said.

Cursing under her breath, Paige gave up.

"Where are we going, Mommy?" Brianna asked as they headed out the door.

Paige sighed. "I don't know. Maybe to Lynda's office."

"Good. I like Miss Lynda's office."

"Okay," Paige said. "That's where we'll go then."

Brianna was quiet as they drove, as though she knew that her mother needed time to think.

But the moment Paige turned onto the law firm's street and saw the fire trucks and police cars surrounding the parking lot, her heart leapt in fear. Forced to stop in the line of traffic, she rolled down her window and stretched as far out as she could to see what the problem was.

A car alongside the building was on fire.

Terror ripped through her, and she covered her mouth, muffling a scream.

Brianna started to cry. "What's the matter, Mommy?"

But Paige didn't answer, for as the traffic began to move, she saw the car that was burning.

Lynda's car.

Trembling, she pulled out of the line of traffic, did a quick U-turn, and headed back to the house as fast as she could, trying with all her heart to fight the certainty that Lynda was dead.

CHAPTER SIXTY-FOUR

Keith had watched and waited from three blocks away, knowing that the moment the car went up, he'd know it. And he'd been right.

He hadn't expected it to happen so soon. He'd figured he would have to spend a few more hours sitting in his car watching, but she had made it easy on him.

He laughed now as he drove to the house where his wife and daughter were hiding. Paige was defenseless now, both in court and out. Brianna was his. All he had to do was tie up these loose ends.

Boldly, he turned down the street that he hadn't dared to drive down before and passed the trees he had hidden in as he had stalked them over the last week.

But Paige's car wasn't in the driveway. Only the red Porsche sat there—the car that hadn't been moved since he'd first noticed it.

Disappointed, he turned around at the dead end and left the street. Okay. So he would park and watch for her to come home, then. And the moment she did, he would grab Brianna before Paige could get inside. There would be nothing she could do. Absolutely nothing.

CHAPTER SIXTY-FIVE

I t's Keith Varner." Lynda's voice was dull and without inflection. "He did it."

Larry had just shown up on the scene after getting the urgent message from Lynda — one that had to be delivered by another detective since he and Tony had been working on an undercover case in which they couldn't carry their radios. "What?"

"He was an aircraft mechanic in the Navy. It's him, Larry. He's the one who's been trying to kill me. I thought you had the right guy behind bars! I never would have let Sally go out there if I'd known—"

"You didn't know. You couldn't have known. You don't even know now."

"Then explain this!" she screamed at him. "Something seems to go up in flames everywhere I go! If the guy you've got in jail is the right one, then why did this happen? I'm telling you, it's Keith! He's crazy!"

Larry looked up at the other officers who were filling out reports. "Put out an APB on Keith Varner. If he did it, we'll know it soon enough."

"Do you honestly think you're just going to go get him? He's not sitting at home waiting for the police!" Lynda shouted.

"We'll find him. Just calm down."

"I *can't* calm down! My secretary is dead in my place! She was my friend!" She collapsed in tears, then shook her head, trying to pull herself together. In a cracked, high-pitched voice, she said, "I have to tell her family. They can't hear this from just anyone."

"Well, you'd better do it soon," Larry said. "Before the authorities tell them."

"Would you—would you take me?"

"Sure." He took a deep breath, then walked her to his car and set her inside. Then he turned and gave a few more instructions to the deputies still on the scene.

As they pulled away, Lynda glanced back at the crowd that had formed around the parking lot. Another gruesome sight they would never forget. Another incident Lynda Barrett had escaped.

She didn't know how many more she could take. Especially not at this cost.

CHAPTER SIXTY·SIX

Keith got tired of waiting and decided to park his car in his usual spot on the street behind Lynda's house and cut through the woods. Then he would sneak up on the back of the house, look through the windows, and find out whether anyone was home.

He made his way to the fence enclosing the back yard, the same place where he'd talked to Brianna just a few days ago. Satisfied that no one was near, he climbed the fence and cut across the yard.

Boldly, he crossed the patio and peered into the kitchen window. The lights were off. He moved past the back kitchen door and looked through the living-room window. No one was there.

Stepping quietly, he made his way down the length of the house to the other back door, the one that went into the master bedroom. Peering through the glass pane in the door, he saw that the bed was made and the lights were off.

So they were gone. He tested the door that led into the bedroom. Locked. Going back to the kitchen door, he tested it, too.

The house was empty. When Paige came home, it would be just the two of them—and Brianna. He found a comfortable seat behind the house and waited for Paige.

Jake heard the screeching tires as Paige pulled into the driveway; as quickly as he could, he pushed himself out of the recliner and into his wheelchair. He rolled to the door—but even before he could turn the knob, he heard Brianna scream.

Through the door's window, he saw that a man had grabbed Brianna out of Paige's car and that Paige was fighting and clawing and kicking him with all her might.

His heart jumped, and he twisted the knob, ready to burst through the door and defend her—until he was hit with the crushing realization that there was nothing he could do. He couldn't walk or fight or defend anyone.

For a moment, he sat stunned, watching Paige fight for her life, watching as the man—he assumed it was Keith Varner—held Brianna roughly around her waist with one arm, and with the other pulling Paige by the hair to the door, making her unlock it. "You have ten minutes to pack everything she has here," he said through his teeth. "And then I'll decide what to do with you."

Jake roused himself, knowing that regardless of his limitations, Paige and Brianna needed his help. Flying back to the small kitchenette, he pulled the biggest knife he could find from the drawer, set it in his lap, and headed back to the door.

He heard the house door slam. He hoped that, with all the screaming inside, Keith wouldn't hear him if he went out and tried to reach his car phone. Jake guessed that they were in the bedroom at the back of the house, getting Brianna's things.

As quietly as he could, he opened the door and rolled out onto the driveway.

Paige's screams still sounded from inside the house, and something crashed. Jake's hands trembled as he opened his car door as quietly as he could then slipped inside. Pulling the door shut, he checked to make sure that Keith had not heard him. Apparently he hadn't.

He dialed 911 and keeping his voice barely above a whisper, told the dispatcher that Paige and Brianna were being held hostage inside the house and that Keith was dangerous. When he told them it was the home of Lynda Barrett, the dispatcher hesitated.

"Barrett? The same woman whose car blew up today?"

Jake clutched the phone. "What?"

"Is it the Lynda Barrett who works in the Schilling building?"

For a moment he couldn't find his voice. "Yes," he said. "What happened to her car?"

"Uh—there was an accident. An explosion."

Trying to steady his breath, he said, "Was she—was she killed?"

"There was one death in the accident," the woman confirmed hurriedly. "Do you think the person in the house could be a suspect in the explosion?"

Jake felt as if he were falling, falling, and there was nothing he could grab to stop his fall.

"Sir? Can you hear me?"

"Yes," he breathed. "Yes, it's him. Hurry, or he'll kill them."

He punched the end button on the phone then sat still, trying to grasp everything she had said. Explosion. Lynda's car. One death.

For a moment, he considered putting his key in the ignition, turning on the car, and ramming it headfirst into the house. Maybe he could get rid of Keith and himself in one quick action.

It was too much.

Not Lynda. She couldn't be dead.

He covered his face with his hand, too shocked to weep or scream. It had to be a mistake. She wouldn't die on him just like that. She would fight and survive. Somehow she'd make it.

So caught up was he in the turmoil of his raging thoughts that he didn't hear a car pull into the driveway behind him. But he jumped when he heard the car door slam and wrenched his neck to see. Lynda was walking toward the house, and a car was backing out of the driveway.

He flung the door open and almost fell out. "Lynda! You're alive!"

She looked pale, and there were red circles under her eyes. "Yeah," she said, and tears came to her eyes again as she reached for him. "Sally's dead."

He wanted to fling himself at her, hug her, but there wasn't time. "He's in there, Lynda. He has Paige and Brianna."

"What? Who?"

"Keith! He caught her getting out of her car and dragged them in. I've called the police."

Lynda stood shocked for a moment, then turned frantically toward the street, lifting a hand — but the car was already gone. Jake pulled himself into his chair then rolled around a corner of the house where Keith couldn't see him if he looked out. Lynda followed him.

"That was Larry who dropped me off! I should have made him stay, but he had a lead on where Keith was — " She looked around for a weapon then saw the knife Jake clutched in his hand. "But surely the dispatcher will let him know—"

"We can't wait," Jake said. "We have to do something! I think they're in the bedroom getting Brianna's things. If we can figure out where they are, when the police get here they can go in another door and surprise him."

Lynda nodded. "I'll go look."

A shadow of frustration crossed Jake's face. He wanted to go. But he couldn't.

"Be careful," he said.

Lynda crept along the side of the house. Peering around the corner nearest the bedroom, she saw them.

Keith stood in front of the screen door that opened to the patio. He held Brianna with one arm while he pointed a gun at Paige. She was on her knees, throwing clothes into a suitcase. Lynda could hear Brianna screaming. And through it, their voices.

"Please," Paige begged. "Just put her down, Keith. Let her go!"

"Shut up," Keith snarled. He grabbed Paige and pulled her up. "Now, where's the rest of her stuff?"

"The living room," Paige choked out. "Her dolls are in the living room."

As soon as they were out of sight, Lynda dashed back around the house to where Jake waited.

"They're headed for the living room," she whispered.

Something else crashed inside the house, and Lynda jumped. Brianna's blood-curdling scream cut through the air.

"He'll kill them," she whispered loudly. "He's insane. What are we going to do?"

"First, we're gonna calm down," he whispered. "And we're gonna think."

"I can get in through the back way," she whispered. "The door to the master bedroom."

"And do what? You don't have a gun. And even if you did, you couldn't use it."

"Then what do you suggest?"

"Let me go in that way," he said. "You wait here then create a diversion at the front of the house when the police get here."

She looked at his functionless legs, at his wheelchair. "No, I can't let you do it."

There was another crash, and Brianna's screaming stopped short. From the house came nothing but dead silence.

"That's it! I won't let him take another of my friends!" Throwing down her purse, she sprang toward the kitchen door.

"Lynda, stop!" he said in a loud hiss.

But she burst through the door before he could reach her. "Stop it!" she screamed. "Let them go and take me instead! I'm the one you really want!" The door slammed shut behind her.

For a moment, Jake sat frozen. He thought of going in after her, giving the fight everything he had. But that wouldn't help anyone. In the distance, he could hear sirens, but they were still too far away. Lynda's purse lay on its side on the ground; he reached for it and dug for her house key. Gripping the knife, he rolled around the back of the house, through the dirt so he wouldn't make noise. As the sirens got louder, he unlocked the master bedroom door and rolled inside.

He heard Keith cursing at Lynda, and Paige starting to scream again; things crashed and fell. Outside, the sirens seemed to have disappeared; had they gone the wrong way?

What if it was all up to him?

Grasping for help, Jake closed his eyes. *If you're up there, God, I could use a hand. Just make my body function well enough to help them.*

In the living room, Lynda tried to breathe, but Keith's arm was brutally tight against her throat. Paige's face was bleeding where he'd hit her, and Brianna sat hunched under a table with her arms covering her head.

"At least let Brianna go," Paige was crying. "Please, Keith. She's your *daughter!* If you really loved her you wouldn't make her watch this!"

"You don't know the first thing about love," he bit out. "She needs to know what kind of a tramp her mother is. She needs to see how weak you are. And she needs to see you dead, so she won't keep expecting you to rescue her when I take her. That way we can start a new life together, and she can depend on me, and I can clear her mind of all the brainwashing you've done."

Lynda struggled to loosen his hold on her. "You won't get away with this," she said. "You think they'll let you keep that child after you've killed two more people? They'll never let you out of here with her."

"Who won't?"

"The police!" she shouted, but Keith just grinned down at her insanely.

"The police are idiots. They already had me twice, and they let me go."

"Don't you hear the sirens?"

For the first time, he listened. The sirens were loud now and sounded as if they were right outside the house. Venomous rage reddened his face. "Then I have nothing more to lose, do I?"

Throwing Lynda down, he grabbed Paige's hair and put his gun to her head.

The doorbell rang, and a loud banging followed. "Police department! Open up!"

The gun fired, and Paige collapsed. Lynda screamed and dove for Brianna, who clung desperately to her, shivering. Keith kicked Paige, and when she recoiled, it was clear that she hadn't been shot. Thankful, Lynda tried to catch her breath and whispered to Brianna, "She's all right, sweetheart. Mommy's all right."

"The next shot goes through the door!" Keith shouted. "And then I'll kill both women!"

"We just want to talk to you, Varner!"

Lynda recognized the voice outside the door — Larry. She prayed that he hadn't come too late.

"Where's the phone?" Keith asked, sweat beading on his face as he looked from one side of the room to the other. "I can talk to 'em — negotiate."

"We don't have one!" Lynda threw back. "We used the cellular phone in my car, but you blew it up!"

"Shut up!" Keith bellowed and kicked over the table they sat under.

It didn't take another gunshot to tell Jake that there was no more time. If he were going to act, he had to do it now. Opening the bedroom door as quietly as he could, he wheeled into the hallway, holding the knife in his fist.

Keith picked up Paige again by the hair and arm, and as she struggled to free herself, Keith's hold tightened and Paige let out a muffled scream.

"In the name of God, let her *go*!" Lynda cried. "Think of Brianna. Look what you're doing to her!"

Jake silently wheeled to the corner where the hall joined the living room. Staying as far back as he could, he saw Brianna crouched beside Lynda. Keith stood nearby, still holding Paige with both arms. He let her go, and she fell to the floor. Bending down, he reached out to touch Brianna.

Curling into a tighter ball, she strained away from him.

"Brianna, it's just Daddy," he said in a quiet voice. "I'm not gonna hurt you again. Don't you believe me?"

Jake's gaze narrowed to the revolver hanging in Keith's hand, muzzle toward the ground, as he reached for Brianna with the other.

Slowly, Jake came out of the shadows and began to move across the carpet.

Tears started down Keith's face as he touched Brianna's hair. She hunched her shoulders higher, and her mouth grew even wider in terror, but her heaving sobs were silent.

First Lynda then Paige caught sight of Jake moving across the carpet in his wheelchair, and they froze, not certain what to do.

"It's not too late, Keith," Lynda said, keeping her timbre steady and low, trying to draw Keith's attention. "You can change your life. You can be the father she needs. Just let her go for now."

Keith dropped his head and began to weep; the gun slipped slightly in his loosening grasp.

Jake pushed his wheels gently one more time, easing closer to Keith's side, holding his breath to avoid any sound that would give him away—

And swung his arm with all the strength and speed he could muster. He hit the gun, sending it bouncing several feet away across the carpet, then swung back to grab Keith's wrist and twist it behind his back, forcing him to his knees. "Didn't know I was here, did you, pal?" Jake asked through gritted teeth. "Recognize me? I'm the guy you maimed in the plane crash."

304

Keith couldn't move; the strength Jake had built in his arms over the past few weeks was overpowering. "Let me go!" he screamed, but Jake forced him forward until his face rested on the floor. Paige scrambled after the gun and stood up, aiming it at her ex-husband.

"Take her out, Lynda!" Paige shouted. "I don't want her to see me kill her father."

Lynda grabbed Brianna and rushed for the kitchen door. Paige waited until they were out of the room before she pulled the hammer back. "I could pull this trigger right now!" she said through her teeth, "and they'd call it self-defense. I'd be a hero for ridding the world of you. And my daughter could finally learn what it's like to live without terror."

Keith struggled against Jake's grip and tried to look up at her. "You won't do it. Brianna would always blame you—"

"Shut up!" she cried.

There was the sound of splintering wood, and the front door burst open. Larry lunged into the room then stopped when he saw Paige holding the gun on Keith.

"Paige, give me the gun," he said.

Paige shook her head. "Stay back. Jake, move away."

Reluctantly, Jake let Keith go and slowly rolled backward.

Her face was red and streaked with tears. "If I blew you away," she said, her voice trembling, "it would be for all the pain you've caused Brianna. All the nightmares. All the trauma. It would be for her peace of mind." The gun began to shake.

"Send him to jail, Paige," Jake said carefully. "Don't let him die knowing he finally broke you."

Her face twisted as she struggled between the emotion of the moment and the hope of the future. Finally, she breathed in and out deeply, her breath catching as her tears flowed anew. "He's right, Keith," she said. "You're not going to break me. You're just going to rot in prison."

When she lowered the gun, the house filled with deputies. Larry handcuffed Keith, jerked him to his feet, and took him away.

CHAPTER SIXTY-SEVEN

As low as Lynda's life had gotten in the past few weeks, she was certain that Sally's funeral was the lowest point yet. As if even God mourned her passing, the sky opened up with torrential rains that morning, and it stormed throughout the day. Lynda sat between Paige and Jake, holding hands with each of them, trying to rein back the tears that had controlled her since the day of the explosion. Even Keith's confession and guilty plea to felony murder had not relieved the pain.

She watched Sally's parents weep over their daughter. Sally had been close to them, even though they lived several hours away.

"At least she didn't leave a husband and children," Lynda heard someone whisper behind her.

Lynda quelled the urge to turn around and tell them that Sally had had many people who'd loved her, that she'd had as much of a family as most people had, and that her being single didn't make it any easier to say good-bye.

The car ride home was quiet, and when they had been back at the house for a while, Paige came out of her room with her bags packed.

Lynda had known they were going back home today, but she'd tried to put it out of her mind. Now there was nothing she could do but face it.

Dropping the bag, Paige reached out to hug Lynda. As they clung together like sisters, Lynda realized that, for the first time in her life, she didn't feel like an only child.

"I'm gonna miss you," Lynda whispered.

Paige wiped her tears. "Me, too. I don't know how I'll ever thank you for what you've done for us."

Lynda tried to smile. "Well, for starters—I need a new secretary." Tears rushed into her eyes again as she got the words out. "And frankly, I don't think I can get used to someone new right now. How about taking Sally's job?"

Paige seemed confused, wary. "Do you really mean it?"

"I sure do."

"But how do you know I'm qualified?"

"You can do anything," Lynda said. "I have a lot of faith in you."

Again, they embraced, then Lynda stooped to kiss Brianna. The child had been quiet and withdrawn since the scene with her father, but she'd already expressed her wish to go back to "school" soon. Paige thought it was a good idea to get her life back to normal as soon as possible.

Jake offered Brianna a final ride on his lap as they hurried through the rain to the car, and Lynda smiled sadly as he hugged the child who had brought him so far, gave her a quick kiss on the cheek, and then helped her into the car.

The rain poured harder as the car pulled away, but neither Lynda nor Jake made a move to go inside.

"Are you all right?" he asked when the car was out of sight.

Lynda was still gazing in the direction they had gone as raindrops mixed with the tears on her face. "I was just thinking."

"About what?"

"That day in the plane," she said. "When they asked us if we had anyone to contact. Neither of us had anyone, really."

"You had Sally."

"Sally the secretary," she whispered. "But not Sally the friend, not then. I didn't really have any close friends then. I thought I was happy, all alone."

"We've both come a long way."

She looked down at him, saw how wet his hair was getting, how soaked his clothes, but he didn't seem to mind. He wasn't the same man who had gotten out of his Porsche that day wearing his designer clothes, expecting crowds to part and women to swoon. "I like having people to love," she said.

He nodded, swallowed, and she knew that the mist in his eyes had nothing to do with the rain. "I like it, too."

For a moment, they smiled at each other as the rain dripped down their faces, and finally, she said, "It's going to be awfully quiet around here without them."

"Well, I'll see what I can do about making a little more noise." She wiped her tears. "You'll have to eat my cooking now."

"I've been keeping it a secret, but I'm a pretty talented cook myself," he said. "As a matter of fact, I was thinking of making my special Texas stew for you tonight. Paige left all the ingredients in there. I already checked."

Slowly, the despair left Lynda's eyes, and she began to smile. "Then we'd better get busy peeling potatoes. You do have potatoes in your stew, don't you?"

"Among lots of other things, which shall remain secret."

"Well, I've survived four brushes with death in the last few weeks. I guess one more won't hurt me."

His smile faded. "That's not really funny," he said softly. "Matter of fact, it's downright chilling when you think about it."

"You're telling me." Looking around at the trees surrounding her house, she rubbed her arms and shivered. "Let's go in before we get sick and your chair starts to rust."

"I'd better change clothes first," he said. "If I don't, I'll ruin your kitchen floor."

"All right," she said. "I'll meet you in the kitchen."

She went back into the quiet house and felt the assault of silence again. But it wasn't so bad because she knew Jake was coming. Quickly she changed out of her wet clothes and towel-dried her hair.

When she went back into the kitchen, he was already at the table, peeling potatoes.

The sight of him there stirred her. Feeling awkward, she pulled out a chair and sat next to him. There were things she needed to say, things he needed to hear.

"We haven't talked much about that day," she said. "It's been kind of busy, and Sally's been on my mind. And we were all worried about Brianna...."

"Yeah. There hasn't been much time for reflection, has there?"

She looked down at the table, tracing the pattern of the wood grain with her fingertip. "I've been meaning to thank you."

"For what?"

"For coming to the rescue when Keith was here. My bursting into the house was really stupid. If you hadn't come in when you did—"

"I got lucky," he said. "If he had turned around and seen me coming, things could have turned out a lot differently."

"No, I think you would have been able to defend us even then. I didn't realize how strong you are, Jake. Even without your legs, you overpowered him. He couldn't fight you."

He smiled, but that smile quickly faded. "I just kept remembering that morning, when Brianna agreed to go outside because I was with her. I realized that she *expected* me to protect her. My legs weren't a factor to her. If I was to help her, then they couldn't be a factor to me, either."

She leaned on the table and faced him squarely. "Did you learn anything from that, Jake?"

His smile was subtle, but it reached all the way through her. "I think I did."

He didn't have to explain. She already knew that whatever he had learned, it was miles ahead of where he'd been before the plane crash.

"The important thing," he said, returning to his work, "is that that slimeball is behind bars." He finished peeling a potato then grew still for a moment, staring down at it.

"What's wrong?" she asked quietly.

He shrugged. "I was just thinking. That day when I called the police about Keith being in the house. They told me about the car blowing up, and said there had been a death."

Stillness.

"You thought it was me."

His facial muscles shifted with emotions he could not have named. "I was so glad when you walked up."

For a moment their eyes locked, and she wanted to reach out and hold him, cling to him. She had done it before when he'd needed comforting. But this was different.

This was more dangerous.

This was more important.

He reached out and took her hand, and squeezing it tightly, brought it to his lips. "You're a miracle, you know that?"

Coming from a man who didn't believe in miracles, that statement overwhelmed her. She saw the way his eyes misted as he gazed openly at her without the barriers of pride or humor, with only the honest glisten of pure affection.

Was he going to kiss her? Did she want him to?

She wasn't sure.

When he let her hand go and picked up his paring knife again, she breathed a sigh of both relief and disappointment. For as much as she'd feared that moment of truth between them, she regretted that it was over before it even started.

CHAPTER SIXTY-EIGHT

David Letterman was almost over when Jake started getting ready for bed. Turning off the lamp and leaving only the light of the television, he glanced out the window to see whether Lynda's light was still on. It wasn't. Was she sleeping? Or was she lying awake, struggling with her grief, needing the same kind of comfort she'd offered him more than once?

And then he saw movement in the darkness on the patio and realized she was sitting out there alone, her feet pulled up and her arms hugging her knees. Moonlight played on her hair and touched her face, and he wondered why he hadn't been struck by how pretty she was the first time he'd met her. She was beautiful to him now.

Wanting to be close to her, he rolled out his door. Lynda looked up at him as he came around the house.

In the moonlight, he could see that she'd been crying. How did one soothe a grief like this one? How did you offer comfort when there was none?

"Need company?" he asked softly, rolling up beside her.

She smiled. "Yeah, I could use some."

He remembered the old days when he would have eagerly held a woman with tears on her face — but it would only have been so that he could use his hundred-dollar-an-ounce charm to work her vulnerability to his favor. It had been so easy for him, then, to make them trust him, count on him, believe in him — then to walk away without looking back the next morning.

Things had changed. Nothing was that easy anymore. He knew that all the introspection of the past weeks had given birth

311

to something new in his life: a conscience. And he didn't think of Lynda the way he'd thought about any other woman in his life.

"I was just thinking about Sally," she whispered.

"Not beating yourself up again, I hope."

She looked out into the shadows of her yard. "I was thinking how unfair it is that she should die because of Keith's vendetta against me."

He turned his chair to face her, then reached out and took her hand in both of his. "Well, call me selfish if you have to, but I'm not going to feel guilty for being glad you weren't in that car."

"What could make a man want to kill?" she asked. "How could he have believed it would set anything right? Didn't he understand that he lost Brianna because of his violence in the first place?"

"He must by now, or he wouldn't have confessed and pled guilty."

Lynda shook her head. "No, I don't think he did that because he understands. I think he did that because McRae dropped his case, and he wasn't getting a lot of sympathy from his public defender."

Jake thought about that for a moment. "Not to mention the little fact that he was caught red-handed holding you all hostage, and he'd admitted, to all of us, that he'd done the other things."

"I think it was more a matter of defeat than regret," Lynda said. "He knew he couldn't win."

"Well, I guess our revenge is in knowing that he's behind bars and that he'll probably never see his daughter again."

She shook her head slowly. "I'm not supposed to want revenge."

"Why not?"

She looked up into the stars as new tears rolled down her cheek. "I'm supposed to pray for my enemies. I'm supposed to love them."

"Yeah, well, 'supposed to' is a long way from being able to. Look at all he did to you. Look what he did to me. I can't forgive him for that. I don't want to. But if I ever get the chance to meet him alone—"

"You won't," she whispered. "He'll probably get the death penalty. Unless I do something … say something…."

"Lynda, you can't."

Her sudden surrender to her tears surprised him, but without giving it a second thought, he gathered her up and pulled her against him. She closed her arms around his neck and wept against his shoulder, and he found himself weeping with her—*for* her. And he remembered how *she* had held *him* when he'd wept, how right it had felt, how much it had comforted him, how it had seemed like light seeping into the darkened chambers of his heart. That, more than her heroics in the plane, had probably saved his life.

"I came out here to pray for him," she whispered. "I made up my mind that I would. But I'm having trouble. It's the hardest thing I've ever done."

She wilted against his chest, and he stroked her hair. "It's okay, Lynda. It doesn't matter."

"It *does* matter."

"Why? Tell me why it matters."

She sat up then, breaking his hold on her and looked him squarely in the eyes. He reached up to wipe her tears away with the back of his fingers.

"It matters because Christ forgave me."

"Forgave you for what? What terrible thing have you ever done?"

"Oh, Jake," she cried. "I do terrible things all the time. And the morning of the crash when we were in that plane, knowing we could die the minute we landed, I just sat there. I didn't care what would happen to you if you'd died. I didn't even try to tell you what I knew. What could save you. But he didn't turn his back on either of us. He forgave me and let me start over. He let me see—"

"Lynda, you couldn't have saved me if you'd tried. I thought I had all the answers. Maybe I still think that. I was a creep then, and I'm probably still a creep, and you were justified in how you felt about me in that plane."

She shook her head. "You don't think it's important because you don't believe. But I do. And I want to obey now, but if it means forgiving Keith ..."

"Keith Varner hasn't asked for your forgiveness."

"That doesn't matter. I still have to forgive him. And I hate myself for not being able to do it."

Later that night, when she had gone back into the house and lay awake in bed, staring at the ceiling and wrestling the monsters of memory and despair, Lynda tried to tell herself that she *could* forgive Keith, that maybe she already had. But as she drifted into a shallow sleep, she dreamed about cars blowing up and planes crashing and houses burning and about that panic that comes right before death between realizing it's going to happen and surrendering to it. Like a running theme through those images, Keith appeared here and there, laughing, cursing, escaping....

She awoke in a cold sweat and looked around at the room full of distorted shadows; she had left the lamp on. Trembling, she reached for her radio and turned it on. Maybe the noise would block out the fears, override the terror.

But her heart was beating too wildly for her to go back to sleep, so she got up and wandered around the quiet house. What if the dream were a warning? He is smart, after all. What if he *had* found some way to escape?

She went back to her bedroom; the dresser mirror caught her reflection as she passed, and she stopped to study it. She wasn't the same person she'd been before the crash. She was different. More fragile in some ways, tougher in others.

Would she ever stop being afraid?

Sitting down on the end of her bed, she pressed her face into her hands and tried with all her heart to pray for peace of mind. But the words wouldn't come, and she found herself unable to pray, unable to ask for help, unable to surrender.

She thought of going to Jake's door and waking him up, but the idea seemed crazy. She would have to wait until morning. And then, perhaps she'd look into counseling. Maybe she needed professional help. Maybe she needed her preacher to teach her to pray again. Maybe she needed a gun and a security system and a bodyguard.

Maybe none of this was really over yet.

CHAPTER SIXTY NINE

I wish I'd killed him."

Paige's words would have surprised Lynda if she hadn't struggled with the same thought herself. Paige sat at her new desk—Sally's desk—with dark circles under her eyes, indicating that she hadn't been able to sleep either.

"I had the chance," Paige added quietly.

"Don't say that," Lynda whispered without much conviction as she sank into the chair across from Paige's desk. "You did the right thing. The only thing you could have done."

"Brianna's still having nightmares."

"Aren't we all?"

Paige's tired eyes met Lynda's, and she shook her head. "The DA asked me to testify at Keith's sentencing. It's amazing that he confessed and didn't even try to negotiate away the death penalty. I think maybe he really wants to die."

"The DA called me, too," Lynda said.

"So I guess, indirectly I have another chance." Paige propped her chin on her hand. "I keep having visions of sitting up there in front of him, telling the judge to give him the chair while he watches me with those persuasive, hurt eyes. He'd be so shocked that I went through with it."

"So are you going to?"

Paige shrugged, despair evident on her face. "I don't think I can."

Lynda was quiet, not questioning, for she knew the dilemma.

"He's Brianna's father. I don't want her growing up with that kind of stigma. And I guess when I come right down to it, I don't want that guilt. I don't even know if I believe in the death penalty."

Lynda was quiet for a moment. "I used to be against it right across the board. But now I'm not so sure. I've never been the victim before." She thought that over for a moment, hating herself for not being able to choose one side of the line or the other. "I guess it's time I decided what I really believe."

"Are you going to testify?"

"I don't know," Lynda whispered. "The judge's pre-sentencing investigation has already probably told him all he needs to know. My testimony wouldn't make that much difference." She sighed. "Maybe I'm just wimping out. I don't know what to do."

Paige accepted that. "Jake probably will."

Yes. That would be his way of getting some measure of revenge. She almost hoped he did.

But the reality of that hope only drew her deeper into a pit of depression that seemed impossible to escape.

Lynda didn't sleep for the three nights before the day she was to testify at the sentencing, and that morning as she drove Jake to the courthouse, she still wasn't sure whether she would even go in when she got there.

Her dejection hadn't escaped Jake's notice, and reaching across the seat, he stroked her hair. "You don't have to do this, you know."

Lynda nodded. "I don't know if I will." She glanced over at him. "Do you think I'm a coward?"

"No, Lynda. When I think about you, a lot of different words come to mind, but coward isn't one of them. I don't think it's fear that's keeping you from wanting to testify."

"Then what is it?"

"Indecision, maybe? Those people in there want to know how we, the victims, feel about what should happen to Keith Varner. And you can't really tell them if you don't know yourself."

She reached the courthouse and pulled into a parking place then sat there for a moment, making no move to get out. "But you're sure, aren't you, Jake? You think he should be put to death."

Jake's face hardened slightly. "I'd do it myself if I could."

She dropped her head back on her headrest and stared at the courthouse—the same building where Keith had attacked Paige and tried to take Brianna such a short time ago. She remembered Brianna's terror that day—and on another day, cowering under a table....

"Let's go in," she said quietly.

Jake shot her a surprised look. "Really? You're going to testify? What are you going to say?"

"I'll decide when I get in there," she said.

Jake got his wheelchair out of the back and slipped into it, and she followed him in. The building seemed too warm, and she found it hard to breathe. At the entrance, a few reporters rushed toward them with questions about their testimony, but they both threw out "No comment," and kept walking.

By the time they reached the courtroom, Lynda felt as if she might hyperventilate. Jake glanced back at her and noticed the perspiration on her temples and above her lip, and he handed her a handkerchief. "You okay?"

She sat down next to him. "Yeah. Fine."

The DA spotted them and came toward them. At the same time, the door at the front of the courtroom opened, and the bailiffs brought Keith in.

His eyes were bloodshot and he hadn't shaved. He searched the room frantically. Lynda knew he was looking for Paige, but when his gaze rested on her, her heart jolted.

All her anger rushed back in a tidal wave of memory, and she thought again about Brianna and Sally. Yes, he deserved death. And he deserved to hear her say it.

Why then did she still feel so divided? Could she really get up there and say what the DA wanted her to say?

Standing up, she pushed past the DA and Jake. "I'm sorry," she said. "I can't do this."

Jake caught her arm, and the DA looked crestfallen. "Lynda, what's wrong?"

Tears came to her eyes, and she glanced back at Keith, whose back was to her now. "I just don't know what I believe anymore," she whispered harshly. "And I can't sit up there and say something if I'm not sure." She looked down at Jake, expecting condemnation, but all she saw was concern. "You do what you have to do, Jake. Call me when it's over, and I'll come back to get you."

And before he could respond or the DA could talk her out of it, she shot out of the room.

At home, Lynda sat in the quiet, trying to decide why she was so angry with herself. Was it because she thought she'd wimped out or because she hadn't? Or was it even deeper? Did it have to do with this forgiveness issue that had plagued her since Keith's arrest?

Praying for her enemies had always seemed so logical, so easy — when she'd had no enemies. Loving had been a breeze — when she'd never really hated.

Now she was being tested. She had been tested before, but those other tests she had failed, and God had taught her through that failure how fruitless she was to his kingdom. How useless.

And if she'd learned anything in the past few weeks, it was that the only true joy she'd found was in being obedient to him. Maybe that was why her heart was so heavy now. Maybe it was because she was resisting.

Pulling her feet up onto the couch and wrapping her arms around her knees, she dropped her head into the circle of her arms and tried to pray again.

But this time, instead of praying for her fears and her trauma and her decisions, she prayed for Keith.

And as she did, his tremendous guilt became real to her, as did his grief. He had lost his wife and his daughter. Even though he'd caused those losses, that didn't change the level of pain he suffered. She didn't pray for his release or for some miraculous acquittal — for she knew that God was a just God and that crimes held consequences. Instead, she prayed for a change of heart, for light in his darkness, and for his salvation.

And she prayed that God would help her find a way to forgive him.

The moment she ended the prayer, she felt a great weight lifted off her, and peace replaced it.

A car door slammed. Through the window, she could see Jake getting out of a car. The car backed out of her driveway, and Jake rolled toward the door.

She opened it before he knocked. "Who brought you home?"

"One of the guys from the DA's office," he said. "Are you all right?"

She smiled, probably for the first time since Sally's funeral. "Yeah. I think I am."

Jake came inside, and he gazed at her for a long moment. "I was the last witness to testify, so they gave it to the jury right afterward. They agreed unanimously on the death penalty. The judge accepted their recommendation, Lynda. He got death."

She pulled out a chair and sat down slowly. "I figured he would." She let out a long breath. "It sure didn't take long."

"No, the jury wasn't out very long," he said. A slow, gentle smile changed his expression. "You really are better, aren't you? What happened?"

"I had a long talk with the Lord," she said. "And we got a few things straightened out."

"That's good." Then, as he gazed at her, he saw the pain return to her eyes. "What is it?"

She let out a deep, ragged breath. "I have to go see him," she whispered.

"What?"

"You heard me," she said. "I have to."

He rolled closer, as if by touching her he could chase away this madness. Taking her hand, he said, "Lynda, you can't. No one expects you to do this. Probably not even God."

"You're wrong," she whispered. "I think God does expect it. And I'm going."

"What will it prove?"

"I don't know," she said. "Maybe nothing."

Jake looked out the window, and she saw the intense struggle on his face as he groped to understand. "This is crazy, Lynda. I want you to think about it."

"I already have," she said. "I'm going tomorrow, before they transfer him to the state penitentiary."

He gaped at her again, his face a study in disgusted bewilderment, but after a moment, that look faded, and he sank back in his chair. "You can't be talked out of this?"

"No," she said. "If I could, I would have talked myself out of it already. It's not something I *want* to do, Jake, believe me; it's something I *have* to do. I was going to let a man die unsaved once before—I can't do it again. That's as clear to me as it was to you when you testified today."

Silence screamed out between them as he stared at her, and finally, he broke it. "All right," he said finally. "But I'm going with you."

Back in his apartment that night, Jake searched the New Testament for the reasons Lynda might have chosen to pray for her enemy, to visit him in prison. As he read through Matthew, Mark, Luke, and finally John, he saw it there over and over. This was why, then, she felt that God wanted her to go, why it was so important to her.

When she'd left the courthouse that day, she'd been confused about what she believed. She must have come home and decided. And tonight, rather than depressed, she seemed centered, peace-filled, and eager to do what she'd decided to do.

He lay awake for a long time that night, thinking back over Lynda's active concern for him and for Paige and Brianna, her determination to do God's will even when it meant sacrifice, and the way she had made him feel less like a shell of a human and more like a man with a spirit. A man with a soul.

And as he reflected on those things, that slow, deep, burning ache began to spread farther up his legs.

He lay there, knowing what it meant, knowing that maybe it would help him to finally take that first step....

Tomorrow, he thought. Maybe he would do it tomorrow.

But first, he would keep his word to Lynda. First he would go with her to see Keith.

Because Keith had not yet been transported to the state penitentiary—that event was scheduled for the next day—the visitation room at the St. Clair Correctional Institute was not the maximum security sort where plexiglass separated them. Instead, Lynda used her attorney's credentials to meet with him on a day that wasn't a visiting day, so the room was empty. The fact that she and Jake were his victims complicated things somewhat—but Lynda had known the warden for years, so he allowed the visit to take place with the stipulation that two of his burliest guards would stand watch over them, just in case Keith tried anything.

It was clear from the disappointment on his face as they brought him in that Keith probably had expected Paige and Brianna. His face twisted in a vile sneer at the sight of Lynda in the chair across the table from him, and Jake in his wheelchair beside her. Muttering a curse, he pulled a chair out and dropped into it.

"You've got a lot of nerve coming here."

Lynda had gotten up early that morning and prayed that God would give her the words she needed when she came face-to-face with Keith, but now she found her courage faltering. "I know we're the last ones you expected to see, Keith. But we're not the reasons you're in prison. You're the reason."

"I did what I had to do for my kid!" he said, hammering a fist on the table. "And if you weren't such a bleeding heart fool, you'd see that Paige drove me to this, and you helped her. You're as much to blame for that plane crash and that woman's death as I am!"

"Wait a minute, Varner!" Jake blurted, but Lynda touched his hand to quiet him, and he flopped back, rubbing his temple and gritting his teeth. Jake had had enough. It had been all he could do to come in with a facade of civility, but Lynda knew he was aching to hurl himself across the table and shut Keith up once and for all.

"I didn't come here to answer your accusations, Keith," she said. "I don't even care what you think of me."

"Then what *did* you come for?"

Looking at this angry, hostile, deluded man, his face rigid with hate, Lynda suddenly felt a deep compassion for him, a compassion that she couldn't explain, for it wasn't something she had pulled out of any human part of her. She leaned on the table, getting closer to him. "I came here because you're going to die, Keith. But I wanted you to know that you don't have to die alone. It wasn't too late for the thief being executed next to Christ on the cross, and it isn't too late for you."

Reaching into her bag, which the guards had thoroughly searched at the door, she withdrew the Bible she had brought for Keith. "This is for you, Keith. I hope you'll read it."

He stared down at it, raw but undefined emotion tugging at his face, and for a moment, she thought he was going to take it. But suddenly that stricken look changed to potent rage, and he ripped the Bible out of her hands, spat on it, and flung it hard against the wall.

The guards rushed to grab Keith, and fury shot through Lynda as she sprang to her feet. For a second, she thought of rushing around the table and unleashing all the rage she'd been harboring for weeks. But she held herself still, and soon a quiet and unexpected peace fell over her. The rage vanished, and instead she felt a deep, abysmal sorrow for him. "I'll pray for you, Keith," she said.

Then she turned and strode from the room.

Jake had been ready to lambaste Keith Varner, the man who had crippled him, with every curse he knew. But seeing Lynda's reaction, he felt suddenly humbled. Without another look at the prisoner, he turned his chair around and followed her out.

When they were back in the car, Jake touched her shoulder and made her look at him. "Are you all right?"

"I'm fine," she said. "Really. I feel good."

He couldn't quite understand that, for he had expected her to be crushed. "But you hoped for a turnaround, didn't you? I mean, didn't you at least go in there thinking that he'd take the Bible?"

She thought about that for a moment. "That was between Keith and God. All I know is that I did what I was supposed to do." Sighing, she started her car. "Maybe he'll pick that Bible up and take it with him, after all."

"But probably he won't."

She smiled sadly. "But he had the chance, Jake."

Jake thought he understood that on some primitive level. She had given Varner the chance to change, even though he didn't deserve it. In that way, she had been like Christ to him.

Just as she had been like Christ to Jake.

"Have you forgiven him?" he asked, amazed.

She thought about that for a long moment. "Let's just say I'm working on it."

Silently, he watched her face with appreciation and deep contemplation as she drove. Self-conscious, she finally shot him a questioning look. "Why are you staring at me like that?"

He sighed and leaned his head back. "I was just thinking. God and I aren't on real familiar terms. Maybe you could pray for me that I'd get my legs back all the way."

"I thought you didn't believe," she said.

He hesitated then said, "Yeah, well. I've seen a lot of evidence lately. Maybe I'm changing my mind."

She smiled. "I pray for your legs all the time, Jake."

"But tomorrow is going to be a real important day. I haven't told you this, but I've been standing."

She almost ran off the road but managed to pull over. Gaping at him across the seat, she asked, "Really? By yourself?"

"Well, I used the parallel bars, but I've been standing on my legs. I'm getting more feeling every day."

"Why haven't you *told* me?"

"I wanted it to be a surprise," he said. "I had this fantasy of ambling out to the car one day when you came to pick me up. But I'm really nervous about tomorrow. I'm going to try to walk, and I couldn't keep it to myself anymore."

"Oh, Jake, can I be there? Can I watch? What time are you planning to get on the bars?"

He almost told her then faltered. He couldn't take the disappointment if he failed in front of her. So he lied. "Probably around ten. They'll put me on traction for a while first and then warm up my muscles."

"I'll be there at ten," she said. "Oh, Jake, this is wonderful!" Reaching across the seat, she hugged him, and he closed his eyes and held her a moment longer than he needed to.

When she pulled back, their eyes locked, and for a fleeting moment, he realized that he would be willing to give up the opportunity to walk tomorrow in exchange for the courage to lean over and kiss her like he had the day he'd gotten his eye. But he'd just been playing then, and this was serious.

Something stopped him.

Fear? The great Jake, who had never met a woman he couldn't charm? The same Jake who had once practiced womanizing with as much devotion as Lynda practiced her faith?

He let her go, and she drove back to the house in quiet. When they pulled into the driveway, she cut off the engine and sat still for a moment. "Well, I guess I'll see you tomorrow."

He caught her hand as she reached for the car door, and she turned to look at him. Her face was expectant as he held her gaze, and his heart sprinted wildly in his chest, anticipating, hoping....

Finally, he leaned forward and kissed her. And at the gentle, sweet touch of her lips, he felt the world settling back on its axis, righting itself and everything around him falling into place.

When he broke the kiss, she looked up at him, soft, humble, surprised.

He touched her face, as if it were something precious, priceless. "Good night," he said quietly.

She leaned forward then slowly and pressed a soft kiss on his scar. He closed his eyes and found her lips again, and this time the kiss was more startling, more telling. When at last it ended, he pulled back and gazed at her, seeing the emotion clearly written on her face.

"Good night," she whispered.

He sat still as she opened the door, slipped out, and started to the house. But before she went inside, she looked back at him.

And there was a sweet, unguarded smile on her face.

Jake found it hard to sleep that night. What had happened between them haunted him—and not in a completely positive way. It didn't make sense. In his "old life," if he'd been attracted to a woman for this long, he would have had more than a passing intimacy with her by now.

This was the first time he'd stopped at just one kiss and the first time he had ever lain awake thinking about one. It was the first time he'd felt such a dependence on another human being, a painful but sweet, heartrending need for her smile, her touch, her presence.

It was frightening. It was frustrating. It was exciting. And it was hard to believe, for no one he knew had had more experience than he had with women. But strangely, he felt as though this was his first experience. As though only now, at age thirty-nine, he was learning the true value of a woman.

As he was learning the true value of himself.

He lay in bed, fighting the searing pain growing more pronounced in his calves—the pain they told him was temporary—and told himself that maybe some good had come from the accident after all. Maybe he was discovering the powerful essence of life, now that the trappings had been taken away.

He sat up in bed, too restless to sleep and thought about tomorrow. What if his legs rebelled and refused to cooperate with him? What if the progress he'd made was as far as he'd ever go? What if he remained a paraplegic for the rest of his life?

For the first time since the crash, Jake admitted that if that happened, he could live with it. He was alive, after all, and things were looking pretty good.

He got into his wheelchair and rolled around the tiny apartment for a little while then restlessly went outside. It was late, and he could hear the crickets chirping and the toads croaking. The wind was strong, whipping through the trees and ruffling his hair, and in the distance, he heard an owl hoot.

It was beginning to feel more like autumn; the wind was brisk and cool as it whispered through the leaves. It never got very cold here, he'd been told, and he wondered what it was like in Texas right now. Was it cool? Were the leaves falling?

He wondered whether autumn was still his mother's favorite time of year.

The moment Doris Stevens came into his mind, his optimism deflated, and he was confronted with all the unfinished business of his past. Before he could clean up his present life, he suddenly realized he would need to clean up his past one. He had skeletons to lay to rest, dirt to wash away, and peace to make.

Going back into his apartment, he picked up the phone that had at last been connected and dialed the number he remembered from so many years ago, the number that had been his in Texas when he'd been nothing more than a poor waitress's illegitimate son. How far he had run to escape that image.

He put the phone to his ear and waited as it rang once, twice, three times....

"Hello?"

The voice was the familiar one he'd had such contempt for before, with its nasal twang and its hoarse brusqueness. Now, it just sounded pleasantly familiar.

"Mama?"

She was silent as he held his breath, then finally said, "Jake?"

That she didn't reject him immediately, as she had so many times before, gave him hope.

"I know it's late, Mama, but I thought you might still be up."

"I just got in from work," she said carefully.

Silence again.

"I heard about your legs. That woman called me."

"Lynda," he said, smiling. "Yeah. She's been looking out for me."

"So … how are you doing?"

"I'm fine," he said. "I'm out of the hospital. I'm getting a little feeling back, and I've been able to stand some. I'm gonna walk again, Mama. I know I am."

He could hear the tinge of emotion in her voice when she whispered, "That's good."

Encouraged by the few words, he decided to say what he'd called to say. His voice trembled. "Mama, I know I've been a pretty crummy son all these years. I don't blame you for feeling the way you do about me."

Quiet again and then, "What is it you want from me, Jake?"

Tears misted his eyes. "Your forgiveness."

"My what?"

"I want you to forgive me, Mama. I turned my back on you."

"You were ashamed of me."

"I was ashamed of me, too," he whispered. "Where we came from, where we lived—"

"I *still* live here," she said.

He closed his eyes. "I know, Mama. But I'm not ashamed anymore. I just want to start fresh. I want to do what's right."

"And what would that be, Jake?" his mother asked.

He wasn't sure, and as a tear rolled from his eye and down his scarred cheek, he floundered for some gesture that would make it right. But he had nothing now. Not a job, not a home of his own, not even a plan.

Yet he had a greater sense of the rightness of the direction in his life now than he'd ever had when there was more money in his bank account than he could spend.

"My car," he said suddenly. "I want to give you my car. It's a Porsche, Mama. You probably don't want a Porsche, but you could sell it."

The idea seemed absurd almost the moment he'd said it, but Doris wasn't laughing. "You'd give me your car?"

"Sure," he said. "It's paid for, and it's fairly new. You could get a lot for it."

"But—what if you start drivin' again?"

"I *will* start driving again, sooner or later. But when I do, I won't want to drive that." He hadn't realized that he felt that way until the words were already out of his mouth.

She was quiet again. He knew that this was as awkward for her as it was for him. He was paying her off, in a sense, or at least it seemed that way—as if the Porsche were a bribe to accept him as her son again. But that was all right. It was a start.

"All right," she said. "I'll take it."

He smiled and restrained the urge to laugh. "Okay, Mama. I can either send you a plane ticket, and you can drive it back, or I can sell it here myself and send you the money."

She thought about it for a moment. "I'll come there and get it. Who knows? I might like to drive it a while."

His eyes welled deeper. "Good. I'd like to see you."

"I'm not being greedy, you know," she said quickly. "I'm thinkin' of this as punitive damages. For all the grief you've given me. And all the years I gave to you before you threw them back in my face. Do you understand that?"

"If I didn't, I wouldn't have made the offer."

"You're not gonna back out now, are you?"

"No, Mama," he said. "I'll have the ticket delivered to you tomorrow. One way. Maybe you can stay awhile, on me. I have someone here I'd like for you to meet."

CHAPTER SEVENTY

Since she'd dropped Jake off at the hospital that morning, Lynda had been praying. She had pled with God, arguing how vital it was that Jake walk again, that he needed a miracle to nudge him along, that he needed to see God working in his life, that he needed to know he had a future.

But as she drove back to the hospital at ten to be there when he tried to take his steps, she realized that God was aware of all of that already. Jake was in God's hands, and God knew much better than she what he needed.

Still, she held her breath as she made her way to the rehab room, where a dozen patients worked on several levels of therapy, each deeply engrossed in the torture required to make one tiny bit of progress.

Jake wasn't in sight.

She looked around for Allie or Buzz but didn't see either of them.

"Excuse me," she said, catching a therapist as he passed. "I was supposed to meet Jake Stevens here. Have you seen him?"

"Yeah, he was here," he said. "I don't know where he went."

"Well, where are Allie and Buzz?"

"In a meeting, I think. Jake probably took a break."

Lynda was confused. Wasn't ten o'clock supposed to have been his big moment? Had they changed his schedule at the last minute? She went back into the corridor. Jake was nowhere in sight.

Maybe he'd gone to say hello to the nurses in orthopedics. Or maybe his morning therapy hadn't gone well; maybe he'd gotten discouraged and had decided not to make the attempt to walk today. Maybe the doctor had stepped in to postpone the attempt for some reason. Maybe something was wrong.

She had worked up a fair amount of anxiety by the time she decided to go to the fourth floor to see if he'd gone to say hello to his nurses. Abby, the nurse who had cared for him in ICU, was waiting for the elevator when the doors opened.

"Abby, have you seen Jake?"

Abby set her hands on her hips, as though offended. "That's it? No hello? No nothing?"

Lynda laughed softly and hugged her. "I'm sorry. It's good to see you."

Abby pointed up the hall. "He's in the chapel, baby."

Lynda glanced toward the prayer room then brought her troubled eyes back to Abby's. "Is everything all right?"

"I don't know," she said. "I just caught a glimpse of him goin' in. He didn't speak to anybody up here. Just rolled right to that room."

Lynda started toward the prayer room, but Abby stopped her. "Lynda, he's doin' okay, isn't he?"

Lynda didn't know how to answer that. "I don't know, Abby. We'll see."

She hesitated outside the chapel door, bracing herself for whatever she might find inside. Slowly she opened it and stepped into the dark room lit only with candles.

Jake was sitting in his chair near the front row, looking up at the cross on the wall behind the small pulpit.

When she approached him, she saw that his face was tear-stained. "Jake, what's wrong?"

His smile was heavy with emotion. "Nothing's wrong," he whispered.

"Then why are you in here? I thought you were going to the parallel bars at ten. I thought—"

"I lied to you," he said quietly. "I didn't want you to see me fail. I've already been there."

Compassion for his disappointment washed through her, and she sank down on the end of a pew. "Jake, I'm so sorry. But it was just the first try."

He started to laugh then, and she frowned, confused.

"What is it?"

"I did it," he whispered. "I walked."

She drew in a sharp breath. "You did?"

But Jake's smile twisted at the corners as a new wave of emotion came over him; new tears welled in his eyes and rolled down his cheeks. "Four steps, Lynda. I took four steps!"

"Four steps?"

"Yes," he said. "They said I'll be able to get around with a walker soon. Then crutches ..."

"Oh, Jake," she whispered and reached out for him.

He accepted her embrace and clung to her tightly, laughing softly into her ear as his tears wet her hair.

"But why did you come in here? You looked so sad when I came in."

He drew in a long, shaky breath and looked at that cross again. "I had somebody to thank," he whispered.

She pulled back to look at him, afraid to make any assumptions, yet hoping....

"It wasn't just the walking," he told her. "I'm grateful for that. But it's the other things."

"What other things?"

"The way he reached out and chose me and worked on me and even broke me, just to get me to the place where I could start really living." He wiped the wetness on his face and moved his wet, red eyes to hers. "And for his forgiveness that didn't cost me anything—not even a Porsche."

As he smiled through his tears, she leaned back into the pew, weakened by her glad amazement over what she was hearing.

"And I had to thank him for you," he whispered.

He pulled her against him again, and this time they wept together, for joy, for sadness, for the future, for the past.

It was a while before Jake could speak again. "Do you think God really spared me because he had a plan for me?"

She felt as certain of that as she'd ever been of anything in her life. "I know he did."

His arms tightened around her, and as he looked back at the cross, he laid his head on hers. "If it was just to give me one moment like this, it would all have been worth it."

330

And though Lynda closed her eyes and thanked God, too, for this very moment, she knew in her heart that there was much more in store for them.

So much more.

AFTERWORD

A year or so before I wrote this book, I became convicted that my Christian walk had been useless. I had never been available to God, though I had called on him often to get me through my crises (usually self-inflicted). My problem was trust. I thought I believed, I said I believed—but I did nothing to put the belief into action. I was neither hot nor cold, but lukewarm, and absolutely fruitless. One day, someone called to my attention something that Jesus had said: "Not everyone who says to me, 'Lord, Lord,' will enter the kingdom of heaven, but only he who does the will of my father who is in heaven. Many will say to me on that day, 'Lord, Lord, did we not prophesy in your name, and in your name drive out demons and perform many miracles?' Then I will tell them plainly, 'I never knew you. Away from me, you evildoers!'" (Matthew 7:21–23).

These words startled me. Was I one of those whom Jesus didn't really know? I finally realized it was only through my knowing him that he would know me as one of his own. And to know him, I needed an ongoing, active, intimate relationship with him—the kind of relationship I would have with anyone important to me. I don't ignore the people I love, and I don't neglect them, and I don't forget them. I talk to them every day, and care about pleasing them, and work hard to be the person they need me to be. If Jesus Christ is real to me, then I have to treat him as a real person.

Once I recommitted myself to making Christ the center of my life, I decided to make myself available to him in every area of my life. That's when the idea for this book came to me. The characters interested me because their own spiritual battles were so much like my own: Lynda, a lukewarm Christian who would let someone die without witnessing to him; Jake, an agnostic who couldn't give up the pilot's seat in his life until it was taken from him; and Paige, a spiritual infant on the verge of belief, who lacked the faith to make the final plunge. I was interested in their awakenings, their spiritual growth, their lessons, and I hoped their struggles might be something others could relate to.

Fortunately, I've finally begun to learn from the lessons God has taught me. I've learned that true Christianity is about going to him on my knees and asking him to fill up all the empty places inside me with his Holy Spirit. It's about asking him to forgive me and cleanse me of all the things that will destroy me—things like greed, apathy, anger, bitterness, fear, malice, and selfishness—so those places can be filled with him, too. It's about deciding what I *really believe*, then relying on it, totally, completely, in every area of my life. This, I discovered, has little to do with sitting in God's house on Sunday mornings. It has everything to do with *being* God's house, every day of the week.

ABOUT THE AUTHOR

Terri Blackstock is an award-winning novelist who has written for several major publishers including HarperCollins, Dell, Harlequin, and Silhouette. Her books have sold over 6 million copies worldwide.

With her success in secular publishing at its peak, Blackstock had what she calls "a spiritual awakening." A Christian since the age of fourteen, she realized she had not been using her gift as God intended. It was at that point that she recommitted her life to Christ, gave up her secular career, and made the decision to write only books that would point her readers to him.

"I wanted to be able to tell the truth in my stories," she said, "and not just be politically correct. It doesn't matter how many readers I have if I can't tell them what I know about the roots of their problems and the solutions that have literally saved my own life."

Her books are about flawed Christians in crisis and God's provisions for their mistakes and wrong choices. She claims to be extremely qualified to write such books, since she's had years of personal experience.

A native of nowhere, since she was raised in the Air Force, Blackstock makes Mississippi her home. She and her husband are the parents of three adult children—a blended family which she considers one more of God's provisions.

Terri Blackstock, a *New York Times* bestselling author, has sold over six million books worldwide. She is of author numerous suspense novels, including *Intervention*, *Double Minds*, the Restoration Series (*Last Light*, *Night Light*, *True Light*, and *Dawn's Light*), and other series such as the Sun Coast Chronicles, Cape Refuge, and Newpointe 911.
(www.terriblackstock.com)

The first book in the Cape Refuge series
Cape Refuge

he air conditioner was broken at City Hall, and the smell of warm salt air drifted through the windows from the beach across the street. Morgan Cleary fanned herself and wished she hadn't dressed up. She might have known that no one else would. The mayor sat in shorts and a T-shirt that advertised his favorite brand of beer. One of the city councilmen wore a Panama hat and flip-flops. Sarah Williford, the newest member of the Cape Refuge City Council, looked as if she'd come in from a day of surfing and hadn't even bothered to stop by the shower. She wore a Spandex top that looked like a bathing suit and a pair of cut-off jeans. Her long hair could have used a brush.

The council members sat with relaxed arrogance, rocking back and forth in the executive chairs they'd spent too much money on. Their critics—which included almost everyone in town—thought they should have used that money to fix the potholes in the roads that threaded through the island. But Morgan was glad the council was comfortable. She didn't want them irritable when her parents spoke.

The mayor's nasal drone moved to the next item on the agenda. "I was going to suggest jellyfish warning signs at some of the more popular sites on the beach, but Doc Spencer tells me he ain't seen too many patients from stings in the last week or so —"

"Wait, Fred," Sarah interrupted without the microphone. "Just because they're not stinging this week doesn't mean they won't be stinging next week. My sign shop would give the city a good price on a design for a logo of some kind to put up on all the beaches, warning people of possible jellyfish attacks—"

"Jellyfish don't attack," the mayor said, his amplified voice giving everyone a start.

"Well, I can see you never got stung by one."

"How you gonna draw a picture of 'em when you can't hardly see 'em?"

Everyone laughed, and Sarah threw back some comment that couldn't be heard over the noise.

Morgan leaned over Jonathan, her husband, and nudged her sister. "Blair, what should we do?" she whispered. "We're coming up on the agenda. Where are Mom and Pop?"

Blair tore her amused eyes from the sight at the front of the room and checked her watch. "Somebody needs to go check on them," she whispered. "Do you believe these people? I'm so proud to have them serving as my elected officials."

"This is a waste of time," Jonathan said. He'd been angry and stewing all day, mostly at her parents, but also at her. His leather-tanned face was sunburned from the day's fishing, but he was clean and freshly shaven. He hadn't slept much last night, and the fatigue showed on the lines of his face.

"Just wait," she said, stroking his arm. "When Mom and Pop get here, it'll be worth it."

He set his hand over hers—a silent affirmation that he was putting the angry morning behind him—and got to his feet. "I'm going to find them."

"Good idea," Morgan said. "Tell them to hurry."

"They don't need to hurry," Blair whispered. "We've got lots of stuff to cover before they talk about shutting down our bed and breakfast. Shoot, there's that stop sign down at Pine and Mimosa. And Goodfellows Grocery has a light bulb out in their parking lot."

"Now, before we move on," Fred Hutchins, the mayor, said, studying his notes as if broaching a matter of extreme importance, "I'd like to mention that Chief Cade of the Cape Refuge Police Department tells me he has several leads on the person or persons who dumped that pile of gravel in my parking spot."

A chuckle rippled over the room, and the mayor scowled. "The perpetrator will be prosecuted."

Blair spat out her suppressed laughter, and Morgan slapped her arm. "Shhh," Morgan whispered, trying not to grin, "you're going to make him mad."

"I'm just picturing a statewide search for the fugitive with the dump truck," Blair said, "on a gravel-dumping spree across the whole state of Georgia."

Morgan saw the mayor's eyes fasten on her, and she punched her sister again. Blair drew in a quick breath and tried to straightened up.

"The Owenses still ain't here?" he asked.

While Morgan glanced back at the door, Blair shot to her feet. "No, Fred, they're not here. Why don't you just move this off the agenda for this week and save it until next week? I'm sure something's come up."

"Maybe they don't intend to come," the mayor said.

"Don't you wish," Blair fired back. "You're threatening to shut down their business. They'll be here, all right."

"Well, I'm tired of waiting," the mayor said into the microphone, causing feedback to squeal across the room. Everybody covered their ears until Jason Manford got down on his knees and fiddled with the knob. "We've moved it down the agenda twice already tonight," the mayor went on. "If we ever want to get out of here, I think we need to start arguin' this right now."

Morgan got up. "Mayor, there must be something wrong. Jonathan went to see if he could find them. Please, if we could just have a few more minutes."

"We're not waitin' any longer. Now if anybody from your camp has somethin' to say ..."

"What are you gonna do, Mayor?" Blair asked, pushing up her sleeves and shuffling past the knees and feet on her row. "Shut us down without a hearing? That's not even legal. You could find yourself slapped with a lawsuit, and then you wouldn't even have time to worry about jellyfish and gravel. Where would that leave the town?"

She marched defiantly past the standing-room-only crowd against the wall to the microphone at the front of the room.

Morgan got a queasy feeling in her stomach. Blair wasn't the most diplomatic of the Owens family.

Blair set her hands on her hips. "I've been wanting to give you a piece of my mind for a long time now."

The mayor banged his gavel. "As you know, young lady, the city council members and I have agreed that the publicity from the *20/20* show about Hanover House a few months ago brought a whole new element to this town. The show portrayed your folks as willin' to take in any ol' Joe with a past and even exposed some things about one of your current tenants that made the people of this town uncomfortable and afraid. We want to be a family-friendly tourist town, not a refuge for every ex-con with a parole officer. For that reason, we believe Hanover House is a danger to this town, and that it's in the city's best interest to close it down under our Zoning Ordinance number 503."

Blair waited patiently through the mayor's speech, her arms crossed. "Before we address the absurdity of your pathetic attempts to shut down Hanover House just because my parents refused to help campaign for you—"

Cheers rose again, and Blair forged on. "Maybe I should remind you that Cape Refuge got its name because of the work of the Hanovers who had that bed and breakfast before my parents did. It was a refuge for those who were hurting and had no place else to go. I think we have a whole lot more to fear from an ex-con released from jail with a pocketful of change and no prospects for a job or a home, than we do from the ones who have jobs and housing and the support of people who care about them."

Morgan couldn't believe she was hearing these words come out of her sister's mouth. Blair had never sympathized with her parents' calling to help the needy, and she had little to do with the bed and breakfast. To hear her talk now, one would think she was on the frontlines in her parents' war against hopelessness.

"Hanover House is one of the oldest homes on this island, and it's part of our heritage," Blair went on. "And I find it real interesting that you'd be all offended by what they do there out in the open, when Betty Jean's secret playhouse for men is still operating without a hitch."

Again the crowd roared. Horrified, Morgan stood up. Quickly trying to scoot out of her row, she whispered to those around her, "I'm sorry, I'm so sorry, I didn't know she was going to say that. She didn't mean it, she just says whatever comes to her mind —"

"Incidentally, Fred, I've noticed that you don't have any trouble finding a parking spot at her place!" Blair added.

The mayor came out of his seat, his mouth hanging open with stunned indignation. Morgan stepped on three feet, trying to get to her sister. She fully expected Fred to find Blair in contempt—if mayors did that sort of thing in city council meetings—and order the Hanover House bulldozed before nightfall.

"She didn't mean that!" Morgan shouted over the crowd, pushing toward the front. "I'm sure she's never seen your car at Betty Jean's, have you, Blair? Mayor, please, if I may say a few words …" She finally got to the front, her eyes rebuking Blair.

Blair wouldn't surrender the microphone. "And I might add, Mayor, that your own parents were on this island because of Joe and Miranda Hanover and that bed and breakfast. If I remember, your daddy killed a man accidentally and came here to stay while he was awaiting trial."

The veins in Fred's neck protruded, and his face was so red that Morgan feared the top of his head would shoot right off. "My daddy was never convicted!" he shouted. "And if you're suggesting that he was the same type of criminal that flocks to Hanover House, you are sadly mistaken!"

Morgan reached for the microphone again, her mind already composing a damage-control speech, but her sister's grip was strong.

"After my parents inherited the bed and breakfast from the Hanovers," Blair said, "they continued their policy of never harboring anybody illegally. You know that my father works with these people while they're still in prison, and he only agrees to house the ones he trusts, who are trying to turn their lives around. Hanover House gives those people an opportunity to become good people who can contribute to society ... unlike some of those serving on our city council."

Again, there was applause and laughter, and Morgan grabbed Blair's arm and covered the microphone. "You're turning this into a joke!" she whispered through her teeth. "Mom and Pop are going to be mortified! You are not helping our cause!"

"I can handle this," Blair said, jerking it back.

Morgan forced herself between Blair and the microphone. "Your honor ... uh ... Mr. Mayor ... council members ... I am so sorry for my sister's outbursts. Really, I had no idea she would say such things."

Blair stepped to her side, glaring at her as if she'd just betrayed her.

"But I think we've gotten a little off track here. The fact is that Hanover House doesn't just house those who've gotten out of jail. It also houses others who have no place to go."

Art Russell grabbed the mayor's microphone, sending feedback reverberating over the room. "I don't think Cape Refuge is very well served by a bunch of people who have no place else to go."

"Well, that's not up to you, is it, Art?" Blair asked, her voice carrying over the speakers.

"If I may," Morgan said, trying to make her soft voice sound steady, "the question here is whether there's something illegal going on at Hanover House. And unless there is, you have no grounds for closing us down."

The crowd applauded again, but Sarah, the swimsuit-clad councilwoman, dragged the microphone across the table. The cord wasn't quite long enough, so she leaned in. "If there aren't any dangerous people staying at the bed and breakfast, then how come *20/20* said Gus Hampton served time for armed robbery and didn't even complete his sentence? And how come your husband was at the dock fighting with your parents just this morning, complaining about Hampton? I heard it myself. Jonathan didn't want you working there around Hampton, and he said it loud and clear."

Blair's eyes pierced Morgan. "Why didn't you tell me this?" she whispered.

"It wasn't relevant," Morgan hissed back, "since I didn't think you'd be the one speaking for us."

The council members all came to attention, their rocking stopped, and they waited for an answer. "If there isn't any danger at Hanover House," Sarah continued, "then how come your own family's fighting over it?"

Blair tried to rally. "Well, Sarah, when Jonathan gets back here, you can ask him. But meanwhile, the question is simple. Do you have the right to shut down Hanover House, and if you do try to close it, are you financially able to handle the lawsuit that's going to be leveled at this town … and maybe even at each of you individually?"

"They can't file a lawsuit," Fred said, his face still red.

"Watch us," she bit out. "And the chances of your re-election would be slim at best, since the people of this town love my parents. Most everybody in this town has benefited from their kindness in one way or another."

The crowd applauded again, and cheers and whoops backed up her words. But Morgan realized that it wasn't the cries of the people that would decide the fate of Hanover House. It was those angry members of the city council, sitting there with their hackles up because Blair had insulted them.

"Some call that kindness, others call it naivete," the mayor said. "They'll believe anything anybody tells them. Just because some convict claims he wants to change, doesn't mean he will."

"Thank goodness they believed your daddy," Blair said, "or you might not be sitting on this island in some overpriced chair!"

As the crowd expressed their enjoyment again, Morgan pressed her fingertips against her temples and wondered where her parents were. If they would just rush in right now and take over the microphone, she knew they could turn this around.

While the mayor tried to get control of the crowd again, Morgan looked fully at Blair, pleading for her to surrender the mike and not do any more harm. But Blair's scathing look told Morgan that her sister was in this to the end. The burn scar on the right side of Blair's face was as red as the mayor's face. It always got that way when she was upset, reminding Morgan of her sister's one vulnerability. It was that imperfect half of her face that kept her unmarried and alone—and it had a lot to do with the hair-trigger temper she was displaying now.

"Order, now! Come on, people—order!" the mayor bellowed, banging his gavel as if he were hammering a nail.

The sound of sirens rose over the crowd's noise, cutting across the mayor's words and quieting the crowd. Those on the east side of the building, where Morgan and Blair stood, craned their necks to see out the open window, trying to figure out where the fire trucks and police cars were heading. As one after another went by, sirens wailing and lights flashing, Morgan realized that something big must have happened. The island was small, and the sound of sirens was not an everyday occurrence. But now the sound of several at once could not be ignored.

When the front doors of the room swung open, everyone turned expectantly. Police Chief Matthew Cade—whom friends called simply "Cade"—stood scanning the faces, his skin pale against his dark, windblown hair.

His eyes fell on the sisters at the front of the crowd. "Blair, Morgan, I need to see both of you right away."

Morgan's eyes locked with her sister's for a second, terrors storming through her mind.

"What is it, Cade?" Blair asked.

He cleared his throat and swallowed hard. "We need to hurry," he said, then pushed the door open wider and stood beside it, watching them, clearly expecting them to accompany him.

Whatever it was, Morgan realized, he couldn't or wouldn't say it in front of all these people. Something horrible had happened.

Melba Jefferson, their mother's closest friend, stood and touched Morgan's back. "Oh, honey."

Morgan took Blair's hand, and the now-silent crowd parted as they made their way out. Cade escorted them into the fading sunlight and his waiting squad car.

Other great books from Terri Blackstock

A RESTORATION NOVEL SERIES

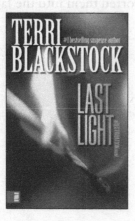

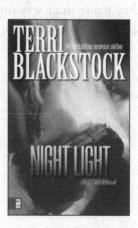

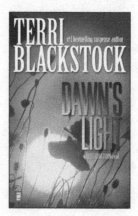

Available in stores and online!

Cape Refuge Series

This bestselling series follows the lives of the people of the small seaside community of Cape Refuge, as two sisters struggle to continue the ministry their parents began helping the troubled souls who come to Hanover House for solace.

Available in stores and online!

Other great books from Terri Blackstock

NEWPOINTE 911 SERIES

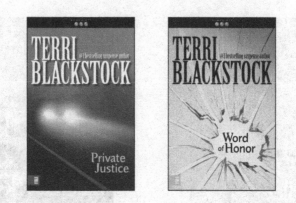

Available in stores and online!

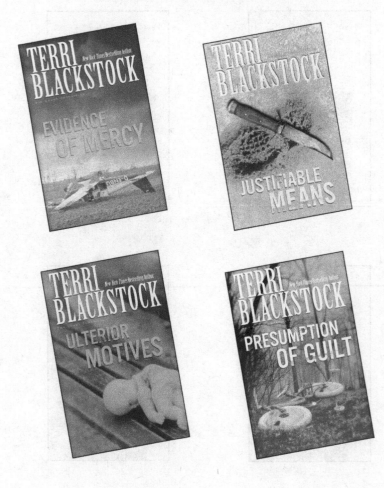

Other great books from Terri Blackstock

SECOND CHANCES SERIES

Available in stores and online!

Intervention

A Novel

Terri Blackstock,
New York Times Bestselling Author

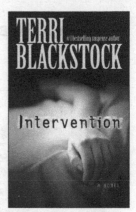

It was her last hope — and the beginning of a new nightmare.

Barbara Covington has one more chance to save her daughter from a devastating addiction, by staging an intervention. But when eighteen-year-old Emily disappears on the way to drug treatment — and her interventionist is found dead at the airport — Barbara enters her darkest nightmare of all.

Barbara and her son set out to find Emily before Detective Kent Harlan arrests her for a crime he is sure she committed. Fearing for Emily's life, Barbara maintains her daughter's innocence. But does she really know her anymore? Meanwhile, Kent has questions of his own. His gut tells him that this is a case of an addict killing for drugs, but as he gets to know Barbara, he begins to hope he's wrong about Emily.

The mysteries intensify as everyone's panic grows: Did Emily's obsession with drugs lead her to commit murder — or is she another victim of a cold-blooded killer?

In this gripping novel of intrigue and suspense, bestselling author Terri Blackstock delivers the up-all-night drama that readers around the world have come to expect from her.

Available in stores and online!